Bell's Landing

THE NOVELS OF GERALD WARNER BRACE

The Islands (1936)
The Wayward Pilgrims (1938)
Light on a Mountain (1941)
The Garretson Chronicle (1947)
A Summer's Tale (1949)
The Spire (1952)
Bell's Landing (1955)

Bell's Landing

A NOVEL

BY GERALD WARNER BRACE

W · W · NORTON & COMPANY · INC · New York

COPYRIGHT 1955
BY GERALD WARNER BRACE

FIRST EDITION

PRINTED IN THE UNITED STATES OF AMERICA
FOR THE PUBLISHERS BY THE VAIL-BALLOU PRESS

PART ONE

PART ONE

✑§ CHAPTER 1 §✎

My Aunt Evelyn walked with heavy steps as though she wore rubber boots; she talked that way too. Her manner was downright. "Now," she said, "I understand that you boys are to be *in bed* by nine *sharp*." She glared at us, I remember, with her lips pushed out, daring us to challenge her.

Harold stood pale and silent, with eyes down as always.

"In summer," I said, "we should stay up later. We don't have to get up for school."

"Nine *sharp!* I asked your mother *twice*." Again the glare and the challenge. "And there'll be no lying in bed in the morning—not in this house!"

I took these fiercely spoken orders as a matter of course; life in the Redfern family, I figured, was like that; but I couldn't repress another try. "Gosh, Aunt Evelyn, aren't we going to have any fun here?"

She made a sudden mirthful cry. Her voice exploded with pleasure, though she did not smile. "Did you *ever!* Do you hear that, Lucy? Any fun, he wants to know."

Aunt Lucy had been reading the *Transcript* and she stopped and looked up with a formal motion, as though she were permitting herself to be interrupted.

"Little Will," Aunt Evelyn explained in a shout, "wants to know if he'll have fun here."

7

Aunt Lucy's austere and elderly face achieved a glowing smile; I shrank a little, knowing how unrealistic her emotions were. "Dear Little Will," she breathed. "Dear boy! Fancy his saying that." She picked up her paper again.

"Why, we can fish," Aunt Evelyn cried, as though that were the one great good thing in the world. "We can row and swim, and you can help James—oh, James can show you lots of things." She made shepherding gestures. "Now say good night to your Aunt Lucy and come along."

This time Aunt Lucy lowered the *Transcript* again and took off the shell-rimmed spectacles and let them hang from the cord fastened to the two bows. Her smile was warm and eager and embarrassing. "Dear boys," she murmured, and we each kissed her brown and freckled cheek. "You do have your father's eyes," she said to me. "So candid and blue—do you see, Evelyn? Do you remember Will just like that?"

"Nine o'clock!" Aunt Evelyn called out, pushing us toward the stairs. "Up you go."

Aunt Lucy's words followed us. "Oh, sleep well, little men!" She spoke as though she were playing a scene on the stage. We heard the paper rattle.

I was first up the oaken stairs; the bannisters were as solid as legs and shone like honey. Aunt Evelyn's voice drove us strongly upward to the wide wall above and on through a doorway to another flight of dark stairs, steep and enclosed, painted rather than varnished. "You just pull the string here," she said, doing so and lighting a bulb in the far upper ceiling. The boards creaked and cracked as we climbed. "You see how easy it is; you can reach it anywhere—" She was puffing a bit, but the voice was full of vigor. "Woosh! Just wait till you're sixty two!" The last words came out like separate missiles.

The air up there was hot and musty, but Aunt Evelyn pushed through it undaunted and opened the door to what was to be our room. "If you keep everything *open*," she said, "you get *cross draughts*." She sounded angry, but I knew she wasn't; she was simply trying to establish the truth. "Now you see this east window is shut here, and you don't get the night air from the water." She opened it with a bang and a grunt. "We always have cool air from the water—why, I should have opened these this afternoon. I supposed of *course* Annie had done it when she made the beds." She rushed out and down the hall to the bathroom at the end and we heard her banging at the window there. "We do have to be careful of thunderstorms," she shouted. "That's the one thing to watch out for —We don't want to ruin the plaster, do we?"

We stood in the middle of the hot and airless room. The furniture was made up of the relics and left-overs—a big straw carpet on the floor, a three-quarter iron bedstead with brass knobs, a wooden cot, a mahogany marble-topped bureau with a carved mirror on a frame behind, an oak washstand with oil-cloth cover and a pink china pitcher-and-bowl set, and a colossal golden wardrobe in one corner. "There's probably a corpse in it," I whispered, trying to frighten my brother. His pale tense face peered at it.

"Now boys, just see here, will you?" The command came from the bathroom. "These are to be your towels," she went on before we got there. "James has moved his things out to his summer quarters"—she emphasized the phrase humorously—"and you can have it to yourselves. Now these here are Little Will's, and these are Harold's, and don't you *dare* wipe any dirt off on them: if you do, I can tell you exactly what will happen: Annie will wring your necks, that's what!" Then she pointed angrily up to the wooden box that held the tank for the flushing apparatus. "Now I want to show you something. That thing has never worked—*never!* I can remember when it was put in, and right off it went trickle–trickle—and it *still does*." She glared at it. "But all you do is jiggle it. Just remember to jiggle it *every time*—like this!" She seized the chain and jiggled, and we watched carefully. "Be sure not to forget or it will go on trickling forever." Because she had been talking about a toilet her face had set itself grimly and her voice was full of challenge; now she turned toward the marble basin and spoke more benignly. "You can usually get some warm water if you let it run, and I must say it will probably get you cleaner, but don't forget that cold water is much better *for* you." She fixed us with a keen eye. "Your grandfather got into a *cold tub* every morning of his life—just remember that!" She seized my arm and gave me a shake. "Remember that, Master William Bolles Redfern!"

I knew she was being jocular, so I grinned.

"On Mondays," she added, "we need every bit of hot water for the washing, so nobody upstairs may use a drop. There's never really enough and Annie gets *very* cross."

She turned and led us back along the barren hall with its closed white doors and musty air. The two rooms on the right, she said, were all full of *things* and probably were hot as Tophet. But in our room a cool air had come in from the sea-facing window and the oppression of age and death receded; the beds looked as fresh and clean as snow.

"Now Harold, you'll have the cot," she was announcing. "Your brother is older, and he'll just have to make the best of this big bed—let's hope he doesn't get *lost* in it."

Harold stayed ghost-like and still, as usual, so I filled in for him. "Well, gosh," I said, "maybe I'll find buried treasure in it, huh?"

"Treasure!" The word came out in a shriek, and a sort of roguish expression touched her puffy features. "Let me assure you, young man, that we don't hide our money under the mattresses." She stared at me with relish, and I could see that she was storing up the anecdote for future conversations.

Then she turned to the windows and adjusted the shades. "Now tell me *frankly*," she said, with even more distinctness than usual, "do you need any *help* in going to bed, or would you rather I just cleared *out*?"

It took me a moment to react. "Oh, we don't need help," I said. "We can do it all right." I spoke with a good deal of fervor, realizing what she had in mind.

She nodded with a certain relief, but then her expression grew dogged and angry again, exactly as it had when she explained about jiggling the toilet. "Now tell me this," she said. "Don't you say prayers? Doesn't your good mother hear your prayers when you go to bed?" Her face was more grim and flushed than I had ever seen it; she looked as though she were ready to strike out with her fists.

"Oh, no," I cried out. "We don't do that—not since we were kids."

"Well, then—be *sure* to brush your teeth." She started briskly for the door, then came back and put her mottled face down so that each of us could give a peck at it. "Good night, boys," she said heartily. "I'll be right under you, you know. Just bang on the floor and I'll be up like a *shot*." Again she made for the door. "You'd better do some more washing—and don't forget about the *jiggling!*"

Except for the feel of closed-in heat and a sort of spookiness on that third floor I didn't mind it too much. The old bathroom and plumbing, and all the heavy old junk of the house, seemed natural to me. The place we lived in in Newton was like that too, only smaller and dingier—and of course I had been out here before: we had always had summer visits with the aunts. Bell's Landing—the name belonged to our lives so inevitably that I had never thought of it as having meaning aside from the ungainly yellow house near the sea and Aunt

Evelyn striding about as though she had boots on and Aunt Lucy with her spectacles hanging from their cord round her neck and James bending over his vegetables. My father always spoke the name as if it were part of his continual reckoning; no occasion or crisis occurred without a mention of Bell's Landing—we might go there, or not go there, or let them know, or not bother to let them know. From the dingy little house in Newton Bell's Landing represented a more splendid part of the world, and of course we had a native share in it. We received strawberries and tomatoes and bushels of grapes. We heard about the people who used to visit there, the Brices, Kossuth, Mrs. Stowe, Sargent—the names all combine into one glittering company. "Papa was always very hospitable," my father used to say.

But the great thing about the place was the sea. For most landsfolk the sea exists in a separate area. It is a place to go and see. It has special properties, like wharves and fish-houses and summer hotels. Bell's Landing, however, was a solid Victorian dwelling house, with a coal furnace, hardwood floors, heavy furniture, and all the apparatus of a town residence, and it stood up alone on a high lawn above a little curve of beach where a wash of surf sounded day and night. From the porch or any of the east windows you looked straight out at water, and for anyone coming from the landward side the experience was stunning: people exclaimed and cried out—even those who expected it. The family called the southeast angle of the porch the Good Lord Corner. "Papa," Aunt Evelyn said, "kept a little *book*." She shrieked at the thought. "He put down what they said and Mr. Norton said 'Ah, Thalassa, Thalassa!' and made a gesture." She lifted her sturdy arm and moved it horizontally. "Most of them just said 'Good Lord,' though the English said 'Oh, I say!'"

Bell's Landing lies between Salem Harbor and Manchester.

There is an arc of sand about a hundred yards long, with a rocky promontory at each end, and the northern one acts as a partial breakwater, so that rowboats can land there. I'm not sure who the Bell was who left his name to that bit of shore, though Aunt Lucy was an authority on him and once read a paper at the Essex Historical Society, but the Redferns had always kept boats there and had a boat-house and a sort of runway on the beach where a skiff could be launched. The shore northeast of Salem Harbor is rocky and bold—with a few beaches like ours—but it is partly protected by the outer ledges and islands between Marblehead and Cape Ann. In summer it is peaceful enough with a wash of small waves coming in from the open Atlantic to the east, and of course on the good days the whole expanse blossoms with the sails of yachts. In winter it can be bleak and wild.

But the atmosphere of sea life is not strongly there. An occasional vessel comes into Salem, but the region carries on no sea business; the shore is mainly owned by rich Bostonians and most of the big houses are closed in winter. The nearest village to Bell's Landing is Aston Corner, a mile or so inland, partly a typical suburban community with a housing developement and a forest of television masts and partly a shopping center for rich people, with branches of city stores and gift shops and an expensive market called S. S. Carrington's.

When you go from Aston Corner to Bell's Landing you go a mile and a quarter along the main road, past estates with high iron fences and granite portals, and come to a stretch of natural forest, mostly pine, where a small dirt road turns left through the trees. No fence, no gate, no sign—just a little road, and you follow it for half a mile, partly in woods, partly across a daisy field, and you see first the yellow barn—or coach house—and James's garden and the chicken yard and grape arbors, and then the high solid front of the house, with porches and ornamental cornices. And you don't see the sea. You aren't really aware of it, unless the surf is booming all along the shore. The effect of the place is pleasantly rural and mellow and somewhat secret, because it seems to be all by itself among white pines and birches and mown grass and gardens with half-wild perennials. Pigeons live in the coach-house eaves and thick hop vines climb on the porches of the big house. The driveway mounts a little hill toward the front door where it makes a circle, and there at last you can suddenly look beyond and down to the vast expanse of the Atlantic. For a few moments you see nothing but the moving water levelling off to merge with the white sky; you catch your breath and exclaim, and the enormity of it comes over you, the power and the coldness and the space. Then you look down at the creamy little beach, and the jumble of gray rocks at the headland with wind-stunted trees above them and a fling of silvery spray below.

My aunts were born and bred in that house, and were to die there, but they exclaimed and caught their breath almost to the end. "Lucy, you simply must come—just for a *moment*." I can hear Aunt Evelyn's voice making little explosions. "Just see those clouds over beyond Marblehead—did you ever see anything *like* them?"

It was religious. The great pictures of nature were the demonstrations of God. Aunt Lucy, passionate and theatrical, daily sent up thanks and praise. "Oh, the beauty," she would murmur, letting her spectacles hang and staring in a sort of ecstasy. "Oh, the grandeur." But then she would turn and look at me as though I were being tried, and of course I shrank away. Her complacent little smile, her narrow far-sighted eyes, tested me. "Dear little man!" she sometimes said, and I understood that I hadn't measured up; I wasn't able to share her vision. "How Papa loved it," she sometimes said. "He walked there winter and summer." She often mentioned how he walked on the veranda. The great ones, I felt, were dead or dying.

CHAPTER 2

WHEN WE came to Bell's Landing on that early June evening everyone was making an effort to be natural. James, who never smiled and who looked upon us as destroyers, laid gentle hands on our shoulders and told us he had a nest of new-born kittens in the stable; his long old face stooped over us piously, with a death-like smile. He had driven to meet us at the station in the old Franklin, and was wearing the black serge and cap as emblems of his office. "We'll have good berries for you in a day or two," he said, nodding anxiously, as though he wanted us to know he was doing his best.

Aunt Evelyn had cried out with controlled intensity. "Well, boys—here you *are*. Now just let's be sure we have everything. Didn't you wear any *caps*? Surely you must have caps to wear on a *train!*"

We shook our heads.

"Gracious! No caps? Well I never!" She gazed at us with thorough appreciation.

The station at Aston Corner is like a bit of stage scenery. Basically it is a smoke-gray pagoda, like all other local stations, but it has been smothered in Virginia creeper and surrounded by greenery and flower beds, and on a June evening such as this it was a symbol of all rural felicity. The few commuters stepped from the venerable little train into a soft air of early roses and mown grass, and strolled off to their waiting cars—hatless, many of them, and visibly taking in the familiar pleasure of their return.

I have always enjoyed the charm of the Aston Corner station, but because automobiles interested me much more I was mainly aware of the rather fancy models that rolled away from the station. But the scene is reflected in Harold's long poem "North Shore"—in fact the place as a whole is created there. He didn't say much, but he took things in. He yearned for order and security and cultivation; he saw Aston Corner, with its flowers and lawns and open cars and rich gentlefolk, as an ideal expression of his classic vision. It all came out many years later.

But on that evening we climbed quickly into the high Franklin, with the bundles and bags Mother had packed for us—I in front with James to watch him drive—and rolled off along the highway toward Bell's Landing. "James is teaching me how to drive," Aunt Evelyn called from the back, "but he says I'm not *reliable*."

"I wish he would teach me," I said.

She made a characteristic sound, partly hoot and partly snort. "You think you are *reliable*, I suppose!"

"Well, I don't know." I squirmed in the seat. "I don't know why not—I guess I'll be reliable pretty soon now."

She hooted again. "Do you hear that, James? He says he'll be reliable *pretty soon!*" Her voice became a shout. "Well, we certainly hope so, Little Will. But until then perhaps you'd better not try to do any *driving*."

Even there in the car, trundling sedately along, there was a strong feeling of tension; we were used to shrieks and hoots from Aunt Evelyn, but now we felt she was almost imitating herself. "Perhaps James can teach you how to push a *lawn mower*."

I studied the instruments and said nothing.

She spoke in a changed voice, husky and deep with feeling, like Aunt Lucy's. "Would that your good mother could be here too—such a time she must be having! Oh I hope you boys have been very kind to her. I hope you've been helpful."

After a moment I touched a black knob and asked James what it was for. We turned into the drive to Bell's Landing.

"We must *all* be helpful," Aunt Evelyn said.

She didn't speak of what had happened, or mention Father. Aunt Lucy did later when she remarked that his eyes were like mine, but for a long time after that nothing was said.

What I most clearly remember is the image of death itself. The real details were all blurred; we were never told the truth, but were protected and deceived. Father had fallen from the window of his office on Congress Street; we were told he was dead, and we went to the funeral service in the chapel at Mount Auburn. We knew that everything was ended. Mother was like stone. The house in Newton, the narrow little slate-gray house, seemed to die—the very air in it was the air of an unused place. It was long afterward that I realized he must have done it on purpose, having lost his money and his job.

But the picture death made in my mind was strong and frightening: somehow I saw bones, skeleton, the terrible dramatics of a Doré engraving. The closed coffin in the chapel gave me nightmares. I made up a twilit landscape, with rocks and black caves and blasted trees, and a half shrouded figure in the shadows, tall, still, without flesh.

This had, I think, nothing to do with the loss, as they called it. It was death itself—all death. It was the dark terror. But the service in the chapel actually did us all good. The minister read very sweetly and rhythmically, on and on like the steady playing of a cello, and created a mood of solemn pleasure. There were about thirty people there. I hardly knew most of

them but I had heard the names spoken again and again—
I can still hear them: The Weldons and "dear Great Aunt
Jane," and the Craigies—often "the crazy Craigies," and
"poor old" Nannie Ewart, and Bolles Sumner, and the Saffords with little Betsy and little Chan—"my age" I was told,
though they seemed hopelessly young—Chan as pale as milk
and Betsy like a stuffed doll with flaxen braids: I remember
how she stared at Harold and me as though we were on
exhibition. I had contempt for her because she was young and
a girl but her stare made me feel important. And I was struck
by the fact that Bolles Sumner had driven all the way from
Cornell; he was a pretty remote cousin, but he and my father
had been at college together. It was impressive to see him
there; he represented an unshaken loyalty.

Mother's only relative was her sister, who taught school in
Hartford, and still does. She came, of course, and stood by
and said almost nothing—she seemed separate from all the
others, and in a way Mother did too. I remember how the two
stood shoulder to shoulder, both rather stocky and a little
gray—Aunt Jean a bit more pinched and grim. It is clear to
me now that they belonged to a different world from that of
the Redferns, not because of any sort of intent, but simply
because of their inherited ways. I suppose it is fair to say that
of all people on earth the Redferns were the most kindly and
tolerant in their intentions. There may have been a time in
past generations when they stood for pride, or even arrogance,
but with the one exception of my brother they seem to me almost foolish in their eagerness to do the right thing. But they
had a little different accent from my mother's, and used different phrasing. She said "Pardon me," and they didn't. They
said "Sorry," or "Do forgive me," and she didn't. She had
been a trained nurse, and worked at it with serious professional purpose; the Redfern and Weldon girls often worked,

but even when they needed money, as they often did, they remained cheerfully humorous about it and tended to settlement houses or good works that didn't involve them in a career.

None of the family ever quite approved of my father's marriage—again I learned this much later, or rather I came to feel it; no one ever said it. But the disapproval was no more than a mild sort of worry. "Dear old Will," they used to say. They admired Mother as though she were a small and virtuous Napoleon. She could do what had to be done. It wasn't that she had more resolution or vigor—Aunt Evelyn, for one, had wonderful vigor; it was that she knew how. She could cook like a cook, and doctor like a doctor; she could make a shirt, or take out fruit stains, or re-tie the springs of a chair, or exterminate ants, or paper a crooked room. The Redferns had no deep reluctance to doing hard and useful work, but usually they didn't know how. "Oh, send for Mary," they cried. "She can do it. She can do anything."

She took things seriously.

But Father hardly did—or rather he had different ideas of seriousness. His little boats were serious—more so to him than to me, even, though of course I thought they were miracles. He made the best sailing models I ever saw—not scale reproductions, but actual little sloops about three feet long, just small enough to get through the back door of our car, and he used all the skill and ingenuity he could command to make them lighter and faster and more nearly perfect.

He must have had a good boyhood at Bell's Landing. He spoke of it a great deal, remembering dates and all related details with pride and delight. His eyes shone. His voice took on a sharp, bell-like timbre that seemed almost falsetto, an eager nice voice. I can hear it saying the names of his father's boats: *Lapwing, Kestrel, Kittiwake*—the old *Lapwing* was his earliest memory, and he told us twenty times at least exactly how he saw her come in to her mooring on the Fourth of July, 1884. "And I ran up the steps to the porch shouting 'She's here, she's here!' and stumbled and got both hands full of splinters and skinned my left knee!" He always used those same words, and then added, "She was a cutter, you know, with a plumb stern and a reefing bowsprit, five tons displacement. Now, can anyone tell me the difference between registered tonnage and actual tonnage?"

He never owned a boat. He might have inherited the *Kittiwake*, but she came ashore in a September northeaster and broke up—and the effort to save her was too much for his father, who had a fatal heart attack. So he spent his life dreaming and planning for a boat, and making little ones. And he was a sort of nautical authority. He read all the books and magazines. He could give the technical details of every America's Cup race; he knew the exact sail area of the *Reliance* and all the secrets of Herreshoff's success. He was well versed in Lord Anson and Captain Cook and seemed to know Joshua Slocum by heart: he read *Sailing Alone* to us at the time we were still getting Mother Goose, and always when he came to the passage about the carpet tacks and the barefooted savages in the Straits of Magellan his eyes glistened and his voice went up a notch and he almost vibrated with delight. He had more fun out of that story than anything in literature.

Most people thought he had been a sailor—or at least "to sea," but he simply dreamed. At first he felt he couldn't afford a boat, and then he felt that his health was too precarious. He had ulcers. For long periods he lived on crackers and warm milk, no matter what Mother said. And he fussed with his little boats, devising new automatic steering mechanisms and experimenting with materials—he made one entirely out of layers of painted paper, and though she came out a little lopsided she was the fastest of all.

And except that he talked so much, everyone loved him. His older sisters doted on him. His sons followed him constantly. His wife treated him like a boy: her seriousness about life was a childish sort of seriousness—she acted like a very good girl in school—and she understood his boyishness. They played cribbage in the evenings, and she was almost light hearted. But he talked all the time. His high, eager, nice voice expressed all the impulses of his heart and brain; he was like a broadcaster accounting for each moment of experience, but never literally or drably. "There now, young Will, she starts, she moves, she feels the life—I suppose you never heard of Longfellow—ah, the puff, the very young willy-wa, and Captain Reece is in full command—see him work her to windward of that stick—by Jove there's a knockdown, and she luffs, she luffs! Very pretty, Cap'n R., very pretty indeed—I'm glad you're out there today. We don't want old Captain Jinx on a day like this, do we young Will?" His eyes would shine—very brown, young eyes—and his long pipe-stem figure would almost prance along the water's edge.

His talk was notorious, and most people took it with affectionate amusement. Dear old Will, they said. The neighbors in Newton liked him—or tolerated him. That Mr. Redfern, he's a one all right. But sometimes women disliked it; he never seemed to hear what they said, but continued his broadcast regardless. Aunt Evelyn always said you just had to shout him down. Sometimes she seized him by the ear. "Now Will, just *listen* a minute! *I've* got something to say." He used to chuckle about it. "Your Aunt Evelyn is a very determined lady. Don't give me away, young Will, but you know whom she reminds me of? The Red Queen. I almost expect her to grab me and start running. 'Faster! faster!' "

When he smiled his face lighted and sparkled. His laugh rang out like high bells. Everything that happened reminded him of something that had happened before, which in turn reminded him—on and on into his past, with dates and hours all precise. "Oh, we had an April snow like this in ought-three—my junior year, and I had started for home—it was the eighth—no, hold on, I remember Easter was extremely late, and Good Friday was the thirteenth—sounds more like bad Friday, heh, heh!—Well it was Wednesday the eleventh, and the train was an hour and twenty-six minutes late getting to the Corner—I never saw so much wet snow: the roof of Driscoll's livery stable caved in, and they had a time with the horses. Fourteen inches fell, but wet, of course, and I waded home and Evelyn said I'd ruined my trousers! But they say the heaviest April snow was back in eighty-two—and I'm sorry I can't remember it, though I was there: at least, I must have been. I couldn't very well have been anywhere else. . . ." He chuckled and made little noises of delight.

Yet he tried Mother's patience almost inhumanly. His wonderful eagerness was genuine, and his charm belonged to his inmost being, but he incessantly worried. He was, I suppose, a hypochondriac. He continually got up and prowled round in the night to make sure the doors were locked, or the furnace was going properly; he investigated little noises; sometimes he called the police station to report suspicious prowlers—he always apologized and explained the circumstances in minute and sometimes humorous detail (he felt very cordial with the police, as though they were all like James). He never went out of the house without discussing the possible combinations of sweaters, coats, and overshoes he might wear, and any longer expedition became a sort of safari of provisions and equipment. And in all these daily emergencies Mother was the agent; she bore the responsibility.

"Mary! Mary!" The clear voice echoing up through the house like a bugle call. "It's out again—it'll have to be dumped and re-built. I knew that last coal you got was poor stuff—I wish you'd call them up right now and tell them. We never had poor coal like this before." If she washed his gray sweater, it was the exact one he needed. If he mislaid a letter, she had been at her everlasting tidying again. If he slept badly, it was the cheese—she knew he shouldn't have baked cheese at night. In times of excitement he called to her incessantly. When we went to Bell's Landing for a day, he bustled about and up and down stairs with intensest eagerness talking to her steadily, his voice sounding from all corners of the house; he expected her to hear and answer wherever she might be, and if later she hadn't heard, and something had gone wrong —forgotten sunglasses or no extra sneakers in case of wet feet—he went over the circumstances again and again. "Oh, but I distinctly reminded you—I made a special point of speaking of that very thing!"

She was as patient and quiet with him as a faithful dumb animal. She seemed to know about him deep down, and to accept him. She always had a terrible temper; she took it out on us sometimes. But I think even Father's worst fussing seemed to her charming—and in a way it was.

❦ CHAPTER 3 ❧

SOMETHING about the eaves of that third floor room at Bell's Landing made the sea sounds loud. When the light was out and we lay there listening, the noise came in with a great whelming rush, like a rising torrent in the room itself. It was a still June night, windless and soft, and the sea below us had a lazy surge that sucked and heaved on the outer rocks and made slow-breaking rollers on the beach. But in the room the noise was amplified almost to an effect of storm.

Doom—nothing sounds more like the very voice of doom. You hear the slow inexorable rush coming at you out of the dark, louder and louder—not a single note, but a multitudinous chord, with lost lone voices mingling and vanishing. You wait for each ultimate crash; you hold your breath and still your heart and lie there in the dark waiting for that final moment of doom.

Our beach there takes the sea slant-wise. The rollers break first on the northern point, farther away from the house— their noise is sharper and fainter, like a portent; and then they roll diagonally on toward the shelving beach, leaving a pocket of lee under the point. On rising tides specially the crescendo is very slow and almost unbearably long; the water seems to come and come and come, and the sound and the

rush and the tension mount—and mount. Often no break
happens at all. The great rushing noise seems to be rising forever. The doom waits. But farther away on the southern
point, when the ground swell is heavier, you can hear the
crackle, the break, the avalanche against rock and shale—it
is there you hear the lone voices sounding out separately
against the solid chords, and the distance seems to make them
unbearably mournful.

I knew how all that noise came echoing into the third floor
rooms, and I had often waked with a shock of terror to feel
the dark waters almost upon me. But on this night the effect
was more forlorn and frightening. We hadn't been there in
many months. We had left home forever, and when Mother
took us in to the North Station, by suburban train and
elevated, through late afternoon crowds, she seemed to be
holding herself in a clamp of some sort. Her body was stiff;
her head didn't turn. She spoke to us quietly and, for her,
tenderly, but her lips hardly moved. She expressed no emotion to us except patient hope and at the last an inarticulate
affection. I realized at the moment of parting that she was
unable to speak; her strong, square-jawed face was spotted
with red and her eyes were full. "Bye, Harold," she whispered.
"Bye, Little Will." She held herself in.

But we were more frightened by that emotional tension of
hers than by anything else. All our lives she had been in command. With all Father's excited planning and directing, it
was she who controlled and took charge. Sometimes, rarely,
she grew fierce and angry, and we all cowered. But there on
the platform of the North Station we saw that she was helpless and somehow wounded almost fatally. To me, for the
moment, it was as though life itself had failed—as though the
most basic of natural laws had suddenly ceased to be valid.

When the train moved out—and on the platform she lifted

one hand—we sat like two little owls. Neither of us said a word all the way to Aston Corner.

It is a shock to a boy to find out that a grown person can cry. When a woman dabs at her eyes on solemn occasions it seems a respectable enough gesture, but when she bows down and sobs it is appalling. I heard Aunt Lucy do it once—she was in Aunt Evelyn's bedroom and I had come upstairs quietly with bare feet: she said in a tragic voice, "Oh, I had *counted* on the Chisholms," and sobbed. I could hardly believe what I heard. "Well, it can't be helped," Aunt Evelyn snapped out. "It's no use to boo-hoo about it." But a more terrible time for me was when I went to the bathroom one night and heard Father crying; it was only about a year before the end, and it must have been the beginning of his financial disasters. It seemed to me like a bad dream, because next day he was as chipper as ever, but there's no doubt that he was actually crying like a child.

Mother stood on the platform straight and square, as she always stood, feet a little apart and head up, but her face was like painted paper and just at the last the tears ran down in quick drops. She hardly seemed to realize it.

I had a five-cent candy bar in my hand—our dessert, she explained, after the frugal supper in a cafeteria. I divided it evenly, as instructed, and gave Harold his half. We sat there for a long time, each holding the piece of candy.

And that night the sea, rushing and rushing into the room. I don't know that I can fairly say that I then had my first premonition of what adult life really means—knowledge of that sort grows like flakes of snow—but now as I look back I single out that afternoon and evening as a time of solemn revelation, and the profound orchestration of the waters seemed to sound it out, again and again. I slept and woke suddenly, lost and alone, and there it was, surging and mounting and swallowing house and land and everything. The room seemed to whirl, and I sat up and stared from window to window and reached out to clutch one of the iron bars of the bedstead: for a few seconds it seemed as though the world was all overwhelmed and carried away into the void. I said—I remember I said it in an actual whisper—"Mother, are you there?" My whole being was shocked, as though an electric charge were striking me. Then I heard Harold flop on his cot in the corner and I was ashamed; I saw the east window, the loom of the wardrobe and bureau, and I lay back in bewildered relief. But somehow it had been like being in hell, or limbo, or some apocalyptic region where the final judgments are supposed to be made.

None of these effects, of course, ever occurred in the daytime. With sunlight the whole tone and timbre changed, the menace of doom receded, and the sea noises grew soothing and romantic. I slept quietly the last part of that night and didn't wake up till Aunt Evelyn rapped on the door, opened it and walked in with rousing cries. "Well, you lazybones, time to be up! It's a *lovely* day!" The shades rattled up and she gave each of us a smart whack. "Now don't forget to do a little *washing* and *brushing* before you come down. And breakfast will be ready in a jiffy—we mustn't keep Annie waiting."

She fussed with our clothes a bit and then left. She had almost no experience with children of any sort, and hardly knew whether to take us one by one to the bathroom and perform each operation for us, or to leave us to ourselves. One thing about her, she was fair and candid, which is what children most need in an aunt.

As soon as she left I went to the window and stared for a long time. The ghosts of the night were still fearsome in my mind; I felt a sort of inner shaking, as though the foundation

of life had been assaulted. The noises themselves now seemed
benevolent, and I looked out at the sea almost in unbelief. It
was a calm June morning out there, and the sun dazzled and
flashed across silvery meadows of polished water. It stirred
slowly, in long ripples and splinters of light; it heaved very
gently, and along the shores the small surf creamed and rolled
without force.

"What's out there?" Harold asked.

"Tide's going down," I said.

"Any boats?"

"Well, a junk boat or something, I guess—an old ker-
chunk, ker-chunk going toward Gloucester. No *Alde-barans*."
That was a little sort of joke, and meant no big sailing yachts.
A few years before some friends of the family named Aspenwall had bought a ninety foot sloop, and Father talked about
it so eagerly and constantly that it got to be a household
familiar. Arthur Aspenwall's *Aldebaran*—she was all that is
splendid in a yacht, and Father repeated her glories, her
bronze, mahogany, teak, her hundred and twenty foot mast,
her winning of the King's Cup and the Puritan Cup, and we
were deeply impressed; we thought she was the greatest wonder of the sea—and she was. When we saw her afar it was
like a glimpse of the true Grail, of the Gleam, the hope we
secretly lived by. But the name sounded and resounded.
Arthur Aspenwall's *Aldebaran*—it turned to pulp in our
mouths. We repeated it with every possible accent. We sang
it, and whispered it in the night, and made it funny and
foolish; and of course we got to calling every tall sail in sight
Aldebaran—accenting, for some reason, the third syllable.
Even Father had taken it up, and from Bell's Landing, looking across to Marblehead, we were constantly seeing Aldebárans, and Father always rushed to the porch with binoculars
and talked out his discoveries—she was certainly *an* Alde-

baran, but probably not *the*—no, you could see she had a smaller fore-triangle, with the stay well aft of the stem (a foolish practice, it seemed to him, probably brought about by some racing rule)—but she was almost as big—why, she must be the twelve meter, the *Starlight*—and goodness, look at that ballooner going up, see her go, like a gull—oh, lovely! Does anybody want to see? She was gone.

Though no white sails gleamed on that June morning, I was filled with a sudden happiness at the sight of the sweet and kindly world. All night I had been terrorized, and there now, basking and purring in the sun, was the beast itself as mild and playful as a kitten. "No Aldebárans," I shouted, "but come on, you lazy Brew, get moving!" I jumped for his cot, hauled the covers off, grabbed an ankle and dumped him on the floor.

He made no move. He cowered slightly, and remained passive, as he always did, expecting the worst. I must have been his greatest trial in life; I was strong and crude and always restless. I bullied him, not, I hope, in cruelty, but he looked upon me as a destructive force. Actually there was little pleasure in fooling with him because he either turned passive, like a stuffed doll, or he lost all control and gave way to madness. Now he simply lay on the floor and waited for me to do something else.

"I'm going to teach you to be a *wrestler*," I said, applying what I supposed was a hammer lock. "You got to learn to handle yourself."

It was no fun, though. He mumbled "Cut it out, will you?" and waited.

In the course of years Harold and I have gone through a good deal of trouble, some of it because of each other, and I'm not only prejudiced but inclined to be jealous—not so much of his wonderful success itself as of the person he has become. My experience with literary snobs is pretty small, but I can't imagine anyone who could surpass Harold. His pose, his rôle, is so authentic that the spiteful little word snob is hardly fair; he is the philosopher-prince of our day, the metaphysicist in charge of tradition. He speaks at commencements, writes for *The Kenyon Review*, lectures at Harvard, and is studied in advanced seminars. He is one of the most serious men on earth. But at the age of eight he was a difficult brother and playmate. He said little, but lived a secret life. He did little; he had to be cajoled into fishing or swimming, though sometimes he wandered off on small solitary explorations. He was vulnerable to the most trifling insult; even a breath of criticism would drive him into quivering silence—he seemed actually to lose his mind and all power of action, and nothing had control in him except the hurt itself. Yet he was never vengeful—not deliberately; except for his frenzies he never attacked or plotted. He may, in a sense, have enjoyed and cherished his many wounds.

"Cut it out, Will." Quietly, with resignation, those were his words.

So we splashed a bit of water on ourselves, brushed teeth and hair lightly, jiggled the chain, got into sneakers and summer clothes, and pattered down the stairs to breakfast.

"Good morning, boys," Aunt Evelyn said with careful formality, as though she hadn't seen us before.

Each of us piped up properly, and gave her cheek a very quick kiss and sat down. There were routines, we knew. We couldn't wander into the kitchen and ask questions. We sat. At each place was an orange cut in halves, and a sharp-pointed little silver orange spoon such as I've never seen elsewhere. Aunt Evelyn sat with an effect of presiding, with considerable silverware in front of her. Aunt Lucy always breakfasted in her room, as advised by a doctor, and when Annie brought in the boiled egg and one slice of toast, Aunt Evelyn filled a cup from the silver coffee pot and then carried the tray upstairs. It was too much to expect Annie to do it. When I got strong and steady enough, she said, perhaps I could do it for her.

The notion that Annie was a dragon was always carefully maintained, not simply to subdue little boys, but because Annie had to be cajoled and flattered. She made life possible for the two ladies. I think James was so much a part of the place that nothing could have separated him from it. But Annie had worked elsewhere and she had relatives in South Boston and she often said she didn't intend to work all her life—there was no sense wearing yourself to the bone in your old age when you might have a nice little place of your own. And this great house was no kind of thing for one woman to take care of; they'd had three in the old days, and now they expected her to do the whole of it. They kept telling how they'd help, they'd do the upstairs work, but Miss Evelyn handled a broom like it was a rake or a pitchfork and Miss Lucy was no earthly use at all. Annie talked a good deal about working herself to the bone, but she had a body like a bolster with an unexpectedly small and anxious head on top. Almost everything about her seemed to be in contrast: she was both neat and slovenly; she worked faithfully and faithlessly, and she loved and hated, gave and took away, trusted and feared, all at once. The Irish can be like that, more than most; little boys can get along with them, because they are that way too, and though I never grew fond of her, or she of me, we had a sort of understanding. I knew when I could visit her in the kitchen—in the early stages of getting a meal, but not when the crises came; I could look for cookies in the big round tin at mid-morning or mid-afternoon, but not other times— though she was more partial to Harold because he was paler and thinner and she thought I was too hard on him.

And most of the time she loved Aunt Evelyn and hated Aunt Lucy, though the love was tinged with contempt and the hate with respect. At emotional times she spoke out sharply: "The one has to do it all, old as she is, poor dear, and the other just layin' up there in her bed like the Empress of Inja." In all her sarcastic moods she referred to Aunt Lucy as the Empress of Inja, or as the Empress. It seemed to us about right.

At this first breakfast Annie was full of good will. She had made yellow muffins for us instead of the toast we usually had, and both eggs and bacon, instead of just the one or the other, and she brought in a new jar of honey she had hidden away since Christmas. She didn't smile at all, but her anxious face expressed a sort of acceptance of our presence. "We'll not be so dull now," she said to Aunt Evelyn with a twist of her left eye that might have been a wink. "When there's just only us old maids here it's all dull as can be."

The dining room seemed very ample to us, and somehow permanent and reassuring. It faced west with a bay window giving a view mainly of the barn and the yard; no morning sun, no glimpse of sea. The wall paper was brown, with figures; there was a wainscot with decorative plates on display, and there were heavy walnut sideboards, and a table solid enough to hold up a stone monument, and chairs with carved backs and stuffed horsehair seats, very slippery. All the main downstairs rooms had fireplaces with marble mantelpieces, and the dining room and living room ones had grates for coal and were used regularly in cold weather.

But at that time the effect of solidity was comforting. Annie was quite solid as she pushed her bolster-like body through the heavy door from the kitchen. Aunt Evelyn sat with fine solidity behind her pieces of silver. The table was like rock. The chairs had to be moved with both hands. All the hard, stained woodwork about the room looked as permanent as the ages. It was very different from the narrow little house in Newton.

"That was where your father sat," Aunt Evelyn said, nodding to me. "And of course your grandfather sat there at the end." She nodded at the empty space; the armchair had been pulled back against the wall. "And every morning, when we were all here, he said, 'Well, William, what of the day?' He always said 'William' and he always said 'what of the day.' And then your father would report. He'd say temperature so-and-so, barometer so-and-so, wind direction—oh, they were very particular about wind. Why, he used to keep a little book, your father did, and he'd put it all down, wind and rain and everything."

Aunt Evelyn's voice sounds out in my memory as clear and strong as ever. She announced her words, and projected them like missiles; each one was articulated with relish and humor and pride. "Oh, they loved the *weather!* We all loved the weather. I must look for the little book—it's something I'm sure you'll want to *keep.*"

❦ CHAPTER 4 ❧

AFTER breakfast we were sent up to Aunt Lucy. We were herded, as it were, and watched to the very threshold where she took command. "Dear little men," she said, eagerly smiling.

It was the southeast corner room, full of morning sun and fresh air, and inevitably I was drawn to the seaward window to look out. "Sit here, Little Will," she said sweetly, "and Harold here." One on each side of her bed. She sat up fairly high against the pillows, wearing a rose-colored jacket.

"Now tell me, what are your projects for the day?"

We squirmed a little.

"With all this glorious freedom at hand, what will you *do?*" She looked at me with one of her testing looks. "I'd just like to know." Her smile seemed to come down to us from some lofty point.

"Well, I don't know," I mumbled, after a silence. "I guess we'll scout around, sort of."

She evidently expected heroic and decisive speech, and I saw from the change in her smile that I had again failed at the test. But I knew it was inevitable.

She shifted to Harold. "And you—will you just—scout around—sort of?" She tried to make her voice young, as though she were talking our language.

"Well, I like to scout around, Aunt Lucy," Harold said with perfect precision, "but I like to read too. I plan to read some things."

"Aah!" The breath came out with almost lyric effect. "There speaks a true Redfern."

Her voice had something of the same charged quality of her sister's, but instead of the humorous energy it expressed eager emotion. Every word Aunt Lucy spoke was a small theatrical performance; it came out with a release of breath, a vibrant sustaining, a suggestion of rich and deep significance. "Oh, the books," she sang out. "My father's precious books. It would be too, too delightful!" She gazed at Harold with the embarrassing passion that she spent on all the trifles of life. "That I should at last have the joy of being allowed to pass on to another generation something of the heritage of our fathers!" The breathed words were like a prayer, but at the same time she looked at us with that testing smile to see whether we were measuring up. "Oh, we must read together— we must set aside the evening hour and read the great things—" Written words give nothing of the voiced ecstasies of her speech: "the great things" was spoken in a tone of such hushed intensity that it seemed to mean God and all sacred mysteries. We sat like two stones. "*Snowbound*," she said. "*Tales of a Wayside Inn*. Those lovely relics of a simpler world—oh, you must have them before it is too late!"

I never knew the grandfather for whom I was named. The family venerated him so much that I had a curious little sensation of fear whenever he was mentioned; I thought of him as some sort of masculine Aunt Lucy, full of incredibly superior idealism, and I always thought of her as his chief agent. She tested us on every occasion in order to report back to him, and she carried on his intellectual and social habits in a spirit of supreme dedication. Naturally we were scared—or I was, at least. In time Harold made a sort of philosophy out of it—a critical and detached and rather cool philosophy. I simply set myself against the whole thing, as any ordinary boy would have done. Aunt Lucy, I thought, without putting it into anything like rational terms, was not really human.

But actually I didn't come within miles of appreciating her, or the tradition she was so passionately trying to carry on. She dwelt in a wonderful world of international cultural eminence; she read *The Manchester Guardian* and the London *Spectator*; she corresponded with celebrities in many nations, and she had supported and held office in all sorts of high-minded organizations—the International Liberal League, for example, was one of her enthusiasms, and her name appeared on the letterheads and she always attended the New York meetings. There were printed leaflets of some of her speeches, and in the library a filing cabinet full of her correspondence. And of course quantities of serious and unreadable books about the state of the world. I even found a little book by her with a title that meant absolutely nothing to me: *A Rational Approach to Calvary*—and for a long time I thought it had something to do with Cavalry. It was dated 1906, and dedicated to her father with love and gratitude.

"Oh, Lucy has all the brains," Aunt Evelyn used to say, and once under some provocation she let out a sardonic chirp: "More brains than sense, as your father very naughtily put it once." But she devoted herself to Aunt Lucy's needs with life-long patience. She spoke always of Lucy's Causes; in the family plans, the Causes were considered first.

"Your grandfather," Aunt Lucy was saying to us in vibrant tones, "was devoted to the beauty of the spoken language. Oh, the Shakespeare that he read aloud to us, and the *Paradise Lost!* Keats and Shelley too! And his voice like organ notes! We'll try this very evening, we'll read some of those *glorious things* together!"

It took me a long time to overcome that prejudice against

my grandfather. Even the pictures of him were much too noble. There were no paintings, but several old photographs— one or two extraordinarily good, better in some ways than anything done now: something about the whole honest and forthright pose that contemporary photographers don't permit. In the best one, he sat up straight, right hand on the knob of a cane, left hand holding gloves, and his clothes were formal and stiff, with a sculptured look to them. The white hair was long and rather coarse, and was combed sideways across his forehead, and some of it fell low above his right eyebrow and gave him a plain and rugged look. He carried his upright pose and stiff garments without the slightest affectation, and the strong face, clean shaven except for sideburns, was shining with rectitude. He looked like the very pattern of nineteenth-century enlightenment: physically and morally and intellectually he was evidently in top condition, like an athlete. He smiled a little—it was the smile I feared, because it was like Aunt Lucy's and seemed to be testing me. Did I measure up? Did I do right? Did I "understand," as they did?

Aunt Lucy, with all her visions and capabilities, had been cut off from the origins of life. She lived in a delusion of her own importance, and the importance of the little society of eminent idealists of which she was a member. She never forgot that she was a lady and a philosopher, and as time went on she felt herself to be further and further above the realities of modern life. Her little smile found everyone wanting. But as I came to know my grandfather, or thought I did, I realized that he had a humorous and inclusive human sympathy. His was not the smile of superior enlightenment; he simply enjoyed life. His little breakfast table game about the weather was not the discipline of the heavy Victorian father—as I discovered when the little black notebook finally turned up:

it was full of funny line drawings and irrelevant notes by both father and son—for example, "Barom. pressure, 29.96, falling. Lucy's pressure, 2996, rising. Wind, S.S.E., very light. Gale force in dining rm." And then a crude little scarecrow drawing, probably by Father, showing a young woman making passionate gestures and apparently knocking over a milk pitcher. A legend under it adds: "Lowest ebb in the milk, 8 A.M." The word "milk" is printed in ungainly capitals.

They did a lot of funny drawing. Grandfather's letters (there are a great many) are often illustrated. Even after the fatal wreck of the *Kittiwake* in 1907 there is a fumbling letter to his sister Jane describing how he tried to get a big anchor out and simply fell overboard, anchor and all. "I managed to hold on to it, though," he wrote, almost illegibly, "and we hit bottom together. I was determined at least not to let it float away." The first stroke had already come, and his attempt at drawing himself clutching the anchor on the bottom is a confusion of scribbles.

Though we were always given to understand that Grandfather was an eminent person, both in and out of the family, it was a long time before I knew clearly what he did. It was sufficient that he "was," and we always saw him in terms of his books, his letters, his friends, his boats, and his manner of life at Bell's Landing. But he did have a career—or several careers: he began as a lawyer in Boston, and concerned himself with rents, leases, and transactions of property. Before long he found himself deeply involved in questions of conscience and humanity; he took up the cause of the poor and ignorant, and presently became the executive head of the Boston Civic Society, which he managed for the rest of his life. The salary was low, the glory none; what Redfern property had existed up to that time began to diminish, though until 1930 it was a slow process. He had given up his law practice, and the profits of it, and devoted himself to his cause—and to other causes, because he could never resist them. He sat on library boards and orphanage boards and fund-raising committees. He became an authority on social problems long before sociology was academically discovered, and wrote innumerable articles and some volumes—which are now looked upon as important "source material" for research scholars: there's at least one doctor's dissertation on him, *The Social Theories of William Bolles Redfern,* by a semi-literate young woman with a mind like an electric drill who spent several days going through the library at Bell's Landing.

At any rate, it is clear to me now that however formidable his social theories may have been he was a man with a warm heart and a sense of humor. It is probably not just to say that he "sacrificed" anything for his ideals, because he lived a comfortable and rewarding life: he had his beautiful place, his boats, his innumerable loyal friends. But his heirs often use the word sacrifice with various inflections of pride and respect and bitterness. There's no doubt that he spent more than he ever earned, and what was once a reliable inheritance is now nothing. And though he loved his heirs and his place, I have a feeling that if he could live all his life again, he'd live it in the same way. See, if you like, chapter three of the dissertation: "The Problem of Inherited Property," even though there's neither heart nor humor in the text.

It was really my father who lost everything. In his struggle to find his own life he had become an investment expert, attached to a small Boston firm, had taken over the family property and had gone under in 1930.

The aunts, I think, didn't at that time know it. They tried to live frugally, for them; given a few amenities, plain living was their way. But Aunt Lucy, in her bed that serene morning, full of lofty and confident thoughts, had no idea what was really happening. Poor Will had always been too delicate, and he worried himself sick; my mother had nothing, of course, and the gray little house in Newton naturally had to go. It was obvious that we boys should come to Bell's Landing, at least till things straightened out—and perhaps for much longer. That's what Bell's Landing was good for.

"Oh, we shall have such a summer together," she was saying emotionally. "Surrounded as we are by all that is beautiful we shall be healed and made stronger and finer!" When the last vibration ceased, and we sat fixed in embarrassment, she went on briskly in a quite different voice. "And now, dear little men, it's time for your old aunt to bestir herself. Run along— do, but oh take care, take care, the waters here are so dangerous. See that James knows what you are up to!"

Her gesture of dismissal was abrupt and regal. We muttered a good bye and hustled out, and were at once waylaid by Aunt Evelyn. "Now, boys, the *next* thing is to make your beds. Up you go—and do a neat job of it. I'll be up in a minute for *inspection.*"

She made it sound funny, and we clattered up the steep stairs in a good humor.

But the great thing was to get out of doors. We hurried through the bed-making; we received the explicit instructions about boats and swimming and the dangers of the sea, and about helping James, and being on time for meals; we were told there was a "little boy" about our age at the Parkers' on one side, and nice children of some sort at the Stannards' beyond—any children mentioned by either aunt were nice children, an innocent and hopeful phrase that always led us to expect the worst.

So we rushed forth, leaping down from floor to floor and

banging the screen door and dashing full tilt down the steps, down the lawn, down over the long grass and the rocks to the sand beach.

What means most in these recollections is the full-blown beauty of Bell's Landing as it was on such a June day. The house was early Victorian and in itself somewhat monstrous, but the place seemed to absorb it. There were big old trees— a stand of white pine to the north, behind the kitchen wing and the barn, and the largest copper beech I ever saw, and a white oak in the little center circle of the front drive—Father always said it would be ideal timber for ships. Elms and maples stood along the entrance road, and there were acres of natural forest, and hardy, wind-blown pitch pines fronting the sea. And the bulky yellow house seemed half buried in leafy hop vines and honeysuckle and a lilac bush at the west corner of the porch. The landscaping may have been planned long ago, but now it all seemed to grow that way. James kept a few bits of lawn trimmed round the house, but on the sea side the wild grasses had achieved a lean balance among the outcroppings of ledge. On the barn side there were old cultivations: a grape arbor, an asparagus bed, strawberries, and further away a half acre of vegetables that represented James's greatest interest in life. Once there had been much larger cultivation, a small farm, in fact, with pastures, hay fields, potatoes, and chickens, a cow, and two horses (a couple of carriages still stood in the back of the barn, ready for use).

Time had made the whole place mellow and a little untidy. There were no edges and corners. Shrubs grew wild. Weeds made a green mat in the gravel drive. Perennial flowers flourished all over the place, lovingly and unsystematically tended by Aunt Evelyn. At this time, in June of 1930, the forces had almost achieved an equilibrium, though wildness and disintegration were very slowly waxing. The old warriors were little by little retreating; James mowed less lawn than he used to, and the beautiful wild grasses already touched the northeast corner of the house itself. A forsythia bush by the kitchen door flowed out into the yard in a cascade of unpruned branches and streamers.

I'm not sure that they noticed the slow change. It was all like familiar age itself. The three old ones were part of it. Aunt Evelyn always spoke of the place as though it were in the full working order of its prime. She mentioned "the hay" as though it were still a valuable crop. She named the stables or the chicken house or the "oat field" without seeming to be aware of their disuse. She often said that we ought to do a lot more trimming and pruning. "Father believed *very strongly* in pruning—oh, he pruned like everything!" But it all grew too fast.

It was specially beautiful for boys. There were very few formalities: no inviolable flower beds and clipped hedges, no precious lawns. The copper beech could be climbed to its far extremities. The shrubs and bushes offered shelter and secrecy. There were forgotten little glades and lanes and dingles and big trees like a vision of Sherwood Forest. There was even a clear little brook, with moss and cool shadows and rocky pools, and the pleasant fiction that there might be trout in it, though the screen that had once been put across it above the mouth had long since broken away.

But the great thing was always the sea. All of our ventures ended there, at the edge of the beach or the cliffs, where the inland world vanished behind us and we stared and stared, seeing ships and islands and the moving water, and hearing the long rush of waves curling slantwise up the beach and splashing on the rocks with a fling of white spray.

❦ CHAPTER 5 ❧

A GOOD many people came to Bell's Landing even then. Aunt Lucy loved society, and Aunt Evelyn (it is fair to say) loved people. They carried on their lives sometimes separately and sometimes together. People dropped in for tea—almost every afternoon there were ladies chatting and laughing on the screened part of the porch, and we could hear Aunt Evelyn's delighted explosions from afar. "Did you *ever*," she used to cry above all other sounds, like the high call of a seagull. They were all first names, and Evelyn was often just Ev, and there was wonderful warmth of heart among them and humor and life-long affection—I can hear them calling out their good-byes on the steps: "Ev, you old fraud—I don't believe a word of it!" At those times Aunt Evelyn grew shrewder and more ironic than she usually seemed to be, and held up her end of the talk with a good deal of eager wit. And even Aunt Lucy was able to speak with a touch of lightness, though the passion was never far from her surface. "Oh, it was stunning, perfectly stunning, I don't know when I've read so fine a thing! It really gives one a *hope*, you know. . . ."

And whenever we were caught we were introduced and made to shake hands and given some dry crackers to eat. The ladies, and occasional gentlemen, varied a good deal, of course:

44

some were sentimental and some said, "Well, little man," and some were indifferent, but most were as natural as Aunt Evelyn herself. It wasn't bad to be caught, and I noticed that Harold nearly always drifted round to the porch at tea time. He loved to listen to them.

It was not until August, I think, that Mr. Fitch came. He was the head of the investment firm where Father had worked, and of course we had all met him; but his name had been intimately familiar to us for years. It was always "Mr. Fitch," and Father had constantly talked of him—not really as an individual, but as the symbol of the investment business; and the aunts used the name the same way. Mr. Fitch was always invoked in any question of money.

He drove up in such a splendid Packard that I couldn't keep away from it. I sat in the driver's seat looking at the instruments and holding the wheel during most of his visit, and when he came out at the end with Aunt Evelyn I was still there.

"This is Little Will," she said very quietly. Her face tended to be puffy and loose, but usually it seemed full of life and energy. Now she spoke and looked as though someone were ill. "Harold is the younger one, you know. Where *is* Harold?"

"Oh, he's over at Sam's, I guess." I wanted to ask Mr. Fitch about the Packard, but he looked too big and too old. He seemed immense and portly, with a great bald head and a moon-like face that had fallen into deep folds and creases.

"Young Will, eh?" His voice was gravelly. "How's your mother, Will?"

I said she was okay, and slid out of the car.

He turned to Aunt Evelyn. "You say she is—ah—working in Hartford?"

"She's a nurse," Aunt Evelyn said precisely. "A trained nurse."

"She's a *practical* nurse," I said. "That's what she called it, anyhow."

"Oh, she's wonderful," Aunt Evelyn said, still very quietly. "She can do anything."

Mr. Fitch said "Ah." He held out his hand, which Aunt Evelyn looked at in brief surprise and then took. "The final accounting isn't done yet," he said, going through the motion of shaking hands. "But the facts are as I have explained. These are terrible times, Miss Redfern. None of us have escaped. But of course I am particularly sorry in your case—"

He climbed in and started the motor. He made other farewells, but I was absorbed in the Packard until it was out of sight.

Aunt Evelyn stood and stared at the road. "Mr. Fitch," she said, "has brought some serious news."

"I don't like him," I said.

"Well," the ghost of a chirp sounded faintly, "I can't say that I—" She broke off. "Why don't you like him, Little Will?"

It was really because he looked like an ogre, but I didn't say it. He looked like the pictures. "I don't know—he's sort of big and—and old, isn't he?"

"*Old!* Yes, indeed—he's as old as I am."

"Well, I—I mean—it isn't that he's so old, I guess, but he *looks* old." I shuddered at my foolish words, but the ravaged moonlike face had made an impression on me. "I don't know," I mumbled. There had been something miserable and corrupt about him, but I couldn't explain.

Aunt Evelyn had rallied. "Your father always thought he was a very good man of business." Her voice was still quiet, but it vibrated with some of its natural energy. "But things are bad, he says. People are losing everything. It looks as though we'll all be quite poor."

The words meant little. All of Bell's Landing, the solid

house, the big trees, the ledges, the sea, were permanent parts of creation, and whether or not there was money in Boston seemed remote and unrelated. Here the summer afternoon existed for ever, and the crickets chirped and James bent over his rows of beans and a faint southeast breeze brought in the cool taste of ocean.

"Well," she said, as though she had made up her mind, "he says we've lost our money. I don't suppose it's anyone's fault." She looked at the open front doors.

"That was a wonderful car," I said.

She made a faint explosion. "Yes, indeed—a wonderful car." She put one of her gnarled hands on my shoulder and squeezed it. "Do you think our old thing is worth anything?"

I stared. "*Worth* anything!" Any car represented a fortune to me.

But she was staring across to the barn roof. "I'm thankful for the slate. We'll have *roofs* over our heads no matter what happens."

Something in her tone was so intense that I felt a tightness in my throat. I had never thought of Aunt Evelyn as having any special dignity: she was what most young people would call a mess—puffy, mottled, untidy, excitable—but now her voice and her whole being expressed a sort of quality in her that made me feel like crying. I stared at her. "We can face adversity, can't we, Little Will? We can get along without money, if we have to. But I tell you I'm thankful for the good strong *roof.*"

In a few minutes I had forgotten all about it and was trying to persuade James to fix the boat, as he had promised.

"We'll need a bit of putty," he gravely said. "And paint—we haven't the paint yet."

"Well, Aunt Evelyn said for you to get some."

"She did so," he agreed.

"Well, couldn't you get it for us, James?"

"It'll be the next time I'm in Salem, I'll get a quart of Miller's Marine."

"Can't you get some at the Corner?"

"It's not the same kind, my boy. We always use Miller's Marine."

James was as fixed in his habits as a piece of machinery. No pleas or cajolings or reasonings could alter his routines; you could, as Annie said, tell the time simply by looking to see what he was doing. I had been at him for weeks to do something about the boat, but it was too far outside his orbit. And I dimly realized that it was all a vague sort of conspiracy: the longer the boat was put off, the less chance we had to get into trouble with it.

We had been out in it. Aunt Evelyn had taken us. She wore rubber boots and a big straw hat with a ribbon tied under her chin.

I was surprised at the vigor with which she went at the whole job. The boathouse stood well back from the top of the beach, a green shingled building full of boating relics—old spars, a punt lying across the rafters, mooring tackle, and one good skiff such as ladies and gentlemen used for pleasurable rowing years ago.

"Goodness," Aunt Evelyn cried, "will you look at all the old stuff in here! There, did you ever see the Redfern private signal?" She flourished a dingy pennant displaying a red device against a white ground. "See? That's the red *fern!*" She chortled. "Father had it made and flew it from the masthead." She glanced about eagerly. "There should be the Eastern Yacht Club one—dear me, look at the *Kittiwake*'s rusty old stove. We *saved* it from the wreck. And there's that enormous anchor—"

She seized the stern of the skiff and began jerking and hauling it toward the big door. "We'll—puff—need the oars—puff

—here, one of you grab that corner. I used to be able to do it alone, but my goodness!" She paused and looked at the boat as though it had betrayed her. "Heavy as all get out." Her breath came hard for a moment. "Now, Harold, you take the bow there and *push*—when I give you the signal you *push*. And Will, you take the corner of the stern—gracious, do you think we'll *ever* get it up again?"

But we wrestled it out to the ways that slanted down to the water. "You see, there's a what-you-call-it with a long *rope*— you crank and crank and it's supposed to come up—but, dear me, it all looks pretty rickety, I must say. Do you think it'll all fall to pieces?" She stared angrily at the weathered timbers. "We ought to have grease, you know—we always had grease, and it got all over us." She took a new grip on the stern. "Now, come on, boys—it's easy as pie from here down, but for goodness sakes don't let her rip—you'll have to *hold back*—"

So down we went to the sea, with directions and explosions from Aunt Evelyn. She splashed about in her boots ("You see, this is where you *really need* boots") and held the boat while we assembled oars and fishing lines and a bailing can ("Gracious, it's simply *spouting* in—did you ever see such leaks?") and off we started—with Aunt Evelyn at the oars. We could row later, she explained, but if we wanted to do any fishing we'd better get along fast, before the boat *sank* under us. So she rowed with profound seriousness, as though she were performing an ancient ceremony. "You see," she puffed out, "I *feather* the oars. That's the proper way to do it."

We caught no fish because all we had for bait was periwinkles, which were useless. The boat leaked and leaked, and I bailed steadily. Aunt Evelyn rowed back to the landing again (before the boat *sank* under us). It took us about an hour to get it cranked up the ways to the boathouse. At first it seemed hopeless, with the rusty old windlass and the boat heavy with water, and I asked if it wouldn't be a good idea to fetch James. But Aunt Evelyn pushed out her lips and flushed angrily. "Now Harold," she shouted, "you go up there and crank *like mad* until I say to stop. And Will, you hold that side—and we'll *hope* the darned old rope won't break—" But Harold was no good at cranking, and the boat was still too full of water and Aunt Evelyn, still in boots and big straw hat, struggled and pushed and shouted orders as though our lives were at stake.

After it was all over she looked rather pale. "It's all in knowing *how*, you see." She sat on the rail of the skiff for a minute or so, a hunched and rounded bundle under the straw hat, and looked at each of us with an expression of pure complacence. "You just have to do everything the *right way*. That's what my father taught me." Her voice was mixed with her hard breathing. "Now, we can't use this boat again until it is caulked and painted. We'll get after James—he knows what sort of paint to get."

And that was the end of our boating. I went to the boathouse often and gazed at the skiff; I could see the cracks in her, and wondered if I couldn't putty them as well as James. But boat-work was regarded as one of the mysteries beyond the knowledge of little boys. I gazed at the punt on the rafters too, and speculated. But James was slow to move. He saw no purpose in boats anyway, now that the old days were gone.

And then Mr. Fitch came, and in due course Aunt Evelyn explained that we could no longer afford a quart of Miller's Marine. We'd just have to make do with a *minimum*, she said, and I realized that from then on boats were out of the question.

Aunt Evelyn got out the bicycles after that. They had been stored in one of the stalls, three of them, and hers was in pretty good shape; she still regarded herself as an able rider. Lucy had given up ages ago, and her bicycle was a quaint old relic anyway, with wooden wheels and no coaster brake. Father's wasn't so bad, and it was thought I might learn to ride it. But Aunt Evelyn was determined to put hers in good usable condition, and she pushed it all the way to Aston Corner to have it inspected and mended. From the day of Mr. Fitch, I think she never again drove in the Franklin (which eventually disappeared, though I never heard what they got for it).

The first few times she rode, James followed her at an anxious jog-trot all the way to the mouth of the drive—a half mile. He saw nothing funny about it—or heroic; it was just perverse foolishness and added to his heavy anxieties, but he knew he couldn't reason with her or stand in her way, so he trotted after her in a mood of solemn anger. I trotted after him, and I remember him standing at the corner of the highway, tall and curved and black, like a question mark, staring off toward Aston Corner. He always wore a black suit, winter or summer, and a white shirt and black tie, and was as solemn and anxious as a crow.

"She's no business to be doing it, at her age," he kept saying. "We'll just have her laid up with broken bones or worse."

But she did it. She pedaled along with the same sort of concentration with which she rowed the boat, looking neither right nor left, exchanging no social greetings with anyone until the ride was entirely over and she had both feet on the ground. "Oh, I love it," she crowed. "I always loved to ride. But I have to watch what I'm doing—I don't want to tumble *off*." She did the shopping, and brought packages back in the basket carrier, and people in Aston and along the road were delighted to watch her—though they said she paid no attention to other traffic whatever and rolled along as though she were alone in the world. She watched the road, she said. The more her friends cried out and protested, the more pleased she was. There were loud and hearty disputes about it at tea time, and still a good deal of laughter.

The changes came pretty slowly. First no Miller's Marine, then no Franklin, and no cream for breakfast. But suddenly Annie was gone, and everything was different.

Nothing had been said. The aunts always behaved with wholly unsystematic secrecy; that is, they made it a policy to tell children nothing, though in practice they betrayed much more than they realized. Aunt Evelyn especially was one who blurted out the truth. But the departure of Annie was so fundamental an event that no word was said about it, as though it were an unmentionable affliction. I came in about six one afternoon, a long, lovely afternoon we had passed at the Stannards' big tidal pool, and there facing each other across the kitchen table were the aunts.

"Now, Lucy, you know perfectly well you're no earthly good at this!"

"My dear sister, I can do whatever has to be done. At a time like this I will not be pushed aside as though I were a mere incompetent!"

The pitch and accent of their voices were normal; one sounded angry and explosive, the other theatrical. They always did. I banged the screen, called a greeting, blew wind into the sails of the toy boat I carried. "Annie out today?" I asked.

They didn't glance at me, but stood at the table.

"I can't do a thing if you're out here," Aunt Evelyn said with intensity. "Will you kindly just go away?" She was flushed, and her lips were pushed out sullenly.

Aunt Lucy's voice represented the highest sort of rational dignity. "I believe I came here first. There is not the slightest reason why I should not be permitted to do my share—and let me say candidly, my dear Evelyn, that this is no time to be bossy and stubborn. It is a poor augury indeed for our future—"

"Oh, fiddlesticks!" Aunt Evelyn shouted. "You needn't be so high and mighty—talking about *auguries*. Gracious, I never heard the like! And as for being *bossy* and *stubborn*, I'm not a patch on you. Now go along with you, do—it's time this child was fed!"

Neither of them had paid any attention to me, and I was startled and somewhat frightened at being noticed.

Aunt Lucy stood there gripping the corner of the table. "Really," she stage-whispered, "I'd like to *smack* you—if I were younger I'd—I'd *beat* you." She spoke as though neither of us could hear her. "All these years I've had to endure it, and I've tried—oh, I've *tried!*" Her glance was fixed on a far corner of the kitchen; her voice projected itself that way. "But I can't bear it, I just don't think I can bear it." She had become wonderfully aristocratic; her soft white hair was brushed back in gentle wings, her fine nose was lifted, her thin mouth firm and courageous, and even the mottled and slightly freckled skin had a quality of elegance, like old vellum. "You are simply a crass and stupid woman, Evelyn Redfern!"

I backed against the hot water tank and stared. It was one of the times when the firm ground of life seemed to give way. Aunt Evelyn had thrust her head forward, like a fighting animal; she had taken up a small enamelled sauce-pan in her right hand, and it looked as though she might strike with it. Her lips were pushed out angrily and her round face was all patchy. But then instead of blazing out, instead of doing something savage, as her stance proposed, she spoke with the desperate sarcasm of a child. "Oh, you'd like to *smack* me, would you, Miss Lucy, Miss High-and-Mighty Lucy! Well, come on —try it—just you try it. You never could beat anything, and you can't now!" She essayed a smile which became a terrible distortion of her pudgy face. "All I can say to you, Miss L., is *fiddlesticks!* You and your big words—it's just awful snobbishness, that's all it is. It's showing off—coming out here and making all this *fuss*—"

For some reason Aunt Lucy walked out. She held her head high, her mouth tight, and swept out of the door with dignity.

"That's it," Aunt Evelyn flung after her. "Go off and *mope.*"

But for several seconds neither of us stirred. She stared down at the table, and her face seemed to collapse. The angry mouth opened and closed with fish-like motions, and I realized that she was trying not to cry. She looked somehow like agony, or death. I crouched down, watching, conscious of the wrong I was doing by being there. "Oh, dear," she whispered to herself. "Oh, dear," over and over.

Then she saw me.

Her mouth for a moment stayed open, and a wave of color rushed up her throat and cheeks.

"Little Will," she said. "Dear me." Then her head gave a slight movement, a controlled toss. "Go find your brother, will you? Tell him we'll have some supper—" she looked round— "pretty soon." Her voice was low and hoarse.

I ran out without speaking.

ᴇ§ CHAPTER 6 ᴥ

Aunt Lucy did not come down to supper that evening. They had always had a somewhat formal dinner at night, of course, but this summer they had arranged a sort of compromise so that we could have our meal together. Aunt Evelyn didn't seem to care what she ate, but Aunt Lucy expected a procession of courses, with soup and salad and all the rest, including a small cup of coffee at the end for herself. She was proud of her ability to take coffee at night.

But this particular supper was not like anything that had happened before. Annie had left no convenient preparations. It took Aunt Evelyn about an hour to produce scrambled eggs and two glasses of milk for us, and we could hear her muttering and exclaiming to herself. "I hope you like *bread and butter*," she shouted to us once. She sounded quite cheerful, and made a great deal of noise and knocked over at least one bottle of milk.

"Your Aunt Lucy," she announced to us, "is not feeling very *well* this evening."

The three of us were quite companionable and Harold talked more than he usually did. He said the Stannards' pool was like the Mediterranean Sea because there was a long sort of leg sticking down into it like Italy and he had put some

55

rocks where Greece was and made harbors. And Aunt Evelyn said "Oh, Corfu!" ecstatically. We ate preserved raspberries for dessert because they had once had a big patch of cultivated raspberries and put up quarts and quarts of them which no one much cared for. "We can't be fussy about them *now*," she said. "No, indeed!"

Afterwards she set a tray to take up, very quietly, in a hidden corner of the kitchen. The aroma of coffee was strong in the air.

I heard her go up and knock and call. "Lucy? Here's your supper." The voice as chirpy as ever. "You'll be pretty *scornful* of it, but it's the best I can do."

The door opened and the voices sounded clearly.

"Oh, no, dear, I couldn't," Aunt Lucy said in tones of utmost tragedy. "Oh, I couldn't *possibly*—"

The door closed and the murmur of voices went on for quite a while.

It seemed to us for the next few weeks like a series of picnics. Aunt Evelyn achieved a state of good-natured confusion in everything she undertook, but no matter what went on her fixed resolve was to feed us properly. "It's a mercy James has all these vegetables," she fervently said. "You must have *green vegetables* whether you want 'em or not." It turned out to be mostly lettuce and string beans, and we had big daily salads. "Oh, we'll make regular rabbits out of you." We ate them so that she wouldn't be disappointed.

She didn't mention the graver problems, but Aunt Lucy did. To her it was a matter for very serious private discussions, and she arranged to see each of us separately, most often up in her own room where she could shut the door and back us into the corner between bed and window. One of her intentions was to summon up the Redfern past, which she seemed to know as a chain of heroic and dramatic triumphs. "Dear boy,

when you *think*," she often began, "when you just *think* of
the courage and the selfless dedication—oh, when you *realize*—" the prayerful tones still sound in my memory. Her col-
orless little shining eyes watched me; her luminous smile tested
me for signs of that wondrous fibre she celebrated. "Those
great souls—oh, those great souls!" She read to each of us (we
compared notes) poems by Robert Browning, whom she loved
and worshipped. She read and re-read a poem by Stephen
Spender. She urged us to be thankful for the challenge of life.
She asked for our secrets and our hopes: "Tell me, dear little
man, what today did you see that was *beautiful?*"

It was in a way like being operated on. I was a victim, helpless, squirming and shuddering in a sort of agony. I said anything and everything to satisfy her, to win a release. If I
thought it would go over, I mumbled about the beauty of wild
roses along the cliffs, or the rise of the moon out of the sea,
and usually she breathed "aah" and lifted her head eagerly as
though she had found the hidden springs of my being. I was
as solemn and self-righteous as a plaster cherub. But I found I
had to be consistent; she had a habit of mulling over a thought
for long periods. Almost the worst of her beginnings, one that
sent tremors of fear up and down my spine, was the abrupt
call for explanations. "Dear, last week you said a most interesting thing. You said you didn't think your mother would
ever want to live in a place like this, and I've been thinking
and thinking about what you could have meant by that. Do
you remember?" Actually Mother had once or twice said that
she never felt at home at Bell's Landing—she said it half angrily, probably out of jealousy, but all I knew was that she did
in some ways disapprove of the place. It was a feeling, an un-
expressed temper, and now I had to account for it; I had to
think up the words that would render the subject harmless
and turn Aunt Lucy's attention to something else far away

from me. So I mumbled that I really didn't know, but I'd heard her say things about the damp sea air in winter.

It seems in a way that Aunt Lucy's solemn and elevated thinking made a liar and sycophant out of me. Both Harold and I learned to say what was expected of us. But except for the periods of actual inquisition, when I sat and squirmed under the testing smile, I took it as one of the routines of life. Among the realities Aunt Lucy was as fixed and native as the walnut sideboard in the dining room or the copper beech across the drive: it did not occur to me to question their place in the order of Bell's Landing. It may even be that she expressed something inevitable there, as though she were an appointed spirit; her own room particularly seemed to amplify her words. The silver-backed brushes and hand-mirrors, the shelf of poetry in small volumes, the Italian paintings photographed and framed, the Sargent water color (original) of a lady sitting with parasol and veils on a sunny hillside, the Greek urn on the bed table stuffed full of flowers and ferns, the almost black mahogany bed and bureau with heart-shaped mirror—all these surrounded her like reenforcements, and she lay among them in her rose-colored jacket with perfect certainty.

Yet with all my hypocrisies, I felt something I had not felt before—a sort of base or foundation. Her faith was embarrassing enough, but I began to see that a high-minded and righteous life did actually exist in her mind, like a country she had lived in and could describe in detail. At home we had had a big framed photograph of a Yosemite scene, with waterfall and mountain peaks, and to me it was as remote and fabulous as the moon; but Father said he had been there, had stood on that very rock above the spray, and some day of course we would too. Aunt Lucy's vision was like that, and I began to think of it as having some sort of far-off existence.

She had always lived, as Annie used to say, like an empress—though a very small-scale and conservative one. The ways were kept clear for her to follow her causes. She did do a little dusting, with an air of a custodian of lovely things; when she touched a black marble clock or a gilt frame she congratulated herself on being able to make it more bright and so to restore it to its rightful place in the ideal whole. But she had little to do with the facts of dirt and waste and decay.

Yet now she insisted on assuming a sort of moral leadership in the face of our crisis. While Aunt Evelyn whacked about with mops and vacuum cleaner, and clattered and muttered among pots and pans, Aunt Lucy made a cause out of it; this was a time of trial, when the Redfern soul would be tested. She adopted a grim plainness; she pulled her hair back tight, and dressed in dark colors and wore no decorations. Her air was brave. She gave up her evening demi-tasse and began coming down for breakfast. She even walked to the village to do errands, reminding us that for several years her father walked in to get the early morning mail before breakfast, three miles on an empty stomach, as she always added. She considered herself a vigorous outdoor woman, and spoke of the tramps they used to take. "Oh, we were taught that we had perfectly good *legs*," she said with a note of passionate daring. "Oh, we were tireless; we tramped in to Beverly and back. And we rowed—many a time we rowed to Marblehead with two pair of oars, wearing gloves so our hands would be beautiful." Her tone had it that no one now knew the strength and greatness of those enterprises. "Your old aunt," she added jestingly, with almost passionate vanity, "is not quite the useless creature you think she is."

But aside from dramatizing our general state, she found little actually to do. So far as I know, the tense scene in the kitchen was not repeated. She hardly knew how to boil an egg, though she always assumed that anyone with her brains could pick up all such skills whenever necessary; but since Aunt Evelyn had flung herself into the work of the house so bodily, as it were, she had to be content simply to find the most effective phrases and tones for it. She never, I think, praised her sister, or even collaborated with her, though she did include her in the Redfern drama and once remarked that Evelyn was so like their dear mother—a detail I hardly took note of till long after. With all the Redfern complacence, little was ever said about their mother, though of course we knew that Harold's middle name, Craigie, came from her. What she meant was that Elizabeth Craigie Redfern, like Aunt Evelyn, had no real brains; she could act very well as a house manager, but was indifferent to the editorials in *The Manchester Guardian* and took part in few causes. She did have, as one would expect, a sterling character.

Aunt Lucy's one practical move was to see that Harold and I did some work. He had the top floor and I had the second floor, and we were supposed to keep them clean, though she was unable to tell how much time it should require of us, or whether we really accomplished anything. She drew up a written schedule—she always put whatever she could on paper. Once a week we were to do a really big job on the downstairs floor. But it operated badly because we were too young, and she didn't know how to clean a house anyway. Harold despised the work and was useless; I was better at it because Mother had made me do it so much, but even those long and free summer days were never quite long enough or free enough and an hour's bondage seemed unbearable. Luckily Bell's Landing was a very clean place.

I don't know whether they made any plan about James or not, but he stayed. He was simply part of it. For quite a while I didn't think much about him, or how he lived, but actually he began to make a safe dwelling for himself in the barn, like a woodchuck designing and executing a burrow. He collected the necessaries from the left-overs of seventy five years: a wood stove, with pipes; a kerosene two-burner cook stove; insulating material: he gradually lined his barn room with everything he could find that would keep out cold—carpeting, building paper, and a heavy canvas storm trisail belonging to the old *Kestrel*—and he did it all with such patient neatness that the room seemed to be part of an architectural plan. Even in his solitude, James had a strong sense of maintaining the Bell's Landing tradition. The room itself had been well built and planned for a coachman—there were, in fact, two such rooms, but James claimed only his. There was a toilet and running water in the warm seasons; in winter he had always moved into a third-floor room in the house, but now he felt that he might somehow bother or be troublesome to the ladies. He had a sort of instinct for digging in, without saying anything. He rebuilt the long abandoned out-house.

Still in the shiny black suit and black tie—still solemn as a crow. With all his gardening and carpentry he never seemed to be dirty; he often carried a bit of burlap with him to kneel on, and he had a brush on a nail near the barn door—one of his most characteristic acts was to stand just outside the door whisking away at himself.

His gaunt face, long and generally convex, always seemed to smile; the mouth opened a little, the head bowed with a special affability. But I found in time that it wasn't a smile at all. It did represent a kindly intention, but there was not a touch of humor or laughter in him—not normally, at least. The open mouth really expressed a life-long anxiety; it was a grimace of deepest concern and expectation of trouble. If you got close to him and gave him a chance to speak, you saw that he was immersed in concern. The ground was too dry for growth of any sort. His left knee had got so stiff he couldn't do the work he should. Miss Evelyn on her bicycle was in danger of her life. The paint on the south wall of the barn was all scaling. The pests were in the elms. The drive was a cart track. Steps rotted. "I don't know, Little Will—I do what little I can, but it's of no worth any more. I can keep a few things patched up. But it's all going—we'll just hang on a while, I suppose." His whole life was in his face as he spoke. I backed away with a little feeling of chill, and in the night afterward I remember lying awake and listening to the sound of the breakers and thinking of James's sad face.

Aunt Evelyn said he lived on nothing but potatoes and cabbage, and she kept putting out bits for him as though he were a dog; but he made a policy of not taking anything. His sense of what was right and proper was invincible, though many of his decisions must have been difficult. He had money in a savings bank, I think, but the daily source of his living was Bell's Landing and everything that meant most to him was part of the place; yet he declined to take a cold hamburg pattie or a piece of ham from Aunt Evelyn. "But my goodness, you must have meat, dear man. You can't go on with nothing but potatoes and cabbage." She spoke with all the anger and emphasis at her command, but he remained impervious. "Whistling jigs to a tomb-stone," she muttered to me. "I never saw such a man—he acts as though we were all at our own *funeral*." And she was certain he was wasting away—he never *drooped* like that before, she kept saying. Poor dear James, she said.

She felt much better about him when he began to acquire chickens. I don't know how he did it, but I'm sure he was a smart trader. They came almost imperceptibly, one by one; the first appeared in the weedy and grassy chicken run like a forlorn little ghost from an earlier time, and then mysteriously there were two, then three. The grain bins in the stable were still quite full, and apparently the years had done no harm to the dry grain. "You can see," Aunt Evelyn said when the eggs began to come, "that he doesn't droop nearly as badly—oh, it has made all the difference!"

The eggs, in fact, were a great help. Aunt Lucy spoke of them to James whenever she saw him. "I can't tell you, James, what a blessing it is to be able to have a fresh egg again. When I think of all the years we have abjectly endured those horrid store eggs!" She always ate hers very skilfully from an English egg cup, and James was gratified.

She also had some of the same sadness that James had. In spite of her ideals, she expressed a constant tragedy, a sense of doom; you could hear it in her heavy stage-whispers. But Aunt Evelyn expressed nothing but active pugnacity; she charged about the house, talking and exclaiming and making noise, and she always attacked without regard for consequences. I found her one day moving an immense kitchen cabinet, grunting and puffing at it, and she glared at me as though I were somehow preventing her. "Now, Little Will, suppose you just put your shoulder behind that corner there, and *push like mad*: when I say *push*, you *push!*" And we strained and grunted, and the whole thing rocked and the glass and crockery in it clattered about. "What a thing it is! But it went an inch—you can see where it went. Mercy, there's quite a *gouge*, I must say!" She stalked warily round it. "You see," she went on, "this whole kitchen needs a *good cleaning*. Annie was no earthly good at getting *under* things." She pointed angrily at the dust and litter between the cabinet and the wall. "We've got to get *at* it, somehow—" Suddenly she reached down and snatched something. "Did you *ever?* There's my Exposition Spoon! Why, bless you, it's a souvenir of the Chicago Fair back in fourteen ninety *two—gracious*, I don't know as I dare

look any more—I don't know *what* we'll find." But of course
we went at it with all our muscle. "The gouges," she said afterward, "don't really *show*, and I'm thankful to know it's
clean under there. Now while you're here, Little Will, let's see
about the refrigerator. I'm afraid it's as heavy as all get-out!"

When every cranny was finally reached and cleaned, she expressed her sense of triumph over and over. "We did a fine
job, Little Will! Oh, I feel so much *better*. I don't like it when
things aren't clean *underneath*."

The washing machine was at first a more dangerous enemy.
Laundry at Bell's Landing had always been a big and serious
operation, but all the ladies ever did was to sort and count.
Now in the new regime James offered to do it—it seemed that
he had had much experience at it; but Aunt Evelyn decided
against him. "No, James, we can't really let you. We'll be
thankful enough if you'll just do the fires—and it's a mercy we
got in the coal when we did! No, there's no reason why I can't
run that washing machine."

It was the kind with a spinning tub, and had to be loaded
evenly and anchored in a certain spot on the floor. I was upstairs when the thumping and crashing started, and though
the laundry was out in the wing beyond the kitchen the whole
house literally shook on its foundations. We all ran, even
Aunt Lucy; the crashing continued for a few seconds as we
dashed through the kitchen, and then stopped. Aunt Evelyn
was half lying under the tipped-over machine in a pond of
water and wet clothes. "I'm *thankful*," she said briskly, "that
I knew enough to pull the cord out of the socket there." She
held it up. "That stopped it at once, you see." Her voice was
full of bristly satisfaction. "Another time," she went on, "I'll
know how to *work* the darn thing."

She seemed to be all right, but a man had to come out from
Salem and repair the machine. Aunt Evelyn made him stand

by while she washed a batch and dried it in the spinner. "It's just a question of knowing *how*," she told us at supper. "That's one thing we all learned from Father: you have to do things the *right way*."

✑ CHAPTER 7 ☞

MOTHER came to get us in early September.

She had been working in and near Hartford, and wrote that she had rented a "place" there—not very close to her sister's, but not far from a school. She planned everything very exactly, as I realized later: she studied the neighborhood, the reputation of the school, and even picked out the best local doctor and dentist in advance. She already had a lodger, a Miss Gundarson, who had something to do with a hospital and was, Mother wrote, very helpful and reliable.

We still existed in a sort of summer trance, regardless of household troubles. Our small chores interfered very little with the long temperate days that stretched out before and after us—for ever, it seemed. The time was not exciting or even very active; we spent hours wandering from one place to another, mostly along shore—sometimes down on the rocks and beaches, climbing, jumping, looking at the driftwood, and sometimes up on the edge of the land where an old footpath ran all along that part of the coast. We played in the tide pools and sailed little boats (two of Father's big models were at the house, in a basement room, too wonderful for us to touch). We made neighborhood friends and came and went among several houses. Most of the people along there were kindly and untroubled by fear or pride, though a few of the houses were pretty big; but one place a little to the south of Bell's Landing was a huge and formal affair, occupied mainly by arrogant caretakers, and its fences and masonry were like a fortress of some sort. We could get past it only at low tide, and had to plan very carefully about going or coming: if we missed the tide we had to go round the inland side, a matter of two miles. For quite a while I thought its name was Buckingham Palace, since everyone at Bell's Landing (even James) called it that, though I knew the people were named Marburg and had oil wells. I used to sit on a high rock and stare at the rows of windows, dimly speculating about what could be inside, but except for the lawn sprinklers and gardeners the place was as lifeless as a vault.

We did bathe and swim on every good day—mostly in the Stannards' salt-water pool, with four or five other young ones.

I keep saying "we," because the two of us did do the same things, but often we did them separately. Harold had a habit of secrecy; he went off much by himself, without a word to anyone. It was not shyness, because he always appeared with the group again, but he lived within himself; he never revealed very much, except for his spells of insane anger. And in general I was the opposite; I talked a lot, and announced myself to anyone who would listen—I chattered, in fact, and Aunt Lucy tried hard to teach me the reticence proper to one of my age; she advised me to learn to listen intelligently, and kept reminding me that conversation was a very serious matter. "Never speak, dear boy, to gratify yourself." I was even the sort of boy who likes to sell things, and I used to peddle James's extra lettuce and beans among the neighbors—though the aunts didn't know about it and Harold disapproved. He said he wouldn't sell anything for a million dollars.

Mother came the week-end before Labor Day, and we had

to do a great deal of cleaning and fixing up. Aunt Evelyn grew self-conscious about her housekeeping, and kept saying, "Gracious, your mother wouldn't approve of *that*, now would she?" She spent most of a day polishing the massive silver, muttering that it was an awful waste of time and they ought to put it all in trunks. She made me clean and wash the downstairs toilet, and then she cleaned and washed it herself, explaining that it just needed some finishing touches. She looked under our beds for dust. She moved the heavy living room furniture. "*Her* house," she said, "was always immaculate."

Aunt Lucy did nothing of that sort, but she took us each aside and discussed things. And it was then that I somehow felt the real strength of her emotions about us. I had taken both aunts as inevitable family possessions. According to the laws of existence, we all belonged together, and Bell's Landing was simply "home," where we naturally went. Family members were required to love one another—and I had some sort of notion that Aunt Evelyn was required to work hard to feed us, and Aunt Lucy was required to lecture to us about life and behavior, and of course I was required to listen respectfully.

But this time when she cornered me she was a little less formidable than usual, and somehow a little more frightening. Her smile was full of tenderness; her hands hovered over me. "Dear boy, I do hope you have had at least *some measure* of happiness here—oh, I do hope so." Her glance was so beseeching, her words so dramatically uttered, that I looked at my feet with intense embarrassment. "Oh, I know how hard it has been, how *shattering* for you"—she breathed the word—"but do say there have been compensations—do reassure me that it has not been all in vain."

She waited and watched me, expecting me to speak. But her language and emotions were more than I could deal with. She looked as though she might somehow envelope me, and

I shrank away. Her smile glittered, not with any sort of cruelty or corruption but almost with a child's anxieties. "You may not realize, dear Little Will, that your old aunts are—very fond of you. Your father was so much younger, you know— he was always our boy—" Her voice had suddenly ended in a whisper. "Your being here this summer," she went on, "has brought back so much—reading all those lovely things we used to read together, hearing your joyous voices on the beach! Oh, I hope there have been memorable things for you too, dear child."

She waited again, watching me, and I swallowed. "Well, it's been nice here," I squeaked. "I wish we could get the old boat fixed up. It had a sail once, you know; there's a place for a mast, and a rudder."

A long time seemed to pass. Aunt Lucy stared at me with an expression I couldn't understand or face; I wiggled in the chair, then reached down and tied another knot in the laces of my sneakers.

"Yes," she said at last. "Your father was fond of boats—he did have a sail once; I'm sure James knows where it is—" She was being insincere, I realized; she hadn't the faintest knowledge of any sail. But she lifted her head and spoke in a brisk adult voice. "Don't you really think it would be more sensible, dear boy, if you two made this your real *home?*" She stopped as though she saw that the wrong thing had been said. "Oh, we hate to part with you! I had foolishly hoped you might want to stay on—I just wondered how you really *felt* about it. But of course it is entirely up to your good mother; she is the one to decide."

The aunts had worked out this plot together, and they kept at it with tenacity. The idea was to persuade us in advance, and then to appeal emotionally to Mother.

She arrived on Friday after dark—by bus. The aunts were

greatly interested, because they never knew anything about busses, and assumed that they came and went entirely at random, without any concern for the public. Aunt Evelyn always referred to them as "perfectly useless," and was indignant at the way they roared by when she was bicycling. But Mother knew how to handle busses, and was dropped with her one bag right at the Bell's Landing drive. She had written that she'd be there a little after nine, and the aunts were a good deal puzzled—not thinking of the bus; they decided she would come by taxi from Beverly, and were somewhat critical of such extravagance. "Of course," Aunt Lucy said, "she can't bear to delay even a minute. She must be pining for her boys."

So we waited alertly for the sound of a car, and suddenly the bell jangled and she walked in. "Hello—anybody home?" She came into the living room just as Aunt Evelyn was exploding with "Did you *ever!*"

It took a long time—minutes—for the excitement to die down. The aunts behaved as though some sort of miracle had occurred. They exclaimed and cried out their wonder that she was there, that she lived and breathed, that she knew about busses, and carried her own bag, and walked in the dark. She must be tired, starved, exhausted—it's a perfect wonder she found her way—she should have let them meet her—or let James carry the bag, at least—why, he could have put it in his wheelbarrow . . .

Mother stood perfectly still, on both feet, smiling a little, letting everything blow past her. She had kissed everyone on the cheek—she seemed cool, and her face was cool from the night. "Hello, son," she said, pressing her fingers into my shoulder. She never said very much, and she was rather stiff— or perhaps awkward—in the way she stood and spoke. She squeezed Harold's shoulder too.

She wore black in a kind of square, grim fashion—she

seemed almost more stocky than ever, and her face had set itself more solidly. There was some gray already in her dark short hair. "You're brown," she said to us. "You're bigger— you've got more muscle."

For a while there was talk, and it struck me how different she was from everything at Bell's Landing. The aunts were theatrical and exclamatory, and always a little irrelevant. Mother's talk about her work was interrupted by characteristic explosions from one or the other: "Did you *ever!*" from Aunt Evelyn; "it must have been perfectly *frightful!*" And of course Mother answered her literally: No, not frightful, not at all; it was uncomfortable for a while, but not really serious . . . And then Aunt Lucy, with the voice of a tragedienne: "Oh, the devotion, the courage! To deal with pain, with human suffering—oh, I think there's no service more splendid!" Mother was very patient with them, and answered their many questions, carefully keeping herself out of the picture with a manner that was almost professional.

It was she who noted that the time was late and we should be in bed, and she simply stood up and told us to come along. "Can I go up with you?" she asked. "I'll try not to be a bother."

Her seriousness sounds formidable, but she was always a perfectly simple person, and she could be very childlike. She got along better with children than with grown-ups, and when we went up to our room she took a great interest in our small treasures. Harold loved to draw boats, and Mother looked at each picture with care and let him explain them to her—the yawl, the ketch, the schooner, and many of the beautiful *Aldebaran*, which she pronounced the way we did. She had lugged her suitcase up to the third floor, and began taking out little presents for us—mostly five-and-ten store boats, a rubber duck and frog, and a real jack knife for each of us.

"Don't you do any washing?" she asked.

"Oh, we've been swimming," I said.

"Well, wash too. And use the soap."

That made us rather sober. We washed, lightly, without much protest, because she had just come, but we realized how different her orderly habits were from the irrelevant enthusiasms of the aunts, who never knew whether we washed or not.

There were other little issues too. We had had no toothpaste for weeks. My pajama top was split up the back. There were holes in socks, tears in pants, and many missing buttons. The beds were so badly made up that she had pulled them all apart and was remaking them before we realized what she was up to. "I ought really dust-mop you too," she said, peering under things, "but never mind tonight."

She seemed so brisk and quick that we got into bed very quietly, with a sense of being somewhat overwhelmed. She wanted to kiss us, but she didn't; she always felt awkward about kissing. But she stroked our hair and patted us and spoke softly. "Good night, young ones. I'm very glad to be with you again."

When she really saw how things were at Bell's Landing she was astonished. She knew that Annie had gone, but she had assumed it was just a temporary shift of some sort; she had had somewhat the same illusion about the place that we had, and thought of it as existing for ever, quite apart from questions of money. Yet there was Aunt Evelyn bumbling about the kitchen, and Aunt Lucy coming down to breakfast, and the dishes to wash afterward. It was inevitable that she took over; within an hour she was whipping through the kitchen chores like magic. "I shouldn't have left the boys so long," she said, "with all this work to do. I just didn't realize."

But Aunt Evelyn angrily defended us. "I won't allow any such talk! We *like* the work, don't we, boys? Why, you don't know how helpful they can be—you should see them *dry the dishes!*" She made that sound immensely emphatic, as though it accounted for everything.

"Drying dishes," Mother said earnestly, "is nothing."

She had, I realized, a literal mind. She kept trying to make logical replies to the histrionic speeches of both aunts. There's the mending, she said: buttons and socks and torn sheets. There's all the laundry: boys get everything dirty. There's the food, enormous amounts of it. There's wear and tear, sand in the carpets, mud on the stairs, dust on the third floor, grime in the wash bowls . . .

But Aunt Evelyn simply cried out against her. "Now, *Mary* —you just stop! I won't have it! The very idea of talking that way about these *nice boys*—why, I never heard such nonsense! The thing is—you don't believe—you just don't *believe* that we know how to do anything here, but I can tell you that we are *smarter* than you think we are. Now I'll tell you something: Little Will here—all by himself, mind you—Little Will has *fixed the toilet up there so that it doesn't trickle!*" Her tone was one of final triumph. "You don't have to jiggle it, even. Now what do you think of *that*—after all these years?"

"Well, he's good at fixing things. But that really hasn't much to do—"

"Good! I should say so. After all these *years* and *years!*"

"I just had to bend it a little," I said. "All it was was a little crooked."

Aunt Evelyn hooted. "The time we've had with it—and now it's *all* right! I call that pretty good, I can tell you. Why, we've had *men* in to look at it."

Mother couldn't keep arguing after that, but she was not convinced: I could see her little protesting shrug of shoulders. Bell's Landing, she thought, was a place of dangerous illusions.

Aunt Lucy's one idea was the family tradition. "Oh, to *see*," she breathed, "just to *see* these dear little men of yours doing the things their father used to do—oh, I can't tell you what comfort it has given me to know that the precious *things* will be remembered." Aunt Lucy used the word "thing" a great deal, and always gave it a vibrant quality so that it implied wonders. "One can see that they *belong*, in a very real sense; they have their roots here, just as we had—oh, I do think they want to carry on the old ways!"

"They'll have to work for their living," Mother said shortly. It was her basic creed.

But Aunt Lucy didn't hear; she was bedazzled by her own exciting words.

During the day Mother scouted round with us—walked the beach, and along the cliff path, saw the Stannards' pool (where we had a swim), and poked into the boathouse. She at once unearthed some putty and a half can of Miller's Marine white that had been on a shelf for ages, and was probably, she said, as good as ever. She shook the paint and heard it splash inside the can. She didn't see why anybody couldn't put putty in the cracks and paint the boat—in fact, she said, if you put the boat in the water and let it soak a while it wouldn't leak. There was plenty of paint on it.

Her common sense made me feel ashamed, and I stood there thinking not so much of the lost opportunities as of our helplessness.

"Too late now," she said.

"I think they want us to stay on," I muttered.

"Well, you're not going to." She thought about it. "Would you want to, if you could?"

We didn't answer, and she asked us one at a time. "Would you, Harold?"

"Oh, yes—sure." He said it casually, as though it were not very serious. But it was—I could tell, somehow. "Aunt Lucy reads to me," he added.

"How about you, Little Will?"

Suddenly it seemed a big question. I looked at the unpainted boat, and out at the yellow beach and the sea and the curl of a wave coming in slantwise with a long, lazy, cat-like sort of ease. The summer trance was still on me. I was bare-skinned and brown and salty, and I was part of everything I saw; the slow curling wave was like something inside me, and I felt responsible for it and almost proud of it as though I were actually demonstrating how a clean little swell could most beautifully wash the length of the beach.

"I like to live here," I mumbled, not knowing how to say it. A sense of belonging rose up in me like a passion; I felt the swelling of it in my chest and throat. Those same waves, it occurred to me, would sound loud in the night.

I'm sure Mother had no idea about these feelings, or if she had she disapproved of them. She thought well of health and play and nature, but only as agents of the main business of life, which was useful work.

"You boys," she said, "have to go to school—and school starts on Wednesday. I don't want you to miss any of it, specially beginning in a new place."

"Oh, well," I piped, "there's a school here—they asked about it and there's a school bus, or we can ride the bikes, Aunt Evelyn said we could."

"You'll have to learn to earn money," she said severely. Then she broke out with angry intensity: "You boys don't seem to understand that we haven't any money—and your aunts haven't any. They can't afford to have you here."

We didn't say anything.

"This is a place for rich people. We aren't rich. What they'll do I don't know, but I certainly don't intend to make it any harder for them."

We still didn't say anything.

"Besides, I think we ought to be together. As long as we're a family—" Her voice unexpectedly shook, and it made her seem angrier. "You can't just play!" She looked round the boathouse as though it represented something insidious. "It's all very nice if you can afford a vacation, but the way things are you can't—we can't." Her voice grew more rapid and even more earnest. "Your father never got over the idea that he was just playing—that's what he was used to here and that's the way he lived. A little of it is nice—everybody has to play some time—but when it gets to be the main thing or even a big thing, it's bad, it's wicked. We mustn't *let* it be that way."

She spoke so aggressively at us that we both shrank into complete silence. It was she who had to change the subject and ease the tension. "I think you'll like our place; there's a school playground quite near—" She stopped. "We'll just have to like it, I guess."

"Is it like Newton?" I asked.

"Well, for one thing it isn't a house—it's just one floor, and there's a store under us. But the rooms will be nice. We can fix them up."

We walked back along the crest of the beach, taking slow steps in the sand. It was an afternoon with the first cool transparency of autumn in the air; the blue of sea was dark in the westering sun and wind, and made a sharp ruled edge at the horizon. Everything was cleanly and exactly in sight— the far coast of Cape Ann, the harbor mouth of Gloucester, the white shaft of Baker's Island lighthouse, the point of Marblehead and the masts and hulls of yachts and the many sails like paper flakes.

"Is that the *Aldebaran?*" I cried.

"Sure—I guess so," Harold said. "It could be, anyway."

That evening they had their big argument.

Before we got into bed I heard them speaking pretty loudly. I heard Aunt Evelyn's voice cry out with full emphasis: "Now, Mary! Lucy and I are entirely *agreed* about this, and you've just got to *listen* to us a minute. Now don't you dare say a word till I've finished—"

I crept down to the top of the main stairs and listened for a while. They sounded angry and emotional, and they cried out above each other a good deal. But I knew how it would go. In practical decisions no one had a chance against Mother.

I lay awake in bed for quite a while hearing the sound of the water on the shore. Harold was asleep, but he had been in a profound gloom, almost in tears. Both of us realized, I think, that Bell's Landing was not a sensible place for us, and neither of us was passionately attached to it, but we liked its freedom and its beauty and we had learned to be part of it —it was the only thing in the world we were part of. Listening in bed, I knew what the tide was doing, what the sky and breeze were up to; I could assess, somehow, the motion of the sea. The noise hardly seemed menacing any more, but it did seem everlastingly sad; all the crying voices from near and far were somehow directed right at me, at the very base of my throat where I choked and burned with pity for my miserable condition and fear of the future.

PART TWO

ৎৡ CHAPTER 1 ৡ৵

I DID NOT return to Bell's Landing for fourteen years. Harold had gone back once or twice during the thirties, when he was too young to get jobs and was inclined to be unhappy and difficult. I always seemed to be working or going to school or carrying on some sort of project—with Mother's connivance. Then we had the war, and I was in that.

I felt bound to Mother more closely because she and Harold quarreled so much. They didn't understand each other or approve of each other, though Mother's dominant sense of duty prevented her from ever leaving him alone. She had to keep after him, she had to see that he was saved from idleness and pleasure, she had to direct and reprove and work on him no matter what grief it caused. And the two of them had somewhat the same qualities of certainty; they were as fixed in their habits as molded metal—but different and opposing habits, of course.

Harold's biographers may never see his inner self. Perhaps if he were a more important writer they would in the end get through his mask, but the books about him will be by his partisans. He is becoming more and more of a well-known academic character, hedged round by the rituals of literary success—the titles and seminars and panel discussions and lectures and

radio appearances and of course the little cloud of admiring
graduate students and English instructors. But a brother is
probably a poor witness. I am constantly dazzled and astonished by his brilliance, so much so that I can't read most of his
stuff at all—not his poetry or his criticism; I do read his political essays, which are said to be creating a school of new
conservatism. What I'm getting at is that behind all this
dazzle of mind is a quiet and secret self-seeking, a calculated
building up of the part of the aristocrat of letters. I mean, he
is a brilliant and successful poseur.

It came to me most plainly when he let it be known that
he was a high Episcopalian. Our religious habits had been in-
formally Unitarian; even Aunt Lucy, with all her stagy ceremonies, remained a reasonable Unitarian. But Harold, about
the time he was graduating from Harvard, announced his
acceptance of what he called the essential rituals of the true
church. Not that he discussed or argued, of course; he just
became visibly more impregnable; his neck grew stiffer, his
nose tipped back, his tight-lipped speech discouraged any
pleasantries. He wrote about it later on, not in personal terms,
and as far as I can understand him he justifies the pose—any
effective pose, I imagine—as an esthetic necessity (he uses
the word esthetic a lot). Nature is mostly chaotic and men
incline to savagery; over the centuries, however, the trained
minds have devised forms and patterns as bulwarks against
natural chaos. A well-tailored suit, a dark tie, polished shoes,
represent a certain victory over nature. A clipped, precise
academic speech does the same—as do the big words and
critical subtleties. The rituals of religion are symbols of en-
during human virtue, not because they are "true" or in any
immediate sense useful—the reverse, in fact: they are practically useless and false to nature, and are therefore desirable

and technically beautiful. They are what educated man has wrought—as, of course, is God.

These comments on Harold may seem too general and jumbled, and I suspect he is a more profound philosopher than I can understand; he is certainly complex, and his command of language is dazzling. If he weren't my brother I might think his ritualistic habits were more admirable, but as it is he merely seems to me to be trying to avoid a world and a nature he has always feared. His favorite reading was the cycle of King Arthur stories, and later Scott; he read Bulwer's *Last of the Barons* over and over, with all its rhetoric and rhodomontade, its kings and princes and haughty aristocracy and pageantry, and last year he astonished the academic critics by publishing a solemn analysis of it, deploring its style but discovering hitherto unrecognized levels of symbolism. There were months in his childhood when he carried a sword and shield.

We kept together, he and I, through the early school years in Hartford and then in Springfield and Holyoke, but in his last two years Mother somehow got him into a big and notable prep school, which she didn't personally approve of but none the less considered an opportunity too golden to miss. And from there on the way was made for him; he was rewarded and given prizes and he did wonders.

We lived, the three of us—and then mainly the two of us —in a succession of tenements in various towns, one very like another. The tone was generally brown—brown woodwork, brown chairs, brown rugs: a practical shade, Mother said. The neighborhoods tended to be brown, as well as the weather, the seasons, almost everything. We lived, of course, in utmost simplicity and cleanness: whenever we came to a new place, Mother scoured it from the ceiling down to the cracks in the floor before we set up our plain cots and plain brown chairs and tables and bureaus.

I seemed to be the essential housekeeper, because Mother often stayed out on cases and left everything to me—or rather she instructed me in minute detail, with every contingency foreseen and each step listed. "If pudding seems sour, *don't eat* it; open can of applesauce and have w. cookies." I never became a versatile cook, but I can clean a house or wash dishes or make beds with professional skill. I can fix anything and make anything and I'd be a better man on a desert island than Robinson Crusoe—thanks to Mother's training. Our problems were like his.

And certainly during those years the old Bell's Landing ways grew faint and far. Mother sent cards and notes to the aunts, and received replies too illegible for me to understand, though she made them out well enough. Aunt Evelyn's script was nothing but vertical lines, and Aunt Lucy's looked the way shorthand looks to a layman—a succession of wiggles. But in time the only correspondence was at Christmas, and on occasional birthdays: Mother never overlooked a birthday.

We lived, meanwhile, like foragers, though with steely self-respect. Mother would have nothing to do with "relief" of any sort; she worked, or she didn't work, and accepted the consequences. But she never resigned herself. She couldn't ever talk her way into a job; she couldn't sell or advertise or manipulate people—rather she washed pots in a restaurant or cleaned office floors and toilets, for twenty cents an hour. And as long as she felt strong enough and kept going, she was content: not happy—she never knew how to be happy—but any combination of hard work, mean or not, and self-respect was all she asked of life.

For a long time she managed me by the same philosophy. A plain list of my jobs over a ten year period would fill pages, beginning with lawns, snow shovelling, paper route, and running through every kind of contemporary mechanics from patching tires to servicing vacuum cleaners. I also delivered groceries, sold ice cream at fairs, cleaned out oil tanks, and collected garbage, and painted houses. I could usually find some way of earning a minimum wage, but no executive singled me out as a likely young hero to marry his daughter and inherit the business. My chief talent, I think, was to assert confidently that I could do whatever was asked of me— a pose, incidentally, which Mother would not have altogether approved, but I could talk my way into things so easily that I couldn't seem to help it. People who hired me assumed I could fix things, whether I had ever seen them before or not, and the challenge was too much for me to decline. I blew a good many fuses and was scolded by many a housewife, but in the end I learned.

I can't say that Mother and I lived in harmony always; she could be very fierce and certain, and in her certainty she was incapable of listening to any voice but her own. She knew not only what she had to do, but what Harold and I had to do too. With Harold gradually an implacable hostility built up, and he came to hate her. With me there were hostilities but also reconcilements. When I was nineteen I fought against her stubbornly and cruelly.

What with our moving round, and my many jobs, I was a year behind in high school. Harold had gone off to his private school in Connecticut, and was winning fame as a poet and scholar. The times were better then: his expenses were paid and Mother was able to be a respectable practical nurse again. We lived in Holyoke, still in a tenement, but the mills were running and there was work to do.

Mother began arranging a college career for me. She wrote for information and talked about this one and that one. I said no—I'd rather work, I'd been to school too long as it was and was fed up with it. At first she paid no attention to me, and settled things by pointing out to me that the Redferns always went to college—naturally I would. That rather surprised me because nothing much had been said about Redferns for a long time and I had been made to feel that the family tradition was no longer appropriate to us. Now she reminded me that Father would certainly have wanted me to go on to college—in fact, there was no question about it.

But the ten years of her training were potent in me. Work was the thing. I had learned to work, I was good at it—not for any special purpose or ideal, but simply for "work," which meant money and security, and of course self-respect. And I had learned to live from day to day, like a scout or a mountain man, disdaining the ordinary communal safeties—a habit not quite intended by mother, who at bottom had very conservative ideals. She saw both Harold and me as solidly reputable professional men—he a teacher, I an "engineer." That was the term she used, and of course it presupposed a lot of high education. But I didn't think ahead very much, or aspire to any success beyond holding a job and being let alone. My vanity was personal independence and resourcefulness.

The summer after I was nineteen I got to be a good automobile mechanic. I worked for a small dealer who cared more about selling cars than servicing them, but he had two mechanics in his shop—and I was one; by August the other had left and I was supposed to do everything. Rochelle, my boss, kept saying he was getting a competent older man but he put it off—though in time he hired an elderly Cretan gentleman named Constant Sardis to do the washing, polishing, tire repairing, and other odd jobs.

Rochelle was designed to do things in a small way. He had a good location and a chance to expand, but he had a frugal and fearful nature: all his decisions were for less rather than more. Yet it worked out well for me. He ran his business so modestly, with so little expectation, that he left me pretty much alone. He was pleased to have a boy doing a man's job —and a man doing a boy's; he was getting a bargain each way. The shop was in the basement, underneath the office and show-room, with doors opening to a secluded back lot, and though it was dark and damp down there it was also quiet and free. For hours no one else came. When Rochelle looked in he was seldom critical or snoopy; rather he preferred to think that everything was going as well as could be expected. The only hard feeling there was generated by the customers, who complained that nothing was done on time. And Rochelle was good with customers: he had a shrewd Gallic talkativeness that could logically account for everything. He could talk very fast.

But most of the time Mr. Sardis and I were there together. For a couple of weeks I felt almost a contempt for him; he was unhandy and seemed slow-witted and out of place in a competitive world of mechanics. I thought of him as the old geezer. He could wash and polish, but he couldn't do the tires right and I had to keep showing him. For a long time he said very little; he thanked me, and he said he was stupid. But I began to realize that he suffered a good deal, not because he had to work but because he felt he was doing it badly. Old as he was he had a persistent belief in his inferiority. "You do it so well," he finally said in his breathy foreign accent. "If I did it for a hundred years I would still do it badly."

Most of the old geezers who do the unskilled work in shops are as insensitive as so many tools. They do what they do as though they were impelled by reluctant springs and wires. But Mr. Sardis worked in a little flutter of feeling, and he never felt he had really finished a job; he kept going back to it for a last few touches, and he cocked his head at it like an anxious little bird. "Always when I look hard, I see blemishes," he said. His voice was very gentle and deprecating.

He seemed too frail for the work, and his deep-lined swarthy face was always tired, but he had muscular arms and hands and enjoyed using them. "Oh, it's so easy," he said. "Just to use muscle, just to pull and squeeze. I like it—I am ashamed to like it so much, but I do."

The confidences came slowly. For some time he vanished at his lunch hour—partly, I found, from modesty, and partly because he knew of a pleasant bit of grass among trees about a half mile away. He regarded me as a natural barbarian because I was young and profane, and because I was good with machines. "It is the new savagery," he said later, only half in jest. "The metal, the metal, the everlasting metal." I was a sort of god of metal, he said. "I admire you very much." But there was a wry expression on his wizened face. We had our lunch together then, out in a corner of the back lot, but our talk was not only at lunch; it went on all day, in and out of the hammering and drilling. Mr. Sardis, I found, was a scholar and a philosopher, though he made no such claims himself. "In my boyhood," he said, "the good people were innocent. They were instructed by the priests—and naturally the best people, the most innocent, were the priests themselves." When he spoke of ideas his voice grew eager. "It was a life of promises, without thought, without any study of reality. We were children—our teachers were children—"

"It sounds very nice," I said.

"Nice—yes!" His face seemed luminous. "A nice little game. We played life and God." He roused up and waved a finger—not at me, because his intention was not to attack me or anyone personally. "It may be good—it may be the best, but I believe it leads to extinction. My people in Crete—they are the futile ones, the rabbits and the mice of man-kind. They inherit nothing—they are nothing." He watched me with a sort of bright irony. "Yes, yes—better a fool's paradise, you say, than a realist's hell; but I tell you, Will, in this world the fool is no longer safe—his paradise is gone, he is dispossessed or murdered."

I hardly knew what he was talking about then, or why he felt so strongly, and actually he didn't expect me to know. But he kept on talking. He had resolved, he said, to be candid, to recognize and respect every fact and every truth no matter what the consequences were. "It is too late, of course—I cannot escape my criminal innocence! But I do what I can. I polish cars; I mend punctures—"

"You mean," I said, "you do all this as a sort of policy?"

"I do it to make money. We are very poor, my family and I. But I do it with what I believe is realization and acceptance. I am no longer just a disappointed musician, as I was for many years; I am a very little part of the actual world. I tell you this, Will—though you may laugh, and rightly: I am proud that I can do what I do here, poor as it is."

He had been a violin player, I found, until some sort of arthritic trouble made it impossible for him to finger the strings. "You see," he said, holding up his calloused left hand, "I am strong—my hands are very muscular, but something about the movement of the fingers made severe pains in my arm. I simply had to stop playing." Then he smiled with his characteristic gentle irony and went on: "Of course, I was not a successful violinist. I gave a few lessons, and played in small orchestras—it may be that here in the garage I am more candid with myself than I would have been before; it is my new realism, you see." That little irony of his had great charm to it, but there was much sadness underneath.

Rochelle called him Papa, but until he protested I called

him Mr. Sardis. "It is not suitable here," he said. "You must call me Pop. It is the correct name for a useless old man." He kept at me until I did. "A musician may be mister—a good musician, that is, and even if I was not eminent I think I was good—quite good; but a man in a shop must have a quick name, like a hammer stroke."

"Is that what you mean by the new savagery?"

"Ah—yes, exactly. We are in it, you and I. We must behave properly, as it were."

It was the first time I had encountered a reflective mind. My mother thought only along practical lines. My Aunt Lucy had expressed the thought of her father. Harold had not begun to think articulately. But Pop, as I learned to call him, seemed to do nothing but shape and reshape his thoughts. He worked so clumsily that I had to watch him as though he were a child, and he expected me to treat him that way, but when he talked I was the child. He instructed me in what he called logical realism. We destroy our minds with hope, he said; we let desire take the place of actuality; we refuse nature.

I was at first amused at all this, and superior to it. Pop was the sort of man the world looks on as a harmless crank; his toughness of mind seemed absurdly inappropriate to his general aspect of innocence. But the ideas were so shrewd and so thoroughly reasoned that I could only listen.

I finally put the question of my future up to him, and I did it with a sense of my own innocence. Should I behave like a Redfern and go to college, or should I keep on as I was? I said it lightly, of course, not wanting to betray myself. I pretended it didn't matter very much.

At first he gave no opinion. It would be presumptuous, he said. But then he asked questions, and slowly the whole problem absorbed him. I was a symbol of the times, he thought. I was what he called a new type in human history—it was very interesting. I must have, he said, a thorough technical education; I must become a perfect expert. In the new culture I would be the indispensable man.

Why, I asked.

He seemed to think I was destined; he spoke like a delphic oracle. My notion of independence, he said, was merely youthful romance. No modern man could be independent—all this prating about freedom was very unrealistic; the fact was that we were all part of a great machine—we were cogs or wheels.

"It is you," he said, "who must become the big wheel, eh?"

Not if I could help it, I said.

"Ah, but you must. It is the only happiness—to do what one can do. If you do less than the utmost, you fail, you are as we say unhappy. In this world there is no place for philosophical retreat. It might have done in a simpler day—St. Francis talking to birds, Thoreau under a tree—but you know, I doubt it, I am sceptic!" His face seemed to screw up with intensity. "They tried hard to fool themselves."

I said nothing.

"You must be in it and of it; you must accept the reality of it."

"You mean I should go to college?" I asked.

"Not just for irrelevant culture—not just because you must be a gentleman—no! You must be very practical—very realistic!"

But then he smiled. "It is only my opinion, Will. As you can see, I have not been practical myself. In my youth I admired St. Francis."

"And you regret it?"

He spread his hands. "I am by nature an idealist, Will. I hope. I have visions. That is why I advise you to be realistic. But you see—" He twisted his whole body with physical effort as though the thought had to be squeezed out. "The words are so poor—they are *false*." He caught his breath, looked down at his hands, and seemed to begin again. "You can master—or be mastered. You can create—or be created. I mean you, Will Redfern. You can be a tool, like a wrench or a hammer—and be used. Or perhaps—it is conceivable—you can be a little the creator, the maker." He pointed to the motor I had been working on. "Tell me, is it perfect, that machine?"

I looked at it stupidly.

"In twenty years perhaps there will be a better one?"

"Oh, sure!" I woke up a little. "Oh, they'll probably have a turbine drive or something—"

"But who? Who is this *they*?"

I nodded. I saw what he meant.

"It is a vision, Will."

  CHAPTER 2

I WORE AT that time a brown skull cap that I had cut from an abandoned felt hat. It came, the hat, out of a trash can, as did many other useful items (including the fountain pen I'm still writing with); I cut notches round the edge of the cap and wore it at an angle, partly to keep grease out of my hair, partly for the hell of it. My pose was that of careless and jaunty freedom. I refused the trappings of civilization: no neckties, no suits, no coats. I went about with chest out, muscles rippling, and the facial expression of a poker player. Much of this behavior was contrary to Mother's training, of course, and she scolded me pretty sharply, but I couldn't seem to do otherwise.

Yet I don't think I was arrogant about it; I didn't intend to be, at least. There was little time for friends or the usual pleasures, and I had to pretend I didn't give a damn about all that. I paid no attention to athletics, never learned to dance or to go to parties. Sometimes Mother and I went for a ride or to the movies and had ice cream sodas afterward, and actually that was about all the "going out" I had ever done. Because I was a workman I learned about drinking beer, and where I could get it without questions being asked: I was convinced that I looked well over twenty-one, though my light

94

hair and pink skin were babyish and my severe poker face must have seemed ludicrous. Mother, of course, knew nothing about the beer.

But in the main it was an innocent life. I loved girls, but was afraid to touch them. I smoked cigarettes, but never at home. Most of my spare time was devoted to tinkering with radios and motors, and I built up a small neighborhood repair business in my bedroom. Many of our human associations, in fact, were with the owners of broken down radios who hoped to get them made as good as new at little or no cost. It was a fine experience, because they were often very appreciative, and considered me a worker of miracles.

I read quite a lot too, mainly in the magazines.

But there were no friends. Mother had no talent for friends —she was too intent on duty. I developed a sort of solitary pride that was in a way an affectation. It seems to me now that my natural inclinations are sociable.

All these notes are a preface to my meeting the Sardis family, with whom in time I made friends. They lived in a three decker tenement, and most of them were not called Sardis but Anthonakis. It was confusing, but I found that there were at least three family units there. Mrs. Anthonakis, who lived on the second floor, was Pop's eldest daughter; she had a family of four daughters. Other members of her husband's family lived on the top floor. Pop lived on the ground floor with his wife and one daughter, who worked in a paper mill. The place was always full of dark-haired girls.

"Very nice, very pretty," Pop said, "but a problem."

I went there first one Saturday evening, and we had coffee and cakes. Pop was a nervous and eager host, and talked erratically; he kept getting up and offering more cakes and coffee and pacing up and down the small room. His wife sat motionless and white in a wooden rocking chair in a corner, saying nothing and apparently seeing nothing: he had told me she was ill, and had had a heart attack; she could hear and understand, but she couldn't easily speak. "It is still, after all these years, a strange world to her," he had said. "She thinks we live as we did in the old country—she thinks I am the head of the family." His voice had conveyed the absurdity of the notion. "She thinks we are very pious. She thinks the girls are obedient and modest." He spread his hands. "I cannot explain to her how things are."

He was full of little kindnesses to her, and rested a gnarled hand on her shoulder; he told her I was his instructor and guide as well as his friend, but she hardly seemed to see me. She sat there, white and shrunk into herself, wearing an old black knitted sweater.

Anna Sardis had something of the same shrunken look and even the same silence, though there was nothing the matter with her. She moved round vigorously, carrying cups and plates, with set mouth and jaw outthrust like a ram as though she were continually impatient and acting under protest. She hardly sat down, but half leaned on the edge of the chair and kept eyeing our coffee cups and jumping up to fetch and carry. Her expression, I came to think, was one of pure anxiety: she simply worried about everything.

"Anna takes care of us," her father said. "She thinks we are helpless." She seemed to have none of her father's reflective and humorous intelligence, and though she treated him with grave respect she kept an eye on him continually, as though he were a child on the verge of trouble.

I felt for a time quite out of place. The room was stuffy and crowded, the effort to be hospitable made for nervous anxiety, a general sort of sadness hung over everything. It seemed difficult to talk freely, and my companion and friend, whom I lightly called Pop, had become an anxious old man involved in a harsh little world of his own.

But then others began coming in, and a strong family affection grew in the air. There was Mrs. Anthonakis from upstairs, a beautiful woman with pure black hair, large in body and loosely held together by her clothes, easy, overflowing with simple-hearted love. She kissed everyone, including me. We sure need a boy, she said, specially a blond one: any time I wanted to join the family I was welcome. But with all her amplitude she somehow stayed observant; she understood about feelings, and was even a little diffident—or perhaps I should say sensitive. "We are so female here," she said, "we hardly know how to behave. Do you know my girls? They know you, I think. Althea and Sally—"

They stood inside the door like two shadows. Their big dark eyes stared at me with no expression whatsoever and they looked as though they had never in their lives uttered a word.

"So many Greek names," she went on. "Helen, Penelope, Athena, Rhoda, Andromache, Cassandra—and Mike said why don't you call her Sally. So we did."

I had seen them at school, walking together like twins.

Anna was getting more cups and passing more cakes. Pop looked happier than he had, and kissed his daughter and granddaughters and watched them with glistening eyes. "How are you, my dears?" He led them to his wife in the corner, and they made a little ceremony of greeting her. "You see," he said to me, "I enjoy pretending to be the patriarch. It makes me feel wise and venerable and important."

"Well," I said awkwardly, "I think they're fond of you."

It seemed a stupid thing to say, but he looked at me with a certain eagerness. "Ah yes—the Greeks are very fond—very foolish." He smiled at the words. "We live in a sort of—" he hesitated—"a sort of conservatory of family affection. It is traditional."

I thought a moment. "Not like the new savagery?"

"No! It is old-fashioned—I almost said it is foreign, and perhaps it is. The transplanted family is more self-conscious." He looked at the two silent girls. "It is hard to tell—there is more than meets the eye. They are no longer transplanted." He included them in the talk. "You must learn to be very modern, eh? You must emancipate yourselves—you must be like Will Redfern, the young man of the present!"

They smiled in deference to their grandfather's whimsies, but their flushed faces were withdrawn and their eyes veiled; oracular wisdom, they seemed to say, was not for them.

He waited for what might come next, watching us with bird-like brightness.

"Are you twins?" I asked.

Their glances crossed and they gathered themselves closer together for defense. One giggled—it was Althea.

"You must answer," their grandfather said after a silence. "It is your duty." His voice was full of laughter.

"I'm a year older," Althea said, and I was surprised that she spoke out so firmly.

"Different grades?"

She nodded.

"What grades, my dear?" It was Pop's voice again, very gentle.

"Sally's eleventh. I'll be twelfth."

"I used to see you together always."

They made deprecating noises and exchanged glances. Althea was inclined to giggle a little, but Sally seemed to exist in a brooding silence.

"You played the piano, I remember."

They both nodded.

"A duet," I added.

Althea offered a comment. "The bench wasn't big enough. We kept falling off the ends." Sally let herself smile widely, then glanced at me like a startled doe and grew sober.

"Not, I assure you," Pop said, "because they are too big on the bottom."

I thought the girls would be smothered in confusion, but one smiled, the other giggled, and they glanced respectfully at their grandfather.

"No violins?" I asked in the little silence. I said it soberly because I was embarrassed by Pop's remark.

He spread his hands. "For children it is the worst instrument. Better a horn or a drum—anything but a violin. I advise all mothers against it—"

Althea laughed. She understood that he was being ironic— she seemed, in fact, to expect it of him.

He peered at her. "Yes, my dear, I am not at all consistent. I insist on giving lessons to my grandchildren. It is possible, you see, that one of them may have talent—"

"Sally does," she said with a touch of indignation, as though it were a settled fact that he should have recognized.

He glanced at me brightly. "You see how careful we must be! So sweet, so shy, yet so fierce—" He touched her shoulder. "Yes, Sally is talented—so, perhaps, are you, my dear. It is said to be a family tradition—music. But the violin is very peculiar, very maddening; it requires such devotion as a child cannot realize. It is either good or it is bad—there is nothing in between, no pleasant mediocrity, as there can be with other instruments; it is all or nothing." He looked benevolently at the silent and shadowy Sally. "I don't even know whether to hope or not—I prefer to be fatalistic about it."

What she understood or thought it was impossible to tell. Her face, like Althea's, had a beauty of clear skin and bright color and large dark eyes, but there was no expression on it; except for the rare quick smile she was like a statue.

"Do you work at the violin?" I asked.

"Yes."

The girls drew closer again, and that was the end of that.

Afterward, when we were back in the shop, Pop talked a good deal about his family. They were still in a state of transition between old ways and new, which was perhaps why he was so much concerned with what he called the new realities. In the old country the girls were kept in a state of mindless virginity until a marriage could be arranged, and he noticed that his son-in-law, Mike Anthonakis, who owned a grocery store, still felt that way about his family. "They think I'm not serious when I say it is all nonsense—they think I'm always making little jokes." His wizened face, anxious and ironic, peered at me. "I am, in fact, a heretic, an iconoclast, too dangerous to take seriously—remember that, Will."

I tried to make fun of him about his heresies, but he was too sharp for me. At his age, he pointed out, he had the advantage of being able to see all that was wrong: he was like a politician who could find fault with past events. One thing he was sure of—that beautiful women were always a problem. I remember clearly how he said that word "problem" with a quick, throaty, humorous accent. "In my family the men are always ugly, and the women are beautiful: it is a problem."

But in time, as he talked, he really shocked me. The human race, he said, had achieved two colossal failures: one was in the matter of war, the other of sex. War, he said, was of course understandable—it could at least be explained. But the superstitions of sex might have been devised by a Congo witch doctor, for all the sense they made. The whole code, he argued, the right and wrong, pure and impure, legal and illegal, was nothing but a kind of voodoo, a system of curses and guilts and tabus that people had habituated themselves to generation after generation. Everybody, he said, secretly knew it; no one did anything about it. The very word virtue symbolized the whole pernicious nonsense (as he put it): what once was an honest word meaning manliness now meant virginity, and why that should be considered a virtuous condition no one knew.

I tried to hide the surprise I felt, but he realized it. "You see, Will, I shouldn't have spoken so candidly—I am simply a corrupter of youth." His face screwed itself into anxious lines. "I don't dare to speak like this at home—nor of course do I really want to upset them. Truth is sometimes very terrible. Of all our ancient superstitions, that of sex is the greatest, the most deeply rooted—we would not know how to live without the terrors and jealousies and curses of sex." He went on that way, and I listened with intense interest. He advised me not to take him seriously.

Naturally my mother seldom mentioned the subject, except to express disapproval of certain kinds of behavior. But I knew the language, the stories, the folk lore, the code of what Pop called pure hypocrisy that governed the young and the old alike, and of course I had never tried to think systematically about any of it. I had heard others say some of the things Pop said, but they were sly or hilarious or self-indulgent. It had never occurred to me that there might be some truth in them.

"Perhaps," Pop said, "I think too abstractly—perhaps I exist in a vacuum of age and inadequacy, like a foolish hermit deluded by what he assumes to be his wisdom."

"Well," I said finally, "what would you do about it? What would you recommend?"

"Ah, you challenge me, you pin me down." His voice grew more serious. "I tell you, Will, if I could have the omnipotence—if I were in fact a god—" He scrutinized his lifted finger. "You know, I think I would do quite well. I would revise the list of sins, I would eliminate the phony ones . . ."

The more he talked the more persuasive he sounded. I have never forgotten in the years since then how simply and intently his mind worked. I can hear his words, see his face as he shaped them—the wrinkled nut-like face full of eagerness, the small bright eyes watching me. "A girl may be judged on her character—her kindness, courage, intelligence, usefulness, loyalty—many such things. Whether or not she is a virgin is of absolutely no importance—it is in itself not a moral or ethical matter at all."

Was it part of his new realism, I asked.

"Not new, Will—rather, old—ancient, I should say. But we need a new realism—or at least a new candor. There is no doubt about that."

⋅§ CHAPTER 3 §⋅

DURING that summer there was talk of the war in Europe, but it seemed too remote to bother about. Mother paid little attention to foreign news. Harold was away at a camp for artists and writers that one of his teachers operated in the Berkshires. I was alone at home a good deal of the time, and of course I listened to the radio and took an interest in the techniques of both peace and war; but I didn't understand what was happening.

Pop did. Europe, he said, was like a dry forest; once the fire started, once the wind began to blow, it would be the worst inferno ever known. He took it so seriously and brooded so much that people were annoyed with him. "All he talks about," Rochelle snapped. "End of the world, you'd think to hear him. Everything down the drain—France, England—pouf! Nightmares he has. He should keep 'em to himself." Rochelle was convinced that France was safe and sane, and would in time take control of things. But Pop kept on with his gentle certainty of disaster. "They are not sane—they are possessed, like the Gadarene swine." He said it so often and so sadly that no one took any serious notice. "Those who should be wise, who stand for civilization, are insane. It is a catastrophe—the worst, I think, in all history."

I went home with him a good deal, and Anna took a sort of

pugnacious pleasure in feeding me. At the time it seemed natural, but I have since then realized that she might well have resented me. The fact that I was blond and male seemed to give me special status; I was looked upon as a relief to the sombre anxieties of the household. Anna's devotion to her father was so pure and serious that there was hardly room for jealousy. She thanked me for being, as she said, good to him. "You are his friend," she said.

Pop was quite candid about it too. "You are very indulgent, Will; you let me talk." He liked young people, he went on, but they were not patient with a slow-witted and garrulous man and they were too eager to pin him down, to get a quick answer to their questions. "Truth," he said, "has to be turned over and around, it has to be held loosely in the hands, as it were; when you look at one truth—here—you have to remember all the other truths at the same time. It is difficult, I think, for the young."

I found all sorts of things that needed fixing—some of them so simple that only the twist of a screw was required, and I pleased Anna specially by getting her old treadle sewing machine to work. Though she spent her days in a factory, she had no notion of any mechanical process ("old-fashioned," her father called her, "much too old-fashioned—like me"), but the one thing she really counted on was the sewing machine. She worked, it seemed to me, all the time, day and night: she did nothing else. Cooking, cleaning, washing, sewing, anxiously watching to see that her helpless parents were taken care of—she never spent an idle minute. Whatever youth or charm she might have possessed had all been transmuted into her single devotion. Her generous-hearted sister and the other relatives from upstairs did much to help; they kept watch during the day, and they gave her labor-saving devices that sooner or later broke down, though she never spoke of any difficulty about them and went on doing everything by hand, the old way. "My poor Anna," Pop called her.

The two girls, Althea and Sally, kept out of my way with calculated feminine perversity, but there were two younger ones, named Rhoda and Nan, who had no reserves, and some cousins on the third floor wandered in and out with friendly intentions, so that I got to know the whole family. They made fun of Althea and Sally because they were shy and somewhat separate, and called them the "twins" and spoke of them as though they led different lives from the rest of the family. We could hear one or the other practising upstairs, Althea on a rather metallic piano, Sally on a violin—though I couldn't tell if she were "good" or not. At times they worked in their father's store, which stayed open when others were closed. But now and then they'd let themselves be caught, as it were, with the others in the little ground by the front steps, talking or sitting in the late sun, or twirling a rope for the little ones to skip, or playing jack-stones. Sally did that best—they were all proud of her and made her do it and watched her hands flash. She was normally a rather still, grave girl; she seldom spoke, seldom smiled, and looked at the world with steady, dark-eyed intentness as though she were spying on it for some unfathomable purpose of her own. There was a wildness about her; she seemed to be poised for retreat and escape, like a deer. It always surprised me to see her bending over the jacks in the midst of a circle of watching youngsters.

I liked girls but I always had trouble getting at them, as it were. The habits of independence were very strong in me, and it may be that I was reluctant to give up any of it. In a subterranean sort of way I fell in love with Sally when I first saw her. I was very strongly attracted by that secret life that seemed to exist behind the dark watchful eyes; I felt somehow that her personality must have a pure separateness of its own, a perfect independence of all others. It seemed to me that she lived simply for the sake of living, and had no designs on anyone, no ulterior intentions, no predatory calculations.

In a sense I fell in love with both of them. They went together. But because Althea was the leader, in a small way, and giggled and spoke more, I was attracted to Sally. Althea belonged to the world round about her—at least, she seemed to; her eyes were quick to see the boys and men of the neighborhood—very bright dark eyes they were, full of flashes of eagerness and sudden retreats into timidity, with inevitable giggles and self-deprecations. She and Sally seemed to talk to each other by a sign language of their own, with little breathings and unvoiced exclamations to go with it, and Althea kept saying "Oh, Sal" with infinite minor inflections. There was something very pure about the two of them; they were like clear springs in a wood and I loved them in an arcadian sort of way.

It took time to break through the thin wall of transparency that surrounded them, though I had little consciousness of any planned attack. Perhaps it was my car that did it. I had spent the summer putting together the parts of a Ford, not a rattling jalopy but an eight cylinder demon that would "do eighty-five," I let it be known, as quiet as a breeze. The car was as much a part of me as my cap or shoes, and I used it to travel round the block or to the corner store for a loaf of bread, and of course I went to Pop's place in it and beguiled the girls into taking rides. We had ice cream; we went to the movies; we even visited an "amusement park" up the river and rode on the merry-go-rounds. We didn't dance—none of us knew how, though Althea had been to one or two school dances and would have liked to do more. But she didn't want to be seen in a public dance place, and Sally was too shy anyway.

The three of us got along with a special sort of happiness,

and the dark girls grew prettier and more animated. They used no make-up of any kind, so far as I could ever tell, and dressed in the plainest and cheapest things, but the shimmering black hair and large half-shy dark brown eyes made them seem almost legendary, like unrecognized deities. Sally hardly talked very much, and we made fun of her silence, but the smile and flash of her eyes were sometimes joyous.

They were still tied quite closely to their family, and were unwilling to be away more than a couple of hours; even then there were concerns about duties at home or in the store and about how their father would react. They went to the Greek church on Sunday morning, though there were differences of opinion, I found, between the Sardis and Anthonakis households. Pop had become a pure eclectic: he made the rounds of all the churches he could reach in town and inclined finally towards the Universalist because the minister was the only one, he said, who had any interesting ideas. Anna never had time for church. Mike Anthonakis was sternly orthodox, and his wife found it more peaceful to join him, though she had few convictions about it and would have enjoyed any sort of ceremony with music. The girls expressed no opinions except a half-humorous reluctance. No one ever consulted their opinions, anyway, and their grandfather was careful, as he thought, not to corrupt them. "My poor innocent little family," he said. "I only hope they remain in a state of bliss."

But they watched him more than he knew. "Gramp has all the fun," Althea said. "I wish I were that old." She said it just for the extravagance of it, without considering very far, and of course she laughed self-consciously.

After several moments Sally spoke with a little blurt, as though the words were forced out of her. "You don't have to be."

"Don't have to be what?"

"Old."

Ideas didn't come to us very easily, and there was a longer silence. "Well, gee whizz," Althea tried, "there's nobody to tell him what he has to do, so he does whatever he feels like. It must be nice."

Sally lifted her head again, and the words came out with the same suddenness. "It's mostly what he thinks. You can think —or try to." She did not emphasize the "you"; she meant anyone could think—and she said it in such a hopeful sort of way that we laughed.

"Sal tries, anyway," Althea said.

"Is that what goes on inside there?" I said.

"I guess so. Something goes on." Althea giggled.

Sally's face was as enigmatic as Mona Lisa's, but Althea was right. Something went on in there.

"Your Gramp," I said, "is a pretty dangerous man. You don't know—he doesn't talk to young girls like you."

But I felt that Sally knew. Her big eyes watched me with secret knowledge.

She read a great deal; the two talked about it a little bit, and I heard names I hadn't known of. Sappho and Housman were two—Althea somehow conveyed a sort of ecstasy for them by the way she caught her breath. Their grandfather gave them Greek tales—and I remember Sally saying in one of her rare comments that the gods did not ever behave respectably. They weren't very happy, either, she brooded. None of the Greeks were. And her own attitude as she said it, the ancient dark beauty of her hair and face, seemed like an emblem of some classic sorrow. But then she added, smiling quickly, "I don't see why they had to make such a mess of everything. I should think they could have done it better—I mean, they could have—" She left it, not knowing how to finish.

Being city girls, readers and dreamers, they delighted in the country. We lived in a sort of prison-yard of tenements and factories and small stores and taverns, but round about was a region of farms and forests and little mountains; in ten minutes of driving we could be high up on the ridge of Mount Tom or along the wild shores of the river. They had no strong desire to tramp or climb or be strenuous; they were in a way too innocent, and too astonished. A cow to them was as rare a vision as a wild elk. Sally could go into a sort of trance simply by watching a squirrel scurrying about among a grove of trees. They were excited by their ignorance; they laughed at their follies and discoveries and made a game of seeing things and counting and naming—I remember Althea twisting in the seat as we drove, turning on her knees, to count a flock of sheep near Granby. I had to stop near Amherst so that they could get out and smell the apples in the big orchards, and they saw a rabbit and were amazed that it was wild. I told them to watch for deer, and from then on they cried out and poked each other at the sight of phantom deer. They peered into glades and old pastures and urged me along untravelled roads in the woods. Deer had white tails like flags, I told them, but they hardly knew whether to believe me; it sounded like something in a legend or ballad, and they conjured up fantastic visions. We fell into moods of light-headed enchantment as though we were following a gleam or questing for the white unicorn.

On one of these Sunday afternoons just before their school opened we were stuck with a flat tire on a little road high up in a range of wooded hills. It was no more than a half hour's drive from home, but the country round about was vast and wild, covered with stunted hardwoods—birch and red oak, mainly. There were overgrown pastures in it, and cellar holes, and a few abandoned barns, but for miles no sign of human life. I changed the tire, and the girls wandered up a wood road and disappeared.

The feel of autumn had come already. Birch leaves were faintly yellow; the roadside weeds gave out the dried pungent smell that at once recalled all the autumns of one's life—a sere and crispy smell like long-preserved spice of some sort. It was a pleasant cool time to work, and afterward I stood looking off over the low forest to the westward where the land fell in long hazy slopes to the valley of the Connecticut.

There were no voices, but the girls were always pretty quiet. I waited, then walked up the grassy lane where they had gone. The land sloped gently up, then levelled; the road branched into two smaller and grassier roads. It was a region where wood-cutting was done in winter, and the lanes were no more than sled tracks. Here and there were stacked piles of birch cordwood.

I called and whistled, at first reluctantly because of their quietness, but then more loudly. I ran from road to road, stumbling into brush and briars, turning back to try another, stopping to breathe and call, but the region was as quiet as a dream. No life of any sort seemed to stir in it, no wing of bird or chatter of squirrel, but in the last glade I came to before turning back to the car I saw for an instant two small does bounding away over the bushes with white tails flashing.

After I blew the horn, walked up the lane calling again, blew the horn many times, I saw them in the dusk coming up the road we had been driving on. They had been away for nearly two hours. I told them I was just about to go and call for the state police.

They were filled with an intense sort of happiness—they overflowed with it, and talked together in a breathless duet. We were *lost*, they said, really *lost*, like children in a story— it was wonderful and terrible. They went on and on through the unknown, Althea saying this way, Sal that way; they tore their skirts and scratched their legs. And then—how silly they were, how utterly dumb—they came to the road at last (it was Sal's idea they should try to go down hill) and then went the *wrong way*. And they heard the horn blowing, and thought how queer that someone should be blowing a car horn way off there, and finally it dawned, it *came* to them, and they looked at each other and Althea said aren't we *stupid* and they laughed and laughed . . .

"We looked for the deer," Sally said.

"Once we thought we saw—something," Althea said.

I started to tell them, but decided not to. "Maybe you did," I said. "They live in country like this."

But when we got back to Holyoke their father was very angry. He couldn't understand anyone being lost. He said I had no business taking them on such trips—he wouldn't permit it. He paced back and forth and made gestures with a stout arm and looked dangerous.

The girls stood like mutes, side by side, heads a little bowed, knowing exactly how they must take it. After a few minutes they could walk away and it would be over. You'd have thought they didn't feel anything; their faces were closed, their mouths fixed in secrecy, their eyes like dark stones. They didn't resent it, perhaps, any more than one might resent a drenching rain: it was an act of nature—but of course they would never forget any of it. "Lost, you say," he shouted out. "All I know is you go joy riding with this feller, you come home late—after dark." His gesture missed Sally's nose by inches, though she didn't blink. When I muttered something about a flat tire he turned on me in fury, fists closed and eyes burning with passion, and I stepped back and braced myself for an onslaught. He growled and sucked in his breath with a loud theatrical noise. "You—*you*—" His right fist menaced me. "You—"

But Mrs. Anthonakis came in. "All right, Mike, relax, pipe down, everything's fine, isn't it?" She threw a soft arm round my shoulders. "Here we all are, good as ever. You don't know Will like I do—" She smiled and squeezed luxuriously. "Take me next time, huh, Will? I won't mind if you have a flat tire."

"Yah—" He turned his attack fiercely against her. "Who cares about an old woman?" Then quite suddenly he shrugged the whole thing off. "I'm just telling you—from now on no more joy rides, you hear?"

He swung round to address the girls, but they had gone.

So THE summer ended all at once. The girls went to school and the old sober routines of autumn began. That pungent smell of weeds and dry leaves grew and intensified like a mild warning of doom—or of life encroaching. Harold came home for a brief time before going on to Harvard, for which he had been awarded a national scholarship, and Mother discussed clothes with him and they went to Springfield to buy a suit. I remember how set and grim they were when they came back, each one suffering under the implacable will of the other. School clothes, winter clothes, were in Mother's view to be dark and strong and plain; Harold saw himself in soft and creamy tweeds and flannels—though it wasn't so much an opposition of actual apparel as it was of temperament. Harold simply felt that Mother was to be fought at every step and turn.

The realities of autumn weighed upon us. Mother spent the evenings actively getting Harold ready for Harvard, as she kept pointing out to us—a long labor of mending, altering, washing, sorting, deciding. Harold devoted himself with a sort of ritualistic earnestness to reading Proust in French, almost as though it were a part of an initiation. He was not much older than seventeen, and his face had a fine golden transparency to it, a choir-boy look, remote and pure and beyond human concern. He read with wonderful devotion—perhaps partly because he felt it was the thing to do, but largely because he was profoundly immersed in it and lived more richly in the book than he did in the drab little world of our tenement.

Yet that year he looked upon me with some respect and even a little awe. For one thing I had developed a good deal of muscle, and I carried myself with a kind of physical arrogance. It impressed him that I was full grown and doing a man's work and holding the world at bay, as it were. He read his Proust partly, I think, as a counter-measure against my kind of success, and it seemed to gratify him that I didn't try to make fun of him as I might once have done. We had begun to be a little scared of each other.

It was he, I think, who took the first steps toward arranging a college career for me—and his reasons were devious and interesting. In the main, he felt that I would be less of a success in the collegiate world, yet more of a credit to him. He borrowed my car one day and on his own hook visited all the colleges in the area; he had no hesitation whatever about demanding interviews with officials on the highest level—his competence in carrying on worldly negotiations has always been astounding. Mother would have done these things if she had known how, but she couldn't drive, she worked during the day, and she was conscious of being awkward and ignorant. But she and Harold conspired, and before I could resist I was involved. The facts were put before me. Wyndham College wouldn't have me at all at so late a date, but there were others of better hope with more practical programs.

I resisted, of course. The abstractions of a college catalogue meant little to one in full charge of Rochelle's repair shop. But late one afternoon Harold threw a tea cup at the iron sink in a fit of rage and my destiny was somewhat altered. Mother had been going at him rather hard: she couldn't reconcile herself to his idleness, his long hours of reading, his apathy toward housekeeping tasks—he hadn't bothered, she noted, to wash his own lunch dishes. But particularly he had gone out and bought himself some ten dollar shoes, cream-colored and flagrant, less durable than ones she could have got him for three-eighty-nine. It was, she felt, a moral failure, and she attacked him again and again. He didn't know what work meant, what money meant, what she had had to go through to keep us alive. At the time we were sitting at the kitchen table while she served supper, and Harold was very still and quiet. She went on, not with passion but with the intensity of some sort of drilling machine.

He screamed. The white face flamed red, the mouth opened hatefully, and out came a cracked scream. "Shut up! *Shut up!* SHUT UP!" He flung back his chair. "I can't stand you! I hate you! I won't—I won't—" When the words stopped he went crazy and threw the teacup at the sink.

Actually it missed Mother's head by a couple of inches. It was a good teacup, one of a set she had brought from Newton, and she had tried to intercept it: her impulse was to save property at whatever risk to herself. In the critical moment she was more outraged by the smashed cup than by Harold's frenzy. But then he turned and kicked his chair aside with intent to destroy it and rushed out of the room slamming the door with the force of an explosion.

In the silence Mother turned at once to the business of supper. She filled a plate and handed it to me. Her face had puffed out and reddened, and there were queer yellow streaks round her set mouth and chin. Then tears overflowed and ran down in two streams. She went into the tiny bathroom and shut the door.

In a few minutes she was back at work again, quiet and

tense, face still puffy, with the yellow streaks. She fixed no supper for herself, but began peeling the hot boiled potatoes, snatching their skins off with sleight of hand speed. I said she'd better come and eat but she made a negative movement and turned her face away.

Up to then I was partly on Harold's side. I wanted to explain to her that she wasn't handling him right, that she didn't really understand him—and if she had asked me I probably would have literally said so. It seemed impossible that two people so close, so vitally concerned with each other, should have no understanding. They were like metal of different thread and gauge, unalterable, yet at the time I still felt that a few words of explanation would reconcile them. Just let him be Harold, I could have said. You have to anyway, so you might as well do it gracefully. But she stood there stiffly on both feet, silent, peeling hot potatoes with flying fingers, and the tear streaks had come back to her face.

"He didn't mean all that," I mumbled. "It's just the way he is."

Again she made the negative movement. "He meant it. He has always meant it." Her voice was a whisper. She looked at my plate. "There's more if you want it." She went into the bathroom again.

I kept on with my meal, and had second helpings. In those days I was enormously hungry, and unlike Harold I could go on eating through all kinds of crises. But when Mother came back and went to work with stiff, unyielding persistence, her chin firmly set, her face shiny from the washing and rubbing, I felt suddenly the whole ordeal of her life, of all lives like match flames of hope in the void. Not much gave her pleasure; she indulged in no passing forgetfulness, no beguiling of the heart or mind, no appetites or pleasures designed to veil the face of doom; even her short sleep was a duty to give her strength for the day's work. Her life was first being a mother, next earning the money to support us, next taking care of the sick, and beyond those things it was being upright and brave. Yet at this moment her first hope had been killed.

"He goes crazy," I said. "He always has."

But she turned me away. "There's ice cream," she said. "Butter crunch."

"I'll get it." I took my plate to the sink and rinsed it. My impulse was to put an arm round her shoulders, but she didn't look up at me and her stance was somehow unyielding. At all the critical times she repelled any expression of strong feeling, and I stood there between sink and refrigerator unable for a moment to move or speak. She pushed past me with a gesture of impatience, as though I were as usual incompetent, and got out the box of ice cream.

"I'm sorry," I said. "I . . ."

"There's cake too—a couple of pieces. You might as well have it."

So I sat down and ate the dessert.

But I felt a heaviness of spirit, and after supper I dried the dishes and put them away, which I didn't always do. I noticed that she kept some food warm for Harold, but I didn't think he'd be back for a long time. She partly thought of him still as a little boy having a tantrum, though it hurt her cruelly enough; he had had plenty of tantrums before and had rushed off—and had sooner or later come back as though everything were quite normal, but each time more reluctantly. She hardly realized the temper of his mind. That he read Proust in French meant nothing to her.

He probably had gone up on the hills westward of town, I thought, but there was no telling. I went out and looked for him with some sort of idea of talking to him, though I had never been able to before, and for an hour and a half I walked about in the dark peering up and down dimly lighted streets. It was a cool and misty autumn evening, and I had never felt so melancholy. Everyone must suffer at times from despair, and many are proud of it, but for the most part my temperament was a careless one and I took a sort of mindless pleasure in the surfaces of life. What really delighted me most, and filled my days with eagerness, with the infinite inventiveness of the world I lived in: it seemed to me a pageant, an exposition of miracles, and the new cars, the new radios, the new notions, were daily adventures which I took part in. Any future I visualized was composed of incredibly deft and efficient mechanisms.

But on that autumnal evening some deeper human motive seemed to be at work in me. There is no virtue, I think, in brooding about the tragedy of being. A man is no better because he is aware of his doom, but there are times when he must see it and reckon with it. It was through my mother, of course, that I felt it and began somewhat reluctantly to acknowledge it. I used to be either indifferent or annoyed at the harshness of her fate and her own ceaseless battle, but this evening for almost the first time I seemed to be inescapably a part of it; I still couldn't approve of her behavior, but I had to share it.

"This place Harold talked about in Springfield," I said to her. "I didn't pay too much attention, but you seemed to think it would work out best."

She was ironing. When she felt badly she always worked.

"The things are all on the table," she said angrily. "The catalogues and things. You can read them. I don't know anything about them."

"Well, you've been saying I ought to go school."

"It's up to you. I'm not going to argue about it any more."

But when I began studying the catalogues she had a good deal to say. The state college was cheaper, but probably there'd be more of my kind of stuff at Springfield or Kingstown. She pointed out some of the course descriptions, and read a few passages aloud over my shoulder. Both of us were innocent about such things, but she was inclined to take anything in sober print pretty literally, specially the pretensions of a college catalogue. She kept saying that of course I ought to have a cultural foundation—English and so forth—but then she went on and read about the physics and mechanics and electronics with increasing eagerness. "Here, now—listen to this! Wouldn't this be the thing for you? Advanced Automotive Design—" What appealed to us most was a place called the Kingstown Technological Institute, which I knew Harold considered a second rate trade school, as it was, but which seemed to be concerned with the actualities that I understood. We began talking and planning, and Mother remarked that maybe another year I could go to a really good place like M.I.T.—she was sure I could win any necessary scholarship aid—and before I realized it I was committed to a new future. It wasn't so much a decision as it was an inevitable sentiment. Mother put away the ironing board, took off her apron, got me a glass of milk and a box of cookies, and her movements had an effect of warmth and buoyancy again. She even left some things on the kitchen table for Harold, with a note, as though everything were all right, and we went to bed. "Be sure to get him up in the morning," she said. "He has a nine-thirty dentist."

She left for work about half past seven, and I left at twenty past eight. Harold had come in so quietly that night I hadn't heard him, but it was pretty late and he was still asleep when I roused him just before I went off. I had intended to talk to him, but the time didn't seem right. Yet I was in a way angry about the whole thing, not so much because he had had a tantrum, which I could understand and even sympathize with, as because the tantrum had such power over the rest of us. I was rather brusque, in the way of stronger brothers, and hauled the blankets off and left him shivering in the cold room. I suppose he hated me for it. But I didn't say much, except that he had to be at the dentist's at nine-thirty.

I didn't say anything to Rochelle either about going to school again. It still remained a sort of reluctant emotion rather than a decision and I half hoped that if I waited it might go away. Back in the shop I felt secure and strong in my overalls and notched cap, and the routines there seemed to go on inevitably. New models would be coming in soon, and Rochelle was going to an advanced showing, as it was called, in New York. To him, with his Gallic scepticism, a new model was not necessarily any better than the old— though of course he knew he had to pretend it was—but to me it was an event more exciting than Christmas, and touched with the same sort of bright magic. The cars we dealt in were to have a new front wheel suspension this year, and nothing seemed more important to me than that.

I even said nothing to Pop. He felt so definitely about it that he would take any mention of it as a commitment. But some fatal power was at work inside me, because in spite of all evasions I knew I couldn't really escape. The sharp image of my mother swinging shut the old refrigerator door with one hand, upending the milk bottle with the other, acquiring a sort of characteristic momentum and energy, like a motor going smoothly into high gear, made a distinct scene in my mind, like a bit in a play. Yet she didn't really understand anything; she lived in a strange sort of forlorn innocence.

The next day at noon I surreptitiously put on a shirt, tie, and coat and rocketed the twelve miles to Kingstown to see what the Technological Institute looked like.

I was thoroughly disheartened by the place; it seemed more

like an abandoned high school than a college and at the end
of the long summer it gave out an air of dust and death. And
the one official there, a registrar or secretary, alone in a back
office and almost submerged in the noon-time silence and
gloom, answered my questions in such a hushed voice that I
could hardlly make out what he said. There would be no technical difficulty in my entering, of course, but that any normal
youth should want to enter seemed to be a matter of grave
regret to him. He was very tired and hollow, as though the
human substances had gradually wasted away from inside and
left nothing but a collapsing outer shell, but his intentions
were not unkind and when he saw that he had discouraged
me he proposed that I wait for Mr.—that is, Professor—
Chadd, who would be in at one, he believed.

All this would be of no special interest were it not that Mr.
Chadd, when he did arrive, so changed the scene. I had begun
to have a feeling of terror, as though I had been trapped; I
had the impulse to run for the free air beyond the front door.
That anything of human value should occur in such a building seemed impossible, and I'm sure the secretary-registrar,
Mr. Wiggam, felt so too. But not Mr. Chadd. He trotted in
as light-footed as a fox, blue eyes bright with confidence, hand
half extended in fraternal welcome. "Redfern, eh? Glad to see
you. Come on into my room—get out of this dismal old hole."
He winked at the solemn Wiggam. His voice was quick and
light, like the rest of him—he wasn't much more than five
feet tall, though he stood so straight he almost seemed to lean
backward. He snatched out a bunch of keys on a chain from
his pants pocket and whirled them round and round. "Anyone
looks at this dump, he thinks we're still working on gramo-
phones and gas mantles."

He seemed to grasp my problem in a moment and was off

at a trot, down stairs to a basement, through doors, and into a bare concrete and cinderblock wing. "Not very big, you see," he grinned, "not miles of it. But we do pretty well. All practical stuff—internal combustion here, you see, diesels—all the radio and electronic equipment up stairs—" He rushed on down a corridor, swinging his keys like a sling, and unlocked a door. "Here—come in—we can talk a minute. This isn't a college, you know. No Latin, no English—though I guess there's a fellow who teaches you how to write letters—maybe you know, eh? Well, it's practical—just enough math and theory—not enough, in my opinion—but some at least." He buzzed on in a bright irresistible way, not so much like a salesman as like a small boy with a hobby, and most of his remarks seemed confidential and candid. The place had been nothing but an old museum ten years ago, he said, but he and Joe Venuti had got this new wing and some modern equipment and though it was nothing but a trade school—we might as well be frank about it—it did an honest job, and the two-year certificate really meant something. He cited examples of success in the region—the man in charge of Kingstown Electric Power and Light was one, though of course all their boys weren't as smart as that. He found out what I had been doing and regarded me with a wonderful sparkle of benevolence. No reason, he said, I couldn't get through their regular course in a year; I was probably, he smiled, a lot smarter than the average fellows they had—he shook his head. No use pretending they didn't have some dumb ones, though they had all kinds too—some older ones who wanted special work, some pretty shrewd youngsters who had been fiddling with radios before they could read or write. Like me, probably. But I could learn a few things—I'd be surprised at how much.

He went on that way, and I was persuaded. He and Joe

Venuti would take care of me (I gathered that they were most of the faculty): all I had to do was to come on the opening day, pay the fee, and start in.

Rochelle, when I had told him, made a long face of despair and resignation. "Very good," he said. "Very good—for you. For me—" He shrugged and spread his hands. But I made a deal with him to work part time. As for Pop, he shook his head earnestly. "You should do better, Will. You are not seeing far enough." He seemed to feel I was too young to know what he meant. "It is easy for you to be a tool, a wonderful human mechanism, but in the end that won't be enough; you must understand what it is to create—like a god, perhaps." He smiled enigmatically. "Just remember, as you go to your new school, that the wonderful engines of the future are still to be created." Then he shrugged as though he were drawing back from his argument. "Perhaps you will find it out yourself. I think you will."

But Mother, in her innocence, thought the new arrangement was all right.

◦§ CHAPTER 5 ﾞﾟﾞ

IT WAS about then that war began in Europe, though we were too provincial to pay much attention to it. Only Pop was deeply concerned, and of course we hardly took in what he was saying. Later a long letter from Aunt Lucy, from Bell's Landing, seemed filled with fantastic concern about the fate of European culture. We skimmed along over the almost unreadable script and felt sorry for the two old ladies. Culture didn't seem very important, except to Harold, who said little about it. We hardly noticed that young men were already being drafted for army service.

If it hadn't been for Mr. Chadd I'd have given up the Kingstown Institute quite soon. It seemed to be a sort of refuge or trap for failures, and since the tuition fee was almost the only entrance requirement a good many incompetents and half-wits came in. But Chadd was undaunted by anything, and managed to run two schools simultaneously, one for the deadheads, as they were properly called, one for "professionals," of which there were twenty-five or thirty in the various fields. He himself actively taught classes about seven hours a day—an expense of human energy I have never seen equalled: he went from group to group and room to room like a young hound loose in the woods, and he handled everything except electricity and letter-writing. Joe Venuti, his partner, with almost equal output of energy and time, but with grim and sombre temper, had charge of the electrical work upstairs. The deadheads were kept as much as possible in the old building, with elementary equipment.

And Chadd saw that I learned—as he had promised. He taught me descriptive geometry and draughting, and metal work and machine-tool work, and the calculating of strains and stresses. I asked him, when I got to know him better, why with all his talents he stayed on at the school and he grinned as he always did and shrugged and said it was his baby and he liked it. Later he said he loved to teach: it made him feel less like the little runt he really was. Since knowing him I've never tackled a new task or problem without first wondering how he'd go about it, what imagination or wit or ingenuity he would bring to it. He could play with the intractables of metals and mechanics with a sort of poetic delight.

What he and the school did was to make me an incorrigible gadgeteer, a manipulator and inventor of small marvels.

So the routines of fall and winter were established. On two afternoons and Saturdays I worked for Rochelle, and Pop always welcomed me with a shy sort of eagerness. The new regular mechanic, a speechless ferret-like man named Nick (short for Maznicki), had been specially trained by the manufacturer and represented a new service policy that coincided with the new models. He was a tool, Pop said, making screw-driver-like motions with his hand, a set of tools that operated automatically like one of the mechanical marvels that performed all the essential functions at the turn of a switch. Pop seemed to save up all his whimsies and speculations for me; his creative mind needed an outlet, and I was the only available one. Nick, he said, was a good example of the fortunate man who had lost himself, who suffered no agonies of expectation and disappointment. I said he didn't look happy—rather he looked quite glum, like a large muskrat. Pop twinkled at me with a sort of relish, as though he had been waiting for that. It was pure nature, he said, the look of final acceptance, the fixed expression of all that is. . . . I couldn't tell how much he meant, though in a way I knew he always meant everything. Desire for happiness, he went on, is man's fatal weakness, and Nick seemed to be immune—hence one could consider him successful, at least, if not happy.

He talked quite a lot these days about the loss of self. It was apparently the primary necessity in life, and was somehow contrary to man's instinct. If you did what you wanted and achieved what you hoped for, you made yourself miserable. Pure self seems to be insatiable; the more it has the more it must have. But if by resolution or stern action of will—or perhaps by good luck—one renounced the self and embraced instead what must be described as a great project, a large and recognizable good . . . Here he shook his head ruefully. The trouble was that some of the projects were not good. Nick's, for example—and as he said it he looked at me with twinkling brightness. What it really amounted to was an ideal, though he hesitated to use an old-fashioned word like that.

I was as impervious to moralizing as most young people are, but Pop's always seemed different to me; it was home-made and had been tested out in his own candid mind. So after I brooded a bit about what he had said I asked him if he was implying that my ideals were not good.

"What are they?" he asked.

I refused to answer.

"It is wrong, perhaps, to require young people to have certain ideals—as I was required in my boyhood in Crete. But I believe the principle of the ideal should be constantly kept in mind, the vital need of it—and as I understand it, it is not.

The colleges, I am told, teach just two things: one is facts, the other is scepticism—both very valuable. The schools—" He shrugged. "They teach the ideal of what everyone calls Americanism—which is good, perhaps, and necessary, but so primitive, so crude, that it often seems ignoble. But where in our common life are the ideals of the spirit or of great love or great sacrifice? We hear about them, it is true, from anxious individuals—like me—but we live without much reference to them. They are not anywhere in the curriculum, as it were."

He said all this with considerable foreign intensity of gesture and accent, but with the cocked bird-like humor that always went with his speech. I had done so little reflecting about life that I contributed nothing, but Pop pretended that I was an active partner in the discussion. "You may say we are forced to doubt all the traditional ideals—especially of course the ideal of the wise and loving God—" His bright little eyes held me as though I were to be restrained a moment from interrupting. "It is true, I grant you. The old vision of the heavenly kingdom was man's best refuge from himself, and it is dwindling away—" He waved a hand. "An abstract spiritual ideal is very difficult without the white robes and angels' wings, though it is quite possible. But let us be simple—let us say quite literally that a man may lose his baser self in a quest for whatever is just, or honorable, or beautiful, or lovable, or true—" He held up the fingers of his left hand to mark each point.

All this seemed to have grown out of his observation of the imperturbable Maznicki, but I realized that it represented a constant concern like an underground stream flowing in his mind. I began to see that it was his dedication, his own particular release from self.

Yet the idea then had no special reality for me. It could be talked about abstractedly, in the quiet Saturday noons of autumn behind Rochelle's garage. There were problems, I felt, that old men could ponder, and it flattered me a little that I was half seriously included; it was like being in a seminar. But Pop's theories about the iniquities of self seemed quite academic. I was active in what I thought were wonderful adventures, and rushed from one thing to another without a single inward look. In the last few months I had got to know the automobile people of the region—mechanics, salesmen, backroom experts of all sorts—and I spent a lot of time inspecting cars, testing them, listening to talk about them, trading anecdotes and professional jests. I became a sort of boy mascot of the trade, and grew cocky and breezy with a sense of wonderful self-esteem. I spoke the jargon, the secret language of crankshaft bearings and cylinder heads, and I saw that my own Ford displayed itself conspicuously. Pop watched me as if I were a phenomenon that required his full attention, and though he took ironic pleasure in my youth and folly he seemed to be compassionate for reasons that I didn't understand. Life is in some ways a long time, he said. There is much that happens. I thought he was brooding about his own sorrows, and in a way he was, but he was troubled about me too.

It was he who advised me to take Althea and Sally out again. We needed each other, he said. As for Mike, his son-in-law, it was a question of understanding: he thinks, Pop said, not with the mind but with the racial tradition; he feels not for himself but for his people. In a sense he is not an individual as we think of individuals in an age of moral anarchy —and Pop went on at length to reflect about the values of racial tradition and how it provides a refuge, a safe retreat from the dangers of extreme selfhood. More practically, he said, Mike had no real objections to me as a person—except possibly on religious grounds. He simply intended to preserve his daughters from all men until satisfactory marriages could be arranged. Each girl was to remain a mindless virgin enclosed in wax-paper wrappings (Pop made gestures with his hands) until she was legally deeded to a suitable husband. If I were to appear, he went on, as a serious candidate—he looked at me out of the top of his eyes, as though he were peering above a pair of spectacles . . . I thought for a moment he almost meant it: in fact, it was hard to interpret the gleams in his little eyes. "You must wear a dark suit," he went on, "and a white collar and a tie, and bring flowers, and ask politely—with a small bow—for Mr. and Mrs. Anthonakis—" Up to that point he had been full of a gentle irony, but how he stared at the neat cheese sandwich Anna had made for him. "I describe myself to you, one hundred years ago." He looked very sombre and wrinkled. "Like Mike, I was not an individual but simply a small representative of my society. I had no inkling of the dangerous pleasures of anarchy."

"And now you do?" I filled in.

"Yes, now I do." Then he roused up with a stronger thought. "But it isn't me, Will. It isn't Mike. It is the age, the time, the world—you have to be in it, you have to swim in the water of it—anarchy, pure self, and all. I am sorry for Mike. He is a sort of vestige." Afterward, as he thought it over, he remarked that there were those who swam well against the current of the world—it certainly wasn't admirable always to swim with it. The main thing, though, was to be in it.

In some devious fashion he thought I was good for his grand-daughters and he made transparent little plans to get us together. But for a time they seemed to lead invisible lives, and even on Sundays were wholly dutiful and devoted. And of course I was busier than I had ever been. Whenever we both had time I took my mother for Sunday rides in the country and she looked for good bargains in apples or squash or anything useful along the roads: it was her greatest pleasure—not only the bargains, but the golden harvests, the countryside, even my jalopy which she now admired as if I had made it all by hand. But one afternoon on the Mt. Tom road we passed a Buick parked well out in the highway, with several men in it talking to a girl standing beside it, and I tooted with a feeling of disapproval and swung out to pass. The girl I hardly saw, but Mother did—she always had a quick eye. One of my Greek girls, she said. By then we had swept on round a curve, but I slowed: was she sure? Which one? She said Sally at once, and I wondered how she could know one from the other. She had hardly met them, I thought, and generally conveyed a sense of distrust and dislike. My Greek girls, she called them. "Why don't you go back and see," she said without much accent.

I reacted pretty slowly. My first feeling was one of jealous resentment and an electric acceptance of all the feminine perfidies I had heard of. Sally talking to men in a Sunday Buick —the secret and mysterious and serpent-like Sally. "You'd better see, I think," Mother said again, and the words this time had an edge to them. They caused me to swing into a side road and back round.

There were three men in the Buick, two still on the front seat, one standing at the open front door, all leaning to look at Sally with pale, faintly olive-colored faces and those tight little smiles like masks over their mouths. Sally was back a few feet in the short grass on the shoulder of the road, with the Mona Lisa look on her face, except that she was as beautiful as a flower or a new-made young divinity of the golden autumn. Her tan cotton skirt rippled round her bare legs in the light breeze and a darker russet sweater was curved to her soft shoulders and breasts; the black thick hair glinted as the breeze moved it. The three men, in gray and tan suits and hats and sport shirts with long pointed collars, leaned intently toward her, and the scene had a sort of hypnotic fixity about it as though all the details and the characters had been composed and were held just that way. It seemed to me that the three men were somehow exactly similar, like one man in three poses. And Sally herself was doubly bright as the very center and focus: she wasn't quite smiling, and she wasn't frightened, but she expressed some strong inner humor as though she were relishing the scene she was part of.

It all collapsed, of course, when I pulled in on the grass, in front of the Buick but well off the road. Mother was quick to get in the first word. "Would you like a ride home, Sally? We were going that way." She had leaned out to get clear of the windshield, and though the words were mild she looked resolute. And the men shrugged, withdrew, adjusted their hats as a sort of ironic salute, restored their habitual look of self, and roared off with a spatter of gravel. "Next time, baby," the outside one said.

Sally didn't come round and get in. She stood darkly, looking at us.

"Bad men," I said.

She shrugged them off. The inner smile and excitement were gone, and her expression had taken on the brooding secrecy I knew so well.

"Come on," I said. "We'll take you anywhere you say." I was glad to see her there, unchanged in her old clothes and sneakers, full of the same mysterious hidden life. She still didn't move. It was somehow as though she would stand there forever, without explanation.

The afternoon was waning by then. The sun was down behind the yellow woods, and the light was full of the deep autumnal intensities; the last brightness fell on a maple in a field across the road and turned it to fire, and below that in a hollow the shadow was like a violet pond. Cars were driving by, but now and then in the intervals the pure stillness of evening came over us.

Maybe, my mother whispered to me in the long pause, she'd come and have supper with us—we could have waffles and a salad, and I said sure, ask her. So Mother leaned round the windshield and asked her.

Sally's intentions, I knew, were kindly, and when she didn't answer at once it was evident that some sort of struggle was at work inside. But after another silence she came round and squeezed in between Mother and the door. Then almost for the first time she smiled naturally. She had a big mouth, soft and beautifully modelled, and her smile was a quick transformation—though it seldom lasted more than a moment.

All she said was that she was going for a walk; she hadn't been out for ages, and she had a strong desire to go up toward the mountain.

I found out long afterward that in a way she was conducting a rebellion. She had left home disobediently, and she had the dark thought in the back of her mind that she didn't care if she ever came back or not. Suppose, I said, those men had captured her—what then? But she shrugged off the disaster my voice implied. All that stuff, she said, what does it matter. People make so much fuss about it. She could be herself, regardless of men in cars, and that's what was really important.

But that evening she said little, and Mother did a perfect job, as always, of whipping up a delicious supper and making everything seem right and safe. In principle she disapproved of any girl friends I might have, specially ones of alien origins and religion, but she had an irresistible desire to take loving care of any individual and she felt that Sally needed the sort of protection that only she could provide. The picture of the predatory men in the Buick had deeply shocked her. A nice girl certainly ought to know better, she said . . .

I realized as I drove Sally home about nine o'clock that she was full of a good deal of misery, and since I was young and half way in love with her I felt a surge of crusading anger and a passion to protect and cherish her against all cruel fathers and predatory men. For almost the first time, in fact, I felt the full rush of desire, the ache of body and whirl of brain. Her flowing softness and sweetness were overwhelming, and I thought that if I reached out and gathered her she wouldn't stop me—she would melt into my arms as secretly as a dream.

When we stopped near her place she waited motionless in the seat, curled like a cat, watching me with dark-lidded eyes. Neither of us stirred for a minute or more. Then she opened the door and slid out with a slow turn of her legs and body that set off an electric charge below my chest somewhere. I touched for a second the silk of her hair. "Sally," I said and stopped. She let herself smile the wide brief smile that ended more soberly than it began. "They won't eat me, Will. Thanks for everything, and—" Her words ended there. After a second she turned and walked up the wooden steps and through the open outer door of the building. I remember the rather slow rhythm of her walk, the swinging skirt against her legs, and the dark head bent forward.

⋖⟆ CHAPTER 6 ⟅⟆

My mother, as I have said, looked upon desire or passion as outside the bounds of acceptable living. Professionally she had much to do with all the bodily functions, and she had an extraordinary respect for the natural process of birth and growth, but she saw them quite apart from the emotional state that co-existed with them. She approved of mothers and babies, even illegal ones, but she felt that sexual compulsion and indulgence were not decent. The familiar inheritance of guilt and shame was strong in her.

It was in me too. Perhaps it is in everyone. I lived virginally, in some fear of the dark desires that seized me at night; it seemed necessary to avoid female snares and to keep clear of the swamp of sexual self-consciousness that lay all about. Not that I understood anything about it; I simply inherited and carried on certain habits—some good, perhaps. I see, as Pop Sardis used to argue, that sex is a simple and pleasant experience, and the enormous structure of rituals and tabus and dogmas that surrounds it is one of the major insanities of civilization. But I see also that human nature must have a sacred mystery to swear by and against; I see that blasphemy and even a sense of utmost filth are emotional needs, and the secrecies of sex are the best ones we have in a time when hell and heaven are failing. Perhaps I don't see very clearly.

Anyway, though I didn't lay hands on Sally that evening, I was shaken deeply, and my life changed. Outwardly I behaved the same as ever, and proceeded on what I believed to be my admirably masculine way. I worked and went to school and held up my head among my peers and in general acted with an aloof and complacent cockiness that won me no friends—except for Mr. Chadd, who liked me but had no time to show it. Not that I sought friends. It was a weakness in me that I felt sufficient and detached—at least I did on the outward surfaces. Yet it pleased my vanity that so many called me Will in varying accents from mockery to obsequiousness. In any town for a dozen miles round I heard it like a pass-word: "Hey, Will!"

But Sally ran so in my mind that I contrived ways of seeing her. I learned her daily habits—I could pick the two girls up on their way home from school once or twice a week, and sometimes I could time their coming out of the public library in the late afternoons. Althea had a half-secret boy friend and was made more beautiful than ever and was full of a conspiratorial humor that brightened her cheeks and eyes. She and Sally exchanged constant flashes of understanding and laughter, using the deprecating little code they had learned from childhood. They seldom spoke the boy's name, which was Harvey, but he seemed to be the main theme of their signals. It had some of the old eagerness of their twin existence, but I realized that Sally had begun to feel separate and even lonely, though she tended by her nature to loneliness. She pretended that Althea's boy was an excitement and part of the charm of life and youth, but actually she considered him a meagre and foolish high-school kid and was a little bewildered that Althea allowed him to come near her.

It gave me what I hoped was a chance at her, and in the few minutes I could take off during the working week I tried hard to capture her—though I never saw it in that light. I hardly even admitted to myself that she was a girl with whom I was very simply and youthfully in love.

Sally Anthonakis—of all people I ever knew she seemed to have the most mysterious and separate spiritual life: not spiritual in the usual sense of pious exaltation, but in the sense of an inner life that strongly existed apart from the physical and visible. All the vital realities were for her somewhere inside her mind, behind the dark steady eyes. The happiness she sought was seldom an activity or an object of value, but rather an awareness; she could spend a half hour staring at a couple of lines of verse, living it in some inner region of her being. I've seen her entranced by the puff of seeds of the dandelion, looking and looking at the fantastic little structure as though it revealed the universal secret.

Yet she was reluctant to speak. The quick sobering smile, so warm and kind, acknowledged her whim, and begged indulgence. She had no arrogance, but when she did speak usually she was compelled to speak the exact and candid truth—as far, that is, as she could. She left much to doubt.

My unacknowledged campaign made good progress, in a way, yet I never seemed to get closer to a responsive Sally. She welcomed me with a grave smile, without shyness or sign of fear. She said little, as though it were Althea who naturally did the talking. She acted like a secure friend, unconcerned with the fluctuations of personal feeling; she could be silent for minutes together, though it was the kind of silence that led me on to talk—too much, maybe. I was full of so many surface concerns that I assumed she must be too, though of all people she was the least so: yet in a way she seemed amused by what she called my specialties, my awareness of the newest gadgets, or of where to get the best ice cream cheap, or of a mill store that had bargains in damaged goods, or of how to make off with a Buick demonstrator for an hour or two. It is too much to say that Sally at seventeen was a philosopher; no one, least of all she, could have told what all that brooding amounted to—but she and I seemed to approach life from opposite directions. To her I was a boy with toys.

It wasn't easy to be with her very much. She made little effort to help, and seemed content simply to ride here and there for a few minutes out of her carefully timed days. She had two miseries—one her father's jealous eye, the other a lack of any privacy at home. Hence she loved the reading room of the Library, and the front seat of my car—where as often as not Althea was with her. In a hesitant way I went on loving her—the easy cat-like flowing sweetness of her body and clothes, the hidden life underneath. When we finally got together one evening it was Pop who arranged it—with his usual humorous cunning. He had two tickets for a violinist in Springfield, and had made an elaborate plan to take Sally down by train, have supper there, and come back late by bus. He was full of great hope, for he loved Sally and violin music, but when the day came he made me take his place—he said the damp November had given him sinus pains and he'd have to go to bed. She was to be ready at quarter of six, and he had told her about the little Greek restaurant run by a friend of his. So I was off with Sally before anyone quite knew how it happened, and Pop took whatever blame there was and went to bed.

We drove, of course, and I think Sally caught some of my delight in the adventure because she smiled less fleetingly —she glowed in fact with a wondrous warm brightness.

"Pop arranged all this, you know," I said.

She nodded. "He thinks I need a boy friend."

"Well, you do—as long as I'm it."

"He thinks you're it."

These were our most intimate words so far, and I felt eager and reckless.

"Do you think so, Sally? I—I like you, you know. I like you better than anyone." Even then I couldn't bring myself to say love.

She turned sombre. "No," she said with sudden flat accuracy.

"No—what? I—I—" It was a hard word, but I gulped it out. "I love you. You can't say no about that. It's true. I love you." The second time was easier. But the word seemed to bring sorrow to her for a few moments; she bent her head and was lost to me. It may not have been Sally at all that I loved, but simply the vision of a dark and half-hidden beauty and a dreamlike happiness far beyond the flat realities of my world. When she brooded that way, looking down and off, the life I led seemed too dreary to bear and I thought of my mother's labors and all the lost hopes, and in a rush of pity for my own miseries I yearned for Sally's dark eyes and hair and the grace of her mysterious body.

"No," she said again, not to answer me but to make a statement. "I will not be afraid." When she was very serious she tended to gulp out her words abruptly. "I mean, love is a fact—I know it, I read about it. Passion, I mean. Men and women naked together. Everyone, though they never say it—"

She didn't look at me. I stayed as quiet as a stone.

"Us too," she went on. "You and I, sometime. I never want to be afraid, or to be—" She paused. "False, I guess—silly, the way people are." She looked up at me with the full strength of her thought clear in her eyes. "If I loved you, Will, I'd say so."

"But you don't, huh?"

She stared down again for quite a long time. "No," she

decided, and paused again. "Maybe I thought I did—I mean—" Another pause. "I don't want to talk silly about it, but it's hard to know—I don't know much, Will."

"Well, gosh, Sal, I don't want to rush you. After all—"

We were as solemn as young owls, and conscious of the nearness of great truth.

"You don't like poetry," she said.

It took several seconds for me to realize that she had tried to say something very vital to her.

"Well, sure—I like some poetry," I said, but I vaguely knew it was no use. She had noted the barrier between us. "Maybe I can learn—" Again, it was no use. I had understood all along that she lived beyond my reach, though what it really amounted to or meant I couldn't tell. It may have been why I thought I loved her.

"Maybe," she said, answering me, and smiled with the characteristic fleeting seriousness. It was as though she had said all she possibly could. But she added one thing more. "I don't know too much, Will. Grandpa thinks I need you to teach me—about what's real, I guess."

"Well, let's pretend I can."

"Yes," she said.

After that we got to the city and began to feel adventurous again and everything from there on was happy for us. It didn't seem queer to me that she had said what she did, so literally and solemnly. A child couldn't have said it with any authority; an adult couldn't have said it at all. To Sally at seventeen the word poetry had its fullest and most exalted meaning, and she spoke it—not dramatically or strongly, but with the conviction of her heart and soul; and to me at nineteen Sally's conviction deserved solemn respect. I thought she was a wonderful girl, and this was not just a minor part of her; rather it was the essential mystery of her. Nor did I brood very deeply about what seemed to be my failure in her eyes. I felt instead more secure with her, and thought I knew where we were and what my place was.

At least that's how it seemed that night. I took very special care of her, with the pleasure of an appointed guardian or minister of grace, and she responded sweetly. She said at the end that it was the best time she had ever had, and in a way it was as though she had gone as far as she could toward being my girl.

But in the long winter that followed we had a meagre time together. There was no warm room for us, no place to be, except in the cold open automobile. I couldn't take her out in the evening, as the phrase is—which meant a moving picture or a place with a juke box; she wasn't allowed to go anywhere with me, except on brief, half furtive daylight occasions. And I thought it didn't seriously matter to her—not going out with me, I mean. What did seem to matter was the emotion of resentment she had for her father that worked in her—and Althea—like a poison, and not even their mother's flood of affection could neutralize it. To the two of them he was the enemy, to be dodged, deceived, defeated; he had driven the best part of their living underground and made them furtive and infinitely wary like two young deer in a farm country. And Althea, at least, fell abjectly in love with Harvey, her unworthy classmate, and spent her time among subterfuges and intrigues. Yet I think she loved very timidly, and was frightened of sin and helplessly insecure—like most adolescents.

But Sally was different—at least she was as far as my experience goes. We had gone on as best we could being friends —she coming up out of the mid-region of her soul to share a soda with me, or even at times to visit Pop and me at the shop and ride home with us at closing time. But some fundamental emotion seemed to be pressing inside her, some overwhelming question that I couldn't quite grasp or share though in a mysterious sort of way I was part of it. I remembered how in the autumn she had run off on that Sunday afternoon —I never knew exactly why, but she assumed I did, and let me have glimpses of the inner urgency that seemed to be a constant part of her. In the young, I think, the fiercest desires often apparently come to nothing; they are left behind, or they shift and escape and are forgotten. But Sally's were in many ways more formidable.

In spring, on a warm Sunday, she asked me to take her back up to the place in the hills where she and Althea got lost. It was a running away again, though she made no explanations; she simply put it to me, with the little gulp of words that meant she was being most serious. I picked her up about two near the library and off we went. I was so full of a glow of delight at the warmth and the freedom and the girl beside me that I hardly noticed how sombre she was, how she stared ahead with more than usual intentness in her dark eyes and smiled with only the briefest flash. When we got up to the place she seemed for a while transfixed, and studied the leafless trees, the far open view to the west.

"Is that the road we went up?"

It was all different, and she sat for a long time trying to absorb it: somehow she had thought it would be exactly the same as it had been in the late summer. It was sunny there, and we didn't move, yet I began to feel a strong tension in her.

"Could we go up the road?"

"Yes, sure—"

She got out and went ahead of me a little way. She had on the same loose tan skirt and a darker sweater and the gray raglan coat she wore to school and old sneakers and white socks. I had never seen her hair so fresh and shining.

When I came beside her she stood looking at me with a curious sort of softness, and then as we walked she let her hand fall into mine. "Are we really free? For once?" The smile came out full and she tipped her head back in a gesture of release. "I didn't think about the leaves and grass—it's all so open and sunny now. It would be much harder to get lost."

"Would you want to?"

"Yes."

She kept on as though she had a quest, not hurrying or letting go of me—she moved as though she wanted to stay as close as possible to me. But she looked this way and that, and changed our direction with little murmurs of doubt, and at last headed for a clump of white pines that made a green pavilion among themselves. She took off her coat and spread it on the bed of needles. "I remembered this place—I've thought about it all winter. I thought—" She stopped, and sat down with her arms over her knees and looked at me with eyes that seemed enormous.

I sat close to her. She had never been quite like that before with me. It was as though she had for the first time let me into her inner life, though nothing had yet happened or been said. I took one of her hands again and kept it as though it were mine. "What did you think?" I asked.

"I can't tell you yet. Not till I've asked you something."

"What?"

We were far far from the world. The silence was absolute. The sun poured down through the filter of green needles.

"Will you love me? Will you make love to me?"

To describe all the rest is more than I can bring myself to do, yet it should be described; no book that I know of contains it—all the charm, the sweetness, the folly, the simple innocence of our love under the pines. Perhaps no other love was ever like it. "I don't want to be afraid of anything," she said. "I don't want to pretend. I just want—" She stopped, and we kissed each other for a long time with a soft and cool freshness, and she smiled in the middle of it and her eyes were full of tears. "I never kissed anyone, you know," she said. "I never did anything. I'm as ignorant as a kitten. I don't really know what we are doing." She lay back on the ground looking up at me, and I noticed that her words no longer came in gulps and she kept on smiling with an easy sort of sweetness. "I think you are the nicest boy who ever lived, do you know that? It says in books that when a man makes love to a girl he doesn't like her so much any more— but you don't have to like me after this if you don't want to. I mean, I just want us to love each other now, right here, this once—and let's not be afraid or shy about it or worried." She talked along as though she had always talked that way. "Do you know about making love? Did you ever?"

"No," I said.

"Well, we'll have to find out together—we've got lots of wonderful time." She rolled over and started unbuckling my belt. "The first thing is to get our clothes off—I'm sure of that, anyway."

This is the place to stop, I suppose, but some of what followed was funny and in spite of our resolution not to be worried very embarrassing. Yet from the start Sally had a genius for it, and she made even our mistakes and my inadequacy seem natural, and above all she made the whole thing sweetly and freely happy and at times full of ecstasy. We kept at it long enough to find out.

"I remembered this place," she said, "because when I read about people making love I always wonder where they do it.

After all, you've got to be comfortable and alone, and there aren't so very many places—not where we live." Her head was back against the cushion of black hair on the ground. "That's what I thought when I saw this little house of trees. I guess I've thought a lot about love, Will, but I can't seem to help it." She watched me dreamily. The air was cool now, and our bodies seemed almost icy where they weren't touching and everlastingly warm and safe where they lay together. "I guess I'm a wanton, or whatever it is they call it—everything I know about life so far comes out of books." She moved against me and the warmth of it was like a beneficent flame. "I did it all—I made you—I thought and thought about it—and I said I won't worry, I won't worry, I won't. But there's so much I don't know, Will, and the only way to find out is to sort of plunge in—like a fool I guess—rushing in—" She looked for a moment as though she were going to cry. "Do you feel all right about it, Will? Is it sort of good? There needn't be any more, you know—I mean—" She choked and squeezed against me in tears as though she would somehow burrow inside me.

I tried to tell her it was good, and she really knew it anyway—we were half crazy with delight and exhaustion. But then the cold really came and we had to dress, though she made us go over each other once more from head to foot so that nothing would be left out of the experience. We were pretty chilly by the time we went down, and light-headed, but we felt fine.

⋘ৠ CHAPTER 7 ৠ⋙

I KNOW THAT writing about sex is in effect paradoxical. The aim is candor and simplicity and freedom from superstition; the result is often a magnifying of the eroticism it has set out to dispel. But, to take a long jump ahead, what Sally taught me that day was the best lesson I ever had in the whole art of living. Wanton or not, she has always seemed to me the nicest girl I ever knew; I've had to measure every other woman against her, and she still stands out in her own fashion as matchless.

But there were aftermaths. The whole mingling of our beings, spiritual as well as physical, could not simply go behind us like an ordinary day's outing. Sally herself was insistent that it should; she planned it that way, and thought it out that far, but she didn't know what repercussions would follow. And I even began to worry about her having a baby, though she had said she had fixed it—someone in school told her how (they knew everything in school, she said), but I had doubts about it. Lovers in stories seemed to have no concern about such a consequence and went happily to bed whenever they felt like it, but on a sober Monday morning I was troubled. I had the gray reflections—in a very small way—of the married man.

It even troubled me to know what to say to her when we met again, which was one of the problems she had taken special account of. She almost implied, when we parted, that we wouldn't be meeting again—and actually for some weeks thereafter she was virtually a prisoner. Perhaps she had anticipated that.

The gray reflections and the worries, I could see, might well have taken all the delight out of our affair, and I understood why seductions (a word that I hope does not apply to us) are so often so miserable in their outcome. But love and delight were still there like an unquenchable melody, and there was so far no guilt. I wanted very much to see my girl again— to have her, of course: I argued that she was my girl. She ran in my mind and heart all day.

Pop knew we had been off together, against orders, though he didn't know what happened. It seemed wonderful to me, as I looked at his nut-like face, squeezed up to utter the thought that had been building in the busy brain, that the lovely and passionate and forever youthful Sally was really his pupil. I wanted to tell him all about her—he would have understood everything at once—but I couldn't. I still remembered the words he had used about the true virtues: courage, loyalty, generosity, intelligence—big words, and too easy to say, perhaps, but they seemed to be about the only ones that could be said. Some day, I thought, I'd tell him.

One thing Sally did that spring was to emerge as a violinist —and in fact the next time I saw her after our Sunday afternoon was at a school concert, where she played one piece, with Althea accompanying, and of course all the family of Anthonakis and Sardis in the audience. Both girls were very solemn and seemed poised on the verge of flight, like wild things, but it gave me a shock of jealousy to see Sally so absorbed and subdued by her violin, not so much because I felt myself excluded as because her rich and original personality seemed to be bound down to that one thing. She was too evidently a pupil going through her assigned duty, without much joy in it, without mastery, though I know she played well and was commended above the others; the general feeling seemed to be that she had talent and would "go on," as people said. I visualized her in a flash as an eminent musician, playing to great audiences, and I understood even then that she could master that pitiless little instrument, and that the full free quality of her being could express itself without constraint and fear, but that evening it seemed like an indignity that she should be required to perform. It gave me a sort of shock to see her up there in view, lighted for display, as it were, in her only silk dress (the white one she had worn for our trip to Springfield in November) with all her natural loveliness about her, the flowing shoulders and breasts and bound waist (something about her waist always stirred me deeply) and silky legs and her girl decorations of sparkling clips for the black hair and little silver chain and pendant round her neck. Yet she wasn't being herself—nor was Althea; their faces were too solemnly dutiful.

I didn't talk to her then, though of course she knew I was there—it was all like being part of a dream, she said later. I finally got her coming out of the Library in the late afternoon, alone, and without pause or glance right and left she opened the door of the car and jumped in. "He says I can't see you at all," she said.

I had started for the open country, but she made me turn back. "I can't, Will. It's too terrible, all the row." She spoke with little bursts, and I could see she was uneasy.

"Did you promise him anything about not seeing me?"

"No."

"What can he do about it?"

"Beat me. Scold me. Make terrible noises. Stop me from going to music school."

"What school?"

"Oh, somewhere—I had an audition—they said I can go free—" She looked down. "Will," she said with a small gulp.

"Huh?"

"Do you hate me?"

"Sally, for pete's sake—*hate* you? Why, I love you—you know that."

She seemed bowed down with woe. "I thought it would be all right—" She whispered: "There's so much I don't know—I mean about the way people feel. It says in the books—"

"You and your books." I took one of her hands.

And she smiled, the sudden flash that seemed to leave her more solemn than ever. "Well, I did it all—I made you—like Eve and Adam, I guess, though Adam was sort of mean about that—but I know I did it, **you** don't have to pretend I didn't—"

"Sally, stop it!" I was driving slow along a street, and stopped by the curb so that I could shake her—though I didn't. "If that's all you've got to worry about, come on back up there and I'll do it—I'll make you—"

"I said I wouldn't care if you did hate me afterward—it would be all over anyway. But I can't help it—"

"Well, it isn't all over—and I think you're just slightly cock-eyed—"

I felt as though I weren't quite getting to her; my words seemed to be blocked. I took a handful of the thick hair and turned her head with what was almost a yank. "Sally, listen, will you? You started all this by saying you wouldn't be afraid and you wouldn't be silly about anything. You said you'd take things the way they were. And here you are, brooding and worrying—it's just what you said you wouldn't do. We had a

sort of agreement, didn't we? We had a no-worry contract—
you can't go back on it."

She listened so solemnly, with such a depth of intentness
in her eyes, that I leaned over and kissed her. I couldn't tell
what was going on in her; the dark mystery of her nature
seemed to be in the ascendant. I felt myself outside of her—
not wilfully excluded, but inevitably outside.

"I think love is like having measles," she blurted out with
hardly a ghost of smile. "You get it, you have it in spite of
whatever you say or want, you are sick with it—"

"You have it?"

"Yes."

"Is that why you worry and brood?"

"Yes."

"You love me?"

"Yes."

"In spite of no poetry and all that?"

She nodded. "I do feel sort of—" She started to say foolish,
but couldn't get it out. "I didn't know what it all meant,
Will—I didn't know anything."

It would have been good then if I could have gathered her
up and kissed her, but it was still in a public street and time
we knew was going fast. But I said I loved her, and she felt
better and a little of the sweet contentment came back to her
face and body, as though she had been rubbed and stroked.
I convinced her that I didn't resent anything she had done,
that we were in it together, for better or worse, though when
I said man and wife she took some fright again. It wasn't
meant to be like that, she said. It was meant to be young and
simple and not too serious—it was meant to end. Marriage
was something else entirely. She seemed to be alarmed at the
very word.

She was standing on the curb round the corner from her

house, ready to fly. Up to then I had never thought of such a thing as marriage, but the idea suddenly seemed wonderful. "Why not?" I rushed on. "It would fix everything—I mean —wouldn't it?"

All these vital considerations had made us tremulously solemn, as though we were undergoing some sort of confessional, and I was startled to see a gleam of almost laughter in Sally's shadowy face. "I guess you really aren't in your right mind, Will—I mean, you of all people!" But she said it with a flooding warmth that seemed to have her whole self in it. "It isn't the Will I used to know, is it?" Then suddenly she looked back along the street with the fear of passing time in her eyes. "If you're all right, Will, I'm all right. I don't care about the rest."

With that she was off running.

The "rest," I supposed, was what she had to deal with at home.

My only notion of marriage was that Sally and I could live happily together in any small bedroom for ever. Other than that I had no great interest in problems of domestic life, though when I got home for supper and felt my mother's appraising eye on me I knew that the whole thing was probably more complicated than I was then willing to admit. I tried to think of how I might tell her that I was in love, that I might marry Sally, and it seemed literally out of the question.

"Anything bothering you, son?"

"Well, Chadd says he can get me a good machine shop job for the summer—war work."

"Why isn't that a good thing?"

I made myself seem gloomier than I really felt. "Well— factory work—"

She lectured me on the need of doing what had to be done. If I did marry (I had no one but Sally in my head, of course),

I thought I'd have to do it without telling her; I certainly could never make her understand—she seemed almost impervious, somehow, to explanations.

"You get such stubborn notions, Will," she was saying. "No one can tell you anything. You get the notion that a factory is bad and you won't go near it, but it isn't for life— it's just a summer job with good experience and pay. I think you need that kind of experience . . ."

I had even once had the idea of bringing Sally there, but luckily I didn't mention it.

"I just met Sally," I said. "She's planning to go to a music school this summer—she has a scholarship."

"Would you like to have her in for supper again some time?"

"Sure, but her father won't let her."

"Oh, nonsense—of course he would if I asked her."

"He thinks I'm dangerous. He makes a terrific fuss if she sees me."

Mother stood still a moment by the kitchen counter. "Are you? Are you dangerous?"

"Me?" I tried a chuckle.

"Why should he think you are?"

"Oh, I guess any fellow—I mean, he wants either an eligible suitor or no one at all for her."

"He thinks you aren't eligible?"

"Oh, lord no—at least, I suppose not—"

Mother was a great one for literal explanations, and she launched into a discourse on the religious and social traditions of the Greeks. It would be a lot more sensible, she said, if I didn't get mixed up with them, and of course I resented the suggestion and pointed out that the girls, at least, were no different from any other girls (my argument was quite meretricious, though I hardly realized it); and she went on to say that the religious background was much more formidable than I probably recognized. To her, actually, all ritualistic religion was nothing but benighted superstition, and poor Sally, she inevitably felt, was a child of ignorance and darkness. And I couldn't explain to her what manner of man Pop was, either; she would not have understood.

We were caught, then, Sally and I, at the center of a whirl of forces, and for a time could do nothing. I suppose our only positive desire was to love, to go back to the house of pines and stay forever. All the other forces were the negative ones, needless, blind, perverse, part of the colossal stupidity of adult life. It became an ordeal of hope and failure and moral confusion. There was a time when Mother was off on a case for a week and I tried to argue Sally into stealing time to be with me, and was angry with her when she wouldn't—her abrupt no seemed to me infuriating, and she looked at me with almost classic compassion as though I were a little boy having an expected tantrum.

Then came the end of things, and Sally was taken off to a school, or camp, as it was called, for young musicians near Stockbridge, and I became part of a machinist crew in Springfield turning out automatic rifles. And it half troubled me that she was happy there, among the kind of people she was meant to live with—she wrote me very many short letters full of the humor that seemed so subdued and fleeting in her actual self, a shrewd irony that might have come straight from her grandfather. "There are five groups here, each one named after a bird, like robin, thrush, sparrow, and warbler. The fifth group is me. I'm the owl." But I knew she wasn't being sorry for herself; she had too much respect for all those she considered her betters.

When I saw her she seemed happier in ways that made me jealous. We had been alone together, separate from every-

thing, but in the group there she was surrounded and supported. She was brown, wore shorts and a T shirt, was spoken
to familiarly by everyone—there were more boys than girls in
the school, and she could smile with wonderful radiance,
though it seemed to me that she was as reticent as ever. Some
of them really did call her the owl and made fun of her
enigmatic silences.

It was on an old upland farm, the school, with fields and
woods running up to a high hill, and we walked up there in
the two hours we had together. Her days were full of events,
but on a Saturday afternoon we had two hours; it was early
July, and hot and hazy. All I had in mind was Sally herself,
not only the soft brown part of her but the whole being, the
voice, the sober smile, the long contemplation of the shadowed eyes, the inside and isolated Sally that had begun to
share itself with me. But for a time she was all passive and
cat-like, walking softly with downward head and saying nothing at all.

We went up through fields and pastures and glades, and
lay on pine needles in the warm shade.

The only reason for this love story is Sally herself. Everything else about it is clinically familiar, but not I think Sally,
not that inner life of passion and resolution and candor which
seemed to have founded itself partly on poetry and partly on
her grandfather's teaching.

All I could get from her that day was a passive sort of compassion that angered me. We had waited, I thought, with
more than human fortitude for a time to be alone together;
the declarations had been made, the way opened, and there
she lay, the soft and lovely wanton, sunk in moodiness, remote, somehow lost to me. I laid violent hands on her, shook
her, hurt her, kissed her, almost throttled her. "What is it,
Sally? For heaven's sake, what's the matter?" She looked at

me with those dark eyes where the light seemed to be refracted into the farthest deeps, a sombre light, somehow sorrowful.

For a while it was as though she were under a spell. She couldn't even speak; she suffered my anger in acquiescence, and waited for it to pass as she might wait for a gust of wind to finish blowing.

"Sally, will you talk? Don't just lie there like a bag of meal—" The anger drained out and I felt more like tears. I brushed with my hand the clouded black hair.

"I can't love you any more, Will—now."

I knew what she meant, but I said at once, "Don't you love me, Sally?"

She knew what I meant, but for a minute she wouldn't answer.

"It was all right before," I said. "What's happened? Do you—do you love somebody else?" I had a flash of bitter jealousy.

"No. I—love you, Will. But I promised—I tried to make a promise—"

I drew back. "You mean to your father?" It seemed incredible.

"No." She paused. "I promised Gramp." And seeing my surprise she went on quickly. "I told him, Will—I told him everything about us. And we talked—he's been writing to me." For the first time she gave a quick smile as a sort of recognition of the oddity of it. "And we can't get all messed up together, Will—not now."

I felt first of all a betrayal. Pop had done this behind my back. "You mean, he made you promise?" My voice almost cracked with the surprise.

"No, he didn't make me. I just did." Her voice was coming in the gulps that indicated tension. She sat up a little distance from me and hugged her bare knees. "We talked a good deal—" It seemed hard for her to be coherent. "He doesn't make you do anything. I sort of asked him about things—I always have—and he sort of tried to tell the truth—you know that, Will."

I refused to answer. The whole thing had come over me with an almost palpable frustration, as though I had been netted and bound.

"It's life, Will," she solemnly said. "I mean it's tomorrow and next year and ten years. And all the other things besides just us—like work and family—your mother. I don't feel like seventeen—I mean I don't feel any special age—but—" She gulped and was silent.

"What's this promise?" I said after a time.

"Well, just—" She opened her hand. "Wait, I guess."

"How long?"

She turned away, put her head down on her arms, and cried. She was very quiet about it, and we sat there a long time. I couldn't seem to touch her or get at her. What I did next is shameful, but I did it. I shook her in a kind of frenzy; I choked her, threw her on the ground, pulled off her few clothes with a harsh tearing of fabric—and she said nothing and did nothing, but watched me with secret female knowledge. Her body on the carpet of brown needles was the dream all lovers have, and I put my face on it and she stroked back my hair and pressed my head against her. After a fashion we made love together, but when we went down afterward I was afraid it was for the last time.

PART THREE

ᦉ CHAPTER 1 ᦉ

In December, after we declared war, I enlisted in the Navy
and was trained in radio and later radar. And during the
months and years thereafter, spent mostly in the Pacific, Sally
kept writing to me—not love letters, but short and candid reports on what she did and saw. She kept at her violin, and
played at local affairs—they hired her because she was so
cheap, she said. She liked playing in orchestras, and did that
a good deal, generally for nothing. She gave lessons—those
were cheap too, but it seemed to be her fate, she said. "I pretend I don't like money, anyway. I think if I had a religion
it would be to live without money, like the fowls of the air."
She generally signed herself simply Owl.

Both Althea and she had gone to a local junior college, and
Althea had been smart enough to marry one of her instructors, a near-sighted but distinguished young man named For-
rest Witherspoon and was so happy she had become without
question the most beautiful woman in the world. The eminent Witherspoons had been at first horrified, then stunned,
and finally persuaded that their son had married a goddess.
Her own father (Mike) had had no use whatever for any
Witherspoon, and had to be fought and outwitted to the end.

Pop, Sally said, was tired and full of arthritis, but he kept on working. He and she had been reading everything by Bernard Shaw.

But as for herself—nothing except a few outward facts. I asked her if she were in love, engaged, married, and got nothing out of her. I told her she made all other women shadowy and somehow false, and I intended to come back and tell her so—she said nothing, except to sign herself as always, Owl.

But the coming back seemed to take a long time. My ship, a light cruiser, kept on through the Red Sea and Mediterranean, with a long visit to the Bosporus, and finally to Norfolk, where I was discharged.

It was mid-winter. Mother was in Boston, working in a hospital, and Harold had managed to remain at Harvard, where he combined military service with education. He was already being mentioned as one of the younger poets of the post-war era; he was known, I found, as the inventor of a new kind of verse that he called Cryptics which I couldn't understand at all clearly—it seemed to be a sequence of complicated puns. He had published a good deal already and expected to have a book out in the spring. I couldn't ask him very much about it because I was ignorant and he found it difficult to explain things to me. He said it was a very small book and a very small publisher; the title was to be *Redfern's Miter* and was full of secret ambiguities. By this time he had become a citizen of Harvard, and was native to it; he lived in a little third-floor suite with two companions, but it was not the temporary and somewhat sordid bivouac of a student— rather it had a tapestried and settled look to it, with hangings, a piano, shelves of books, paintings, and sculptured wood, and a bar.

Our gulf-like differences made it possible for us to get along as well as casual strangers, but I felt a hard tension when I went to see Mother. She was dietician and domestic supervisor of a convalescent hospital for women in the Roxbury section, and when I inquired for her in the front office I realized that it was a battle ground—or rather a dark arena where too many people struggled against hopeless odds: I could smell desperation in the air, see it in cracked plaster and sagging thresholds, hear it in the voices and the shuffling footsteps. She greeted me with watchful constraint, waiting to see what I did, and when I leaned down to kiss her she squeezed my arm, then patted me, then said she had about an hour, and led me back through tragic corridors to an older wooden part of the building where her own rooms were, a white little bedroom with an iron bed and an "office" adjoining, where we could sit down. I looked at her with the sort of shocked clairvoyance that comes at such a time: the whole reality of her life took hold of me, the fixed set of her mouth, the squarer angle of the jaw, the ashy gray of the hair. "You've been working too hard," I said, and she flared up with the old pugnacity and challenged me to say what else there was to do. Her only interest in life was to be useful—she certainly couldn't see any other reason for her existence. But the anger was like a reflex; actually she was studying me almost fearfully, watching for the good and evil in me, hoping for some sign or token of love but unwilling to believe in it. She kept asking questions—where I'd been, what done, what I planned—and after the first constraint we talked the hour away very quickly. She admired my weight, made sure I had some warm clothes, appointed a time and place to meet for dinner the next evening, squeezed my arm again as we walked back through the corridors, and at last lifted her face for the cool little kiss.

I felt strangely mournful as I walked away through the harsh streets and rode the trolley back to Cambridge. There were things I should do, words I should say to her, but I felt the impotence of someone in a dream.

I was using Harold's rooms as a place to sleep. There was a cot in the study and it seemed to be taken for granted that if I didn't sleep on it someone else would. The place was evidently a microcosm of post-war university life—at least of a certain phase of it—and no experience in my past up to then had been as strange for me. I had lived in a world of constant activity, mostly physical, not only through the war but as far back as my experience went. My hands were dextrous; my mind dealt mainly with what I could see and touch. I had not thought abstractly of myself, nor did I attach myself to any conscious set of values; I had functioned simply as one male among many, without reflecting about my condition. But in Harold's rooms I was as alien as an ape, not because he and his friends failed in respect or tact—they knew, after all, that most of the outer world was made up of people like me—but because I knew nothing about the world they lived in. Names hovered about the room like repeated notes—names like Rilke and Lorca and Guillaume Apollinaire (always spoken in full) and Sartre; they spoke constantly of music, not with affection, but with passionate technical interest—I was astonished to hear Harold discuss the influence of Bach on some part-Indian Brazilian composer, with one-finger demonstrations on the piano. They had a phonograph and many records, and played them often, with an intent awareness of values that escaped me entirely. My one contribution to their little society, in fact, was to eliminate a buzzing noise in the player, and they were as grateful as though I had performed a major miracle. When I said that the buzz had seemed to go nicely with some of the music, they smiled patiently and said nothing.

But as Harold's brother, home from war, I was part of their

duty. It was a time when young men floated in and out, sleeping on couches or floors, with no urgency and often no destination. It struck me in that wholly strange little world that I had none either. Everyone I met was waiting—waiting for money to turn up from the government, for entry into some course of study that might or might not lead anywhere, waiting to be taken care of. Some of those Harvard rooms were like flop-houses where men of no apparent origin or attachment crept in to sleep and let time pass. I knew in a way that I was one of them, and I began to feel self-conscious about it, specially because Harold and his friends so politely took it for granted that I was little more than a savage.

So I began to think of Bell's Landing again, and the secure domain of glades and big trees and sea-facing rock. The image of it had always been in my mind as bright as a colored postcard, with sharp details and a sense of the wondrous about it, as though it were the glory I had come from in infancy and would some day return to.

Harold, when I asked him, was indefinite about it. He had been there a few times, but not since September, and had rather lost interest in the querulous old ladies. "Poor dears," he said. "I doubt if they are quite sane any more, though of course in a way they never were."

I reminded him that he used to like visiting them.

"Oh, yes, of course, I did, but the last time I found it pretty depressing. I decided I really couldn't—" He stopped short. "I mean, there's nothing much one can do about them. They and the house, you know."

One of his later poems is called "The Mansion," and is a nightmarish (and cryptic) identifying of old house and old woman, and though it is pretty sardonic and full of ambiguous wit, it is respectfully poignant. But just then he waved the old ladies away with almost a gesture of annoyance.

When I asked Mother about them she seemed to harden
herself. She had grown more formidable anyway, and had assumed a good deal of authority in her new job; she was impatient with all the fools she had to deal with—and of course
she was tired a good deal of the time, and tense with the
anxiety of duty. No, she said, she hadn't seen the aunts lately.
She tried to help them about a year ago—went out to Bell's
Landing several times to try to get the place straightened out
—it was a mess, of course—and (I gathered) she had finally
had a terrible row with them. They were impossible to deal
with, she said, specially Evelyn . . .

"Why, she's the good-natured one," I said.

"You don't know." There was a bit of contempt in her
voice. "It was fine while they had things their own way—"
She was angry, and checked herself. "I've tried to be very
careful and tactful. You may not believe I can be, but I've
certainly tried—and it's just no good. What it really means,
of course, is that they don't approve of me—they never have;
they never thought I was good enough."

Her voice was as sharp as steel, and I drew back from it.
She seemed to be accusing me. "I thought I'd like to see them
again," I said.

"Well—" She stopped and caught breath with a good deal
of vigor. I could see that she was calculating very quickly.
"They like you—they always have. They kept asking about
you. See them if you like—but it isn't the same old place, you
know. They've had troubles." Then with a visible subduing
of her prejudices she went on more reasonably. Someone
ought to keep in touch with them—she thought Jane Safford
and some of the Weldon cousins went out there occasionally,
and of course they had a lot of old friends, but after all Lucy
was eighty-two. I must be careful, she said, not to give them
any trouble.

I took a morning train from the North Station, and almost at once the old illusion began to be dispelled. I had still been thinking of the trip as rich in expectation: I remembered the smell of the cars, the clank of couplings, the freight yards and factories and marshes, all as preludes to the adventurous journey to the North Shore, but on this steel-gray February morning none of the dream remained. It seemed to me, all that ugly debris north of Boston, the very emblem of human travail, where hope was dead and nothing remained but desperate survival; and I even saw that the conductor, who used to suggest ample benevolence and an almost priestly trustworthiness, was merely a tired old man driven by necessity. Not that this kind of bitter insight was new to me, or surprising; no one can grow up without seeing the life process at its lowest and barest, without putting to himself the overwhelming question why anything at all is worthwhile. But I hadn't expected it so plainly here on the old route to Bell's Landing.

It was partly the winter day, as fixed in its still gray cold as a casting of metal. The little station at Aston Corner was not absurdly charming as it used to be in the old summers; the vine-leaves were dead, no expensive open cars waited, a gritty dust blew up in the little whirls of northeast wind. I bowed my head, turned up the wool collar of my navy jacket, and pushed off along the road—shivering almost visibly. The cold was normal enough for the season, but my blood was not yet ready for it after the months in the tropics.

Except for a rural letter box balanced crookedly on a post, the turn into the old place seemed unchanged—still an unmarked dirt road twisting off into the woods, but beyond the first turn what used to be a pine forest was a waste of stumps and dead brush; five or six acres there had been carelessly butchered of all its trees. Patches of snow and ice were fre-

quent and in several places a hard six-inch bed lay across the
drive, unmarked by wheels though there seemed to be a track
of footprints in it, frozen from an earlier time. It came to me
then strongly, as I mounted the last grade and saw the faded
yellow walls and high mansard roof, that this was no home-
coming, no return or renewal. I was afraid.

The day itself seemed pitiless. There everything stood in
harshest detail, with no shadow or motion, all gray or drab, all
silent except for the pervasive rumble and moan of the invisible sea. The sky was like steel, the earth as hard as stone. But
as I stood looking at the house—it seemed enormous and ugly
up there on its little hill—I saw that the large window of the
upstairs room at the south corner had apparently been broken,
and a white rectangle of cardboard had been put in to cover
the hole. That was Aunt Lucy's room. No smoke seemed to
be coming from the high chimneys, though I couldn't see the
kitchen chimney from where I was approaching.

When I came up to the turn of the drive near the front
steps—hardly visible as a roadway any more—I got my first
glimpse of the sea itself, like a sheet of newly poured-out lead.
The wind had quieted and the surface seemed motionless
though the inevitable rush and break of water sounded up
from the shores.

The front door, I could feel, was not to be used.

A wisp of white smoke curled from the barn chimney, and
I stared at it with a little sense of shock; I had begun to feel
that no life could be here at all. I crossed to the back porch,
where the bare streamers of the old forsythia bush almost
blocked the steps, and knocked at the kitchen door.

Nothing happened, of course. It was an outer door, and the
sound of my knock made no impression on the fixed wintry
silence. I pushed the stiff hinges, went into the entry and
knocked on the inner door. This time there was a stir, like the

scurry of a small animal, then silence, then a muttered voice. I spoke and turned the knob. "Hello, is that you, Aunt Evelyn?"

"Who is it?" came the challenge, fearful, belligerent, with the familiar resonance of old.

"Why, it's Will," I called and opened the door.

It was, at first glance, no one I knew. She stood by the stove with an iron poker in her hand ready to come at me, a twisted little witch with back curved down and bird-like face fiercely glaring.

"Who? Who is it? What do you want?" It was my Aunt Evelyn's voice, strong and articulate.

"I'm Will—Will Redfern," I said slowly, with no smile, no eagerness. "I came out—" there was a curious silence here as I tried to get my bearings—"to see you."

"Will?" she shot back. She had to tip her face up sidewise to look at me, and the sunken eyes were half covered by the straggle of white hair. She seemed no more than four feet high, and though bundled in a brown coat sweater that sagged down almost to her knees she had no flesh, no human shape.

"I've been in the war, you know—in the Navy. I just got back." I shouted this to her as though she were quite deaf.

"You don't have to yell at me, young man. I can hear very well, thank you." It astonished me that the voice I so fully remembered, the resonance, the stout intonation, the wonderful asperity, should be coming from the body of a miserable and tragic old witch I had never seen. I hardly knew how to speak.

"Will!" she suddenly exploded. "My gracious goodness— Will Redfern! Here I stand in a perfect *stupor!* Well, did you *ever*—" I heard the echo of that old cry as far back as my life's memory went and I laughed with a nervous gulp. "Little Will—" She pitched toward me a step or two, then stopped, held out her left hand like a small claw, and assumed control. "Well, I'm very glad to see you—safe and sound, I hope." She squeezed my hand, touched her shrunken cheek with it, but made no move to kiss me. "We thought you had abandoned us, after all this time. Most people have. Now sit down, do—take your coat off, unless you think it's too chilly in here—it's far from warm, I must say—and tell me *everything*."

She took a lid off the stove, poked at the fire with the iron poker, put in one stick of wood, and touched the draught openings. "You see, we are burning wood now—there was quite a bit left over when they did the lumbering, but my goodness, it does burn so fast—oh, it goes in a flash! Poor old James has cut most of it for us, but he can't do *nearly* as much as he used to—so we try to be very frugal." There was no note of resignation in that voice. The little words exploded and crackled. But as she bent to hang the poker on a hook behind the stove, her head as low as the top of the stove, I noticed that she seemed fixed there for a moment. She put a hand down on the lower ledge and slowly pushed herself back in balance. "My darned old back is *no* good," she said. "It isn't as bad as it *looks*, but none the less it's an infernal nuisance. Let me be a warning to you, Little Will: keep a straight back when you're young and you won't have a crooked one when you're old."

It was certainly cool in there, but I took off my jacket and sat in a wooden rocker between stove and window. The aunts, I remembered, had always been proud of their cool rooms and open windows, but the kitchen that morning seemed almost dank. No sun for days, she explained; they counted on a sun— it made all the difference.

With some hesitation I asked how Aunt Lucy was and for a while got no answer. Then the curved little figure turned to me with a gesture of determination. "Now, Will, you'll just have to know that Lucy is not herself. She doesn't see people any more—" The old belligerence was in her voice, as though she were challenging me to take issue with her. "She has failed a very great deal—maybe you think *I've* failed, my gracious, but compared to Lucy I'm as strong as a *mule*. I have to be. But poor dear Lucy is not *well* at all." She almost glared at me, tipping her head from its downward bend, waiting for me to reveal myself. But I couldn't speak—it seemed as though I couldn't speak of anything. "Things are *very different* here," she said.

And then a strange little thing happened. She turned back to the stove and touched the lower draught, and very slowly seemed to be falling toward the stove; her head went lower and lower, her right hand groped forward to reach something solid, and she began to sink downward. I sprang toward her.

"I'm really quite all right," she mumbled. "I do sometimes get a little dizzy, and I'm just afraid of grabbing at the hot part of the stove." She held to the back of a chair while I stood by. Then she made a little chirpy cry of derision. "Oh, I do feel perfectly *foolish*—but really, it's nothing. Now do sit down—sit there, and I'll sit here for a minute. I want to hear all about you—I want to hear *everything*."

THERE were only two warm rooms. The rest of the house on that gray day was a vast icy cavern, strewn with dust and dried flies and moths and old cobwebs. Yet, it was nearly all there as it had been, the oak and mahogany, the books and portraits. Some of the rugs had been rolled up, and some seemed to be gone. Two windows were broken and had been patched up with heavy cardboard. When I asked about them Aunt Evelyn was evasive. "Glass breaks, you know. Accidents happen. And I simply can't put new ones in—and of course James won't." She lowered her voice significantly. "Sometimes James can be very difficult—you know that, I'm sure. He's really getting to be a little *queer*—more than he ever used to be."

She hadn't wanted me to see the house, and she insisted that I must not go to James's room in the barn—he was much too queer, and goodness knows (she said) what it was really like. . . . She exploded into a grim little shriek, as though the worst could not be told. Her utterances were all dramatic, as they used to be, but in a lower key and in a way more ghostly; her bent and shrivelled figure hardly moved, and she stared downward, but the voice emerged with unexpected energy. "Oh, he's cantankerous, James is." There was no complaint in the voice, but only a sardonic relish of the irony of being alive. "I have no illusions whatever about what's the best

168

thing for all of us, but just the same I have to be grateful to James."

It was nearly noon then, and I heard no sound from the next room where Aunt Lucy was. The effect was death-like. Neither had James appeared. In all that wintry place nothing seemed to live but the small bent body of Aunt Evelyn there in the kitchen, standing now uncertainly, as though it had nothing to do. "You do look more like your mother," she was saying, "except that you've got so big and square, and you aren't dark. I suppose—" She hesitated a moment, then spoke with great resolution. "Now Will, I must tell you—" Once again she seemed to waver and then catch herself. "Sometimes," she muttered, "I *just can't think*." She lowered herself to the edge of a hard chair and brushed the straggle of hair away from her forehead. "Sit down, do—take the rocker; I can't *see* you up in the air—you've got pretty big, I must say." She had once been a solid body; I remembered how she walked heavily in rubber boots. Her face had been puffy, and turned red when she exercised. Now it was like a bit of crushed paper, though strangely there was a gleam of mockery in the thin twist of her mouth.

"The thing is, Will," she was saying with sudden strength, "that we can't do much in the way of *lunch*. I suppose you're hungry as all get out—"

I tried to say that it didn't matter—I could get something at the Corner on my way back, but she went on intently, without listening. "We have some tea—you can have tea, goodness knows. And potatoes!" She made the word sardonic. "James's potatoes—we have those. But I'm afraid right now there's very little *on hand*." She held up a claw-like hand and counted off. "No bread, no butter, no milk. No eggs, although James does sometimes bring in a few. But you see, Will, we don't really *need* much to eat—we get along on *very little*."

I said at once that I'd just run back to Aston Corner and pick up a few things—was there anything special she'd like? She said no, there was nothing—they didn't need a thing, and she wouldn't hear of my bringing back a *single item* of any sort (she emphasized this with almost a shout), but perhaps I ought to get a decent lunch for myself. When I came back —and I must, she said, because there were hundreds of things she wanted to hear about—she'd make me a cup of tea, and perhaps I could have a glimpse of Aunt Lucy by then. So off I went into the gray noon and had a drug-store lunch at Aston Corner and bought a bag full of staple provisions, all I could safely carry.

It took a good deal of resolution to face Aunt Evelyn with the bag of provisions. She flared up so strongly that her body seemed unable to sustain her. She put both hands on the table and bent over so that her head was horizontal, but twisted to let the eyes peer up sidewise. "I told you not to bring anything and when I say something I mean it—you ought to know that, Will Redfern. You can just take those things away—give 'em to James if you want to, but I refuse to accept them. I know you meant to do the right thing, but I intend to be just as stubborn as a *donkey*—and I will not accept these provisions from you. Now is that *clear?*"

It seemed to me that her lifetime was in her words. Eighty years. I could say nothing for a moment; the childhood sense of guilt was on me, and I shrank a little from her. "Well," I said, "it's just bread and butter—it's just the stuff you need anyway." Then it occurred to me in a flash that she had no money to buy such things, and I even began to see that she was probably starving. The two hands on the edge of the table were like ineffectual claws.

"Well, we don't," she was saying. "I can't tell you about James—he looks out for himself, but as far as *we* are concerned we don't need these things." She spoke with elaborate emphasis, as though I were a small child. "If you want to make *yourself* a sandwich, just go right ahead. We'll have some tea after a bit, as soon as I can get the kettle to boil." She turned with slow care to the stove and peered at the draughts.

"It's a fine thing," I said, unpacking the bag, "when a chap just back from the war can't bring his aunts some groceries without all this fuss. Maybe you can live on nothing but tea, but I'll bet Aunt Lucy would like some toast and jam—"

She made a little explosive noise which I took for a chuckle. It was her vanity to be stubborn and willful, and she wanted to be appreciated. "If you think you can get *round* me, you're very much mistaken. But I will say that I'm *very glad* to see you, even if I do make a fuss, as you call it. Now I just want you to sit down and tell me about it. Sit over there." She waved at the rocker. "You know, I've heard hardly a thing about you—and as for Harold, I do believe he has abandoned us altogether."

I talked to an accompaniment of exclamations. She believed in the heroic and the fabulous, and my experiences as a tiny unit in a mechanized war seemed to her as astonishing as Sinbad the Sailor's. "Now tell me, Will, when were you the *most scared of all?* Just tell me that, if you please."

But we heard the quaver of Aunt Lucy's voice from the next room. "Evelyn—Evelyn, dear, are you there?" There were scuffling and stirring noises.

Aunt Evelyn was up and off instantly. "Now, Lucy, don't you *dare* get up. You must stay right there—" She went in and shut the door, and I heard the strong murmur of their voices. After a bit she beckoned me. "Now don't stay more than a minute," she whispered. "And remember that she isn't very *clear* about things."

"Dear boy," came the quaver, "are you there?"

The air was stale in the room, with a faint smell of urine, but Aunt Lucy lay against her pillows like a lifeless effigy, whiter and thinner than anyone I had ever seen. Everything was white. "Is it Will?" she whispered. Her pale little eyes hardly seemed to see me. "Is it really Will?" The faint voice breathed rather than spoke, but the intonation was still dimly the same. "Dear old Will!" A lovely world of sentiment and hope clung to the words. "Is it your holiday again, dear boy? We must read together—oh, I do have an exquisite thing I've been keeping for you—" Her white hand groped toward the table beside the bed.

"It's Little Will," Aunt Evelyn said very distinctly and quietly. "He's been in the war, you know—he's been a sailor in the Navy. Do you see how *big* he is?"

Aunt Lucy looked like an alabaster image, but unbelievably thin and transparent and somehow sanctified. She seemed to have gone beyond flesh and blood; her face had sunk tightly against the bone and expressed nothing but a sort of finality. Yet her voice still carried some of its old vibrant sentiment. "Ah, Evelyn dear, you don't understand him—you never did." She turned a little toward me and went on in a rapt whisper: "I often think of those mornings in Taormina—you do remember, dear boy—and reading Shelley aloud, and the ruins —how blue it was looking down from the lovely terraces—" She closed her eyes and lay motionless. "You needn't stay, Evelyn," she said with abrupt authority. "I'll call you. I'd just like a little chat with Will—"

But Aunt Evelyn was already shooing me out, and I called a hasty good bye and said I'd be back later. There was a rusty iron stove, I noticed, with a pipe twisting up to an outlet in the kitchen chimney. "It's very convenient," Aunt Evelyn whispered, "for burning all the *odd shaped* chunks of wood, but it does smoke a little." Her mouth had a sardonic twist to it, as though she felt that nothing in life made much sense any more, but afterward when we were back in the kitchen she spoke earnestly. "You see how poor Lucy has really failed. Her mind is quite confused and she can't do very much for herself. It's just a *blessing* that I can still do what has to be done."

The day already seemed to be darkening when I went out to look round the place and along the shore. It had a queer effect of bareness and smallness. I remembered glades and groves and many hidden places that seemed far away, but now in the bare exposure of winter nothing was hidden. The bleak little shingled boat house stood there in full view—and the runway I could see was partly broken and gone. But the shore itself, beach and rock and headland, remained, and the wash of sea curled in slantwise as it always had—except that all of it was like a world empty of human meaning. An afternoon wind was coming in from the northeast, and no color existed but shades of gray, slate-dark on the sea, pale and smoky across the low sky, with flashes of silver where foam broke on the headlands. No ships anywhere, no white sails.

I circled back through the old garden patches where brown matted grass now lay, and briers and dead stalky weeds that rattled in the breeze. I had almost forgotten how winter could change and destroy, but even beyond that the place had the look of a long abandoned marginal farm. A forest of tough little maple trees grew where the strawberries and asparagus used to be. But the buildings themselves seemed to stand up with incongruous bulk and strength—even the barn with its slate roof and granite foundation looked as though it would endure forever.

It was really James I was looking for, but he kept out of sight, and I finally slipped into the barn and called—and then went up and knocked on his door and called again. I could hear him slowly stir and mutter to himself, and then he asked who it was. The voice was like rust, or the rattle of the dry weeds, and full of a sort of unbelief. It took me minutes to explain, and at last he opened a crack and peered at me. "It's Will Redfern," I kept saying. "You remember, James—I used to be here with my brother Harold when we were boys."

It was dark in the loft—I saw his white face staring out at me. "Do you want me for something?" he said. His eyes glared.

I pushed the door—a surge of stale warm air came out—and I stepped toward him. "Don't you know me, James?"

He had a birch stick in his hand, held like a club.

"What is it you want?"

"Why, I want to see you—I want to talk."

His lips were pulled back in a white grin. "Now stand back," he said.

I explained again, slowly, "Aunt Evelyn says you take good care of them," I said.

His eyes shifted. "They have no money—none at all."

"Well, I want to ask you about that," I said. "I have a little —I've been in the Navy and all: maybe I could leave some with you—just in case of special need."

"Folks say they're rich, you know. That's what they say. Silver and gold hidden away. They'll come looking for it some day. I've told them it has all gone for the taxes—the silver and the rugs—"

"You used to call me Master Will."

He wavered a little as he stood there, thin as a crane, with long down-curving nose and chin. "Is it Master Will?"

"I used to be after you to paint the rowboat."

The pale lips came together and opened in a childlike smile. "And tell me, how is young Master Harold?"

"Well, he has grown big too, like me."

"Is it possible?"

I came in and shut the door, though the air was thick with heat and poison. James seemed to hang there in uncertainty. "It's not a fit place for you, Master Will," he muttered.

I remembered James always as one full of assurance, and as he wavered there in the gray light he seemed like the shadow of what he had once been. I asked him how he was—I asked with serious insistence, and he nodded gravely, turned, put down his stick, and explained with profound gratitude. He was not well, of course. He had had stomach pains for many years, and he used to take Dr. Kiley's tonic for them—but now he hadn't the money, and could do nothing but suffer. And lately his feet had begun to hurt him and the pains shot right up the length of his spine—he couldn't wear his shoes with any comfort and it was hard getting about in the cold weather.

The tale of his ills seemed to strengthen his spirits, and he invited me to take the only available seat—a steamer chair. "I don't expect company in here," he said with a hint of accusation. "There's been no one here these ten years." He tipped his head toward the big house. "I keep *her* out of it, you can be sure. She'd be into it like a demon if I ever once let her."

"You'd better get some fresh air," I said. "You'll die breathing this poison."

He nodded gloomily. "I mind the cold, Master Will. It's that I'll die of, and soon. The chill stabs into me like a knife."

The room was wrapped and quilted against the outer world. Rugs, blankets, old sails, burlap, had been nailed to the wooden walls and floor and even the ceiling, and the window was double sashed. I could feel the heat radiating from the pot-bellied stove. "There's air enough comes in," he said. "You can hear it whistle when the wind blows up." He perched on the edge of the bed, where gray blankets were tangled like a squirrel's nest.

It seemed to me that much ought to be said, but I scarcely knew what. "You've had a hard time," I began. And James nodded in full agreement. The stomach pains were the worst, he added, and then held up his right hand and explained that there were times when his thumb was as weak as a baby's . . .

The ladies, I said, had had a hard time. He nodded and said they had indeed. Poor Miss Lucy was far gone, and he expected Miss Evelyn would drop over dead—it was only the spirit kept her on her feet. The three of them were not long for the world and it would be a blessing to have it all over with. He spoke without much emotion.

"You've taken care of them, James. You've kept them alive through all this trouble."

"I've done little enough. There was a time, Master Will, as you well know, when this place was kept as it should be, and I was the one that kept it so. In my judgment the three of us and the place as well has been dying these fifteen years and I wish to God it was ended." He lifted his eyes to the six-inch crucifix on the wall above the head of the bed. "There isn't a night goes by I don't pray for it."

I tried to get him to say what might be done, but he shrugged it off. There was someone come in the fall, one of the Weldon folk, and said they ought to sell the place—prices were high and all—but you can't tell that to the old ladies. Miss Evelyn got so mad she told him to go on home and leave them alone. "You know them well enough, Master Will— you've got to let 'em be. I don't believe any two people on earth have got stronger wills than those two—and I been dealing with 'em for sixty years." James shook his head respectfully. "Now their father, you could talk things over with him —but take Miss Evelyn, when she gets a notion in her head

God Almighty couldn't get it out again." He relaxed a bit on the bed, and seemed to gather a sort of momentum. "And Miss Lucy—you wouldn't believe it but she fought like a cat to stay up in that room of hers. By God, I come in one day and heard 'em screeching at each other upstairs—I didn't know what I should do, you know. Why they were fighting— I could hear 'em stamping and thumping and yelling—two women eighty years old. I stood there by the stairs, and then there was this crash—you know what one of 'em had done? She threw a stool—one of those wooden ones—and it went right through the window. Well, I started up—I thought they was killed, you know. And out come Miss Evelyn and says would I help take Miss Lucy's things down to the cook's room off the kitchen—they'd broke a big window up there and she'd have to move. She never let on they'd been fighting and screeching—they both of them acted as cool as you please. We decided this and we decided that, and not two minutes after they'd been at each other like wildcats."

I asked him who threw the stool, and he said it must have been Lucy. She went crazy sometimes. She broke up the telephone one day, threw it down on the radiator—he didn't know what it was, but some scheme went wrong, somebody couldn't come to dinner—and there was the time he was driving her to Nahant in the old Franklin, a lunch party with a lot of famous folk, and they had two flat tires—two, mind you, one after the other, on a hot summer day. He shook his head in helpless sorrow. She had had a fit, no less; she wept and called him an Irish blackguard and would have beaten him or shot him dead, though when they got there an hour late in she went as cool as the Empress of Inja, as Annie used to call her. And on the way home she said she was sorry, she'd been a mite upset. Of course, Miss Evelyn could be a good deal stubborner, as I knew—he eyed me with lips pulled back in an anxious grin as if he wanted to make sure I understood. "I wouldn't be telling this to anyone but you, Master Will, you know that. She knows what I think about her—I've spoke my mind more than once, and I know well enough what she thinks, but the fact is I have a higher respect for Miss Evelyn than anyone on earth. Whatever I can do for her, I'll do. There isn't much left for us—it's a blessing young folk don't ever know what it is to be old—" Again the white grin, without mirth.

I asked if they got enough to eat: they were all three wasting away. But he shrugged. They had the potatoes—it's one thing he could grow and store. He gave them what eggs he had, but in winter the hens had no decent feed and wouldn't lay. He didn't need much—none of them did. When I got out the money I had with me, a bit over twenty dollars, he looked almost frightened. "I wouldn't know what to do with it, Master Will—you'll best settle it with *her*. It's not a thing I can take the responsibility of." His expression was solemn. "She's the one to know about money—she has to get the taxes every year, and she's a smart one when it comes to selling a rug or a piece of silver. There's a dark little picture in there she says she can get a thousand dollars for, though you'd never think it was worth two-fifty—"

But I said there'd be emergencies—doctor, medicine, special food—I told him to put it away and say nothing to Aunt Evelyn, but to be sure to use it when it was needed. He could at least get a bottle of Dr. Kiley's, I said. He held the bills cautiously, shook his head, and then slid them quickly under a small Bible on his bureau. It seemed odd to see him dressed in brown work pants, darned at the knees, and a roll-collar knit sweater (from the family store, I realized) instead of in black gabardine suit and white collar. He was uncertain in his movements.

"I do fear for them," he said. "All the countryside thinks they're rich. There'll be thieves, Master Will, you can be sure of that."

I asked him if they had wood enough and he shook his head in sorrow and said up to now by the grace of God he had managed to cut enough—there was plenty of it lying round in the slash, mostly pine that burned up like paper, but some hardwood—but he couldn't tell how much more he'd be spared to do. There were times, he said, when he could hardly hold the saw in his hand. I said I'd come out and do some cutting for them and build up a good supply, and he nodded with gloomy doubt: they'd made out so far, he half mumbled; I wouldn't need to bother with it, and anyway they'd all be dead in their beds soon enough. His tones had an accent of pride in them.

I went back to Aunt Evelyn and had a cup of tea, and made her take a slice of bread and butter, but afterward, as I left, she did up my groceries in a package and asked me to leave them with James. He needed them much more than they did and would appreciate them—he never did eat properly, and hadn't looked well for years. I said goodbye to Aunt Lucy, who held my sleeve with a clutch of frail fingers and asked me to be sure to say howdy-do to Mr. Eliot for her, and then when I went out, with the package for James, Aunt Evelyn came to the steps with me and looked at the weather with a sardonic little smile. "I used to dote on winter," she said, pulling the sweater round her bowed figure. "How we skated—I could do the figure eight and the grape-vine!" She made the words explosive. "I could do the outside edge *backward!*" Then she snorted as though the whole idea had no relevance. "Now do come and see us again, Will—"

I said I was coming to cut wood, and she clutched the rail with both hands, stooping far forward, and shouted, "No—

no, you needn't do that, Will. You needn't worry about us—
we're *all right*. If you come, just come to *visit*."

She turned back to the door, with her chin at the level of
the knob, opened it and went in.

I left the package with James.

⊸§ CHAPTER 3 §⊷

BEFORE I went back to cut wood I bought a car, in the face of my mother's stern disapproval. It took most of my war money, and a week's time, but it was necessary to self-respect—or seemed so. It had been in my mind to go back to Holyoke, and the only way I could conceive of going was in my own car: to take trains and busses, even to walk, seemed unmanly, a mark of helplessness—and I confess that I have the same illusion still. Without an automobile I feel powerless, like an unhorsed cavalier. At whatever cost, I had to get the speed and the power and the eight cylinders, and being a mechanic I know pretty well how to go about it.

My mother's idea was that I should use my saved up money to go to college. The government would pay for most of it, and with what I had besides I'd be well off, and she was sure I could get into a good place like M.I.T.; but I had been living in Harold's rooms at Harvard and it seemed to me that the whole world was going to college—especially all those who felt they were getting something free: they were willing to study anything and everything, and they shopped round from one school to another to find what came easiest. Instead of being carried along with them I turned perverse and expressed a general contempt for academic timeservers. Not that I said much about it aloud: in the presence of my articulate brother and his friends I found it almost impossible to speak persuasively about anything, and instead of recognizing their abilities with intelligent humility I simply withdrew into my own precious separateness. College represented a sort of mass movement to me and I thought I had to keep out of it.

My intention even now seems to be to avoid solemn pronouncements of what the war meant to me or to anyone. It is over and gone—that one, at least—and the personal confusions are on file, and not of much interest. Nothing of my experience needs going over, except that I was confirmed in my desire for separateness—and in my hatred for mass activity of any kind. As a technician I had fared very well in the Navy, but the vision of personal freedom was always with me, like love.

So now in my car, a little '39 coupé of incredible agility, I rode the highways with a heady sense of escape. I had a secret desire to see what I could see, to scout the city, the waterfront, the automobile industry, and all other industries and curiosities. I liked to talk to people—my separateness implied no dislike of humankind—and I could talk in various technical jargons, with the simple-mindedness of the gadgeteer. Before I had finished my deal for the automobile I had been offered at least two jobs, and had declined them with a quick little sense of danger, as though a trap had been set and sprung, though illogically I was comforted by the fact. I'd have to have a job some day, but not now and not like this. As for what my mother called a career, I shrugged off any thought of it.

What I had in mind a good deal was Sally, with all the uncertainties that had built up in more than four years. In the dark watches and solitudes she had been my dream, at first richer and more palpable than the hostile world I faced. Not that I am much of a dreamer, as men go, but there are times when everyone lives most intensely in visions of love and hope, and this was such a time. But then the intensities began to fade, and a shimmer of great distance came between and sometimes I half wondered what it all was; at night I came back to it as though it had been an old book I was reading. It was nearly six months since I had heard from her and now I was almost afraid to see her again. It would be safer not to, yet it seemed to me that Sally, along with her grandfather, was almost the only thing in the world I could go back to, and in a sense I had to.

But I remembered her letters, how cool and candid and amusing they were, how different from the night-time illusions. I set off on a Saturday, with snow falling.

It was one of my conceits that I could drive through anything; the hazards of snow and ice enhanced the adventure and confirmed my pride in the agility of the car, and I shot along through the white with a fine sense of mastery. It was a good sort of day, I thought, to try to find Sally, though I could hardly have explained why.

There were ways of going at this, and my way was somewhat devious. It is to be recorded that one thing I did in the Navy was to win at poker—not spectacularly, but steadily enough, and fairly inconspicuously. I didn't rush in, and I mistrusted my emotions, and I figured with as much shrewdness as I could bring to bear—though it is true in my experience that shrewdness and even deviousness are characteristic of most people. At any rate, I approached Sally with caution and as much suppression of expectation as I could manage. I reasoned that the Sally I remembered had no existence now and that the old love was part of the passing adventure of early youth.

Yet as I rushed through the wall of flying snow an intense

urgent hope burned like a flame, underneath and separate from my figuring. I drove as though my life depended on my getting through to Sally.

Rochelle, the man I worked for, wasn't there any more, though the place still operated as a filling station. The boy on duty knew nothing, had never heard of him—or of Pop Sardis —or of me. He remembered that there had been a salesroom there, but he thought the only agency for that car now was the big place on the Springfield road.

So I circled round through slushy streets once familiar to me, peered at the Anthonakis grocery store—even looked in through the door and saw Sally's father behind the counter, unchanged and still formidable; I kept out of his sight with a familiar little stab of fear lest he catch me and accuse me of wrong. In that brief glimpse he looked as dark and angry as ever, even as he waited on and conversed with a booted and bundled up customer.

I stopped at the tenement house and knocked on Pop's door. He opened it.

The recognition came almost instantly. The nut-like face twisted into wrinkles of delight and he reached out both hands and spoke with a slow husky softness. "Will! I am so happy to see you." There were tears in his eyes, and his face was shining. "Come in, come in—" The voice was very throaty, the words almost slurred, and I saw at once that he had lost some of his old energy. But he looked the same—he had on the same shapeless gray suit I had last seen him in—and his countenance reflected the activity of his mind, as it always had. "You must stay here, Will—you must allow this to be your home. You see I am now in retirement, I am forced to live as a gentleman, in complete idleness—" He spread his white hands, smiling and peering at me steadily. "I have missed you very much." He shut the door behind me, took my coat, and ushered me to the best chair. "I see that you have grown very strong, very—manly." He made the word seem both earnest and humorous. "You must tell me—" He paused and smiled at the enormity of his request. "Tell me what you can."

But it was he who talked. His daughter Anna, he said, still worked at the factory, but was earning very high wages and now on Saturday afternoon was getting double her regular wage. Anna was a miser, he said, shaking his head; she worked and saved—there was money in the teapot, money in the Bible, money under her mattress—and they lived with the utmost frugality. Not, he shrugged, that he cared to live otherwise—but Anna, poor anxious Anna, had no existence but frugality. How could she, he asked, differ so from his other daughter Sandra, upstairs—she who saved nothing and floated along on a cloud of affection and benevolence.

I asked about his wife, who had never existed for me as a person, and he looked at me for a few seconds with a curious sort of speculation as though he were fathoming something in me. She was in a state hospital, he finally said. They wished she were dead. Sandra of the generous heart prayed every night that she might die. "It is to be faced," he said. "All that we consider precious in life is as fragile and brief as a house of cards." They had tried to keep visiting her, as a ritual if nothing else, but she had no mind, no spirit, and was cast away among the living dead. "I cannot describe it to you—I cannot speak of it. I feel guilt, as though I were responsible not only for her but for all the tragic disaster that life must come to." Then he moved and gestured as if he swept away the subject. It was better, he said, to talk about the young— about me and my plans—

But there was only one thing I wanted to talk about. What, I asked, was Sally doing?

He looked at me from the top of his eyes. "You don't know?"

"No."

He seemed to wait a moment for energy to build up a small pressure before he released it in speech. "Sally—she has been exiled, you know; she doesn't come back." His voice expressed affection, regret, humor, and a sort of eagerness. "We see her —occasionally—in secret, against orders. Her mother pays little visits. But I think—" He shook his head. "There is something sad about Sally—in her very nature—an air, a motif, of very beautiful sadness."

I let him go on, but added a question now and then to make a clearer picture. She lived in the city of Springfield and had a job as an assistant music director in the public schools. She was married to a boy—Pop looked at me quizzically as he said the word—named Saul Julian, a writer of some sort, a poet, he understood. There was more to her story than simply that, he implied; she had scandalized her father by consorting with artists and musicians and freeing herself from the strict ways of her early life. She had great warmth and affection, as I realized, and a kind of strength that attracted the weak and the unsure.

I had known that she must have had other loves than mine; I had expected it all, even the marriage. But the news left me with a sudden sense of great defeat and loss, a wholly un-looked-for despair that welled up from some nether part of being that I hardly knew was there.

"Married," my voice said cheerily. "Well, well! Tell me more about it—do you approve? What is he—like?"

He glanced at me, held his breath as though he were about to say something vital, then looked down, spread his hands, even shrugged a little. "I hardly know—I am not, I think, able to judge. You see, marriage has a use, a purpose—I mean tradi-

tionally. It creates the family; it is the unit cell of all society."
He hesitated as though he were constrained, then he looked
up in a sort of surrender. "No, I don't really approve, Will.
But I am too old—I think of them as children—" After a moment he said, "I feel very sorry for them."

He told me about Althea, who lived in New Haven and had
two children—both girls, but I hardly took it in. It would be
well not to see Sally at all, I thought. I shrugged off the neth-
erward disappointment that kept welling up like an insistent
fever and making almost a dizziness in the head. "I'd like a
glimpse of Sally," I foolishly mumbled.

Pop had been watching me with a bird-like steadiness; now
he got up, poked among some papers on a table, wrote the
address on a torn scrap, and handed it to me. I couldn't
fathom his expression, though the gesture seemed quite per-
functory. "It might be better if I stayed away," I said. "What
do you think?"

"My dear boy, I can't tell you. I know very well that Sally
would like to see you, but what is better—or best—is more
than I can say." Then he added as a sort of postscript: "She is
a strong character, you know." His smile was bright.

"Is she beautiful?"

He made no answer.

I stayed there that night—slept on a couch in the sitting
room that Anna fixed for me. I met all the family again—
even Mike, who was hearty and warm in his welcome. They
gathered me in like one of them. The two younger sisters
were full of the same conspiratorial charm I remembered so
vividly in Althea and Sally; they lived among their own in-
communicable secrets, as though the real part of their beings
was elsewhere, and it seemed somehow surprising that they
both had ordinary day-to-day jobs, Rhoda as a telephone operator and Nan as office secretary in a building-supply firm. I

wondered what hopes or loves or passions lay concealed behind their very dark eyes and enigmatic shy smiles. Their father, I thought, regarded them with profoundest pride.

The youngest, Pop said, are the fortunate ones; they are given what the oldest had to fight for. But then he reflected and amended: perhaps not so fortunate after all—perhaps it is not well that the way be made easy. Rhoda might have been as fine a musician as Sally—she might have used her contralto for a better cause than answering telephones.

All that Sunday morning I made up my mind not to try to see Sally. Instead I drove over to Kingstown and visited my old teacher, Mr. Chadd, who at once, at first glimpse, offered me a job. He surrounded me, in fact, and if it hadn't been Sunday I should have been put to work then and there. The school, he said, was overwhelmed; every hopeful veteran in the country wanted to learn an easy trade at government expense. Joe Venuti had gone—he was making his fortune in the electrical business—and there was no one to take his place—no one really competent, that is. Money was too plentiful elsewhere—

Chadd's magnetism was part of his being, and it always won me. He lost himself in his cause, and he did it with gallantry and courage and humor. The bunch of keys whirled on its chain, even on a Sunday morning, the blue eyes flashed, the small figure bent backward and the chin lifted high. The enterprise was really booming, the game was being won— Chadd's own game of showing the world that he could create and carry on a successful trade school. Had I seen, he asked, their new stuff? They had taken over the garage across the street, steel and concrete, two floors, and put in war-surplus tools: he rushed me out, forgetting hat and coat, ignoring the winter wind, and drove me over there. Seventy-five a week, he said, and I could start next morning—he dashed on ahead, unlocking doors, whirling the fat bunch of keys like a sling shot. He had three good men—pretty good men, that is; but there was just too much, they needed three more—and I was the three. Chadd, then and always, could persuade me to do anything. It was a challenge, a dare, a game to be shared by the courageous, and there was no argument about it. His sharply cut, boyish face and blue eyes, the upthrust of his chin, the blade-like smile, all conspired in a wonderful certainty, a foregone conclusion. There were no complexities about Chadd, and very few hesitations. "I can get engineers, Will—I can even get M.I.T. graduates and technical big-shots, but can they teach anything to a bunch of farmer boys? They can't even talk that language." He fixed me with his shining blue eyes. "You can teach 'em, Will; you can talk to 'em. I *know* what you can do."

I resisted, of course. I feared the trap. I protested my inabilities. Chadd applied no pressure, argued little, but simply waited for his certainty to make itself felt. It surprised me, I remember, that he seemed older and quieter; I noticed the web of wrinkles in his face, the lines of resolution at the corners of his mouth. It struck me that he was a man of character and not simply a phenomenon of energy, and I was reassured and comforted by his faith in me.

"Tell you this, Will," he said. "You can learn about yourself here. I mean, you can see what you have to do—maybe what you are good for. It will give you a scale." He smiled at me with a curious little wistfulness, as though he were seeing himself in me. Then he tossed up his keys. "Me—I like to teach, I like to run this outfit. No regrets." He shrugged. "But you—I don't know. You'll have to do some thinking—and do it pretty quick. You hate to, I guess: everybody does, specially now, after a war." His blue eyes seemed very sharp as they studied me. "Ever fool around with ideas, Will? I mean—designs, dreams, perpetual-motion machines—" He smiled quickly. "All those years in the navy, eh?"

I remembered Pop's gestures in pointing to the motor in Rochelle's shop—it seemed ages ago.

"Well," I muttered, "sure, I guess so." I gathered courage. "They still go on building water-cooled motors—year after year for ever. I argued about it for six months with a guy aboard ship and he kept proving that I didn't know a damned thing about it. But wait till I show you—I mean there's no reason why the idea won't work—"

Chadd's smile was like a blade. "Okay, Will. You've got pictures of it, eh? We'll look at 'em some time." He paced the floor. "You want to go to Tech, do you?"

I watched him. "What do you think?"

The keys flew up again. "You can't go now anyway. The term started a month ago. Come and look at the auto shop—that's where we need you right away." He trotted ahead. "Tomorrow at nine, that is." He grinned back at me. "Just old fashioned water-cooled stuff, Will."

"That's only one thing," I said. "Wait till you see the new carburetion system I figured out."

"Half the fuel and twice the power, I suppose!"

We went back to his house, an iron-gray two-family affair with wooden porches before and behind, and I met Mrs. Chadd for the first time. It startled me that she seemed ten years older than he, and both heavier and stronger, a slow-moving rather monumental woman with a craggy face—I even supposed at first that she was his mother, which was the name he used for her. He let her direct him in all the small acts: it seemed that he would never think of washing his hands until she ordered it, or of attending to my needs, and she kept a sort of top-sergeant eye on both of us to see that all was done.

Chadd himself was full of smiling brightness, like a boy, and she was patient with him and rather stern, as though her only refuge from the long ordeal of life was in pure duty; I felt somehow that he was daring too much when he made fun of her. It seemed that a grand-daughter had been born, and they were immensely preoccupied with the fact—it was what made me understand that they were husband and wife: "Mother," he said, "keeps at me to steal the baby—she wants it for herself. Fact is, she doesn't think anyone else is capable of bringing it up. Now, my idea about a grandchild is you can enjoy it without any of the bother of raising it." She eyed him stonily, and I felt a touch of embarrassment; but then a softening, a faint twitch of the mouth and melting of the corners and angles, and Chadd nodded and glanced at me with a quick little signal of satisfaction as though a point had been scored. Mrs. Chadd froze again at once.

But there was a good dinner and before I could think fully of the consequences I said I'd be at the school at nine the next morning. The decision, I told myself, committed me to nothing permanent. I was free, I could do it—or not do it. The thought gave me a sort of giddiness and when I took leave of the Chadds I had no serious view of the future whatever.

What I intently thought of was Sally, and I found myself heading for Springfield, still in the mood of giddiness as though nothing counted.

CHAPTER 4

Yᴇᴛ ᴡʜᴇɴ I found the place I sat a long time in the cold car, shivering a little and staring at the slush-covered wooden steps that led up to the house. The day had been cold after the storm, but the afternoon sun was melting the snow; in the city the freshness was already gone, and snowy surfaces were specked with gray and brown. In this side street slush churned under wheels. A few patches of cleared walk were dry, others wet and sloppy; as I sat there I was acutely aware of all such things, the unclean look of old city snow, the mess of the narrow street, the wooden tenements as drab as unused warehouses. Ugly as sin, I kept saying to myself.

A three story box, and theirs was the top floor.

After a while I drove off, turned corners reflectively, finally stopped at a drugstore and looked up the name in a telephone book. Julian.

She was, I remembered, beautiful and a little wild, like the deer we always looked for. Secretly beautiful, half hidden from the world, and somehow very valuable, like treasure. But I thought how long ago it was, in the time of her girlhood, in the poetry of her life. I thought of her body, and tried to be clear with myself about it—I even tried to see what my intentions were, but I seemed to get nowhere. I pictured myself

192

driving off, leaving her unvisited—and knew I couldn't. I reasoned that the issues were unclear, that it would be well to go on, that nothing decisive was at stake. . . .

The double ring made a forlorn sound over the wire and no one answered. Sunday afternoon, I thought. Empty rooms, empty city, everybody lost in the immense voids of Sunday in winter. I hardly believed in a live Sally any more; the double ring sounded like a knell, and I hung up to cut it off. But I drove back along the dismal street where she lived, and saw them coming from the other end—I saw Sally walking just as she used to, with a slow cat-like ease, head bent a little forward, eyes down, black hair thick and unbound, not speaking or smiling. She was hugging a violin case in both arms. She wore a gray shapeless wool coat, no hat, no rubbers—her low shoes, I thought, must have been soaking.

I had had inevitably an image of the man, but the actuality was nothing like it. Even at a distance he looked like a lost boy, tousled and thin and tired and in some mysterious way miserable. He was not much taller than she, with narrow hollow shoulders and a shuffling gait—he too with wet feet and bare uncombed head. He wore glasses.

For a hundred yards or so they came along, and I watched. A brief impulse came to me to say nothing, to sit anonymously in the car and let them go on up the steps—she might, I thought, stare right at me without realizing who it was. But there she was, outwardly and bodily the Sally I had had in mind all the four years, and some sort of rushing dizziness seized me, and I opened the door and got out and spoke.

I said, "Hello, Sally. I'm Will Redfern." In the odd pause I explained that I had seen her grandfather.

It seemed queer to me that I had introduced myself to her that way, but I had an impulse to soften the abruptness of it, to make her understand as quickly as possible. It was probably needless, because she always knew how to control herself, and I saw that she recognized me at first glance, before I spoke at all. She smiled. It was only for a few seconds, a quick flash of passionate brightness against the dark background of her being—darker now, I felt at once, than it used to be.

"This is Saul," she said with the characteristic little blurt I remembered. "My husband." It was a serious moment. We shook hands.

His look was still that of an adolescent—face with unformed features, white blemished skin, a look half way between misery and cynicism. His mouth didn't quite close, and though the lips seemed to smile, they expressed a sort of bewildered contempt—at least that's how I came to think of it later. Just then I could hardly take it in that this miserable looking schoolboy was Sally's husband.

We stood there in the cold in uneasy attitudes. Even Sally seemed nervous, and her dark eyes stared at me with uncertainty, as though she were looking for a clue.

"You—been playing?" I nodded at the violin.

"Rehearsing." She gathered herself together. "Come on up —I—we'll make some coffee. I knew you were back—from the war, I mean—"

She climbed the steps, and we followed and kept on up the three flights, creaking and clumping in the semi darkness, stumbling on the gritty boards, pushing up through the dungeon air, saying nothing till we got into rooms where they lived.

And there we stood in silence. It seemed to me that Saul, with hunched shoulders and wet feet, was shivering, though the heat from an oil-burning iron stove poured over us in a choking wave. For a moment the air could hardly be breathed; I felt the sting of it in my eyes.

With a sort of effort Sally put her violin down on the floor in a corner and walked into the next room—I watched her intently and she seemed somehow slow and dreamlike. "It's too hot in the kitchen and too cold in here," she said with a detached humor, as though she didn't mind how it was. "But you can breathe better here." She waited for us to move in, and though it was chilly a westerly low sun brightened the plaster of the walls and fell warmly on the uneven floor-boards. "We sort of shuttle back and forth, hot to cold, cold to hot."

Saul at last spoke. He nodded to a big square of orange cotton tacked to the wall beside the door to the kitchen, glowing now in the sunlight. "Radiant heat, that is. Warms the fancy." It was a deeper, more masculine voice than I expected, but bitter and heavy with irony. He hunched further into his coat and peered downward at the bare floor. Yet his words revised my notion of him. He smiled ruefully, almost with a confiding charm. "Fire and ice," he rumbled, as if it were a tiresome incantation that he was forced to say. "Sally's immune to both."

He stood like one who had nothing else to do or think of. Sally had gone to make coffee, but looked in again with a sudden wide smile and said we could sit down—as best we could, that is. There were two wooden chairs, two boxes, and a slatted rocker—and also a table with a typewriter and phonograph on it, and piles of books along the floor against walls. I remember one title staring up at us: *Troubled Sleep*, by Jean Paul Sartre. But Julian made no move, except to huddle further into his overcoat and let his slack mouth fall vaguely open as though he were going into a trance. I took a chair and thought of what to say: was he going to school some-where? was this his native town?

It surprised me a little, then and later, that he answered so shrewdly. He looked like a persecuted adolescent, full of sul-len misery, but his voice came out with baritone energy and a kind of sneering competence: He had been separated from three colleges, he said, stressing the words; he wasn't the college type, they told him—he smiled, thinking of it, bared his teeth not in pleasure but in defensive irony. Then with sudden intent seriousness he said that there was a man at Columbia he liked—taught a class in modern French drama, the only course he ever had that was worth doing any work for. The man was fired too; he wasn't the college type.

The sun by then had faded away; no glow lingered on the scarred and dirty plaster, nor even on the square of orange cloth. Saul had collapsed into the rocking chair, still bundled in his coat, and sat with half smiling relish of his condition. I suggested that he might feel warmer with dry feet, but he took no notice; he had a strange trait of staring downward, open mouthed and unmoving, yet giving an impression of some sort of inner activity. He seemed miserable, inside and out, and the room seemed miserable. In the silence I was con-scious of a stinging in my eyes and a dull ache above them. The air was bad.

But Sally brought in coffee and crackers and cheese. I saw that she was slimmer, firmer, more muscular, though still ample enough, and her face was more subtly modelled, her mouth larger and more expressive, her eyes deeper. She seemed very beautiful to me—more so than any woman I had ever seen, but also formidable. The dark glance revealed little of her inner being, though now and again she smiled with that flash of brightness that came and went in an instant.

She asked what I was doing, and we talked on for a while

about such things and I half forgot the ugly tenement room and the bad air. But when she said that Saul was writing a novel it came back to me with a double impact of self-pity that I had no home, nowhere to go, no Sally to be part of. Something in the way she enveloped him with her glance reminded me of everything, though she revealed no special feeling; but there he was, at home with her, sharing with her his destinies as a person and a novelist. Even though it seemed pitiful that he should be trying to justify his existence in a novel I had to realize that he not only lived and breathed, but possessed the mysterious potentialities of a man—and he might, for all I knew, have some sort of divine gift that I couldn't see.

He bared his teeth again and sardonically remarked that he was only doing it for the money he hoped he could make— he was supposed, after all, to be supporting a wife. But as he glanced at me with a calculated sneer his face curiously dissolved into that of a small boy; the smile appealed for confidence and comfort and even affection. "I guess it sounds pretty damned foolish," he muttered. "Writing a novel— that's what they all say. No trick for a man of my talents— easy money, really." His ironic tones seemed to combine childish petulance and grown-up awareness. He even giggled. Then he slumped down lower in his rocking chair, half buried in his coat, and seemed to go off into a sort of doze.

Sally had been serving out coffee and crackers and moving about; now she settled down with a cup and saucer on her knee and took note of me, as it were. Her eyes were darker, steadier, more profound than ever, and the black hair and wide mouth made her seem somehow Egyptian. You couldn't tell what went on, I thought—you never could. I had a sudden clear image of the head lying on its cushion of shining black hair on the pine needles.

No thought formed itself in my mind, but it seemed as though blood whirled and rushed from heart to head and roared within. The room grew dim and strange.

"What are you going to do, Will?" she was saying in a voice that seemed to come from far away.

It couldn't really *count*, I thought suddenly to myself. Even though they slept there in the next room it couldn't be what I always had conceived of as marriage.

I said Chadd wanted me to work for him, but my words sounded thin and far through the rushing inside me; I stood up without volition, impelled by force of blood, walked to the window and peered at nothing, walked to where my jacket lay on a pile of books in the corner, picked it up with a hard clutch of the blue fabric. "Got to go, I'm afraid." My voice came from a distance, but it sounded all right. The emotion in me was not quite an angry one, not quite savage; it was, I suppose, at war with itself, and made a turmoil without direction. But it had exploded with no warning, touched off apparently by the clear vision of Sally's head cushioned on the black hair on the bed of pine needles. "I told Chadd I'd be there," I mumbled into the corner. "But I don't know— seems sort of funny—I mean—"

It was as though at that moment Sally was life itself, all the good of it, air to breathe, sweet sleep, music, the bright colors of the days and seasons, all the comfort and beauty the world could hold. I hadn't remembered—I didn't know she'd be like that. I had supposed it was just a young dream, the unreal part of childhood that inevitably passes; but there she was in the room, a grown woman more beautiful than all the queens of the Nile, there were the dark steady eyes and the warm mouth and the hair, and I knew as sure as truth that all that loveliness in her face and body was the true emblem of her inner being.

Come down again, she was saying. Sundays and evenings —except for when she played: better telephone first. They had parties sometimes—Friday or Saturday night. She got up and came to the door, watching me with profound feminine appraisal.

Saul nodded from his chair and smiled with a suddenly childish and helpless smile, appealing for indulgence. I probably looked surly, or even angry, but the rush of blood was still in me and I hardly understood what I did, except to mumble and nod and blunder out through the kitchen and down the long creaky stairs.

Outside, in the winter air, I stood a moment half stupefied, already beginning to doubt what had happened. The cold was like a shock of water over me, and I looked up at the drab tenement almost indignantly as though somehow it had taken me unawares. It wasn't, I thought, quite believable— it wasn't real.

I drove off in a mood of cynical self-justification, asserting myself against the icy roads and the intense cold of the coming night. The car rushed like a weapon in my hands directed at an almost visible destiny. It was a waste and a folly, and on two or three glare corners it almost destroyed me, but I felt compelled to it; the recklessness was like an electric charge crackling along my spine. No thought remained in me, no special awareness of Sally or of what I would do.

When I got back to Pop's about nine he was reading and Anna had gone to bed. It seemed astonishing to me that he was reading *The Descent of Man*, a heavy yellowish book that looked as though it had never before been read by anyone. He half apologized for it and held it up as an object to be marveled at. "I was curious to see what the new world comes from." His voice sputtered a little and gave the words unexpected accents. "Darwin—the architect of modern life:

see!" He pointed to the fly leaf. "Nineteen eighteen—the last date. Twenty six years on the shelf—unopened: yet everyone knows about Darwin—everyone talks about him." His nut-like face expressed the eagerness of his thoughts. He roused himself to the edge of the chair and gestured with the book. "It is a great pity that we simply take him for granted—we make an abstraction and call it Darwinism; but the man is a wonderful man, Will. His mind—it is like light—it is like—" He stared at me without seeing me. "It is what we have instead of God, perhaps. More than reason and more than knowledge: there are moral qualities—there is devotion and humility and integrity. I tell you, Will, it is good for a sorrowful old man to read Darwin. It would I think be good for a young man too. You see the only true divinity." He looked at the book once more and then put it aside. "I must confess to you that I don't read it all. My own devotion is imperfect. My capacity is small." He made a throaty chuckle as he said it. "But I feel—" He spread his hands. "I feel as though I have perched for a time on a giant's shoulders."

Then he asked me what I had done and I told him about Chadd and Sally. I could see his mind begin to take it in and work on it, and he nodded and peered round at the meagre little room we were sitting in. "I wish it could be a home for you, Will, but it is not enough."

I said I planned to rent a room in Kingstown, but he went on as though he hadn't heard. The Greek people thought in terms of family, he said; life was best at home. But I had no home. I wandered. I adventured. This job with Chadd—it was just an accidental job. I would live in a rented room—I would go on to other rooms, other accidental jobs. I was a sort of picaresque character, he said, like the comic adventurers in old books—but he said it with speculative irony, waiting for me to respond. I shrugged. Adventure on a pretty small scale, I said. But even so, why not? You almost had to keep going, didn't you? It wasn't a good idea to get stuck in a hole—

"There—you see!" He broke in, holding his hands wide apart. "The two ways of living—the going and the staying. You—and me!" He didn't say it seriously, but he looked round at his forlorn little room. "Home," he nodded. "This is it. This is my hole. You may be right, Will—it may not be a good idea. But I have this in mind: the wanderer is one who tries to abandon his soul. He runs from it, as it were. As long as he escapes he is always young, he has very little sorrow, a very small conscience—" His face was twisted with the humor of his words, but he had moved to the outer edge of his chair in a posture of tension. "He has no love, though I suppose he may lust—he is free, like the fowls in the air—"

It was meant for me, somehow, but I couldn't take it in.

Is it better, he ventured, to stay and be burdened with the weight of conscience and love, or to escape—but then he stopped in sudden negation, with a horizontal motion of his hands. The mind, he said, makes everything into poles, like north or south, or positive and negative, but as far as he could see the one great aim of man and nature was to have it both ways. The bondage and freedom occurred together in an impossible union. Man ran from his soul in order to find it; he left home to seek a home. He reserved to himself the benefits of all extremes.

Is that, I said, what he thought I was trying to do?

He remembered, he said, an old tale in his part of Crete about a boy named Val who fell in love with a mountain girl. He was a shepherd, like many boys in old stories, and very charming and talented, and he could sing tenor and play the flute and dance. But in the mountain pastures where he tended his sheep he felt very lonesome. He dreamed of love, and made songs of his yearnings, and he would have left his sheep and run off into the world if he hadn't come upon a girl sleeping in the soft grass under an oak tree. He watched her a while, then played a tune on his flute, and when he saw her eyes open he kissed her. It was very lovely and happy, and it was almost as though she expected him to be there. They talked and sang together and played at love. She said she lived higher up in the mountains, and in the evening she left him, but she smiled and kissed him and said she'd be back. He went home with a vision of her warm lips and dark eyes and her black unbound hair, and next day he came eagerly back to the oak tree but she wasn't there, nor did she come that day, nor the next. Just as he resolved to go and search for her in the mountains—many days later it was—he came upon her again sleeping under the oak tree. But when he ran to embrace her he saw that her hair was golden—like ripe wheat, the story says—and when he kissed her eyes open he saw that they were blue. Yet she was the same girl, and she knew him, and they talked and sang and played at love as they had before. When he spoke of her eyes and hair she mocked him a little and said he must be thinking of some other girl. And they were as happy together as lambs in spring and the day passed like a melody, and when she departed, with kisses and smiles, she said she'd be back. And he went home again with the vision of her warm lips and blue eyes and golden unbound hair. But it all happened as it had the other time: days passed, and he resolved to seek her in the mountains, and then she was there again, under the oak, only this time she was all brown, with gleams of chestnut in her hair. Yet it was the girl he loved—it seemed to him that he loved her more than ever, and the parting at evening was harder. He asked her if he couldn't come up into the mountains where she lived, but she said no—her family were out-laws and enemies of all the valley people. She promised to come back to him, but she had to be careful and secret.

So it happened, again and again. And each time she was curiously different, but always lovable and always radiant with youth and beauty. But as weeks went on, and even the seasons, young Val grew less and less satisfied. It made him uneasy that his love was dark one day and fair another, though the change each time was a miracle of delight; he him-self, he thought, couldn't have dreamed of such infinite varia-tions on the classic pattern of a beautiful girl. And in the soft grass under the oak on a summer afternoon she made his little world a paradise. But down in his village his friends and relatives were living in other ways: they worked, traded, farmed, acquired property; some of the young men went to school, learned professions, and some married and had chil-dren. They asked Val what he planned to do: was he going on being just a shepherd? They wondered why he didn't ap-ply for a scholarship to study music in Athens—they re-minded him of his talents and abilities. So his secret love grew less satisfying to him, and he tried to persuade her to marry him and go back and live among his people—and per-haps go to Athens with him and study music. And of course for a long time she laughed and put him off, and then she said she would and she wouldn't and from one day to an-other he couldn't tell what she meant. He grew more sombre, and she more petulant, and their play under the oak took on the intensities of passion and anguish. Even the girl, who had been as lightsome and free as the meadow flowers, began to brood, and her beauty somehow deepened; she appeared more and more in her darker guises and she looked at Val in sorrow.

When he got to this point, Pop cocked his head at me. "Perhaps," he said, "you think this is simply a child's tale; perhaps I shouldn't be telling it."

"What was her name—the girl's name?"

He reflected a moment. "Her name at that time was Amaryllis."

"And did she leave him? Did she fade away into the forest?"

"No. She loved him. She married him. He was a very attractive boy, don't forget."

"What then? Did they settle down in the village, or go to Athens and study music? Or did they build a cabin beside the oak tree in the meadow? I have a feeling that it is a sad story. It begins much too happily."

"He took her back to his village and introduced her to his mother, who hated her at first sight—at that time Amaryllis was a brown girl, and rather severe and nun-like, with hair braided and tied; but at the wedding, when she appeared in the bridal array the family had provided for her, she was a dazzling blonde, with hair like white gold curling to her shoulders, and scarlet lips and darkened lashes. No one there had ever seen anything as spectacular, and they stared at her in silent awe. And Val himself looked handsome and happy, and after the ceremonies they went off to a seaside cottage that belonged to Val's great uncle. Everything went well and they had a fine night together, but next morning when they woke up she was a stranger to him. She was a rather stocky girl, sturdy in the waist and hips, with brown hair cut straight round her head. Her features were a little pudgy. Are you Amaryllis? he asked. And she smiled cheerfully and said that's what he kept calling her last night—and of course it was a much prettier name than Meg, specially on a wedding night.

Did he like his egg boiled four minutes? She wanted to be sure to have his first breakfast just right for him.

A very sad story, I said.

Pop shrugged. "It is true they didn't go to Athens and study music. They didn't venture into the great world at all. They inherited a small farm and lived on it for forty years and had many children. It is a story, Will—but not necessarily a sad one." He peered at me from the top of his eyes. "I believe he was a very fortunate young man. She might have been a vampire, you know. Or at least she might have been incapable of boiling an egg."

He didn't go on with it. I supposed it had something to do with me and I asked him what it really meant, but he spread his hands and shrugged. "I am like the Delphic oracle, Will. I speak mysteriously." His smile seemed childlike in his wrinkled face. "It is one thing to theorize about human nature and repeat old tales; it is quite another to account for particular individuals like my grand-daughter Sally—or my friend Will Redfern." He brooded a moment. "Perhaps you can find a blonde girl, Will, with blue eyes and hair like ripe wheat."

✌§ CHAPTER 5 §✍

FOR THE next few days Chadd took charge of me. He flung me into the mid-stream of his school, not recklessly but with tireless advice and consideration. He had the faculty of making me feel like an extension of himself. I had expected to blunder; I went into the job with a sort of bland carelessness, with crossed fingers and little concern for the outcome; but Chadd seemed to know what to do with me, and by the time I was there half a day I was his confident deputy. It was partly his organization—he always knew exactly what had to be done—and partly his vitality. He was all over the building at once, explaining, instructing, setting things right, patting backs, generating confidence and good cheer.

He found a room for me—he knew the people who could do things for him. The town was still crowded with war-time workers, and rents were high, but Chadd made two or three telephone calls and sent me to a house on the western outskirts where the shops and factories stopped and the truck farms began, a dismal area in winter where the barns and sheds and shops and dwelling houses seemed all forlorn and shabby in the gray weather. It was dark when I got there, so I couldn't tell much about it except that the house was very old—at least the front was: a plain square farm dwelling of long ago—but so added to and reshaped with bays and bulges that it had become a hive of tenements. At the old front door were name plates, bells, and mail-boxes, and there seemed to be other side doors and in the rear a collection of dark and slanting outbuildings. Mr. and Mrs. Harkins, Chadd said, and they lived in the wing on the south side—she was the one to deal with, she handled the rent business: his second wife, and a sharp one. Chadd always admired competent people.

The room was under a gabled roof, one window facing south, one dormer facing west. Iron bed, wicker rocking chair, bureau with marble top, bulb hanging from ceiling, and a floor lamp with pink shade. It was right over their kitchen, she pointed out, and kept warm in winter and the two windows made a cross draught in summer. Bathroom at foot of stairs—I'd have to share it with them, which was one reason they didn't rent the room to anyone who came along. Mrs. H. was all starch and asperity and had no reluctance about asking for the rent in advance. "We've had some of Mr. Chadd's people here before and they've been quite satisfactory," she said with quiet threat. But she refused to be personal, or to smile, and asked me to be very careful about smoking.

It seemed all right to me—the barely furnished gable room with the straw carpet on the floor, the drab outskirts of a factory town, the very competent and impervious landlady. I had few expectations in life, and a warm room, a bed, and freedom were the only necessaries I then cared about. It was a snug place in winter, as she had said, and I spent a good many evenings lying on the bed and reading. I still indulged in magazines where all the mechanics of modern life were pictured, but Pop had taken it upon himself to educate me in what he considered the essentials—which seemed to consist of European history and philosophy. He provided me with a heavy volume of each. The history, he said, was straight meat and potatoes—I had to have it. But the philosophy—he shook his head over it. It was, he said, the greatest paradox under the sun; the more he read of it, the more baffled he felt. Most of the great philosophies were, as far as he could see, perfect nonsense. Plato's ideals and Aquinas's realities were manifest fantasies, the dreams of imaginations that verged on insanity. Yet all western culture rested on them. And the chief function of all subsequent philosophers was to point out the absurdities of their predecessors. I remember how he peered at me from the top of his eyes as he handed me the book: the supreme greatness and the supreme folly of man in one volume, he said, and smiled with that gentle sweetness that concealed so much strength: the one, he went on, seems necessary to the other; the mind of man was compelled to push itself beyond and beyond, regardless of sense or reason or truth itself. I had to know this, he explained, and he had picked out a volume that summed it all up—though it said nothing about supreme folly: that was just his idea. I wondered as I read it why Pop didn't write a book himself.

I may have been led to read by various impulses—affection for Pop, consciousness of my brother's superiorities, a notion that Sally would think well of me because of it—but though it began as a duty and a vanity it went on by its own momentum. I even ventured into a public library and found books that summed up all sorts of things—the books, I learned later, that my brother scorned as mere popularizations; but they seemed fine and valuable to me, and I read through the late winter evenings with a good feeling of adventure. The history went best, and I began to see old events not as fables but as part of the warring world I had actively been in—it came as a grim discovery that violence had always been the rule. History, I noted, said very little about suffering. Hostages were killed, towns sacked, armies destroyed, peoples massacred, but what human profit or loss accrued was seldom made clear. Power and money were the forces at work, and as I lay snug in my warm room under the pink lamp I felt contempt for the great ones of recorded history. Philosophically, I thought, they were no better than juveniles fighting for street-corner prestige—fighting with the same methods and ends. But when I began struggling with the philosophers I found that they were very little concerned with the question of human success. The happiness of men was the least of their concerns.

It took me a good while to arrive at these ideas, and even now I have no special confidence in them. But I keep wondering why philosophers have been such indifferent teachers of the art of civilization, and why mankind again and again gives itself into the hands of the savage and miserable. I should like to ask a real philosopher about it—one I could reasonably understand. My brother Harold talks of sin and suffering and ritual and redemption in a language I don't grasp.

Meanwhile I went back to Bell's Landing to cut the wood. I couldn't stay the night there—it would have been too much for Aunt Evelyn—so I slept Saturday night in Harold's rooms and spent most of Sunday at the sawing and splitting. It seemed to me that the old ones must die, all three of them, especially in that dismal chill of late winter by the sea, but they were fixed in their habits of life. "If we all froze *solid*," Aunt Evelyn said, "it would be so much the better." They were like parts of one organism, each necessary to the whole, with no other purpose than survival. When one failed it would be the end of all. Yet something more than that existed in Evelyn, some spark of immortal spirit that sounded in her voice. "I declare, Will, you've brought us in some good hard *maple*. It'll be a pleasure to burn it, I can tell you, after all that pine—Papa *always* liked maple for the big fire place. Oh, he delighted in hard maple!"

I brought the last of what I had cut and stacked it on the porch near the kitchen door—some maple and birch and a good deal of pine. James had kept himself out of sight most of the time, not, I felt, in disapproval of my work but in a sort of shrinking from my energy. "I can see you've got to be a strong boy," he said almost sadly, as though he were commiserating with me. I had thought of asking him to work the two-man saw with me on some of the big pieces, but I didn't mention it.

In late afternoon, about when I was wheeling in the last load, an old black Chrysler drove into the yard. The ground was frozen, but soft on the surface, and the tires made conspicuous tracks. I thought they were curious Sunday drivers, but they got out and walked somewhat uncertainly toward the porch where I stood with the wheelbarrow. Though I hadn't seen her in sixteen years I knew it was my cousin—or second cousin, I was never sure—Jane Weldon. She had no chin, and years ago had seemed to me conspicuous and pathetic; now, with middle age, it was the same face, but lined and somehow molded into a trustworthy homeliness.

"Do you know if Miss Redfern," she began very gently and coldly—and then eyed me with a gleam of inquiry. A girl and boy were just behind her, and they all paused and looked at me.

When I said who I was, Cousin Jane nodded calmly. "How good of you to do this"—her voice was level. "This is Betsy and Chan—we're perfectly good cousins, aren't we—we know Harold, of course, but it must be years and years—" She went on with the calm and level appraisal.

Chan looked about sixteen, and seemed thin and droopy. His head was thrust forward on a rather small neck, and without cap or warm jacket he looked defenseless against the cold—though I found out later that he was a hardy nature lover and was training himself to be very tough. Betsy, hatless, in gray sweater and dungarees, looked about fourteen, all natural and pink, and pretty. I couldn't think of their name and I tried to hear in my mind the old voices—Jane, Jane Weldon—married Walter Somebody.

"We can't persuade them to leave," she was calmly saying, as though it were a Sunday afternoon trifle. "If they'd only sell the place they'd have plenty—they could be comfortable somewhere. You know how they are, I expect."

Safford, I said to myself; Walter Safford—at least I was pretty sure. They had been at the funeral, long ago. I remembered Betsy, the stuffed little doll with flaxen braids. Jane was asking me what I did, and invited me to "come and see them"—they lived in Dedham. "Your brother is very talented, isn't he—we hear about him a lot—Betsy has brought him out to dinner a few times—" She went on placidly. She asked how the aunts were, how James was and what he was doing—suffocating himself in his air-tight room, no doubt. Life stretched round her like a well charted plain. "Aunt Evelyn gets so mad at us when we try to suggest anything—she and Mother really had quite a row. You know we call them aunt, but my grandmother was their father's sister—so we're really cousins, but I never know what kind—I mean how many removed and that sort of thing. I always think of that English story of the children who thought that their cousin was 'removed' because it was carried off by the nurse when it was naughty—was that one of the 'Would-be-good' books?"

"Mama, we're freezing," Betsy said, dancing up and down.

"E. Nesbitt, I remember. Do you suppose anyone reads

them any more? It's so English, isn't it—the E. Nesbitt, I mean. You don't know if it is male or female, Edward or Eleanor, though of course you suspect it is very respectably female."

Chan was visibly shivering.

But the door to the porch opened and Aunt Evelyn's head appeared, not much higher than the latch. "Well, did you *ever!* Standing round in the cold like *penguins.*" Her white face had a ghostly gleam to it. "Tea is brewing, I'll have you know. Do you see what this boy has been doing? Mercy, look at all the hard-wood—I don't dare ask where he got it. Now come in, all of you."

We perched ourselves round the kitchen and had steaming cups of plain tea. All the talk was of people. Albert's wife. Agatha's swollen joints. Addison Sumner's divorce—"I was perfectly shocked, I can tell you," Aunt Evelyn said. The crazy Craigies—Cousin Jane spoke the phrase as though it were a proper name: the Crazy Craigies had bought a second-hand hearse, she said, and were going to New Mexico in it—a most elegant Cadillac with a black plush interior and room for all four to sleep—they made port holes in the sides and had a galley. And Bolles was retiring from Cornell this year —he already had an apartment on Brimmer Street. . . .

Betsy talked a good deal too, with an accent and flow like her mother's, and the same assurance—there were no little-girl gasps and flutters and no folly—she went on like a competent adult, and after a time I began to be aware that she was in college and was probably twenty. When we were stirring round to depart she asked me if I were going back to Cambridge—and if so I could take her to the dorm and save her mother the trouble. "Maybe we can be friends," she said briskly. "Who knows? We can give it a try. Your brother is a bit alarming, I must say—I mean he talked about nothing but Saint John of the Cross last time I saw him; he made me feel like a sort of embodied seminar."

Theoretically I knew a good deal about Betsy. She—or what she represented—was part of my childhood: she had the assurance and accent and the very quality of old Boston. She was cool, candid up to a point, plain in her adornments—light brown hair cut short and left alone—complacent in a nice and humorous way. She could probably play tennis, sail a boat, and identify birds. But impersonal, even in her proposal of friendship; it was in her voice that she had many friends and she led a busy and secure life—she was safe in the fold of family, college, the Vincent Club, and a house in Dedham with a horse in the stable (a humble stable, as I found out later—no grooms or gardeners, no riding habits or red coats—but a live horse none the less).

She started talking of college affairs in a brisk and confidential way, as though I shared all the well-known secrets of the academic life of Cambridge—we were driving back through the dark and dreary wasteland north of Boston, and at first I thought she was making conversation in a fashion she considered suitable for the occasion. But the talk seemed to be a natural part of her being, and she went on about her course in baroque art and the visiting Irishman who read *Finnegans Wake* and her effort to learn to play a viola da gamba (or something like that) for a concert in the Fogg Museum where Stravinsky was a guest—those ancient music people at Harvard are so serious about it, she said. . . .

When I explained finally that I knew very little about all that, and spent my time on radios and automobiles, she hardly hesitated. "Oh I know—it's perfectly dreadful; all we do is go on and on about Radcliffe and Harvard as though nothing else existed—we get so provincial about it, though I must say I can't seem to help it—it's so fascinating, you know. But tell me—I simply must have a car—something that runs—and Father says we can't afford it and I don't need it anyway and I can't have *both* a car and a horse and all that—but it's such a bore trying to go home on the train, there never are trains when you want them, and I'm sure if I knew exactly what sort of car to get and how much and all about it I could talk him into it. I don't mean anything super, like this—but just an old thing that would chug along—why Sam Prescott said he got one for fifty dollars, only he had to do things to it, and I know a boy who actually got a Rolls Royce for *nothing* —someone *gave* it to him—it looks like a royal coach and it really runs but of course it must take mints, I mean think of trying to buy a tire for it. . . ."

It was after six by then and I suggested that we stop for supper somewhere, and she said fine, she was starved. But then I felt uncertain. She represented habits quite different from mine and I had a sense of being a sort of country cousin. Where, I wondered, would she expect to be taken for supper on a Sunday evening, dressed as she was in sweater, jeans, and sneakers. But I realized that she was equal to anything—there were several joints just beyond here, she said, one called McGinty's Diner she'd been to, but if I wanted beer she didn't know—there were a couple of dives in Cambridge, of course. I began to like her about then. There's something very nice about being brisk and healthy, I thought —and competent: we went to McGinty's. She glowed. "I do love good hamburgers with onions—cooked ones, like these. Do you mind if I have two—and two cups of coffee?" I had been out of touch with girls like that—in fact, as I thought of the young ladies of my boyhood, it seemed that Betsy represented something new. If she had vanities or affectations she concealed them. "I have an enormous appetite," she went on. "I'll probably look like a barrel someday. Why don't you come and see us, Will—I mean come and visit? Next week, for instance—no, I can't be home, come to think of it—I have to play my darned old ancient instrument again, with hours of rehearsal—but two weeks, how about it? You can ride Eddie, and we'll get Harold out on Sunday. You can talk to Father about cars. . . ."

When I left her at her dormitory a good deal later she said we were friends: she said it in the cool and social accent that had at first seemed a little inhuman to me, like some sort of mechanical articulation. "It's so nice having another cousin—I love having cousins. It's one of the nice things about Boston, don't you think?" But her smile was warm and the color flowed more brightly into her face. Her gray-green eyes were steady, as though she willed herself to conceal nothing. She looked very naturally the way a girl should look. "We'll expect you—any time Saturday. Better bring a necktie and jacket—Father expects it at dinner, poor dear." Then she looked at herself. "Great Scot—I almost forgot: I'll have to sneak in—I'm not supposed to be seen like this." She was still sitting in the car, and peered up and down the drive conspiratorially. "I'll just have to—hey, psst! Jean!" Two girls stopped and looked our way. "Jean, lend me your coat long enough to get in, will you?" She was briskly rolling up her dungarees. "Bye, Will—thanks for the ride and all." She buttoned herself into Jean's coat, and the three disappeared into the dormitory door.

ও§ CHAPTER 6 ৪৵

MRS. HARKINS, my landlady, kept things going with strict discipline. Her weeks ran from Saturday to Saturday, at least as regards the single rooms: the tenements, as she called them, had different arrangements. On Saturday morning she changed sheets and towels, cleaned the room, and collected the rent, and she made it clear that the operation would take place between nine and ten. It behooved me to be out of bed and ready for her—or if I went out earlier, to leave the rent money. She preferred not to have more than a week's rent in advance—it seemed to interfere with her system. On other days I was to make my own bed and keep things tidy, as she said—and please remember if I came in late or went out early that other folks were trying to sleep. Formidable she was —and not happy in any positive way, but certainly successful. Her discipline was military—her order, her uniform house dress, her hair like cast iron: she operated somewhat the way my mother did, but without the drive that made Mother a positive force. And without any love. She expressed nothing but contempt for Mr. Harkins.

I mention this because it was Mr. H. who gradually took shape in my mind as a man of human and dramatic value. For a time I hardly associated him with her—I thought he was a workman of some sort. He looked like a stoop-shouldered Lincoln, very shabby, with earth-stained knees; he seemed to say nothing, and his gaunt face with a drooping gray mustache—a sort of comic-book caricature of a walrus mustache—was unutterably mournful. I saw him occasionally by the kitchen stove and realized he belonged there, and once I met him in the doorway fumbling with the button of the electric bell—he was applying a foot-long screwdriver to it. "She can't seem to get it to work," he mumbled sheepishly, with a quick glance at me. "Have to have an electrician, I fancy." His gaunt features were somehow wild and secret, like a large forest animal's. I felt that he was on the verge of running.

"Let me look," I said. "The button's probably corroded." I had a pocket knife with a small screwdriver for just such events, and in a moment had the thing apart. "See, it works when you connect the wires—all you need is a new button like this."

He looked at it in solemn bewilderment. "I don't know," he said with an accent of grief. "I don't know about such things. Can you—" he jerked his big hand toward the button—"can you buy such a thing—in a store, that is?"

When I said I'd get one and put it in for him he stood motionless for a time. Up to then I had hardly felt that he was human, but slowly his face softened—it was like a sort of natural force at work—and an expression of anxious whimsy touched the gaunt features. "Tools aren't right, I can see that." He held up the powerful screwdriver. He sighed. "It all seems new-fangled to me—has for thirty years. Bell buttons like that, I mean. I learned to dig and chop and hoe —that's about all." He backed away with a questioning eye on me. "I'll be grateful if you—that is, if it isn't really any trouble—any expense, of course—we'll make it—I mean, it's a service we'd naturally expect to pay for—" With a desperate final nod of the head he disappeared.

A few evenings later, when I came in about nine and was turning to the stairs, he appeared again in the kitchen doorway. I felt at once that Mrs. Harkins was not at home— something in his face indicated extraordinary freedom and boldness. "Didn't know but you'd like a cup of tea," he mumbled with a sort of question mark at the end. He left it at that, and stood half inside the door as though poised to escape; yet his face was lighted with hope.

It would have been impossible to decline.

The big kitchen was a mixture of the oldest and the newest —in one part an iron sink and pump and an iron range with a rocking chair beside it; in another part a porcelain-white refrigerator and electric stove and fully equipped enamel sink. The bright lights were off, and a single yellow bulb shone from a wall fixture near the iron stove. The rocker was still rocking slightly, and a curl of vapor rose from a white china mug on the edge of the stove.

"I most generally like it," he was saying to fill the moment. "She's from home—she visits her sister over at East Meadow. These bags are handy when you're alone—" With huge hands he manipulated a tea bag and cup and saucer and steaming water, spilling and sizzling on the stove top. "Milk from the can—that's all we have—sugar here—" He waved me into the rocker with a sudden grace of motion that startled me. "You'll enjoy it, I believe—the chair, that is. Fits the frame—I aim to hold on to it long as I can." He brought up a small wooden chair for himself. "A few old things still here— stove's just as old as I am, you wouldn't believe it: in better shape, too. Pump there—my father put in a cistern—right under here; rain, you know—nothing better for washing— she don't use it much: easier to run a faucet . . ."

His quiet shy voice went on, making tentative questions, expressing small whimsies, brooding over the past. The gnarled hand holding the cup seemed like a great brown root. "You wouldn't think of it as a farm, would you? Over where the Pickering Belt plant is—used to be cow pasture. That street there with the new houses was the lane—it turned through the bars to the barnyard: Edwards Lane, they call it now—he was the one laid it out, though two or three had owned it one time or another. My father was a great hand to sell off property—said he never wanted to be tax poor. I presume all in all it would be worth quite a sum now—the old farm, I mean. . . ."

They used to tell him, he went on, that the first Harkins had taken up the land there as early as seventeen twenty—how much he didn't know, but there was a time when they had twelve hundred acres running westward across the flats there—used to be considered good soil—and up to the ridge of hills where they pastured sheep: he remembered the sheep, all right—they used to do well with them before the Australian wool came in. The best time for the farm he supposed was back before the California rush—back in the thirties, say, when the main part of the house was put up, with the front rooms and all: his grandfather, he said, was a grown boy at the time and helped nail on the laths—he must have described nailing on the laths a hundred times. Farms in those days were pretty prosperous—you see those big old dwellings, some with four chimneys; this one was good sized—had eight fireplaces once, not counting the kitchen stove—most of them blocked off now, of course.

Mr. Harkins talked for an hour or so, with a mild and deprecating sadness. He didn't want to bore me—old men and old farms, he said, were not very interesting to smart youngsters like me. But he thought about it a good deal—he was seventy six, and when he passed on no one would know how it all had been. He wished he could write it down. It didn't seem right, somehow, that the life that had meant so much—all those generations of a family, all the work, the plowing and building and planning, and the beautiful land, the pastures and mowings and cultivation—should all be forgotten as though it had never been. He carried it all in himself; it filled his mind and heart.

After that evening I often talked with him—"visited," he called it. I found that his business was to run a greenhouse—and if his big hands were too clumsy for small tools, they were deft with seedlings. He had about a half acre out in back, and the greenhouse stood partly on the foundation of the big cow barn—good rich soil there. It was his father's idea—he had lived to be eighty five and was full of ideas right to the end, though it was he who sold off the land; he speculated—and no Harkins was cut out to speculate. The greenhouse did all right—it paid for the coal it used; a really smart man could make a good thing of it, but somehow he never felt very smart. He used to hope his son would take an interest in it, but he was probably better off—he was a shoe salesman in St. Louis. There was a daughter too in Paterson, New Jersey —but she almost never came back, not since he married again. They didn't seem to get along. He meant his present wife, of course, whenever he used a pronoun. He never said her name, but he assumed I knew what he meant.

I used to visit in the late afternoons, on my way back from school. We sat on hard chairs in the furnace room—once a carriage house—at one end of his greenhouse: the office, he called it. There was a desk and an old safe. He had some rum —it came cheaper, he said, and tasted just the same to him. They all tasted the same in spite of what folks said—and tasted pretty bad, at that. As a young man he hadn't ever indulged; his folks considered it wicked, except for the hard cider which came with the farm, as it were. But after he got to be seventy he couldn't see that it made any difference—except to ease the pain a little and he thought an old man had the right to ease the pain if he felt like it. He said this with a roguish expression on his tragic face, a sideways sliding of the deep-set eyes, an upward wrinkle of the weathered forehead and a movement of the grizzled mustache that concealed the irony of his mouth. His voice was always quiet but irregular in its volume, as though years of disuse had made it rusty; it had tones of long-suppressed eagerness, of a humor that had lain hidden since he was a little boy. "I can't say I don't still feel wicked—I keep an eye on the door in case my father should walk in. I wouldn't care for a strapping—he had a temper, you know. Restless, he was—always into things—you never knew when he'd turn up. I believe he'd take a nip himself—he'd get so blue about things: oh, he'd be the most discouraged man you ever saw, and he'd go off into the barn and take a nip. But he didn't believe in it for anyone else—he thought it was all wickedness." He reached a long arm and took a dusty brown bottle from a shelf and handed it to me with a sort of reverence. "They tore it down—gave us five-hundred for it and tore it down. I found this in the corner of the oat bin. Father was bed-ridden then—I never said a word to him—he never asked. I kept it hid for quite a while and then it seemed a good idea to try it—I missed him, you know, and then I missed my wife and the boy went off and the girl was married, and I thought I'd just drink a little toast, as they say. Here's to the old man may he rest happy wherever he is—he had a temper, but we got along fine together: he never thought I had enough git-up-and-git to me—that's how he said it—but we made out all right. He was mighty fond of my wife—he thought she was all right." Mr. Harkins paused for a full minute or so. "I don't mean *her*, of course. He never saw her. I mean Persis. It was stormy weather in those days— she had a temper too, she made the pots rattle—but they seemed to get along. Lively is what it was, with the youngsters round."

From then on the vision of the old farm was with me. Traces of it still existed among the industrial debris—a few fences, walls, gnarled apple trees, empty pasture-land along a winding brook, a plank bridge where a lane led toward the westward ridge of hills, though beyond the brook on the rising land a real estate development was growing up with a row of identical small houses. The road past the old house was a street much used by heavy trucks, and there were garages and used car lots scattered along it. But a mile or two beyond, farther to the northwest, the countryside lay pretty much as it always had. You could see where sheep might still find summer pasture on the hills.

My own time moved along easily these days. I must have worked hard at Chadd's school because by five every afternoon I felt a sort of sensuous weariness, the emptiness of mind and sluggishness of blood that come after hours of work. Some moralists, I noticed in my reading, advocated work as the cure for human doubt and failure, and I had to agree that there was a profound pleasure in the cycle of weariness and recovery, discomfort and ease. The effort added much to my self-esteem too. But Mr. Harkins set me to meditating in darker ways. If he had been an insensitive man, existing only fom one sleep to the next, like a retired ox or horse, I could have taken him for granted as part of the human landscape, but I had begun to feel his loss and loneliness as though they were mine. On a Sunday in April when the ground had dried he took me along the inner bounds of the farm: he strode ahead of me with long slow steps, with a relentless intent to locate each corner and turn, though we were stopped by many obstacles—houses, garages, a high chain-link fence round the Pickering Belt plant, and another solid board fence surrounding a used-car lot. It wasn't that he complained or mourned aloud—if anything, he admired, was astonished by the new world: all the quickly built little houses seemed miraculous to him. But he was like a man who had died and was condemned to walk the earth unrecognized and unattached; it seemed to me that I was the only person in the world he communicated with. "You'd hardly believe there'd be twenty or thirty down here by the stream for a picnic on the Fourth—my wife's folks, the Deanes that is, were great on picnics. We'd play ball in the pasture—near where those empty tar barrels are. I was quite a ball player—my brother was too: he died long years ago, but he pitched and I was first base for the Kingstown Redwings—we had a uniform with a red bird's wing on the sleeve here. I fancied myself at baseball, I tell you—I was a good deal better at that than I was at farming. I can remember my father playing too —at the picnics, that is: he was always in on any sport going on. Hunted in the fall, fished in the spring—used to catch trout right here along the meadows: nothing he liked to do better than fish."

It was almost as though his communication were secret and forbidden. He seemed to have a feeling of kinship with me, but when we met within hearing of anyone else he might have been carved out of wood; he was as grave and sad and motionless as a statue for a tomb. I never heard him speak more than a monosyllable to his wife, though her sharp voice sounded often enough. In the early evenings he sat in his kitchen chair and after her dishes were done she retired to a cozy sitting room she had made for herself. If she went out— she drove a good-sized Oldsmobile—he and I often shared a surreptitious drink of tea. The rum, even more surreptitious, we had only before supper in the office. He was usually in bed by nine thirty and up before six—I heard the ring of his coal shovel as he tended fires.

One afternoon in the office, before the glass of rum and water, he handed me a paper—thrust it at me awkwardly, with what was meant to be a jocular wink. "Just tell me if you think this will do." His rusty voice made a half question out of it, and his whole figure seemed to lean in an attitude of solemn anxiety. "It may not signify," he said in a tone meant to be casual. "I just thought I ought to do something about it—you read such advice in the newspaper all the time."

It was a pencilled will. The paper was a printed form for bills, with Benj. Harkins, Florist, at the top. "After funeral expenses are paid, what money I have in the Kingstown Savings Bank is to be divided equally between my son Lester and my daughter Caroline, now Mrs. Henry Voigt. The certificates for stocks and bonds in the metal box in my office safe were left to me by my father, and I believe are worth nothing, but if they have any value they should be divided between Lester and Caroline. Lester is to have any of the tools he wants and can use." There followed a paragraph about the house and real estate, to be left for the use of his "present" wife, Myra Strout Harkins, during her lifetime, and then to go to Lester and Caroline, to be disposed of as they jointly decide. "I believe they won't fight over it," he explained to me. "They'll take what they can get for it." Then he leaned closer and spoke in a heavy whisper. "She's got a boy, you know, name of Alfred—Alfred Bannerman—and she keeps him going: he's hardly twenty yet, wife and baby and all—he works in the A and P in West Springfield—when he works, that is. Maybe you've seen 'em here—they drive up Sunday sometimes, nice new car. She'd like him to have the property—he'd like to have it sure. He's bright, no question, but he'd rather get along without doing any work."

I knew nothing about wills, and advised him to see a lawyer, but he hardly seemed to hear me. He brooded in silence above his pencilled sheet of paper. I said I thought he should name an executor—I said it several times before he took notice. He stared at me as though I were part of another world. Someone he could trust, I said. It was the usual thing. But after a while he shook his head with a mournful impatience: the old neighbors were dead and gone, he mumbled; he had a cousin out in Worthington but he wouldn't hardly trust him; some of the Deanes were honest folk, no doubt of that, but they thought he did wrong to marry Myra—as he spoke, somewhat absently, he began to write out a copy of his will in ink. "It's the best I can do, I guess. I don't know why it isn't plain enough the way it is. Father, he never made a will at all, but there wasn't any question who was to get it. Maybe it doesn't much matter, the way it is now, I mean. All it is is an acre or less, and an old house in bad shape—" As he wrote, bending over the scrap of white paper, moving his big hand in a slow jerky scrawl, like a child's, he seemed to be carrying all the heavy years of his life. The shadowed lines in his face had no bottom. I looked down at the gray thin hair and the leathery neck and felt the shock of mortality as I never had before, the long slow death, the loss and the clear knowledge of loss.

"I never wrote a neat hand," he said in a mocking tone. "Persis used to say a scare-crow would write as well. But they won't doubt I wrote it myself, that's sure." He held it away from him and read it over. "Maybe I better say I'm of sound mind, the way they do in books. I believe *she* doesn't think I am, though what good it does to say it I don't know—"

"Put the date in," I said.

"That's in books too. Dated this twenty third day of

April—" He bent himself to the writing, looked at it again, and with larger and heavier jerks of the pen signed his name. "Big as John Hancock," he muttered, "but not half so handsome. Nothing I can feel proud of, either." He sat motionless for several seconds. "That's it, I expect; nothing I can feel proud about. What I've done is let everything slide, right from the start: down hill all the way, the whole thing—about hit bottom, I suppose. Used to wonder why anyone would want to go out to St. Louis to sell shoes—used to think the only thing was to stay and hold on here—I was pretty disappointed, I can tell you, when he left home. He did right, I guess." He gave a shrug of his wide slanting shoulders and made a little whistling sigh. "So here we are. You put your name on here as witness—that ought to be legal enough for anybody."

He opened a small old safe—with gold letters still legible on the door: Jabez Ellwood, Hay, Grain, and Feed (his great uncle, he had told me)—and put his will in a black tin box with other papers. His father, he explained, was always fiddling with papers—deeds and stocks and receipts—and a lot of them were still there, mostly worthless, no doubt.

Then we drank some rum with a feeling of solemnity. "Seems cold for this season," he said, taking a second glass. "We'd do well to finish up the bottle." I said it was my turn to bring one and he looked at me again with a strange preoccupation as though there were distance between us. It was the first time I had seen him take more than one glass. "She came in to do for me, as they used to say. We'd had a few roomers and I didn't manage things very good and Caroline —that's my daughter—said I had to have a housekeeper and got hold of her. She can do, all right—I'll say that for her." He took a third glass of rum. "Persis drove a Ford, you know, a Model T—I never tried; I believe my feet were too big—

but Persis was bound and determined—she liked to ride better than anything, and we went all over; why we went clear to Barre, Vermont, one time, had three or four flat tires—that's one thing I learned how to do: I could fix a tire. Oh, I tell you now, it was mighty pleasant riding through the country in those days. Persis was a one to see the sights—never missed the Eastern States Fair, drove the whole lot of us over to Pittsfield one time to the Ringling Brothers."

He made a grave gesture with his glass. He hardly knew I was there. "It was a good time, I guess. I haven't done much to be proud of—I've just let go, let slide. Those Gravenstein apples were the best in the country at one time—Persis was so proud of them she'd send some to the fairs: she got two or three blue ribbons—but you've seen the orchard, what's left of it, a couple of blighted trees, the rest gone to building lots —more money in lots, of course." He made the whistling sigh, almost a little tune. "That's how it is, I guess. She's a mighty sharp woman, give her credit. She put it plain—she wanted the legal right. She wasn't going to do all this just for wages, no future for her, and you can see she's made quite a thing out of it with those additions and tenements."

His voice had blurred and at times faded to almost a whisper. I thought he might doze—in the dim light I couldn't see his eyes. His face was deeply shadowed. "It don't signify," he blurted out. "I see that good and clear. The spirits make me light, as though I might be floating in air, but I see how things are—no question about it."

After a while I left. He had said nothing more, and I was sure the rum had put him to sleep. I went off for supper, came back fairly late and noticed the light still on in the carriage house, a dim yellow gleam through one of the dusty windows. My only thought was that he was still sleeping off the rum, but I went to see.

The chairs had been knocked over, and a broken glass and small bottle were on the floor. He was lying, not prone, but twisted inhumanly, knees drawn up to chest, head turned far to one side and facing the light. The massive features were wrenched in pain, the mouth fixed in an open position as though it were about to shout. The bottle had contained insect poison—there was a red skull and cross-bones on its label.

There was a note on the desk—I saw the Benj. Harkins, Florist, at the top, and the big angular signature at the bottom. "I do this because I have decided it is what I want. I have lived my time. Don't anybody feel bad about it. I shall be better off. My will is in the box in the safe." I made sure he was dead, and left everything untouched. But as I started out the door I wondered what had happened to the rum bottle, and I looked back to see. It was standing inconspicuously on the shelf beside the dusty brown bottle he had found in the corner of the oat bin.

◦§ CHAPTER 7 §◦

THE NEXT evening I drove down to see Sally. The night and day had been occupied with the muster of all defenses against death and disaster. The police took charge with relentless routine. Questions, reports, forms, a succession of officials and experts, cars coming and going in the night, an ambulance, doctors, attendants, anomalous observers of all sorts, and finally the clergy and the undertakers and grave diggers. The whole busy sequence absorbed and transmuted the fact; everyone who was at all concerned about Benjamin Harkins was swept along in a succession of necessary events. At the time I took an impatient and even cynical view of the rigid routines: the legalities seemed childish, the formalities crass. I despised the whole works, the official faces, the cruelty of some of it, the falseness of some of it, but I can see that it all in the end distracted the attention and filled out the time.

What impressed me more than the official side of it was the succession of friends and neighbors who turned up. They brought dishes of food and some of them went to work with brooms and dust mops; the terrible event seemed to call for thorough cleanliness everywhere, and I found a stout and muscular woman polishing the windows in my room—a Mrs. Deane, she said, Josephine Deane, whose husband was a nephew of the first Mrs. Harkins. They all had thought a lot of Uncle Ben, she said, though he was shy, of course—he never said much. He looked like Abraham Lincoln, people used to say—except for the funny old mustache: but he did seem sad always, specially these last years—it was an awful pity. The only thing he took an interest in really was his flowers—had I seen all the spring jonquils and hyacinths he had in the hothouse?

I had felt that Mr. Harkins had gone down to disaster as a symbol of his time and family, and so he actually had, but the buoyant Mrs. Deane was not haunted by any such shadows. Her husband worked for the electric light company and one son was in college. Caroline, she said as we gossiped, took after her father—shy, quiet, and, I gathered, inclined to sorrow; but Lester was like his mother, full of go—did I know that he'd got to be manager of a shoe store in St. Louis? They were all sure he'd do well—and he wasn't even forty yet. Uncle Ben had married quite late—at least he was thirty-five, she thought. Aunt Persis had been a good deal younger—and it was such a shame she had to go. Everybody had loved Aunt Persis.

The widow remained mostly secluded that day, but was represented by her sister from East Meadow, who had the same cast iron look; she took on a sort of official appearance and manner, very much like that of the policemen. She repeated one speech to all who came: "There will be a short service at McTaggart's Funeral Home tomorrow at two o'clock P.M."

Since my visit to Sally two months earlier, I hadn't known clearly what to do. I had a strong physical awareness of her: there she was, twenty miles away, breathing and speaking and being. She occupied the same space I did, somehow, and I lived with that in mind; it was as though I could touch and feel her presence. But I didn't see her. I visited Pop a few times in Holyoke, but any talk of Sally was oblique and unsatisfactory. I thought of her always at night.

So in the early evening I found myself on the way to her apartment without any reasonable purpose or decision. The image of Mr. Harkins was very vivid—not only in the agony of death, but in the loneliness of his life. I kept seeing his gesture as he held his will at a distance from his eyes and read it over with ultimate acceptance. I see how things are, he said —was that the last thing he ever said? In the adventures of my youth whatever loneliness I felt had been temporary and even gratifying, like the hunger of late afternoon. I naturally felt that some sort of happy fulfillment lay ahead; I believed in the swing of the pendulum, the restoring of the balance, even in the inevitable bettering of circumstance. I had somehow explained away the fate of the old ones at Bell's Landing, partly because something in Aunt Evelyn's spirit seemed to hold out against the worst, and partly because I had the cruel notion that Aunt Lucy deserved what she was getting—not that I recognized such a notion at the time, but rather irrationally felt it. But the last days of Mr. Harkins had drawn me in as a participant. I felt as though I were the only sharer of a tragedy in which there was no redress, no balance, no ultimate making good. My affection and deepest concern had gone out to him —not that he had ever asked or expected it—and I had been beside him, as it were, in his last stand. Time and the world had shown themselves as the immortal enemy.

I looked for comfort—not from a rational mind like Pop's but from the one person I knew who might give love and compassion. It was only when I came to the drab street and the match-box building where she lived that I had a sense of my folly. I sat quite a while looking up at the lighted windows on the third floor, thinking how I could rightly go up there. And then of course I went up rehearsing the speeches of a casual call. There were no bells, as in apartments of better class, no telephones or clicking latches; I walked up the gritty stairs and knocked.

A movement and pause, and she asked who it was. The words came in the familiar little blurt. When the door opened she was smiling with the brightness I remembered but somehow hadn't expected, the glow that shone out against the darkness of hair and eyes. She looked domestic and uncombed and to me very beautiful. Thinner, I thought, not so soft and billowy. There were shadows in her face.

We could say almost nothing except a few murmurs and fragments. She shut the door behind me and I said I should have thought the oil fumes would smother her and she said they weren't so bad in the other room. . . .

Saul wasn't there—he had gone to New York. At first she said little about him or herself. She made me take the rocking chair and she sat on a pillow on the floor—her smile still lingered and I'm sure she felt no constraint or strangeness because I was there. There was always a watchful stillness about her. The room seemed very still too. The harsh world surrounded and pressed it, but just there between us was a center of quietness. The place, the building, the very walls and floor, were all part of the functional ugliness of human living; they sagged and rotted and bred dirt and vermin, and it seemed morally wrong to me that Sally was required to live there. In my mind I saw her in Greek sunlight among colonnades, with music and flowers and white garments, and the rich blue of the sea beyond. Yet the squalid place actually gave her a special sort of beauty in my eyes. Her own quality was brightest —so, at least, I felt that evening as I sat with her in the intense stillness and isolation of the third floor room. What thinking I did at first was in the blood and body where life went on with its own eagerness. I was impelled to ask her if she was happy, and if she didn't dream of better things—as though somehow I had the power to offer better things. What was Saul doing in New York? I hoped he had gone forever, though I didn't yet say it.

But in some implicit fashion she made me tell her about myself. I had come down there with a mind full of Mr. Harkins, but he had receded—he and his life were twenty miles away from where we were sitting. I talked for a long time about the Navy and about the places and people I had seen, specially the extremes in the Far East of savagery and fastidiousness—a matter I had brooded about a good deal. Our enemy had seemed cruel beyond belief, beyond what I had thought were the human possibilities, yet at home they lived in what looked like lovely innocence, with flowers and kindliness and rituals of civility. I kept wondering whether all civility, ours as well as theirs, was false—or at least how much falseness was inevitably in it. One of the men at Chadd's school said there was no true virtue; the only consideration is survival and success, and all professions of integrity or kindness are simply matters of policy, and every act, however sacrificial it seems, is an act of self interest. He said that the notion that human life is sacred or even valuable is a Western illusion and that as far as the processes of nature went it didn't matter at all whether an individual lived or died in agony. I suppose these arguments are familiar in colleges, but they came to me with fearsome strangeness, like half-seen monsters in the twilight. My brief solitary readings had only created new mysteries.

Not that Sally did much more than lead me on. I hesitated here and there, thinking she'd find it all naïve—I remembered that she had been to college. She looked as wise and enigmatic as an oracle; her eyes were dark with ancient knowledge and her wide mouth shaped into a sombre half-smile. On her pillow, legs curled under and back against the wall, she seemed like an ageless and beneficent goddess. And when she spoke it was in figures and riddles. Life is a composition, she thought; it is what the mind makes—it is a house, or a fugue, and there are laws. . . . But she didn't argue abstractly or consecutively; what she said came out as tentative and whimsical metaphors.

We talked nearly all night. She made coffee and got out crackers and cheese and jam. I felt the strong desire to touch her and make love, but at the same time she seemed inviolable: it was that I didn't understand her, I couldn't get at her inner being, and I had a strong sense of her mystery. I remembered Pop's story of the shepherd and the nymph, and I looked at her wondering how much of her reflected my desires and how much existed in reality—if there were such an area as reality, which I had begun to question. I told her the story, as best I could—skirting close to the edge of why he had told it—and she smiled with dark radiance, then sobered suddenly and wondered why it was supposed always to be a man's problem. Did woman have more sense and less beguiling dreams?

It was then that I said it. Was she happy with her husband? Did she love him? I felt odd to put it so literally, but I went ahead. After all the night's talk and the coffee and crackers it came out easily enough—I felt again, as I used to feel, how easy it was to be candid with Sally. She invited it.

"Happy—I don't know," she said. "It would be foolish—wouldn't it?—for anybody to say so. I mean, if someone asked what kind of music you liked and you said you liked pretty music. You think of happiness as like sweetness—"

I said that's all very well for talk, but misery was a real enough condition, and whatever was opposite to misery must be real too—it wasn't just sweetness. Wasn't her mother happy—and Althea—and a man like Chadd? They had a chance to do the best they could.

She couldn't in the end apply any such words to herself. She did her best in some ways, and trying to be a musician was a sort of happiness to her. If she did better she might be happier—she didn't know: but anyway, art—music—was what she most liked. It was why she left home.

But of course she had married—that was what I was driving at. She was evading the main question. I said it lightly, or tried to, but she wouldn't smile. Her look enveloped me with a sort of solemnity.

"When you say things, you—" She paused. "Well, if you say you are this or that then you think you have to be what you say you are. I don't want to put myself into the power—" It seemed to embarrass her to talk soberly and she smiled at me suddenly. "It isn't you, Will—I mean, I'd like to tell you anything—you know that. But words—tie you up. If I told you about Saul it wouldn't be true—whatever I said would somehow be wrong, specially anything about being happy or unhappy. Everything about him—and me—depends on something else—it all has two sides or three sides—" Her smile almost broke into a laugh. "There—that's what I mean, and it sounds sort of foolish." But she went on and talked a good deal about him. He thought he wanted to live in New York, and had gone to do some prospecting there. He was determined to write and publish, but he was worried about not earning anything and wanted to find a job. Some of his friends had gone into advertising, but she knew he couldn't stomach that; actually it made him sick. If he had the degrees he could teach—he liked youngsters, really; she thought he ought to go on at college. He used to be impatient and furious with his teachers—he always fought with them, but she thought he was more restrained now. So if he could get an unskilled job, maybe . . .

"What about you?" I said.

She gestured at the room. "Nothing could be much worse than this—I mean to live in. I don't know—maybe New York would be exciting. Wouldn't you think so?"

There, I thought, it seemed to be. I got up and walked round. I said I'd better go, but it was impossible for me to go. She watched me in a long silence, and slowly I began to realize that she too was caught in a current of emotion. Her eyes and mouth were softer and younger than they had been. She might have been crying.

"I love you, Sally."

She bowed her face and the black hair shaded it. My words went on as though they came out of me by a hypnotic process. I loved her still and always, I seemed to be saying; life without her would be worth nothing . . .

I think I expected her to break in and stop me, or to act decisively. I had thought of her always as a character of greater strength and wisdom than mine, and all that night she had seemed possessed with the detachment of a minor immortal. I realized even as I spoke—or heard my words sounding out— that I had a sort of fabulous feeling about her, as though she naturally lived on the higher slopes of Olympus.

"Sally, darling," I suddenly said, thinking of her as a girl, my voice choked with an access of tenderness. "Sally . . ."

It was necessary to touch her, to brush back the heavy hair and turn her face. The compulsion was a dizziness in me. Words came to praise her beauty and spirit, to celebrate the wondrous happiness of our youth together, to affirm our destiny. Her being had become in my eyes and under my hands the very essence and secret of life; I remember watching the fine modelling of her expressive mouth as though all fate somehow was to be revealed in the changing curves. My friend at Chadd's school, the talkative cynic, usually cited woman's beauty as his basic example of nature's immorality; the feminine externals, he said, are simply man-traps, without any relation to moral or spiritual value, and deception in a pretty girl is almost part of her duty. He said it so fiercely that he made it seem true; I thought of it as I pushed the heavy silk of the black hair back from the shadowy cheek and leaned down to put my lips against it—beauty like this, I felt, almost smiling, doesn't count in a cynic's logic.

But she turned, stood up, put the table between us. Her eyes seemed very dark and large, and glistened a little from the brief crying. "What is it you want, Will?" The words sounded almost fierce, but they weren't; a tension was in them, and an accent of grief.

I said I wanted her, of course; but it was far from a heroic assertion. The room, the scene, was like a dream where curious events go on with a perverse logic. After all those hours with her I was possessed by love and desire, by the flood-like sense that all life, all beauty and good and purpose, were visibly and palpably embodied in her. Perhaps, as I think of it with an effort of detachment, my emotion was the universal one of passionate love, but the experience is so sharp and strong in my mind that inevitably it seems unique. I hadn't intended it, of course; I assumed that I was there on a reasonable errand. And further than that, and aside from passion, I found myself looking across the table at Sally with an almost tearful tenderness. Her life, her sorrow, her beauty, her very mysterious soul, all seemed precious, in need of care and nurture, like a rare flower. I even felt a tenderness for her marriage and for the unhappy boy who was her husband. In the flood of my desire for her I thought of all those things, and how she was years ago as a young girl looking out hopefully at the mysteries. If I could only be a god, I thought, even for a few minutes, I'd do something—I'd give her everything . . .

"You don't want a wife, Will."

That too was like a dream—the word *wife*.

"Remember how you used to look for the deer, Sally?"

Her eyes were like shaded pools. She didn't smile, but her mouth softened.

I had a quick little vision of my mother washing and waxing floors. The idea of marriage nearly always carried that picture with it, and the food and the money and the little notebook of expenses.

"You grow up thinking it will be all right," she was saying. "You'll be sensible and faithful—or try to be—and you won't ask for too much. You won't make all the bad mistakes, like other people. You'll be as good as you can. You won't be afraid."

"I remember how you said it."

"I won't be afraid. I won't—" She smiled at the words. "I said it all right. I guess it was a good thing to say, but the brave ones don't have to say it at all. Cowards do."

"People have to say it."

She stood up straighter and seemed to brush aside her moodiness. "Fools too—they rush in. But all these words, Will —here it is almost morning."

"Do you love Saul?"

"We live together, Will. If I didn't—"

"Why did you, Sally? Why did you marry him?"

"Do you think I could tell you at this hour of the morning? Would it do any good to tell you?" She sounded sharper with me than she really was. She seemed almost visibly to be trying to control her own mood. She lifted her chin. "It's easy to say that nobody who marries has any sense about it. It's easy for me to be sorry, too. But we had to do it—I had to save his life, I guess he had to save mine—"

"I don't believe that."

"You think of me as something I'm really not—" Her smile came out as a flash. "I don't mean a blonde nymph or anything. It's nice, in a way—I feel almost exalted sometimes, but it isn't quite true. Saul knows how weak I—or at least how—" She stopped. "He'd be a wreck now if we hadn't married—I mean he'd be dead or crazy. No one has ever loved him—or even liked him."

"No one but you."

"We were like castaways on an island—we had to."

I brooded over it. "You won't always be on an island." But there was nothing I could propose, not at four in the morning. "I tell you this, Sally. I think of you as my girl. I can't believe you are anyone else's. I live with you in my mind all the time and how I can keep away from you I don't know—" The words ended in a gulp. "Should I keep away?"

She didn't answer.

I wrote the name of Chadd's school on a scrap of paper.

But something, I thought, would have to come of it; something would have to be proposed.

PART FOUR

OF THE OLD ones at Bell's Landing, James died first. It was the last bitter weather of the season, a long spell of cold easterlies in May, with more rain than anyone ever remembered. There on the coast the raw damp seemed like a permanent climate, and the fogs and mists made the lonely promontory as remote as an outpost in Baffinland. The trees and bushes dripped continually, the brook ran turbulently, and the surf boomed and rumbled day and night.

James had come out of the winter barricades to go through his life-long routines of spading and planting. The plot had diminished each year, but the methods were unchanged. In late autumn he wheeled barrow loads of seaweed up from the beach and spread it on the land; he used also a mulch of old leaves and weeds, but it was the seaweed that he almost fervently believed in—and in his great days he had been famous in the region for the miracles he could work with seaweed. And in those days of course there had been a horse and plow and wagon and a man or two in addition: now it was a matter of slow wheeling with a hand barrow and in spring slow digging with a spade. The garden earth was of course tame and tractable, with never a pebble or root in it, and he took his time and dug as slowly as an aged tortoise might, but even so it was a heavy task. There was the raking to be done, and the furrowing and planting.

This spring he had tried to do it all as before, but the sombre wet days made him sadder and more discouraged; he was delayed by the wet, and finally in May when a day or two of drier air came along he went at it with angry recklessness; he finished digging and began breaking the damp clods with the rake. But he grew suddenly tired, and felt a dizzy weakness take hold of his body. The rake hardly seemed to do its work any more. So he sat down on the wheelbarrow, between the handles, and waited for the dizziness to pass. It was still a gray dank sort of day, with the easterly chill setting in from the sea, and before very long he felt the cold like an icy hand on the skin of his neck and chest. He got up and started raking again, but the fatal blow had been given. He went to his room shivering, contracted a fever, and lay all night in a dream of death. He drank all the Dr. Kiley's he had, and in the morning tottered over to tell Aunt Evelyn about it and died before she could even set out for a doctor.

"I wasn't surprised," she explained, "not in the least. I had been expecting it for months. I knew I'd have to go out to the road and flag down the first car that came along—it's exactly what I planned to do. But of course it was too late." She spoke as forcefully as ever, with a glitter of hard humor in her eyes; she looked at me almost with a sardonic challenge, as though she might have asked me how I liked that for a sample of what life could do. "We can be thankful it happened the way it did," she announced. "Oh, it could have been much worse for poor dear James: he's out of it at last." She looked at me with the little glitter of her pale eyes and withered smile. "Don't think I'm complaining, Will. I'll do what I have to do to the end. And it'll be summer pretty soon too, if we can only get rid of these confounded east winds—you do forget how nice the summer is. But it will seem mighty queer not to see poor dear grumpy old James coming in with his lettuce and beans." And later she said it might seem pretty funny to me, but she always thought of herself as young—somewhere about twenty five, say—and she thought of James then too; it seemed no time at all since they used to go fishing together, or row all the way into Salem Harbor among the schooners and barges. "If I only got started, I think I could still do it!" But then she hooted at herself, glancing up sideways at me from her bent over position. "Well, I just hope I'll go off with as little fuss as poor James did."

There were questions about his burial: he had not been to church for years, and had acquired a few heathen habits from the Redferns, Aunt Evelyn said, but she summoned the parish priest and as far as was possible he was returned to his fold. Except for Aunt Evelyn and me, he had no family and no friends.

At once after his death the warm weather came, the southwest airs and the hot noon sun. Bell's Landing made itself benign and beautiful in the restrained way of spring with new grass and young golden leaves and lilacs and fruit-tree blossoms, all with deceptive garden-like orderliness. Aunt Evelyn allowed herself to be beguiled by the sweetness of it and opened her doors and windows and came out into the sun: "I know perfectly well that by autumn this will be a *jungle*, but I must say it is beautiful—will you look at those red tulips by the barn: James kept them going for I don't know how many years—he was proud of them, I can tell you. Fireman red we always called them. And that mass of lemon lilies there, they'll be out in no time. Really, you know, he loved his flowers *more* than his beans. After all this wet everything is bursting open—see the coral bells, my goodness! He did manage to keep things a little in order, but now that he's gone I just can't think what will happen. We'll be in the midst of a *jungle*. But do look at that quince—did you ever see such blossoms!"

I came down on week-ends and slept in my old top-floor room where the sea-noise still echoed and boomed in the still night hours. The main part of the big house was filled with damp and cold, and no outer warmth seemed to penetrate, but the third floor drew heat from the sun on the mansard roof. Getting out of bed on the bright Sunday mornings and looking from the east window across the silvery dazzle of sea, I remembered all my own old days, and the days of Bell's Landing as far back as I knew about. I marked the spot where the mooring used to be, and the sloops that lay there, *Kestrel*, *Lapwing*, and *Kittiwake*; and my eye inevitably spanned the horizon from Gloucester to Marblehead to spy out the tall triangle of the *Aldebáran*. Even then, with James gone and the old place crumbling to epic ruin, the shining sea and coast pulled at the heart like hope, as though all things were new and fresh and full of wondrous possibility.

Aunt Evelyn could do no more than walk into the yard. She talked of mowing grass, of weeding and cutting, as though she felt fully capable of doing the most vigorous tasks, but she stood bent and wavering, with the glitter of an ancient smile on her papery face, and then turned and reached a groping hand for the railing at the steps. At times she held to things with both hands and waited for weakness to pass. When Cousin Jane arranged for a man to come on three afternoons a week, Aunt Evelyn said "no" with the full double-noted strength of old, but then after Jane's quiet persuasions she stared at the floor for several seconds. "I can't *think* as clearly as I wish I could. I must say, it's most annoying. I suppose the place will really go to rack and ruin—I suppose I'm not being very *practical*." The glittery smile was not there at all—only a weary uncertainty. "It's very good of you, Jane."

We didn't see Aunt Lucy at all. Jane kept saying to me that she ought to be in a "hospital," but Aunt Evelyn would permit no such talk. "What would be the sense, I'd like to know. She's a good deal happier than the rest of us, and she wouldn't be anywhere else. I may be losing my mind about some things, but not about that, I can tell you." We arranged to have the laundry sent out at least.

I saw a good deal of Betsy these days. We spent a June Sunday cleaning out the big house, opening it wide to the warmth and westerly breeze, battling cobwebs and flies, burning up accumulated trash. She went at it not so much out of respect for cleanliness as a principle as out of loyalty to the house itself. It wasn't as though anyone were going to eat off the floor, she said, or even look under the beds, but after all, the place was a family monument and had dignity—you simply couldn't let it stand there with a patch of cardboard in the front window. As always, she spoke with the brisk sharp-edged articulation that reminded me of tinkles of ice in a glass, and she sounded as though she were taking a part in a comedy of manners. "But what will future generations make of a lavender majolica umbrella stand? Really, Will, if we could take all this stuff out and drown it in the sea we'd be doing our descendants a great favor. How could anyone conceive of so much carved and varnished oak?" She made her words brittle and faintly laughable, as though they were addressed to an appreciative audience, and my first impulse would have been to take them as affectations; but it began to seem to me that actually she had few or no affectations. She cleaned the house like a dedicated demon. There was no water in the main bathrooms, but she carried up pails from the kitchen and washed bowls and toilets. She saw that the rugs were properly rolled up with moth preventatives. She put in screens—and commissioned me to fix the broken windows. She thought of everything—clogged gutters, loose shutters, damp cellar (a vast black cavern with a monster of a coal furnace and the faint sound of dripping water). In the end we even tackled James's padded chamber in the barn and broke open the sealed windows and threw out the moldy bedding. "I just feel somehow that Bell's Landing is important," she said. "It's an awful old elephant, and Papa is convinced it ought to be sold —I really think he'd offer it to the nearest junk man if he could—but I love it. I mean, I keep thinking of all the stalwart old great-grandcesters and the good times they had and the boats and funny old bathing suits and rowing to Marblehead with gloves on and ladies sailing with parasols—oh, I really love it—and the books, the library! Did you ever see such wonderful things—those first-edition Dickens and the inscribed Kingsleys and William Jameses!"

At that time in June Chadd's school in Kingstown was closed for a couple of weeks and I shuttled round a good deal, partly at Bell's Landing, partly at the Saffords' house in Dedham. Betsy kept urging me to become a professional hobo— go west, she said, and live off the land: pick peas or beans now and then, be a mechanic or a fire lookout in Oregon . . . Her bright ironies implied that I was at heart a drifter. This eastern life must seem very stuffy to me, she suggested. If she were I, she'd do wondrous things—she'd go to Alaska and Mexico— As it was, she planned to go to summer school and learn French so that another year she could study in Paris.

Her family had a place on Martha's Vineyard, near Edgartown, and Betsy and Chan and I went down (in my car) to open it for the summer—and again she attacked the job with cool and humorous zest. Chan devoted himself to wildlife and a sailboat somewhere in a local boatyard, and Betsy wrestled happily with rusty plumbing and mice in the mattresses. In the sun and wind there she turned a golden tan and her beauty flourished like an emblem of health. She did everything well, as though it were native to her to row or walk or cook or handle a Stillson wrench: her mother had been brought up to be a lady, she said, and expected to get a man to do things; Chan was hipped on birds and mollusks and paid no attention to life's needs; Papa was too busy, of course—so it was up to her. But what luck, what heavenly luxury, to have a real mechanic, a *professional* on hand. She could clean out traps and poke wires through pipes, but she had no idea about the insides of the electric pump—all those washers and valves and things—and now I had fixed it all like new and found out why the fuse kept blowing and everything.

She still seemed to me invulnerable, without weakness or even softness. Except for the lovely rounded body and creamy skin, she might have been fashioned out of stainless steel. Her mind was a perfect mechanism, observant of everything, retentive, constantly busy. Her taste had been precisely fashioned: she knew all the shades of excellence and folly, all humors and ironies, and she valued the classic simplicities. Her body was a model of health and energy, and delighted in food and sleep and the hardest activity. I could see no dark corners of fear in her, no bad dreams, no shifts of vanity and deception, no color of passion. As a companion she was like a trained angel of some sort, with more sharpness of wit than most angels—I realized that she had had several summers of experience in girls' camps and had risen to the position of leader and counsellor. She treated Chan and me and everyone with the same good-humored tireless common sense.

"Oh, I shall marry somebody—I don't know who: I'd like to wait three or four years because I do want to go to Paris and I really want to work on my piano—you just can't do it with college and all. And Bill Borden wants me to climb in the Canadian Rockies with him, and I love to climb—and I probably can't if I start babies—I want at least four."

"You could marry him, maybe."

"Bill? Heavens no—do you know Bill? Not a brain in his head, poor dear, but he's a wonderful climber—he did terrific things on McKinley. He's nice too—he doesn't expect you to sleep with him the way so many do. I really don't know what to do with these people—maybe it's the war or something, but you can't even walk round the block with some men without practically being attacked."

It wasn't that she invited seduction, as is the fashion with girls: for the most part she and Chan wore the same clothes and had the same personal habits, and almost from the first she behaved as though I were another brother—though it amused her that I belonged to what she called the older generation: Uncle Will, she called me in her comedy-of-manners mood. So far as I could tell, she behaved exactly the same with all men, of whatever age or connection. But notwithstanding the sweatshirts and mussed hair and the cool ironies and good sense, she inevitably looked as lovely and seductive as a harvest queen. It occurred to me often that she would fulfill any or all specifications for wife or mother or life's companion, though she expressed nothing but contempt for the sexuality made current by the entertainment business. "I was brought up to be sort of ashamed of being a puritan—one of the inhibited, warped, frustrated old New Englanders: you know the stereotype. Aunt Evelyn, I suppose. They think she hasn't lived. Well, from here on I'm for Aunt Evelyn. I'm for character. It's more fun that way—I mean you have the only freedom that's possible: at least, I think so—don't you? Don't you really, Will? I hate to say discipline—people assume you are completely pre-Freudian and hopeless if you even breathe the word, but it's the one thing that counts—not the *only*, but the essential. I mean, it's the way you made the pump run; you subdue yourself for the sake of a good result. It's what I ought to do about the piano and don't."

For those few days we were together continually, working light-heartedly in the early summer freedom, housekeeping with experimental humor, walking the beaches, swimming, basking, idly talking. We laughed a good deal, skipped stones, picked up flotsam, whittled, sailed little boats, and the hours passed like pleasant music. Chan, though he did nothing very useful, kept us eagerly informed of all the natural events and as a sort of climactic gesture pointed out a nest of four spotted eggs belonging, as he precisely said, to the semi-palmated plover. But on the last evening, after the supper things were put away and Chan had gone to bed—he intended to be up at four, he said, to do some bird watching—Betsy turned silent and sombre. It was unexpected. Brightness had been like a glaze on her; she had taken nothing very soberly, not even her reflections on discipline. People who talk about character, she said, are simply unbearable . . . Now she brooded at the fire-light and asked me how old I was. When I said twenty-five— and four months—she seemed to turn it over in her mind for a long time. She was lying on her stomach, chin on hands. Was I planning to get married—or anything? She looked at a finger, then gently gnawed it. No—no plans, I said. Why? She rolled over and sat up, with crossed legs like a tailor. The fire-light made her face seem pink and childlike. Wasn't I even in love with anyone? Didn't I have a—she hesitated—a best girl of some sort?

"Well—" I said. There was a long silence.

"It's against the rules to say it, but I want to anyway. I—" She stopped. "It's just that—if you did marry, you'd be better off." She said it in a literal and constrained way, with face turned downward.

"A while ago you were urging me to go to Alaska," I said, with some notion of teasing her out of her solemnity.

"Oh, you know what nonsense I talk. But really I suppose there's a time to go and a time to stay. You can have it both ways—sort of—if you do it right—and are lucky. I mean—" She took breath and glanced at me. "Well, here you are, Will, with all the abilty in the world; you can do anything—really *anything*. You can be what you want to be—"

She felt me withdraw from her words. "I know—it's awful to say these things, but I can't help it. I'm compelled." She gnawed at her finger as though she drew nourishment from it. "I don't think you'll be happy, Will—I mean just going on by yourself, being a sort of lone wolf; you won't have any purpose, or not enough. You won't use all your ability. I think you'll feel badly about it."

"And would a wife make me do it?"

"I don't mean being a success and a leading citizen and all that, I mean doing something worth doing. I mean a good big purpose. As it is, you're just sort of filling in." She frowned down at her finger. "A wife would help—a good one, let's hope." She flashed a troubled glance at me. "You really ought to go to school—a grade-A engineering school; you ought to go *on*. If you had someone to work for—and with—"

Something more than ordinary youthful seriousness enveloped us, a tension and emotion that I felt rather than understood. Betsy's bowed head, her brooding and gnawing, the constraint in her voice, gave a strange solemnity to what had always been a light-hearted companionship.

"What about that 'well'?" she suddenly said. I knew what she meant, but waited. "A man of twenty-five is usually interested in some female—"

It would be better, I felt, if I said nothing about Sally to her—the atmosphere was not favorable, but I went ahead and said it anyway. There are times when confession can't be resisted.

Betsy stared at the fire for quite a while. "What do you do about it?"

"I don't know—I haven't any plan."

She stood up and seemed to shake herself out of a trance. "Will."

"Yes?"

"When you do have a plan—will you let me know?"

"All right, but I'm not very good at plans."

"Well, don't just drift. Great Scot—you—" She pressed back her hair. For a moment she looked tired and even pale. "But let me know anyway. I'm going to bed." She went off without another word.

❧ CHAPTER 2 ❧

THAT SUMMER I lived at Chadd's house in a hot third-floor room. It was Mrs. Chadd's proposal. She had been looking me over carefully to make sure that I wouldn't come stumbling up the stairs in the middle of the night. Not that she said so —she said little; but she alluded several times to O'Leary. He had roomed there, and had stumbled once or twice in the night, had even lifted his voice in profanity and song, and had been expelled. I said that I might come in late now and then —it occasionally happened that way, and Chadd assured me I'd be all right as long as I didn't stumble or sing. Or swear, Mrs. Chadd put in. O'Leary had said terrible things.

But of course she was never quite as grim as she looked. The craggy face had been bestowed on her by whimsical fate, and any effort at feminine softness seemed useless; as long as she had to look like an old soldier she inevitably had to behave that way. Her intentions were kindly, and by the third day she insisted on giving me breakfast—though all meals had been excluded from our arrangements—and as often as not she said she had plenty of supper for three and wanted me to help eat it up. Chadd, she said—she always called him that—needed a youngster to keep him lively: she was too old for him. So we did well together, except for the heat. The house was the southern half of a two-family affair, and that summer particularly the sun poured down with tropical power. My room under the roof was often too hot to live in—at least until midnight or after—and I spent most evenings in cooler places.

Sally, I found, had disappeared, apparently without a trace. Pop didn't know, her mother didn't know—except we agreed that she must have gone to New York where Saul wanted to live. I even wrote to her, hoping the letter would be forwarded, and since it didn't come back I assumed it reached her, but there was no reply. The tenement in Springfield was already occupied by others and it was as though she had never been there.

Melancholy, Pop said: with all her beauty and purity of spirit (that was his phrase) there was something tragic in her nature. "It is foolish and fanciful," he said, "but I see her as one of the symbols of ancient sorrow—as a beautiful Medea, perhaps. You know, Will, I love her especially much—especially tenderly." He said this with the foreign little sputter that expressed the candid earnestness of his thought. "Her sadness, you know, might well be a sort of fulfillment, a beauty, what one could call a most satisfactory happiness." His face made itself up into intense furrows and wrinkles; he held his hands as though they would grasp and twist the thought, and his breath kept the words in suspension. "It could be happiness, you know. It could be the adagio mood. You know in Berlioz—" The wrinkles turned quizzical as he looked at me from the top of his eyes. "Perhaps you don't know Berlioz, but there is the beautiful sweetness of sorrow—like the sound of twilight—like—" He turned his bent hands with an effort. "It is like Sally—it is like her smile—her dark eyes—"

During the hot evenings I went to see Pop quite often. His ground-floor rooms were a trifle cooler than others; I even persuaded him and Anna to go for occasional rides—he in front with me, Anna always alone and silent in back, but quite satisfied with the arrangement. She had the soul of a servant; she rode with us simply to be behind her father, to see that he was cool or not too cool, that he observed the views and noteworthy scenes—she interrupted him now and then with a little nudge and nod left or right; her plain sexless face expressed approval of our being there by tiny smiles and bobs of the head, like a figure in a cartoon symbolizing pleasure—the thin line of mouth turning up at the corners like a pencil stroke.

Mostly Pop talked, of course. I can hear his gentle and speculative and slightly sputtery voice going on and on, always humorous in the manner of the true philosophical mind, and often under a pressure of energy that made him turn on the edge of his seat and manipulate the air as though his thought could be visibly shaped. He talked about politics and people, and the fatal weakness of the civilized and the power of the savage—he used the word "levelling" a good deal, and explained that he had been reading political history and observing how dangerous the idea of democracy had seemed: it would give power to the ignorant and savage, they used to say, and would bring out the worst rather than the best. "It is true, Will—there is mankind's greatest danger. But the fault is not in democracy—it is in man's own nature—it is the barbarity in men, and the love of barbarity. There are too many men—here in Massachusetts as well as in Germany and Russia—who desire cruelty and evil, who in a sense worship brute force as they might once have worshipped Satan. I am not hopeful, Will. Science has given such men the power . . ."

But of course he talked about me too—asked me what I intended in the world and scolded me for my aimlessness. Already, he said, I was depending a little too much on gadgets and surfaces—he paused here in a knot of concentration. It was good, of course—the pleasure of the thing, the moment, the speed or the cool drink or the view or the new car: his hands grasped and turned all such things and he peered at me with special intensity to see that I understood. One must be alive on all levels— "as I am not," he added. "I am only alive abstractedly, like a hermit without dedication." He held his breath for an instant in order to savor what he had said. Then he grinned: "Except, of course, that I have the honor of being a patriarch. Perhaps you can look forward to that dignity—" he twisted his hands as though they were adding to his humor —"but somehow I doubt if the future will tolerate patriarchs. It is a pity. I am already an anachronism, and I must say it is a little bit like being a king. I hardly deserve such a high station—and I certainly haven't earned it—but it can be very pleasant."

But it wasn't a question of convincing me of anything. When good people argue, you can only agree: they are as right as possible. The reach must indeed exceed the grasp; the heaven must be projected above and beyond. So it should be. My mother had told me, and Betsy and Pop, and even Chadd in his way. Subdue yourself for the sake of a good result, Betsy had said, confirming her puritan faith. Yet I felt no strong push toward such ends. I dreamed of my lost Sally. I drifted round among the automobile folk, drank a great deal of beer and other things, and traded my pre-war jalopy for an almost new convertible. In our school there were three or four resolute girls, mostly doing electrical and radio work, and one of them took a resolute fancy to me. I think she was frightened at being twenty-seven; she felt that her life depended on her marrying before thirty. Angelica Bovaird—as dark and angular and thin as a scarecrow, or young witch: ugly yet sentimental and soft-hearted and attractive. She had sharp bones, warts, stringy hair, and an enormous capacity for whimsy—every day she appeared with gifts and notions, a wind-up mouse from Woolworth's, a chocolate man, a comic car, a lolly-pop, and with an April-fool secrecy concealed something on my desk. Her study of the mechanics of radio reflected a strong whimsy, and though she was shrewd enough to do passably well, her main motive was otherwise. For most of her youth, I gathered, she had dwelt in expectation of romance, and now at twenty-seven she had taken stock and was alarmed.

I had supposed that a man could easily defend himself from the dangers of such a woman as Angie, but my experience was almost that of a fly in a web. Angie was never absent from my daily routines. At lunch she was there—with a special ice-cream soda or frappé. At any moment of need during the day she was on hand like Gunga Din to fetch or carry or bring water to the parched. At closing time she was my shadow—and after the gentle amenities quite insistently so: a nice little restaurant she knew of—the best pizza somewhere—a Chinese place in Northampton—a little Greek hole-in-the-wall—and why not drive to the Worthington Gorge?—and so far into the night: the only deterrent to her going home with me was Mrs. Chadd.

It may be that other men could have dealt cleanly with such a problem—have loved or not loved, said yes or no. If Angie had been mean spirited or stupid, the case might have been simpler, but she behaved generously, even gallantly. Though she had the face and hair of a wicked witch, her intentions toward life and the future were warmly honorable: she desired a legal husband and children and all the burdens and duties and travails that went with them. I liked her, was fond of her, enjoyed her whimsies, but had in the end a primitive feeling of repulsion. It should be added that she continued long enough at the Kingstown Technological Institute to marry a capable radio and television man—small of stature and somewhat defenceless, and she is happy with a house of her own, three children (the oldest is five and a fourth is coming), and a cat and a dog. She still sends me whimsical cards.

My mother wrote faithfully—generally on Saturday or Sunday—except for the few weeks when I stopped and saw her. It was still hard for her to let go her hold on us: she wrote to Harold too, of course, though she seldom saw him, and she kept sending clothes to both of us—the bargains she had shrewdly picked up in the Boston stores: shirts or pajamas or pants or sweaters, and for me a cool summer suit with a Lord and Taylor label she had paid twelve dollars for. She knew exactly what would fit us, and she tried to please us though she felt that I was much too slovenly and Harold much too fastidious—he poured scorn on her selections and I maltreated them. She expected to do all our mending still, and was flattered and heartened if I brought her socks with holes or shirts without buttons.

It was her constant desire to get the three of us together; she had a forlorn little vision of the family, of mother and sons making a natural unit in the hostile world: she knew in her mind that no such unit had existed for a long time, but her heart and conscience refused to give it up. As long as she lived she would perform the duties of a mother.

So on occasion she had taken us—by means of my car—to one of the country inns where huge and expensive dinners are provided in antique surroundings. The difficult element, I think, was Harold. I share with my mother a literal interest in trifles; we are both, as Harold would reasonably say, vulgar—we comment on waitresses and bus-boys, we prefer the plain and solid foods, we mispronounce French, and sometimes we exchange banalities with people at the next table. On these few occasions Harold had been coldly patient and forbearing, but finally he refused to join us at all—at first on plea of engagements, finally on the ground that he was bored.

He still managed to keep his rooms at Cambridge—he had a sort of faculty status, I think, and was a very official Fellow and Scholar—and I stopped in late July to see him. He was assisting in a summer-school course, and would later attend one of the writers' conferences in Vermont—still in official capacity as resident younger poet. At this time he was alone—a rare state for him—though I felt at once the insistent pressures of his world, the letters on the desk, the invitations, announcements, cards stuck in mirror, even the ring of telephone. I didn't tell him I was an emissary—and of course I had no relish for such a task. Mother had spoken to me bitterly about Harold and I had said the only thing to do was leave him alone, but she hardly heard me.

Harold always seemed as impregnable as a statue. He had a long face, in the fashion of the British intellectual, but without the wide mouth or mussed hair—I fancied he looked a little like Aunt Lucy in the thinness of his nostrils and the beautiful strength of his chin. He was a good deal browner than she, and quite tall and flexible. But he revealed nothing, not even hostility; his face seemed to be waiting, reserving itself from any present commitment. He wore tan gabardine trousers and a very white oxford-cloth shirt with long sleeves and cuff links. It was mid-morning, and he held a green silk tie in one hand and a jade figurine of a horse in the other. "Green," he said, "is lovely, isn't it—specially in mid-summer."

"Are you wearing the horse too?"

He held it up, a charger, very stylized, with great arched mane and flaring nostrils. "It's wonderful, isn't it, how a horse can look Chinese. It's a sort of dragon, you see—it has the terrifying look. It's very potent, and yet the green is so innocent." He set it on the desk and looked gravely down at it; it was as though he were waiting for me to take the bait. Then he went on: "The horse is already a myth—much more than the tiger, say." He shrugged and began putting on his green tie, making the knot large and neat. He had some conferences at eleven, he said.

When I asked if he'd like to go down to Bell's Landing with me after lunch he studied his tie very carefully in the mirror. "No, I couldn't," he said. "You don't really want me to anyway."

I said somebody ought to keep an eye on them now and then—for all we knew they might be dead: but he hardly listened. "That's your little province," he said, "not mine."

"Why mine? Why not yours?"

"You'll have it, won't you?"

"Have it?"

He brushed his already neat hair, slipped on a brown jacket, and began putting some papers in a briefcase. "There'll probably be people this evening," he said. "Not the sort you'll much like—bird-brained esthetes and poets like me, and a lot of chatter—but if you want to sleep here it's quite all right. They'll be clearing out by one or so."

"Keep out of the way till then, eh?"

"Don't be touchy, Will. You'll be welcome any time, of course—come and talk and drink whenever you feel like it—but there's no use pretending you like that sort of thing. It's a literary barnyard—though Betsy may be round, if she hasn't gone to the Vineyard: you like Betsy, I hear."

I did feel a flow of anger in me, and I waited for it to subside. Damned arrogance, I said to myself. He acts like— "You act like a fish," I almost snarled. It seemed an absurd thing to say, and I felt the warmth rush up to my face. "A cold fish," I added.

He waited with an appreciative smile for me to go on, standing by the desk with his case of papers as though he were giving me an extra moment before he was off to his duties.

"You pay no attention to anyone in the family. You don't give a damn about the old women at Bell's Landing. You won't go near Mother any more. What's the matter with you?"

His smile continued very gravely, with no apparent irony. "It is a reasonable question, Will. What *is* the matter with me? The answer is by no means easy, and I fear I have no time now to go into it. Mother and I don't get along—that's quite obvious; we'll both be happier for the time being if we don't try. There's no use forcing it, you know."

"Forcing!" I snorted. "Making a little effort to be decent, you mean. Other people can do it."

Again the grave moment of attention. "I'm afraid I can't discuss it, Will. It is rather more complex than you realize."

His manner was impregnable as he turned to walk out. "Make yourself at home, do—"

He might, I thought, be jealous somehow, or resentful—he had always, I supposed, been the touchy one; he had wanted affection but had repelled it—he still repelled it. And now he had it in mind that I would inherit Bell's Landing, as though I had worked for that, excluding him. The idea was like a stab. It seems naïve, but it had never occurred to me before. Bell's Landing had been simply an institution—not the sort of place an unimportant individual might own.

Harold thrust his head in the door for a last word. "By the bye, there's a curious chap who may be here tonight—says he

knows you. Name is Julian. A writer of some sort—he's in this
course I'm assisting with—"

"Is his wife here too?"

"Haven't the vaguest."

"Why, it's Sally Anthonakis. You knew her."

"Well, dimly—I certainly don't know anything about her
now."

He was off in a hurry.

◄§ CHAPTER 3 §►

So IN THE evening I came back to Harold's rooms, or rather at first to the narrow street outside where I sat in indecision for a long time watching the door and listening for sounds from the open windows high above. I knew nothing of my intentions, except that they were subterranean; for a time I behaved as though I were a spy, ready to trail Saul Julian to his hiding. Then without any conscious decision I went up the flights of stairs and stood at the closed door for a minute or two. Finally I tried the knob and went in.

I had been up to that moment very self-conscious, partly because of Saul, partly because of Harold's literary society, but I might have been an invisible man as I stepped in. The room was focussed on Harold and an angular woman with a sheaf of papers in her hand: "The bone erect and septic," he was saying—or it sounded like that—"yes, good, very good, one accepts it, but you can't possibly use the word 'gods.' How did it go? 'The pancreatic gods'—very clever, really, but you simply can't . . ." And she cried, "Oh, I know—gods are outrageous, but there's simply nothing you can *do* . . ." And others spoke with intensity, leaning toward the focal center, overlapping one another. "The old names," Harold said, "the gods, fates, immortal powers, the *élan vital*, the chemisms, are all useless. The key to the future is the new word, the one word, in biblical terms the Word that will name it: whoever finds the name will inaugurate an age. . . ."

"Pretty thick going for you, Will old boy," a voice whispered below me and I recognized Betsy Safford on a stool. She reached up the half-full glass in her hand. "Here, you'll have to have this at least." Then she moved and exposed a few inches of sitting space. "You can share my seat too—it seems to be the best we have left—" The talk went on above our whispers and chuckles. Saul Julian, I saw, was sitting in a sofa close to the center of things, still looking like an anemic school-boy, with slack mouth partly open, but I heard him say in a resonant voice that you had the problem of naming the anomalous, which was rationally impossible, and others cried that nothing was impossible for metaphor, and Saul grinned with cynical relish and reminded them how silly the metaphors really were—"the President of the Immortals and all that stuff," he said.

"Very thick," I whispered to Betsy. As usual, she looked quite cool and poised and pleasantly amused. "Gods," she said aloud, "did pretty well for a long time—as a metaphor, I mean," but no one paid much attention.

Later the talk broke into fragments and trivialities and I tried to speak to Saul, but he looked at me with indifference and kept his mind on literary matters. It was only when he was going, in a general breaking-up about two o'clock, that Harold spoke effectively to him. Was Sally really his wife —the Sally we used to know in Holyoke? He remembered that she was beautiful. Saul half smiled with the moist look of a child with a naughty secret, but he offered nothing in reply. "Where is she?" I asked. "Is she in Cambridge with you?" I tried to keep a light and level tone, and I felt Betsy's eyes on me—I felt for a moment conspicuous and naked.

Betsy knew, Saul must know, even the imperturbable Harold. "Oh, she's still in New York," Saul finally said with slow indifference. "She—" He paused as though reminding himself, turned a little with eyes downward, and was absorbed in the general departure and the goodnights. He said no more. Betsy touched my sleeve. Would Uncle Will mind seeing her home —in his new convertible? Not, she went on, that she'd ever forgive me for not letting her have the old jalopy: she was very cool and natural and familiar, as though she had no need of pretenses with me, and when we got outside she said she could have walked back to the dorm with some of the others but if that was the Sally I loved I probably needed a little ride: and what an *odd* creature her husband was—what made him so discontented and sort of underdone? Had he abandoned her, did I think? You'd suppose he'd be happy to have such a girl for himself—or maybe of course she couldn't put up with him. He looked as though he really needed a mother . . .

I didn't mind her talking about it; in fact, I suppose her candid interest flattered me and gave me cause to feel sorry for myself. She behaved, as always, with a wonderful precision. When she got out of the car at the dormitory she said she'd been trying to figure out what sort of cousins we were. Her great grandmother was my grandfather's sister: would that make us second cousins once removed, or what? I said I had no idea, but since I was getting used to being her uncle it would make it easier just to go on that way. In these times it wasn't necessary to use the formal title: she could properly call me Will. She thought about it a moment, then nodded without smiling and turned to go.

Two weeks later I was back in Cambridge, and stopped at Harold's room to try to persuade him to come for dinner with us, and there curled up in his comfortable chair was Sally. No one else was there.

It seemed to me that I stood for minutes looking at her. She had smiled at first, the fleeting giving-away smile like a promise of warm surrender, then she let the shadow return to her face and waited.

"Did you get my letter?"

She nodded.

"You look as though you lived here."

"It would be nice to." Her glance took in the books and piano, the tapestry and wood carving, the pictures.

I looked with a fresh curiosity at the room—and at her. "You suit it very well—" Her physical being seemed astonishing to me, the black rich hair, the dark eyes, the mouth, the coil of her body and the folds of her cotton skirt. "It's you, isn't it?" I moved closer and touched the shining hair for a moment. "I suppose you are just a mortal sort of woman, with arms and legs and normal temperature and maybe a tendency to hay fever, but all I can see is a miracle." I walked suddenly to the window, then back again, unaware of what I did: my words seemed foolish and I searched for something better.

"Saul thinks he wants to live here somewhere," she said with the little effect of effort and abruptness that I liked so much; it was as if she fashioned the words specially for me. "He seems to approve of Harvard this year—and he's staying here in Harold's extra room—" She smiled at my surprise. "I'm in the room he had rented—a tiny place, and sort of hot—so I read here a good deal. I'm trying to find a job—in fact I guess I have one beginning Monday in Filene's store, if I want it."

"You mean selling things?"

Something in my voice made her smile. "More likely errand girl," she said. "Selling is what I work up to."

"It's hard to visualize," I said. "Couldn't you sit in the lobby with a tin cup and play the violin?"

The smile broke almost into a laugh, then sobered quickly.

"It's so queer, Will—everything, I mean. Living. Here I am—" She pushed back the thick hair and looked round Harold's room. "There's so little wholeness—I mean, it's all in little pieces; there's one thing, and then another thing. You go along like—" She stared at her quiet hands. "Like a child, I guess. All the unconnected moments. You wonder sometimes if there isn't some secret you are missing, a motive that would make the whole thing mean something."

I watched the shadowy face for a few seconds. "Well, I suppose some people—"

"Oh, Harold—he does, he has whatever it is. He's wonderful, Will. Did you know?" She held up what she had been reading, a folder of scripts. "He let me have these. He has a sort of system—I don't understand much of it, or all this business of what he calls cryptics, but I can see how it is all part of the world and life he has made—"

I walked to the window and looked at the summer sky, then took Sally's hand and pulled her out of the chair. "Come along," I said. "I'm taking you for a ride." I knew if I said it that way she would come without asking any questions or hesitating. "You like moments anyway, don't you?" I said. "You like what happens."

"Yes," she said.

I drove her through the miserable streets and wastes toward the North Shore with a feeling of giddy triumph, as though I had captured her. I could take a handful of her skirt as a sort of security; I could verify her presence by glancing and touching. I drove her right down to Bell's Landing, not knowing exactly why: I had told her about it—and told her more on the way, and I felt a compulsion to take her there. I think I dreamed of somehow having her there like a captive princess. It was the only place in the world I could go.

And in summer it seemed benign and soft, with long grass and leafy bushes and tiers of little maples pushing up where the larger trees had been. The greenness covered everything. Even the cut-over places seemed to have reverted to a natural wildness where birds and rabbits could hide. And grasses and weeds grew in the roadway, with golden feathery tops in the afternoon sun. The big house that had risen so starkly against the winter was now hidden by hop vines and unpruned lilacs and branches of the beeches and oaks. Growth and green had taken charge with full authority, as though human arrangements no longer mattered.

"It's like a legend, isn't it!" she said. "Long ago there was an old castle in a wood—near the sea—"

I thought of witch and princess and the old enchantments: the deep rote of the waves made a very faint doom-like sound under the surface of the afternoon.

"Go and explore," I said, stopping in the grassy yard. "Look out for big waves and goblins." I waited a few moments to watch her walk toward the shore beyond the front corner of the house; she turned her head toward me once with a little ducking motion and smiled briefly—it seemed somehow a smile of bewilderment as though she were about to be lost. Her black hair lifted a little in the southerly breeze at the corner and the loose skirt blew against her bare legs. She had a legendary look to her, the ample softly-molded body like a very old painting, the bent and brooding head, the darkness clinging to her. "I've never been to the sea," she said, rather quietly so that I hardly heard. She went on round the corner.

I glanced at the closed kitchen door to see if Aunt Evelyn had noticed us, waited a few seconds longer, and followed Sally.

Beyond the outer edge of the house the wild grass, brown

and dry, sloped to the rock of the headland, and she was
sitting cross-legged, head on hands, where the grass ended.
The rock, corrugated gray and white with rust marking, fell
steeply to the waters below where the waves sucked and
streamed in the crevices and curled along the arch of the
beach beyond. Sea and sky merged in an infinite misty blue.
And just a few hundred yards out a white yacht, a schooner
with all sails curving to the summer breeze, dipped and
surged with lovely grace like a miracle evolved out of the air
itself.

She didn't turn when I came up. Her face was wet, and
hearing me she dried it with her skirt. "I didn't know," she
said with a gulp. "I didn't expect to cry. I don't cry very much,
not any more—I thought I didn't, anyway." She pushed her
hands up under the hair at her temples. I remembered all
the gentlefolk who had come to that corner of the house for
the first time, and Mr. Norton calling out "Thalassa,
Thalassa!"

She brooded without speaking. She was not one to dissect
her own emotions or give them a sort of literary existence in
words, but I could feel how strong the experience was in her.
Once she turned with a bright flash of smile: "I wish Grandpa
could be here."

I was comforted that we had as much as that in common.

"We've always lived in ugly places," she said, "but he can
remember Crete—he has had that in his mind like a sort of
theme. The rest of us have just had the ugliness as though it
had to be. Tenements and dirt. You do nothing but struggle
with it from one moment to another. And all the time this is
here." She looked off at the horizon. "Clean, clean, clean—
and as bright as heaven." She hugged her knees and laid her
cheek on them. "Bigger than heaven though. I couldn't have
imagined it so big." She lifted her head with a quick thought.

"Maybe this is the secret we need to know. Cleanness and brightness—blue brightness. Like a motive."

She seemed very close to me for a moment. She had taken me into herself again, and I had the brief feeling that we were lovers. Without quite realizing it I said it. "Sally, you know I love you."

Her head rested on her knees again. After a while she said, "Grandpa would tell us it all comes down to what's in the mind anyway—whether you live in a tenement or here. Cleanness and brightness are good—they are the secret, maybe—but they don't really exist out there. He used to say a melody exists only in the heart—or whatever it is in us we call heart. Everything in the end is inside, like—" She broke off as though she were not thinking much about it. "It has to begin somewhere, though—on the outside, like a bullet I suppose." She looked up and listened a moment. "It sounds like a hushed bass harmony—"

I told her how it used to sound at night up in the top floor room. I tried to describe the effect it had on me, the terror when I woke suddenly and the sense of doom. I grew solemn as I spoke, more so than I expected or intended; the dark figure of Sally against the rocks and sea intensified my feeling about the place and what it meant to me. A tightening came in my throat. "I always wanted to bring you here," I said. "Even years ago, it almost seems, before we actually knew each other."

It seemed to me that she understood me and even shared my feeling, but she said nothing and sat as motionless as stone.

I left her there and went back to find Aunt Evelyn. The afternoon was full of summer mildness, with hot sun here on land and the silvery mistiness of the southerly breeze over the water. Other white sails off Marblehead made the great expanse seem beneficent, and my eye searched for the one big one that might be the *Aldebaran,* the dream of our childhood.

As I passed the porch I noticed the rotten wood at the base of the posts, and the paint scaling off on the weather sides. Water had splashed down along the front and I realized that the gutter had clogged again. The house seemed huge up there among the trees.

At the back door all was motionless and silent. I knocked and then went in. Normally in summer Aunt Evelyn kept things open, even to the east wind and fog.

The door to the other room, where Aunt Lucy was, stood open, and when I spoke I heard a movement and step and Aunt Evelyn looked out, bent far over as she was and holding to the door frame.

"Oh, it's you." Her white face had the gaspy look of a fish. "Well, I'm thankful." She groped for a support and came tottering through the doorway. She held to the table a moment and then turned her face sideways and upward toward me. "Now, Will, I need your help." Her voice was as commanding as ever, but solemn and fateful; the words had a special force to them as though each one were to be uttered once and for all. "It has come at last," she went on. "Lucy—" She swallowed and her face twisted with a sort of anger. Her mouth opened and closed. She tried to stand a little straighter. "I must tell you that Lucy died *early this afternoon* and I want you to notify Dr. Barnes—Dr. Harrison Barnes—he's the one we have to notify. And you tell him that I just couldn't get word to him any sooner; I felt I didn't have enough strength to walk so far: now be *sure* you tell him that." She seemed to brace herself for some sort of opposition; her speech was almost belligerent. "Have you got that clear, Will? I think you'd better go right away."

We stood a few seconds as if we were fixed there. Aunt Lucy seemed for an instant almost like an abstraction, a final symbol of duty and will.

"Could I see her?" I said, feeling that I had to break through her guard.

After a moment she turned, and swung her bowed head and shoulders toward the other room and went ahead of me. "You see," she said, "she's been very *quiet* these last few days; I'm thankful to say that everything was as easy for her as possible. Some of her memory stayed, you know, and she kept having little glimpses of things that happened long ago. Learning to swim, for example: she had a dreadful time learning how to swim . . ."

The window was wide and some of the sea air blew in. The room was tidy and the remnants of the long struggle with mortality were hidden away—all but the head and shoulders of Aunt Lucy against the white pillow. She wore a rose colored jacket, all fresh and smooth; her white hair made two neat little waves on each side of the part and swept back above her ears. Her thin face was ivory white with a few brown freckles that gave it a peculiar aristocratic quality like authentic markings of some sort, and all her features were spare and very fine, as though delicately drawn and carved. I looked at once for the little testing smile, the mark of her romantic vision of the better life—I expected that she would have it with her at the very last and beyond, but her mouth was fixed in austerity. No gleam touched her, no inner light of any kind. Her face was distinguished by a sort of elegance and fineness, but it was impersonal and closed. In a way it looked unlike the Aunt Lucy I remembered, and reflected a helpless and common mortality that she would have refused to admit in herself. I had once resented her illusions, and had been contemptuous of them; she had lived, it seemed to me, in a dream, but as I looked at her dead face I had a frightening glimpse of all human dreams and death.

Aunt Evelyn was making a little bustle of work. Her expression was determined and executive. "Now, Will," she said in her most emphatic voice, "you'd better let them know —I mean Jane and the others. There'll have to be a good many *arrangements*—and of course there'll be all sorts of legal fuss. There's a man in the village who did our wills for us, and he ought to be told—he'd better come out and see to things: Guptill, Orrin Guptill." She pronounced the name with fierce emphasis. "I guess he's all right—he seems to know about estates and wills. I'm going to write it down for you—I'll give you a *list*." She swung herself toward the kitchen and muttered "Guptill" several times as she went out. "There's a great deal that has to be *seen to*, you know."

She went to a kitchen table and I saw her reach out for a pencil. She tipped slowly forward toward it, her right hand extended; then her left hand came up to the edge in a groping gesture and she pitched right against the table and her knees crumpled. I was able to prevent the crash to the floor and picked her up and laid her on the cot she used as her bed. She was inert, and I thought she must be dead—it seemed impossible that life could continue in the ancient and twisted little body, but something still fluttered inside her and I covered her with blankets, looked for a stimulant of some sort— fumbling among pantry shelves and old bottles and jars, and failing to find anything—and ran out to fetch Sally.

I CAME TO her—she was on the beach with an orange crab-shell in her hand—with desperation. I called and waved. But then suddenly the monstrous events took clearer shape in my mind and when she walked back toward me I stopped and turned away as though I were retreating. She walked along with a lazy rhythm of body and clothes, tipping her face to the little breeze, watching the water creaming and flowing along the edge of the sand.

It was difficult for me to speak. She seemed entirely free and placid; she had nothing to do with the old sorrows of Bell's Landing. I had brought her out there with a careless notion of happiness.

For several seconds we walked along the top of the beach, and she asked finally what it was. "It's something very bad, isn't it?"

"You shouldn't be in it, Sally."

"Are they sick, Will? Are they dead?"

I told her, walking ahead on the narrow path up the hill to the house, but there was little she could do except be there while I drove off to Aston Corners for the doctor. She did find some brandy in a medicine bottle in the closet in Aunt Lucy's room, with a label inscribed in Aunt Evelyn's vertical

scratches: *Papa's brandy*—FOR EMERGENCY USE. She admin-
istered a few drops from a spoon, and when the doctor came
Aunt Evelyn was conscious and her face worked in an effort
of speech. "We're—all—done—at last." A little edge of wry
humor cut through the whisper. "A very good—riddance."
She waited for a last breath. "Dear old—Will—you'll have
to—see to things—" She intended to say more but couldn't.

It seemed remarkable that she continued to live until after
midnight. The doctor came and went several times. I had
telephoned various people, including the Saffords, who were
all at Edgartown, and Harold to explain about Sally.

But after the doctor left at last, we were there alone, in the
dark of the great house with the two dead ones. Two oil
lamps glimmered in the kitchen. Aunt Evelyn lay shrouded
on the iron cot she had used for her bed.

"I can take you back now," I said. "I ought to be here in
the morning."

We had been sitting on the hard chairs and waiting, and
had had tea and pilot crackers and some scrambled eggs—
there was a big china bowl of eggs in the pantry, and almost
nothing else.

"I'm sorry about it, Sally." I felt curiously hollow and
shaky as I spoke. "You shouldn't have been in on all this. I
just thought you'd enjoy seeing the place and the shore, and
I wanted to be with you. I keep wanting to steal you from
Saul. I haven't any sense about it, Sally; it's a habit or an
addiction or something, but I can't help it—" I said all this in
a ghostly mumble that seemed to come from some other
source than my own mouth.

She tried to say it was all right. I remember how her big
dark eyes enveloped me—in the lamplight they were deep
with shadow, and her wide soft mouth expressed so much
patience and awareness and knowledge that for a few seconds
I couldn't speak.

"You're new to me, Will," she said. "I mean—you have all this behind you and I didn't know: the place and the house and the family and the old ladies and I guess even the tragedy —if that's what it is. It seems ancient, somehow—the whole thing, like parts of a classic story—like—" She touched my hand with a light caress. "Don't think about me being in it. I feel really—" She hesitated. "I feel almost proud about it, being with you and—helping a little. It's queer to say it, maybe, but I feel that something profound has happened. I guess I'm not afraid of death, Will. I know about it—somehow I understand it: at least, I think I do. . . ."

"You'll put it into music, maybe," I said as a way of catching my balance, but I said it seriously enough and she understood and nodded.

"There are two worlds," she went on rather hesitantly, with a little smile at her effort of thought. "One is the old way of family and home, the chain of fathers and children never to be broken; the other is the way most of us are now, living from day to day and job to job—improvising, I guess. Drifting. It's what I chose—I had to, or thought I did: the old chain was more than I could stand, and it didn't seem to be necessary any more. I think you are like that too—you improvise and drift and in a way you are free. But you have all this—I didn't know you had it." Her smile widened for a moment. "I suppose I'm hoping we can have it both ways at the same time. A little bondage and security for comfort, a little freedom and adventure for pleasure—not too much of either."

I said that "all this" had pretty much come to an end; I said it so gloomily that she touched my hand again in a gesture of sympathy. An end in one way, she said—people had to die and property grew old, but in the mind and memory, in the composition of life, the old way needn't end at all. She felt that I was in it and part of it.

Actually I hardly took in what she was saying. But her presence there, her voice and being and all of her, was so pleasant to me that it was all I could do not to wrap my arms round her as she sat on the wooden kitchen chair by the wooden table. I felt a lassitude and emptiness in me, and a compelling need for Sally that was like the workings of a drug.

"We'd better start back," I said, watching the effect of lamplight on her face. "Saul will be coming after you—it's nearly two, you know."

She had been looking at me quite steadily—it was her habit to envelope me in a steady and mysterious contemplation that seemed to delve into the inner parts of my being. When I spoke of Saul she stared downward at her hands. "He won't come for me—he doesn't care very much where I am. I mean—" She looked up and took a breath. "You know, I like Saul—it seems funny to you because you don't—I guess you sort of despise him. People do, almost everybody. He complains and sneers and acts like an unhappy child and he hasn't any virility or muscle. But he has a—I don't know how to say it, but I like his mind, I admire it, I wish I could set it free—free enough to work. I wish he could be my child or pupil—or—" She paused. "In a way I think Harold is taking my place. Harold likes him too—or whatever it is in him, and the fact that Harold is a poet is terribly important to Saul. I'm sort of out of it—I mean I don't count for very much with them."

"Do you mind—being out of it?"

"Well—" She studied her hands. "I do feel like a mother more than a wife. I say to myself 'poor boy—poor kid'—that sort of feeling, and I think if Harold can do things for him— bring him out as a writer, or even as a person—it will be all right. No—I don't mind in the way you meant." After a bit she said, "If we lived in a house, in a place, everything might be different: but we couldn't, we aren't the kind. It's sort of funny, I guess, to feel so maternal in a little furnished room. Maybe it's funny that I should be maternal anyway; I never expected it."

It was Sally, I realized, who was keeping us there. She made no move. And then I had my arms round her and my head in her lap. It was for a few seconds as though I let myself go in a rush of current and was being carried along without any motion whatsoever. It felt like a spell of sleep and dream. But of course it didn't last. I pulled back. "Do we get in the car and go, or do we sleep here?"

She touched my face as though she were shaping it a little. "I like you best of anybody in the world, Will; I always have —ever since. Except maybe Grandpa—I love him too; I think of you together." She was quite serious. "You, the two of you, are sort of what I live for—I mean you are my strength and my help in time of trouble and I guess my faith: without you I'd be nothing—or that's how it seems." She stood up and looked a long time at the shrouded figure on the cot. "We'd better sleep here, Will." The words came out in the solemn little gulp that was sometimes characteristic of her. Then she smiled. "I want to see it all—the house, I mean. I couldn't go without seeing it."

"It's pitch dark, you know."

"Well, people seem to think I'm one of the creatures of darkness. We can be ghosts for the night, can't we? Maybe we can grope our way up to that room of yours in the eaves where the sea makes a noise like doom." Her voice was low and calm, and touched with some quirk of humor, but her face in the lamplight had taken on the contours and shadows of tenderness and beauty. She sounded, I said, like the Sally I remembered of old, the one who would not be afraid, but she looked more than ever like one of the immortal dark beauties of the legends—maybe the black-haired Isolde, I said, trying to remember who they were.

I blew out one lamp, held the other high and took a last look at the cot in the corner, and led the way through the pantry to the wainscotted dining room of the main house. The air was fresh now from the open windows of summer, but the big rooms were heavy with walled-in silence, and the great pieces of oak and walnut stood about like memorial monuments. We made a noiseless little procession through the rooms, hand in hand, peering ritualistically at portraits and cabinets and book-cases, and there was nothing eerie or ghostly about any of it—not in the ordinary way of ghosts: we had the feeling, both of us, that we were rightly there, part of it, somehow essential to time and place; our mood was relaxed and compassionate, and in the lamplight the oaken banisters marching into upper darkness seemed to be arranged like a piece of familiar staging. The house enclosed us, separated us from the outer world, became a place of pleasant enchantment. It was what we dreamed, a castle, a night-time vision, with glimmering treasures and carvings and delightful dark halls and chambers leading us on from one to another. I told Sally I had never seen any of it before. The majolica umbrella stand in the front hall was darkly beautiful in our moving lamplight. The huge walnut desk in the library was like a carved gothic altar, and behind it the tall sashes and inside shutters of a great bay window reached into the shadows above. When we came to the grand piano in the parlor Sally let her left hand run up the keys in a gentle cascade of bass notes that made a muffled out-of-tune harmony in the darkness.

"Aunt Evelyn used to play *John Peel*," I said. "Long ago. We sang it. It was the only thing she could play." Another world, another life and time. Far, far away. Aunt Lucy had read us a story of Sir Percival and a castle by the sea and a dying maiden and the cold wind blowing night and day.

Through the open window we heard the slow wash of waves on the sand.

I led her up the stairs, following the golden oak banisters to the second floor, and round the circuit of four rooms, through the big closets from one to another—closets full of bags and ancient garments and shrouds. We stopped at the big east window of Aunt Lucy's room and looked over the sea where a waning yellow half-moon made long splinters and swords of light. "I've never seen the sea," Sally murmured as though it were a small ritual she had to say. "I've never been in a big house like a castle. But I've dreamed it— I must have, because I know about it. All the old books, I guess—the gray sea and the long black land and the yellow half-moon large and low: I seem to remember everything— bits of it come jumping in to my memory." She took my left hand and squeezed it as hard as she could, with all the muscle of her strong fingers, watching my face and smiling like a kindly witch. I held my breath at the pain. "It's to remind us," she said. "We might forget we're alive—and mortal. It's better if we know, if we remember. Now squeeze mine—do it so it hurts." But I couldn't. I took a firm handful of the thick hair, pulled her head back and kissed her, holding all the time the small kerosene lamp in my right hand. "We might get to thinking it doesn't count," she said. "We might think it's all a spell." She twisted her head against my grip. "I want to *know*," she said.

We went on up the steep and narrow stairs to the hot hall of the third floor, more remote and more silent than anything below. I put the lamp down on the bureau in my old room, opened both windows and felt the fresh easterly air come in exactly as it always used to come in on the quiet summer nights.

Sally prowled round in the shadows of the room, and leaned on the sill and looked out. "It's all quiet now," she murmured "—almost quiet. And far—everything is far away. No life, no world, no time—" she turned and blew out the light. We lay on the bed and slept and a long time later I felt her hand on my cheek and heard her say something. The sound of water was loud now; the flood tide had come with swells that broke slowly on the rocks and made long slanting rushes up the sand and pebbles, a steady blending of chords that came whelming into our room. The sound of space, she said, of infinity, of the end of all things. All you had to do was surrender, surrender—she whispered the word until nothing was left of it but the strange sound. We slept together, holding out against time and change—until I awoke slowly to a strange bright room with a wash of rosy light on the wall. I lay for a second or two, squinting into the dazzle and still inert from deep sleep; then I felt the emptiness beside me and in a flash was out of bed. Sally had gone, her clothes were gone—she had never, it suddenly seemed, been there at all.

I pulled on some things, ran down the flights of stairs, through the rooms—glanced at the books and the piano— out to the rocks and shore. All was as it had been. The morning serenely brightened, and water and shore lay all empty and mild in misty sunlight. No change anywhere. I looked in the kitchen, in Aunt Lucy's room. Two clocks ticked. I listened. The beat of pulses sounded both loud and precarious in my ears and I looked fearfully at the sheeted body on the cot; I could hardly believe in its stillness and I made an effort to see and accept all that had happened. It was death, I said; it was fact. Dust to dust—I actually used the phrase, almost said it. It had to be. But Sally—

I got as far as my car, started the motor, backed it round in the grassy yard. It was eight o'clock, I noticed. Sunday morning—I was supposed to have dinner with Mother and hadn't called her: I should have called her the afternoon before. Bodies had to be taken care of on Sunday, I thought, and at once the whole thing came over me in a flood—images of decomposition and worms, coffins and graves, undertakers in black suits, officials, clergymen, lawyers, courts and legal fuss. I turned off the motor. She couldn't be very far away—it was only eight o'clock and all she could do was walk: or pick up a ride, I thought. I sat with head and arms on the steering wheel remembering Sally and the quiet night up in the third-floor room—as quiet and safe as a womb.

I looked round at the large reality of Bell's Landing, the house and barn all solid in the morning air, the great oak and beech and maples, the sparkling grasses and the acres stretching off to ragged fields and woodlands. Pieces of slate from the mansard roof had fallen here and there on the grass, I noticed, and the back steps sagged a bit.

It was still early, and the morning was full of innocence. There'd be a little time, perhaps, before anything had to happen. I pushed it all away with almost a physical gesture—the duties and rituals and men in black. Sweet sea air filled my lungs and seemed to flow all through me. I must still find Sally, I thought, moving the gear and clutch. The dream still possessed me.

But a flashing of sunlight darted from the trees of the driveway and a heavy black car trundled into view and turned into the grassy level beside me. The two men in black looked at me with formal appraisal. I nodded and switched off my motor.

CHAPTER 5

THE FIRST question in dealing with death and burial, I found, was money, and luckily both Mother and Cousin Jane were shrewd bargainers. It was assumed by the undertakers and casket makers that a Redfern funeral would be a big thing, with a formal procession to Mount Auburn in Cambridge; but Jane, who took charge in her cool and level fashion, explained what was to be done and trusted that Mother—or someone—would see to it. They did well together. Jane's directions were so mild that the busy professionals hardly noticed them: they assumed that everyone naturally began with timid references to plain pine boxes and no Cadillacs, and everyone in time realized the need for satin and bronze and mahogany and the luxuries of a decent burial.

I never knew all the details of the affair, but once Mother found out what was wanted she saw to it. She decided that a battle had to be fought, and she went into action with an implacable mistrust of the enemy. The dead were buried in Aston Corners as quickly as could be and the matter of the headstones was left for later: but a service was held in the old Unitarian church in Beverly, and fifty or sixty came. I had to borrow dark clothes from Harold.

And of course I went reluctantly, with distrust of religious observances. Death, I thought, was not to be mollified. But

284

I reckoned without the human qualities of the gathering. They were mostly old, the friends and far cousins of long ago, and they came to acknowledge and accept their own mortality; as these old ones are, they silently said, so we shall be —quite soon. But they said it, I strongly felt, not in grief and pity, but with pride. They hadn't seen Aunt Evelyn for years, most of them, but they knew she had lived to her last breath without once betraying their common heritage, and they came together to celebrate as best they could the ways of life they believed in. I felt all this quite clearly, even though their controlled faces expressed nothing but solemnity during the reading and prayers. The service went on impersonally, conducted by a young man with a young voice who had never known the old ladies at all. But afterward, as the aged and infirm made their way bravely to the doors, an effect of solidarity was there. "Pity it had to be now," an old voice said with knife-edge precision. "Autumn's the best time at the Landing. I'll never forget that line of maples on the road." "They cut a lot of 'em down," another said. "Too bad. Used to be such lovely woods. Can't think what'll happen to it now —have to be sold, I guess. Such an elephant, after all—but that wonderful library . . ."

No one but me seemed to be surprised at the numbers who came. Jane Safford knew them all, and Betsy seemed to: well, that generation, she said as though it were all recognizably here. I knew Bolles Sumner, didn't I? And Dr. and Mrs. Edmund Craigie from Quincy, and poor old Miss Nannie Ewart who was ninety-two and her companion, Miss Hitchcock, who must be eighty herself and had been a "companion" for fifty years at least, and the Trasks, of Manchester, and surely I knew her uncle Albert Weldon and his family—she guided me from group to group and I bowed and shook hands very stiffly because of Harold's tight charcoal-gray coat.

"So you're young Will, eh?" It was a Mrs. Fairchild who said it, but others had looked at me with the same question and implication in their eyes. "You'll inherit the old place, they say. Is that right?" Her deep voice and bulldog face challenged me, and I pulled back in alarm. I supposed she was another cousin—Betsy had left me—and I mumbled that I knew nothing and expected nothing, but she went on accusingly: "Well, I hope so—I hope you do. It needs to be looked after. You look capable enough, I must say. You took care of poor dear Evelyn, they tell me—which is more than anybody else did." She seemed to glare at me with jaw outthrust. She had a white mustache and mottled leathery skin, and her blue eyes were almost out of sight under the wrinkled folds—but I could see a small twinkling gleam in them. "We're all cantankerous as mules, of course, but Evelyn was the worst—though I must say Lucy could be a trial too. Poor dears—I'm just thankful they don't have to suffer through another winter."

She was, I found out later, another Craigie, a cousin of my grandmother Craigie. I felt like a neophyte among them all: their lives and experiences had woven together like an animated tapestry, and I was out of it. But for the few minutes we stood about the vestibule and steps they hovered round me with visible curiosity. They didn't forget that the occasion was funereal: there was no social release—voices were low and dry, gestures few, motion rather formal; but they spoke with the sharp candor of self-possessed and confident members of their fraternity. "Will Redfern, are you? Remember your grandpa—used to sail with him: tried to teach me how to stick a cringle—can you stick a cringle? I couldn't either—haven't the least notion about it . . ."

It seemed as though they were trying me, not with hostility

but with wry hopefulness; they were full of a congenital
scepticism about the way of the world, specially about a young
outsider, as I felt myself to be. They all had a clear vision of
the beautiful and trustworthy life they had been born to, the
respect and family security, the code of gentle chivalry, the
humor, the confident individuality, and they had no real hope
that the old ways would continue. ("That house," Uncle Albert Weldon said in his driest voice, "better burn it up. Save a
few books, perhaps.") But none the less they looked at me
with a sort of ironic warmth. Another Redfern anyway, they
seemed to agree—better than nothing, and healthy at least—
plenty of muscle: perhaps—perhaps—

They knew all about Harold, admired and accepted him as
a natural family phenomenon, but they disliked him. I could
hear it in the way they said how'd-ye-do, the clipped coolness
of it. He had a right to be Harold, and it was suitable that he
should be at Harvard and publish poems in *The Atlantic*, as
he had recently done, but he might just possibly be a poseur:
no honest Redfern, they felt, could be quite as well dressed
as he was—nor an honest poet, either. "Those things in *The
Atlantic*," I heard Uncle Albert say to him, "astonishing, I
must say. I'm too old for 'em—brain petrified, I expect. You
never knew Briggs at Harvard, did you? Nice old boy—I never
knew anyone better—used to have a class in writing: I had
no business to be in it, but I was—and we had a poet, brilliant
chap named Proctor. I remember one thing Briggs said on one
of his poems: 'It might help if you used a little more soap
and a little less ivory.' " As Uncle Albert said it he flashed a
cool glance at Harold's bland face. "Couldn't resist a pun—he
was good at them, of course: not the thing now, I'm told—"

Harold, of course, was fully equal to Uncle Albert. The
whole art of poetry, he murmured, was a matter of balancing

the soap and the ivory—and as for puns, they were very much the thing; they were, in fact, the essential gamble a writer had to take.

Uncle Albert raised his hands in a small acknowledgment of defeat. His impassive face crinkled with a brief appreciation, but his appraising glance seemed shrewd and cold.

Mother got us away as soon as possible. She was always uneasy among the family, and took a defensive stance with her weight equally on both feet a bit like a wrestler awaiting the attack. The ironies, the understatements, the private humors, all bothered her, and she turned her head watchfully so as not to be surprised. Yet they were kind to her—perhaps too kind. They made an effort. "The one really competent member of the family," Mrs. Fairchild said to her quite loudly, so that all heard. "I do hope you'll take charge—you and your strong boys." She smiled horribly and bobbed up and down with exaggerated nods, as though she were speaking to someone who couldn't understand the language. Mother grew very red, of course, and remarked with extreme quietness that she'd do what little she could. Her hand on my arm made a pressure and we edged away toward the car. It wasn't right, she said, to stand round talking after a funeral service—the sooner we left the better. Sometimes of course you went to the cemetery, but they weren't doing that, and there was no reason for staying.

I don't know that I had any plan whatever about the future: it was a Monday afternoon late in August and we were to meet with Mr. Orrin Guptill at four o'clock at Bell's Landing. Mother had taken the day off from her hospital, Harold had come back from his session at the Writers' Conference, and Chadd's school was closed for the two or three weeks before the opening of the fall term. Beyond going back to the Landing I had no notion of what would be done. It is fair to say that in spite of the general certainty among the family I had no expectations and no desires, and certainly no intention of taking on the responsibilities of property.

Mother had got a hand under Harold's arm too, and he acquiesced with a sardonic little smile and came with us. Others would be going, I supposed; it would be a scene from a novel: the mansion, the will, the lawyer, the eccentric family. But not greedy, not avid for property—unless for a rug here and there, a painting, some of the first editions: mainly the thing was an elephant, nor was the family specially greedy in the manner of people in books.

So we all gathered, Mother and I in innocence, the others in their various degrees of experience: the Saffords, including Betsy and Chan, Uncle Albert and a middle-aged daughter (Cousin Harriet), Dr. and Mrs. Craigie (not very closely related), and Bolles Sumner, my father's classmate and third cousin (I think) and warm friend. The house was well aired and clean: Mother had spent the morning putting it to rights, though there was still no electricity or running water (except for the cistern pump in the kitchen, which Aunt Evelyn had made do for all her needs). There was no special drama, no revelation: Mr. Guptill behaved with quiet competence, though he stumbled over my father's middle name each time he came to it: Ee-wart, he called it, paying no attention to Bolles Sumner's modest correction to Ewart.

But I listened with increasing wonder. The property came to me—all of it, with the very earnest request that I would do my utmost to keep it intact. Everything there was to be entirely mine: the silver (in a trunk behind some old boards in the northwest corner of the cellar), the furniture and books and pictures and "papers" (Aunt Evelyn had a strong conviction about the value of her father's files) and everything else including the contents of the barn and carriage house and the old boat still in the boathouse. She urged upon me the need of discretion and wisdom: if I wanted to distribute some of the things to other members of the family I could, but I was to consider the matter carefully and not act hastily. She advised me in the end to take my responsibilities seriously. She had great confidence in me.

It came, not the things but the confidence, as an astonishment. She had absurdly misjudged me, I thought, though I realized that it was characteristic of her; if Aunt Lucy had had the final say there'd have been little or no confidence—and for a moment it seemed to me that Harold was a much more appropriate custodian of the tradition and the property. I had a sudden image of him living there in eminent retirement—not yet, of course: he was too young and ambitious for country life, but in time he might become a solid and celebrated literary squire.

Not me, though; I thought of myself still as a stray, a social wanderer, a boy staying out of school. "It's crazy," I said. "All this place—what could I ever do with it?" It was a matter for lawyers and brokers and people with offices. "Holy smoke—the taxes alone—and upkeep—slates falling off—paint—" It ought to be sold, I almost said.

But no one in that company seemed in the least surprised or troubled. There was even a little half-humorous handshaking and congratulating. Betsy kissed me with a cool sort of benevolence and advised me to marry a rich wife, but at the same time she seemed both affectionate and solemn, and stood by me faithfully. Her mother and father expressed a placid approval, and I looked hopefully at him especially because he had been named executor and I considered him a very bulwark of reliability: one could tell at a glance that he managed everything correctly and simply; his egg-shaped head, for example, seemed neat and reassuring with the round bald crown well tanned by the Vineyard sun, and the circle of gray hair and the matching mustache, with an overall expression of self-control. It occurred to me surprisingly that they were friends as well as distant cousins—I called them Jane and Walter and dropped in at their house and was accepted. "I count on you, Walter," I said. "You'll have to execute everything." And he nodded with the quick firmness that was part of his pattern, and then he smiled his dry little smile. "Squire Will, eh?" He understood—I saw his eyes take in the library, where we all were, the heavy furniture and cabinets and books to the ceiling. "Remember Thoreau's pity for the poor civilized devil who was condemned to push a house and barn through life. You're in for it now, Will—I'm sorry for you." Yet his little humor reassured me. The burdens of property, he implied, were the inevitable lot of civilized man: with patience and common sense there was no reason why I shouldn't civilize myself. Dreams of freedom and "happiness" were strictly for the self-centered young.

Mr. Guptill pointed out that there were pretty heavy taxes to be reckoned with, but he added that Miss Redfern had a savings account in a Salem bank of over eleven hundred dollars, which she intended to be used only in extreme emergency: it had been untouched for eighteen years. Some of it could be applied, of course, toward expenses as soon as the will was probated and the estate transferred—he used more suitable technical terms perhaps, but it sounded pretty much like that. "The poor sweet old thing," I heard Jane say. "What do you suppose she thought an extreme emergency could be?" I remembered the little bottle of brandy.

After that various individuals cornered me for earnest low-voiced consultation—it almost seemed to be an art with them, the quiet little manoeuvre of cornering, the casual words, the point made, the general effect of good will. Walter Safford

reminded me in the mildest of tones that of course I'd have
the right to sell: no one could be required to keep property he
couldn't afford, and actually the place was worth a great deal
on the present market—the land alone was as valuable as any
on the North Shore, and the house could perfectly well be
modernized. The dealers and buyers would be hounding me,
he said.

Uncle Albert got me in among the books and warned me
about sharks and sharpers. I could make money on the first
editions, he said, but it was a mighty tricky business and he
advised care. *He* didn't know enough to handle them and
he'd been messing round with books all his life—had a *Robinson Crusoe* first in his safe right now simply because he
didn't know what else to do with it: no sense in 'em, actually
—a book was a book, meant to read, not put in a safe. Of
course that *Pickwick* first there was very nice, pretty hand-
done water colors and all, and the *Vanity Fair* had Thack-
eray's own drawings, poor as they were—they were amusing
to have on the shelf, but he presumed I'd rather have the
cash—a good bit, he should think. The main thing was not
to turn them over to a jobber or broker. Better ask Bolles
about it—Bolles had nothing to do now he'd retired . . .

So Bolles joined our low-voiced consultation, and said he'd
ask old Jim Quackenbush at the Athenaeum—he knew everything about old books, how to buy 'em or sell 'em though he
himself never did either. Uncle Albert said that's the kind of
chap I needed—better get him out here.

And presently I found myself in another corner with Bolles
alone, who leaned close and reminded me that my father had
been his oldest and best friend and if I needed any assistance
—any that he could possibly give, that is—I was to come to
him. Bolles had just retired from the Cornell faculty—I think
his special field was colonial history—and lived alone in a

Beacon Hill apartment. "I'm not well to do, Will—you don't mind my being candid, I'm sure; after all, it's almost as though I were part of the—well, of course, I *am* part of the family—but I do have a moderate annuity as well as a bit of an investment fund, and I could easily lend you a little something. It would be very pleasant if I could—don't hesitate an *instant* if you—that is, just keep it in mind that it would give *me* pleasure." He spoke moistly, with pudgy and slightly pop-eyed eagerness and emotion. He must have been in his late sixties but you could still see how he had been as a baby and small boy. His good will was almost tearful and his voice seemed ready to crack with the significance of what he said. The family, I remembered, all spoke of him with affectionate indulgence: poor dear Bolles. "I just hope," he went on, "that the old place can be kept going—it meant so much to me as a boy, you know—and all through college: I came out with Will very often." He shook his head reminiscently and his mouth seemed to glisten. "Your Aunt Evelyn was very sharp with me, I can tell you. To be frank, she always rather frightened me—I'm afraid I never quite measured up to her expectations, and she could be *pret–ty* formidable!" He wagged his head as he spoke the last phrase, and then added a kindly "heh-heh" to assure me that all was long ago forgiven. "But your grandfather, Will—I've always considered him the finest all-round man I ever knew. A very few people, I often think, ought to be permitted by providence to live for ever—and he is one of the few." There were visible tears in his eyes as he said this.

Harold had been edging along the shelves, looking at titles, taking out volumes, and Bolles stepped back in a way to include him. "It's pretty scattery, of course," Bolles said, nodding at the library and making his tone quite professional and even pompous. "But the nineteenth century items are remarkable: some of the material on the opening of the West, for example, is quite rare—I doubt if Harvard has all of it." It was a literal classroom voice, and he looked almost like a small boy trying to imitate a professor. But Harold responded warmly, his face brightened and he smiled—it struck me as he did so that he had a sort of beauty about him, a balance and fineness that made a sculptured harmony. Yes, the books, the rare and lovely books—all of the romantic poets, every one of them. "Don't you dare sell a single volume, Will!" He looked at me with an expression of ironic challenge—at least that's as close as I can come to describing it. Often he made me feel like an enemy, or a despised object, but I tried to believe that he had no personal animus against me; he had tastes and values, very clear in his mind and supremely important to him, and whatever failed to pass his test of value became in his eyes contemptible or at best indifferent. Just now he was eager about the books and annoyed because they had legally passed into unworthy hands. I said he was welcome to make use of them, though it seemed foolish that I should have to say it and I half choked on the words. We were actors on a stage, I thought, and I was cast as the young heir and playing it badly—and of course Harold didn't help with his ironies: "It's very kind of you, brother. Perhaps you might give me a borrower's card—I think Cousin Bolles might be included too. We'll be respectful and appreciative, though I should warn you that I shall probably steal a good many books. What about you, Cousin Bolles? Have you got your eye on a few?" But then he smiled with a more evident warmth. "It's the one thing I'm jealous about, Will. All the rest you can burn up or sell for junk, but the books—" He shrugged. And I almost told him to take them; I began to say the words—he surely had a better claim to them. . . .

But Betsy appeared between us, sun-brown and healthy and

full of friendliness. "Can I have the boat, Will? The good old four-oared skiff? I've always admired it—through the window, that is. It even has a rudder—I used to think a boat with a rudder was wonderful. Isn't that what they call stern sheets in books—I mean the little ropes to steer with?"

I grinned down at her and reminded her that the will advised me to keep things intact. But I appointed Harold special custodian of books and Betsy custodian of the boat—stipulating that she paint it once a year with Miller's Marine. I gave her arm a little squeeze—a golden-brown and competent arm.

~§   CHAPTER 6   §~

So THEY ALL went away, except Mother, who agreed to stay for the night and be driven to her hospital early in the morning. She said I'd have to make plans—I couldn't go on drifting as I had been. But it seemed impossible; I avoided discussing it in the serious way she wanted, and slipped out to walk among the trees and glades.

It was late in the afternoon and the sun slanted down with a rich gold light like a visible wash on grass and leaves and tree trunks. The eastward sea was as dark and flat as blue paint, flecked with the white of little triangular sails. All the fresh coolness and shining color had remade the world; the old white half-dusty haze of summer mid-day had vanished, and the brightness seemed as new as the beginning of creation. Even the great house had lost its look of neglect and stood up proudly in the brave new light.

I walked about as though I had never seen any of it before. The inland fields were over-run with weeds and little trees—a good many grayish-green junipers and scrubby birches: I appraised them and noted that they were beautiful if no longer useful. The woods were a sorry mess: if I put in a month of steady work, I thought, I could clean up a good deal and give the new growth a fair start—and I felt almost a quiver of desire in my arms to get started with ax and saw. My notion of ownership was still on the level of touching and manipulating: I even broke a twig of pitch-pine with the awareness that I owned it, and I looked at the ground I stood on and kicked at the stones and picked up a nugget of quartz and held it as though it were everything.

Along the shore I had the strongest sense of security and permanence. Nothing there needed to be done. The beach remained inviolable, the high rocks held out against time and the sea and the headlands endured. The old wooden ways below the boat-house had nearly gone, I noted: only a few of the posts still showed in the sand. It was simpler this way, I thought: let the shore be a shore. If Betsy and I ever got the boat in we could use rollers—I filed away a little image of the two of us heaving away at it. The thing to do, of course, was to get a light boat, something of plywood or fibre or aluminum. With an outboard motor we could do wonders—zip over to Marblehead or up into Salem Harbor or Manchester. There might be delightful adventures for us.

But the boat-house did sag a bit in one corner (simple to jack it up, I told myself) and the old shingles had begun to blow off (hardly a day's work to put on a new asphalt roof): it should be painted too. In its day it had been a solid little house: no sense in letting it go to ruin. The window sashes were badly weathered.

Yet in the benign light all seemed hopeful. Even the big barn had been built like a church. Paint would make it as good as new: a lot of paint, though—a terrific job, I realized: ladders, scaffolds, platforms—and the whole thing would have to be scraped and brushed. I could do it—I once had a job painting houses when I was seventeen—but it would take weeks. And of course the house would be worse—I hardly dared looked at the eaves and cornices and fancy windows and acres of high walls. It needed a crew, of course, with a lot of equipment. . . .

All these reflections and impulses came in a series of eddies and whirls, but what seemed to count most just then was the evening light. The whole of my life was somehow refracted through that pleasant lens—and even my future, as if I were looking into a bright and burnished landscape. No train of thought carried me along, no seriousness of reason—I had no practical view of the actual problems of my lifetime; I simply felt beguiled and delighted by what was there, by the clean sky and the evening air, the coppery grasses glinting on the edge of the cliffs, the line of jumbled trees and junipers against the luminous blue. The quiet yard muffled in weeds, the barn door, the back steps with the cascade of forsythia, the plot of James's garden, the big oak and beech, all seemed to make a sort of pattern of security, like the courtyard of a modest castle where years passed almost unnoticed. I remembered a word from the old stories: pleasance—a green place, I supposed, beside a manor house where life was most pleasant, specially in the shady time of a summer afternoon.

Perhaps I knew I was being beguiled. The green place was weedy, the old ones were dead, the costs and taxes were heavy. In winter the rain might leak around the slates and the snow back up above the gutters. The world outside would wait—not with enmity but with certainty of inevitable loss and failure: the lawyers, sheriffs, tax-collectors, bankers, would see how defenseless and discreditable it was, a weakness in the bastion of North Shore property. Not half a mile away was Buckingham Palace, with terraced levels and sprinklers running all day and famous chrysanthemums.

I sat on the steps in a dapple of low sunlight until Mother looked out and said she had supper ready. She seemed very staunch there in the old kitchen, and pointed out the soundness of her manoeuvers: she had a fire in the wood range because it was really getting cool and we'd be glad of the warmth, but she used the little one-burner kerosene stove because it boiled water so quickly. She sent me to draw a bucket of water from the well north of the barn—the cistern tasted very brackish. She noted that the hand pump didn't work right and would I fix it after supper—she had actually a little list of things to be done, hinges and latches and loose shutters and cracked glass, and she had organized the laundry to be sent out, trash to be burned, cans and garbage and all the by-products of existence.

But I could tell that she had been systematically thinking about the realities of my inheritance, and later in the evening she argued her case. It was up to me to be as generous as possible with all the family valuables: she supposed a lot of the things had sentimental value (a phrase she used many times), and if Jane or Bolles or Harold wanted them they should certainly have them: or me too, of course—in time I'd want a great many of the things. The silver should be put in a vault somewhere—right away: it was very dangerous to leave it behind old boards in the cellar. But as for the house and land, I couldn't possibly make proper use of them. Even renting them would be impractical, since everything would have to be renovated at enormous expense. It was too bad, she said— especially as the old aunts wanted to keep it all in the family, and the tradition meant so much to all of us—but it seemed senseless for me to have to take on any such burden. Aunt Evelyn would certainly understand—so would the family as a whole: Walter Safford had already spoken to her about the advisability of my selling the property. It was, she reiterated, the only sensible thing to do.

I could say nothing in answer. She bored in with the effectiveness of a power drill. I mumbled that we'd have to wait and

see, and she flashed back at once that I had no time to wait—
I ought to be applying at Tech right now—I needed money to
put me through, and this was my chance. I'd get in—she was
sure of it, had no doubt whatever; supposed in fact that the
Tech scouts were already seeking me out: she lectured me on
my careless disregard of my own abilities, my irresponsibility
and lack of seriousness. I still behaved, she said, like a boy—
racketed round in my car, had no aim or ambition, and it was
high time I settled down to the hard work of a career.

Yes, I muttered, she was right—I saw, I understood. I bowed
my head as though a cold rain were falling on it. It was dark
by then and we had the two oil lamps on, and my little vision
of the bright pleasance of Bell's Landing had faded away. I
conceded that my notions of life and the future were no more
than the trifles of youth.

"You see, Will," she said with deeper, more solemn tone,
"your father never really faced his responsibilities. He was
gifted and capable—you know his memory was remarkable
and he could do almost anything he wanted to do, but of
course he kept putting off any serious work. The thing he
worked hardest at was those little boats. . . ."

They still stood in a cellar room, near the closed bulkhead
doors, the wondrous boats like a boy's dream, with dusty decks
and mildewed sails: I had thought of them with little gleams
of pleasure and visions of sailing them again on sunny waters
—I had saved from a popular science magazine an article on
a new self-steering mechanism for sailing models, with dia-
grams and illustrations.

"With all his charm and enthusiasm," she went on, "he was
never really happy—not as a grown man should be
happy . . ."

After all those years I could hear his excited laugh and flute-
like voice calling to his boats. "She moves, she starts, she feels

the breeze—see her luff to the catspaw! By George, that was pretty—did you see, young Will?"

She spoke of my capabilities, how much greater they were. She went on with it until I said I'd better put up the top to my car, and slipped out into the starlit night. It was cool out there and enormously dark and silent, with the first feel and smell of autumn in the air.

I slept in the top-floor room again. It seemed to me that I was wrapped in a secret life—more so than ever before, and more bewilderingly. Everyone, I supposed, must be: there was always an inner desire and an outer command. But the two might be reconciled—at least, so it seemed in the lives of the well balanced ones. Up in the high room, with the old sea sounds quietly echoing through the open windows, I thought so acutely of Sally that she seemed palpably there, on the bed where she had lain two nights before. I thought of ourselves—the two of us—here in the fortress of Bell's Landing, not against the world but independent of it, indifferent to the commands of the lawyers and bankers and all the lay officials in and out of the family; even of Betsy Safford, whom I liked and trusted and felt strongly tied to. I thought of the remoteness of the place, the womb-like safety of the high room, the harmonies of sea and air that surrounded it. I lay half awake for a long time. I remembered how she had said the word surrender over and over, and her voice was still in the room—at times as faint as breathing, and at times sounding clearly in the orchestration of the night.

And even when I did sleep that night, the dreams were so much a part of my inner living that I hardly seemed to lose consciousness at all. I painted the boat with a new can—a huge gallon—of Miller's Marine, and Aunt Evelyn and I carried it down, she in her big rubber boots but as old and twisted and frail as a puff of smoke. We had my father's boats to sail, but alas they tangled and broke like cobwebs—all but one, that sped away across the flashing waters and became beautiful and perfect and presently turned into the *Aldebaran* dashing to windward with sails curving like white wings. At another time I lay on the warm sand with Sally, and a voice called from the cliff above, strained and angry and accusing, and I saw old James standing above us like a furious prophet, pointing a long finger and shouting (though we could hardly hear him) that the roof had gone—he had warned me and warned me, and now the slates were coming down like rain and suddenly I could see gaps and rafters open to the sky. And everyone told me what to do—Mr. Guptill and Walter and Mother—and there was talk of a mortgage, as though that were the one great thing, and I signed papers as fast as I could, and then Mr. Harkins took me aside and explained how it all was: you made apartments, he said, and there were doors with name plates and people going in and out. . . .

About then I half woke up, with the sound of Mr. Harkins's voice still in my head. I remembered everything about him, and in the night as I lay and thought, partly awake and partly bemused by dreams, I saw him very clearly: I had a vision of his farm in Kingstown as it had been in the old days, with sheep on the hills and cows coming up the lane toward the great barn, and the ripening Gravensteins, and the corn and potatoes. I thought of the family gathering by the stream—where the old oil drums were piled now—and the picnic and ball game on the level green of the pasture. I couldn't help thinking of how he looked after his death, lying twisted on the floor of his office.

But in the last few hours of the night I slept more soundly and woke and looked out at the peaceful morning waters with a sense of relief. The ghosts of darkness had all gone. It was early and the air was piercingly fresh; when I came down

Mother had the eggs and coffee and toast all ready and we ate and were off for town with a fine feeling of briskness. I remembered as I drove that Sally would be at her new job at Filene's today. Harold was due to go visiting somewhere, but I wasn't sure: I had tried to tell him—without too self-consciously sounding like a new heir—that he could stay at Bell's Landing. It occurred to me as we locked the door and drove away that it had probably never been empty before.

I dropped Mother at her grim-looking institution in Roxbury ("Go over to Tech *today* and see about admission. You can't afford to wait a *single day*.") and went on from there westward ninety miles to Holyoke and Kingstown. In the sunny morning the distance seemed very slight.

"The thing is," I said to Pop Sardis, "I've got this big house and place and I don't know what to do about it." I said it lightly, as though I had just happened to think of it. But Pop looked at me keenly: the small and nut-like face scrutinized me for several seconds. Was I asking his advice? I said sure, of course—I always wanted his advice. He waited longer, and I told him what had been happening, and he said he was a ready giver of advice—it was about all he did anymore—but he observed that people seldom took advice; rather, it often impelled them to do the opposite. The young ones, who most needed it, assumed that he was too old to know anything about life—their lives; the old ones wouldn't take it anyway, were fixed in their habits. As for me, he wasn't sure what my case was—

He said these things to make the talk easy for us and to avoid solemnities and certainties, and yet he was so glad to see me that his face shone and his voice sputtered and caught in his breath. He needed vocal exercise, he said. Reading made him dull, and he was getting too lazy to go to the lectures and meetings he used to enjoy. So he held me there and made me tell him about everything, and we shared the frugal lunch Anna had left for him.

"Everything," he said, with his rush of breath, "everything in man and nature is in a state of tension and balance—like—" he modelled the air with his two hands "—perhaps like a suspension bridge with all the wires and beams straining simply to stay there quietly—or like a bird floating and soaring . . . One force alone is destructive—like love, or freedom, or even virtue. You, Will Redfern, are at the center of all these strains and stresses, like all the cables of a bridge—" He fixed me with a pointed finger for a moment. "You are not peculiar, Will: everyone is the same. But you are conscious of it. You belong to all that is new—your talent is for the new: yet now you are checked and balanced by the old—you even brood about the beauty of old times, your friend Mr. Harkins's farm and your grandfather's house. And you want freedom—you want to live entirely by your own wit and strength, like Robinson Crusoe, but you know you can't, not in a world of motor cars and electric power. You have tried to escape your family and now you are almost captured by it . . . You thought you could be happy by avoiding responsibility, and now it seems you can be happy only by accepting it. It might even be that to make a success of love you must first renounce it."

He said a good deal more, of course, and it all whirled through my mind. I couldn't take it in clearly. But what did he advise, I asked.

Well, he advised patience, he said with a small twinkle in his eyes to suggest the irony of any such advice. He advised a good deal of acceptance. It was all very well to reject the bad things or the foolish ones—but you had to use what was given. Not that he meant resignation—or defeat—but a realization

of what you had to work with: steel had a breaking point, and
so did flesh—he was alluding to the bridge again.

"But," I said, "what do you *advise?*"

He shrugged. "I advise you to do your utmost. The unhappy
man is the one who knows he has not done what he might
have done—like me, perhaps, Will." He spread his hands.
"When I came to work in that shop I was spiritually miserable. It is an unhappiness you must avoid—the realization that
you have no function. In my case it was perhaps bad luck—I
have not allowed it to destroy me: there are compensations,
such as a leisurely talk with Will Redfern. I've always felt
that you had a talent—more than that, of course: a calling,
perhaps, or even a genius—and I can only advise you to do
your utmost with it."

What I wanted, of course, was specific advice that could be
literally taken or not taken, but Pop would have none of that.
He merely remarked that happiness, such as it was, generally
came the hard way. At the end, when I left, he said I under-
rated myself—not from lack of confidence, but from lack of
vision. "You must see, Will: see yourself, your function or
power or whatever it is in you that can be brought to fulfillment." He stood on the steps in front, a wizened nodding little figure, blinking in the light of day and smiling slightly at
the earnestness of his own speech. "I fear it is unpopular advice, and unhelpful. But I think life has you in hand, Will.
You have less choice than you perhaps realize." He waved and
watched me drive off.

I had intended to ask Chadd about my problems too, but as
I drove to Kingstown I realized that I couldn't—or shouldn't.
It was a sudden little discovery, and perhaps it was the first
result of the talk with Pop. Or perhaps it was merely that life
had charge of me, as he said. When I came to the house I

stopped the car and sat there for a strangely long time, not thinking very consecutively or rationally but in some fashion becoming more certain of a few things. The whirl, the drifts and eddies that had bemused me, seemed to flow more clearly.

"Chadd," I said later, when I had him alone, "can I get into Tech?"

He gave a bright smiling nod as though I had asked him to share a bottle of beer with me. "Sure—why not?" I realized that to Chadd, anything was possible: he could be wrong about this, but he was so full of cheery certainty that I began to believe him. He'd back me—he'd see that I had the best recommendations.

But what about my job there? School began in two weeks.

I remember how he looked at me, smiling and cocky. "Never mind that," he said. "You tend to Will, I'll tend to school. If it's what you have to do—why, do it. Besides, I've got a man anyway. You don't think I didn't expect this, do you?"

But then, when the decision was made and recognized, he touched my shoulder with a sort of boy-scout formality as though he felt the need of making an official gesture. "I the right thing, Will. For you, I mean. It's the chance you have to give yourself. Maybe in the end you'll decide to open a bicycle shop after all—or even get a job with old Chadd again. But a man has to give himself every chance—a man like you, that is." He tipped his head back and grinned. "I've been for it all along but I hoped you'd see it that way on your own."

DURING the next couple of weeks I painted the barn, two coats of "colonial yellow." I did nothing but that from the time the dew dried in the morning till late afternoon, except for a day and a half of rain: early September it was by then, a dry sunny time with a tint of gold among the leaves and the fragrance of autumn grass. There were ladders and ropes and tackles, and except for the high part of the gables it was simple enough to reach, and I worked at it with devotion. The round of the day, morning and night, was like slow ritual: I grew hungry and tired, I ate and slept, I worked while the sun moved, and the whole project of the new-painted barn occupied my being as though nothing else had any existence at all. Except for trips to the village to buy food—I concentrated on ripe tomatoes, corn, and hamburg steak—I saw almost no one. Mr. Guptill drove in once with papers to be signed. And the Saffords turned up on a Sunday afternoon—they had closed up their place at Edgartown—and we had a picnic on the rocks.

By then the job was almost done, and they looked at it with a good deal of wonder. "You did all that?" young Chan squeaked—his voice ranged from bass to soprano—and Walter appraised it as a five hundred dollar project, at current prices.

On the rainy days I cleaned out the furnace and got a rope

down the chimney and hauled a juniper tree up and down—
and carried out many buckets of soot and ashes. The top of
the roof was fairly flat—covered with copper sheets soldered
at the edges—and I inspected everything and mended some of
the gutters and flashing and admired the good work that had
gone into the whole affair; it was all meant to last forever. A
few slates had broken from the steep part of the roof but not
enough to matter. What the house most needed was paint,
and I made a beginning on some of it—mainly window sills
and casings on the south side.

It was a sort of retreat, I suppose, a time of devotion and
ritual. I enjoyed the virtues of a hermit's life, the day-long
silence and the meditation, and I subdued myself to steady toil
with no alternative but food and sleep. And I was conscious
that it was a stolen time, separate from all other times: for the
two weeks I was Robinson Crusoe, as Pop had said, surviving
on my island.

But I had notice that Tech would admit me as a freshman,
with other advice and instruction that filled me with a sense
of doom. I had gone to war still as an individual, maintaining
a sort of bubble of personal inviolability inside me, but now
I was committing myself to a more demanding authority.
Probably I was making too much fuss about it—within my
self, that is: discipline is expected of the young; authority is
necessary, institutions are necessary, and the breaking-in of
Will Redfern should have come as a matter of course. But the
fact is that I dreaded it, and began looking for ways of escape.
There were jobs to be done, money to be made: an after-the-
war rush was on and I could have flourished as a radio man
or automobile mechanic. I cruised round with that in mind,
and fancied myself as an independent operator of some sort.

And one day Walter Safford came to the house with two
stout and prosperous men—one of them a real estate dealer

from Boston, the other a possible buyer. I had been scraping and brushing the old paint round the second floor windows; I wore a pair of dirty pants, no shirt, and was plastered with sweat and paint-dust. The arrival of three city-dressed men in a black Cadillac seemed surprising enough, but I felt a childish sort of irritation as I went down the ladder from the porch roof. Here visibly, in flesh and metal, was the official outside world: I even had a shock of fear that they had come to attack me with legal power of some sort. But Walter was as modest as ever, and hoped I'd let these gentlemen look round a bit—Mr. Upshaw was interested in North Shore property and Mr. Singleton (the real estate man) had suggested that they all come together; it was a pleasant afternoon to be out and the air was delightful here by the shore.

For a moment it seemed to me that Walter had done me a grave wrong; even his mention of delightful air might have been calculated, and I felt myself rushing toward anger and churlishness. Yet I knew also that his intention was kindly and reasonable. "Mr. Upshaw is just exploring," he said.

"Used to live in Salem—as a boy," Mr. Upshaw said with mildness. "I always liked this shore—I had a little old tub of a catboat one year and used to sail round and think how happy the folks must be who lived in these houses. Kind of a dream, I had. Thought maybe I'd try it and see."

I said he was welcome to look round, of course. I felt foolish about being angry, and hoped they hadn't noticed.

But later, when they had gone, and I stood in the sunlight of the yard and looked at the shining paint of the barn, I felt some of the fear again. They did have power, after all: they had money—Mr. Upshaw, I was given to understand somewhat cryptically, had all the money in the world—he owned everything worth owning. If he really wanted the place it was obvious that I couldn't afford to stand in his way.

So my time of retreat ended. I cleaned up, shaved, and went back to town to find Sally.

It almost seemed now that everything depended on Sally. I had seen her a couple of times, but not alone, and I had heard that she and Saul had gone off with Harold for a weekend at Truro. I tried not to think about it, but inevitably images flashed in my mind of Sally alive in the ways I couldn't share. She spoke to others, smiled, was kind or affectionate—or even passionate: I didn't know.

But now on a Tuesday evening in September she might be found and captured; she might at last save me, solve my life for me, bring happiness-ever-after out of the uncertainties of property and career. With Sally, I thought, all would come clear, like crystals in a cloudy solution.

I drove to the house where she roomed and she was not there. I tried Harold's rooms. I peered into eating places where they might be, wondering how I could get hold of her alone. At last I simply waited in my car in front of the rooming-house. About nine o'clock she came along, with Saul. I sat there, and they went in without noticing me or the car. It was an hour before he came out.

I had been watching the door all that time and noticing that it swung shut and latched itself very slowly. There were no bells and clicks, as in an apartment house: this was a large warren of a rooming house, and the way for a stranger to get in was to ring for the janitor (a very stout female one), as I had done before. But now I waited for a chance—a long wait —and when someone unlocked the door at last and went in I caught it before it latched itself.

Third floor, she had said, and I prowled among dark halls and doors—and finally in desperation spoke her name aloud. I remembered as I spoke it all the dismal third floors of her life, the tenements and rooming houses and anonymous halls with

close air and oil fumes, and the strangers below or above.
"Sally," I called in a muffled voice, listening to movement behind the doors—and one opened a foot or so and a wrinkled
witch peered out and told me I was a disturber of the peace
and if I didn't keep quiet she'd call the police; she glared at
me for a moment with malevolence, then closed the door with
a quiet click. But by then Sally had heard, and was looking at
me from a shadowy end of the hall; her black hair and dark
blue robe were almost invisible, but the relaxed wide smile
changed the scene for me entirely: the limbo of bad air and
decay and doomed humanity no longer seemed to matter. It
was partly her pleasure in being surprised by me and partly a
recognition of how lost I was in the third-floor wilderness.

"You need rescuing," she said. "It's a dangerous region—I
don't know how you ever penetrated so far."

There I was, anyway. The room was hardly longer or wider
than the iron bed along the wall; it had a slanting ceiling, a
small window set in a narrow alcove, a bureau, a straight chair,
some hooks behind a curtain, a naked bulb hanging from a
wire with an extension to the head of the bed and a shaded
bulb for reading. The green bed spread was rumpled; a book
lay open and face down on it.

"I had to see you," I said.

We sat on the bed, one at each end—Sally curled against
the pillow where she had been reading. She waited for me to
go on; she could wait, I felt, with infinite patience, like a cat.

"Would it be better if we went out? My car is outside—"

"Whatever you like, Will. No one will bother us here—if
we don't make a racket."

"What about the witch?"

"Oh, she's just crazy. We're all crazy up here. It doesn't
matter."

Sally's calm, the quiet voice and motionless body, settled

over me. I had come with urgency; everything seemed to de-
pend on my finding her. But now I lay back, watching, feeling
the silence of the room. Her clothes, I saw, lay on the chair in
a little white pile. She wore light blue cotton pajamas under
the dark blue robe. I wondered how she kept things clean in
such a place. "Here you are twenty three," I said, "with a
mind and a heart and a soul. You are very beautiful—not in
the way of bathing-suit girls, but in the way of legends and
classic heroines. You are married to a man unworthy of you,
and even unappreciative of you. You live in a temporary furnished room with yellow marks all over the ceiling and you
work in Filenes for a small wage. Is all this inevitable? And
where does it lead? Will you spend your life in a furnished
room?"

She said nothing.

"Will you always be temporary and poor? You said it yourself: you fight against dirt and ugliness and never quite win
or get anywhere. No victory, nothing achieved. No beauty."

I had no intention of talking this way, and felt annoyed at
having done so.

"It seems to me," I went on, "that there ought to be some
sense to life, specially to your life. You could at least live in
a clean place and play your violin and have a couple of babies
—that wouldn't be too much, would it?"

There was a choke of anger in my voice and I tried to control it.

"You could have grass to walk on now and then, and air to
breathe, and people you liked—"

She couldn't answer me, I knew—or wouldn't: she looked
at me patiently. Out in the hall footsteps padded up and
down, doors clicked and bumped, water ran in the pipes.

I told her about myself, and she asked questions and made
me tell all the details. We spoke almost in whispers, in a

conspiracy against the world of the rooming-house. It grew late, and I began to think I was talking too much, but there was something almost hypnotic about being alone with her in that small alien place. We huddled into it and whispered like children in a cave or a tree hut. But she said finally we shouldn't be talking; people were trying to sleep and even murmurs carried through the walls. They might start banging, the crazy ones—they had done it before when Saul was there, I supposed.

I said then that she was to come with me. It was the reason I was there. She wouldn't even have to dress: just bundle things up and come. I touched her, not with passion but with a sense of our affection and oneness. We should be together, I said, for always. We could breathe good air and walk on grass and do some of the things we enjoyed doing. We could find a way to marry and have a family and live like human beings.

For a while she didn't answer. She had the old owlish look to her, steady and solemn.

I spoke—or whispered—as urgently as I could. We were friends, companions, lovers. We belonged together. We were destined to make a life together.

"Where?" she asked.

It seemed an odd question. Anywhere, I said—except a city tenement: no third-floor rooms, no oil fumes and dirt. I'd build her a house if she liked. Bell's Landing could be sold, I explained: it was worth more than I had realized, and we'd have plenty to get started with. We'd have to work it out together: that was really the point of the whole thing—to work it out together.

She was so still that my eloquence diminished and I watched her questioningly. She looked like the sphinx, I said. Her head was bent a little forward, and the heavy hair enclosed her face.

My words had not effectively penetrated, I thought. I shook her a little and pushed her hair back to reveal more of her face.

"Did you hear all I said?"

She nodded.

"Well, it's a very important and serious proposition. I've been thinking about it not only for years but for days and nights. There's every reason why you and I should be together, and no reason why we shouldn't—"

"Did I ever promise anything to you, Will?"

"You promised you wouldn't be afraid."

"Anything else?"

"Well, yes—sort of. You promised you'd always be Sally, without pretending."

"Did I say that?"

"No—but it's how I understood you."

She looked down at her hands for a few seconds. "If we were to—go off together, as you say, would you sell Bell's Landing?"

I nodded. "Walter Safford has advised me to anyway."

"And you'd go to work—somewhere?"

"I could work for you, Sally. I mean, I could make a living for you. We could live like people. Music—" I gestured. "Violin. And all those books—they're still ours, you know."

She hardly smiled. "I'm trying—not to be afraid," she said with a gulp. "You see me as the sort of person I don't deserve to be. I think you see me as a good wife and mother living in a pretty suburb—" She hesitated. "I could be, I guess. I don't know. But things happen to me, Will—foolish yearnings and longings and desires. I love you—in a way, an ideal sort of way, as though you were my better half, or my reasonable half. I love your common sense and your muscles and the way you laugh and drive a car and eat and do things with your hands. You make me feel a little the way the sea did—" She smiled quickly. "We have illusions about each other, I guess, but mine are a sort of reality, like faith."

"Don't talk so much, Sally. Just—please—come along. You can, you know. You aren't afraid."

I knew as I spoke that she wouldn't come. I knew that I'd never really have her. She had already slipped a little out of my hands, though I didn't know how it happened or why. I had an overwhelming sense of her, the secret being that lived behind the dark eyes and quiet mouth, the sadness and warmth and awareness. All the longing of my life was there, visibly and actually curled up on the iron bed, body and soul in one. I could say nothing.

We lay for a long time—perhaps five minutes—without a word or motion.

"Sally," I said finally in a voice that broke harshly out of the silence, "I want you more than all the rest—" The sudden harshness seemed wrong, and the words seemed useless. I stopped.

She moved a little, pushed back her hair. "Saul was here—just before you came," she said, trying to keep her voice quiet. "He wants to go to Mexico."

"Not you, Sally—you can't go."

"Well, he has it all figured out. He didn't get into Harvard, you see: his record is pretty queer, I guess, though he has some good recommendations. But he thinks Mexico is the place to go—he knows some writers there, and they say it is cheap and warm and the scenery is beautiful. He's all excited about it. His mother—she has another husband and lives in Passaic—sends him money now and then. And he is sure he can write in Mexico. It's the ideal place, he thinks."

"What do you think?"

"I promised to go, Will—or at least I said I would—"

"How about Harold—did he advise it?"

She waited several seconds before answering, and her glance enveloped me with a steady and mysterious solemnity.

"Harold thought it was foolish. He said Mexico is where the failures and dead-beats all go—the ones running away from themselves and life."

"Harold is very bright," I said.

She waited again, then spoke with sudden strong effort. "Harold has fallen in love—or says he has—with me."

I sat up as though the point of a small knife had touched my back.

"He wants me," she went on, "to be his mistress—that's what he calls it. It sounds sort of grand and literary like a French novel."

At first, after the sharp stab, I couldn't take the idea as anything but part of Harold's theatricals. "Mistress!" I snorted. I made the word preposterous. But then I stared at her, dark and secret and withdrawn. "Sally," I whispered. "You—" She looked at me for a long moment.

"Harold," I muttered with sudden reflective bitterness. "What do you do about it?" My voice sounded loud in the room's stillness.

"Go to Mexico." She read my expression and smiled. "I haven't been your mistress, Will. I've just been your girl, I guess—like the first time; it's different from anything else—it always will be. But I could be a good mistress in the old-fashioned sense—a kept woman; it's a side of me you don't see, or want to see, but Harold sees it—he's very shrewd, as you say. If he were richer it might be tempting, but of course he couldn't really set me up in a handsome establishment, as they used to call it."

I couldn't tell how she meant it. She spoke with a gentle smiling seriousness.

"How much do you like Harold?" I asked.

"I could almost love him—but I guess not quite. He has a cold heart, Will. But he is the most formidable man I ever met. You don't really see him, you know—not the way most people see him—" She said it hesitantly. "I guess that's another thing about me—I mean the way I feel about what he does and is. He may be a literary snob, but he is good at it— oh, he's better than good, he's the best. He can be very nearly irresistible—to any one as susceptible as I am, at least. I guess it's lucky for me he isn't rich too."

"Lucky?" I couldn't keep an edge of bitterness out of my voice.

She watched me somberly for a moment. "Don't desert me, Will—I mean don't—" She couldn't seem to say it. "I'm not any different. I'm exactly what I was, only more so. I try to tell you just how it is—I keep that promise: I won't pretend with you. But none of it is simple—I mean love and desire and loyalty and duty: they all pull in different directions, and you just have to improvise as you go along—I do, anyway. I can't seem to help being temporary, as you called it. People like Harold—and your mother—are able to follow a clear pattern—at least it looks like it. I think you need to too—"

"Need to! We all do, I suppose."

"Well, you can, Will. It's possible for you. Career, family, even the place there—you could do your way as well as Harold does his—oh, better, I think, because you won't be heartless—"

It was then that the knocking started on the wall beside the bed. I looked round at the drab room and felt a stab of guilt. I had forgotten the place and time. Sally's face was full of resignation and acceptance of all conditions.

"Come on," I whispered. "All we have to do is walk downstairs and go." I said more than that, not very articulately. The knocking started again more irritably.

"If I didn't have Saul, I might—I probably would come, though it wouldn't be right—not for you, I mean. But—" She stood up. It was the end.

She walked all the way down to the front door with me, both of us tip-toeing on the creaky boards. She held my hand tightly, and at the last kissed me. We were melancholy and unable to speak. Her warm mouth, not passionate or demanding, seemed unwilling to let me go. "You make me feel so sorry for myself, Will." Her face glistened. "It isn't sensible— it's bad, I guess. I try not to—I will try not to." She backed away and said no more. I remember her in the dim hall light standing motionless like a strangely humanized and melancholy goddess of romantic legend. Tears had given her shadowy face the quality of sculpture, though her mouth quivered a little—partly in an effort to smile.

৩ CHAPTER 8 ৯৯

My cousin Bolles Sumner wrote to ask me to lunch at his club: he assumed I'd be in Cambridge all next week for the opening days of the term, and gave me a choice of dates and times—realizing, he added, that my schedule would doubtless be crowded, but hoping we'd have enough time for a chat and smoke afterward. Another cousin, the very aged Miss Nannie Ewart, sent word by means of her companion that they were at home for tea on Tuesdays. The Albert Weldons invited me to Sunday dinner in Milton. There were other overtures. I seemed to be carried along by a large tidal flow. One involvement led imperceptibly to another, and I found myself sailing in a schooner out of Marblehead or spending a Saturday night among cordial strangers on a modernized farm in Dublin, New Hampshire.

It was the Saffords who took charge, of course. They had no doubts, fears, hesitations, or uncertainties about life; they flowed along at an even pace, with even keels; they lived with such expertness that there seemed to be nothing left for them to learn. Jane and Walter, I sometimes felt, had reached a point of complacent serenity, like well protected cats: they had eliminated the hazards and emotions—at least to outward view, but there was no such resignation in the young ones.

Chan seemed to be destined to almost fanatical zeal as a naturalist, and Betsy—it was impossible to find anything wrong with Betsy. In most of the old novels I have read it seems to be assumed that the heroine can be nothing less than perfect. She is trained from childhood and she plays the part of perfect ladyhood, without flaw or falseness. But of course in our times the certainties have been destroyed. In her own way, though, Betsy was achieving a kind of perfection—a better kind perhaps, if that is possible: like the ladies of old she seemed sure of her aims, and her speech, her accent, her taste and personal accomplishments, were all carefully developed. It was her duty and pleasure to study French and play the piano. Her manners, apparently careless and casual, were the result of long training and shrewd intention. There was actually a firm traditionalism in her behavior, well concealed by the modern surfaces; she respected integrity in a way that is looked on as unrealistic and outmoded. Like her brother Chan, she trained herself in hardihood; she took cold showers early in the morning, she wore thin clothes in winter, and never rubbers or hats, and she slept with all windows wide open and shades up; she walked and rowed and skied and managed horses. At Bell's Landing she worked one end of a cross-cut saw. She swung an ax, not powerfully but skilfully enough to cut off branches. She dragged brush and logs. And she did these things without the arrogance of muscular girls. She did what she did easily, and took delight in air and earth and all the creatures; she got tired, hungry, scratched, bruised, all with good nature and relish, even with a sort of deliberate appreciation like a pupil of old idealists. But she seldom phrased it; she never used such a word as nature or explained what she felt to be obvious, nor did she allow herself any solemnities. "This plain living is very nice," she said. "Health and muscle and appetite and all. But don't you think we should give high living a try too? I mean things like truffles and champagne and music in the night. We'll have to do it this winter—once or twice, anyway, all in our best clothes—" She glanced appraisingly at me. "You don't have any, of course —wouldn't be caught dead in 'em." I could see that she intended to do something about it.

But she worked on me with gentle art. She had, I found, numberless friends: each time she came to Bell's Landing she seemed to be in a different car with different companions and when I began to rally her on it she said she was bringing the world to my door and I might as well take it gracefully: I liked people, anyway, she said, and these were mostly very nice people. Some of them came several times and the young ones got to calling me Uncle Will—with a sort of affection, as though they knew all about me and had no fear, and they had the piano tuned and played ancient music with flutes and recorders, and sometimes they stayed all night without going to bed and drank coffee and ate hamburgers.

Between these doings I brooded a good deal. The house weighed on me. The property made demands. Taxes, they said, were high and would be higher. Once I started on my college work there'd be no time to paint and mend and cut wood—in fact I'd be living in Cambridge. I had a few hundred dollars in the bank and the government was paying my way at Tech, but I was poorly equipped to be a North Shore squire. The only reasonable solution was to sell, and Mr. Upshaw had returned with an offer. My response should have been simple: the offer was large, the arrangements wholly generous, and Upshaw himself seemed full of kindly recognition of all my problems. But I could not open my mouth and say yes. I agreed with his reasonings, I noted that the money would be wonderfully useful and comforting, though in my innocence I hardly conceived of a large sum of money as an actuality; I had no petulant hostility to the man—but I could not just then say yes: nor, for that matter, could I quite say no. I must have been an exasperation to the patient Upshaw.

On the Saturday before the opening week at Tech (a sort of initiation period for freshmen had already been going on, and I was oppressed with a sense of the incongruity of my age and condition) the Saffords had arranged a family picnic at Bell's Landing in celebration of what they said was its centennial. They may have made up the occasion; at least they seemed to feel that a family party was desirable. I knew the house was ninety-one years old because the date of its building was plainly stated in the begining of my grandfather's journal, where a number of vital facts were listed—including the dates, dimensions, and sail area of his boats. But Jane said they had acquired the land nine years before they built on it and therefore we could properly have a centennial now; how she knew all this she didn't say except that it was what they used to tell her.

It was the twenty-first of September, a day so still and clear that I shall never forget it. There were clouds overhead, matted and ridged in an unnatural way, though in the mid part of the day the sun shone warmly and mild little breezes seemed to blow from various directions; but the clearness was not that of bright northern air, rather it seemed to lie low along the water and it gave a steely sharpness to the edge of the horizon. It was almost as though distant objects were magnified by a lens. "Weather breeder," Uncle Albert said. "What we used to call it, though it was half superstition. Tropical storm on the way—heard it on the radio this morning: that's how I can tell it's a weather breeder. Hurricane down south—" He shrugged. Others had heard too, but took little stock in it; hurricanes hardly belonged here—line storms, yes—it was the time, in fact, of the equinox, and an old-fashioned southeaster was to be expected, but not a hurricane.

We were on the beach, with a fire and a boiling pot of lobsters—the family, fourteen or so—even Harold—but mostly subdued and autumnal: I remember the dry voices of the Weldons, the fussy eloquence of Bolles Sumner, whose accent reminded me of my father's, and the curious explosiveness of Mrs. Fairchild as she cried out in the old phrases my Aunt Evelyn had used: "Well, did you *ever*—" They were, I thought at first, too old and unyielding for a picnic on the beach, but they went at it expertly, like trained performers. "The pride of the Redferns," Uncle Albert said, "was always the ability to eat a boiled lobster on a sand beach. Your Aunt Jane wouldn't have me till I could. I had to qualify, as they say of doctoral candidates. The thing is to get every last edible scrap, but no sand, no grain of sand . . ." His voice kept on steadily, like a dry obligato. But he was rejoicing. His wrinkled face had set itself in lines of approval.

"It's too bad your mother couldn't come," Jane said in placid tones. "She'd manage everything much better." It was a flat and literal statement, without irony.

I knew that Mother disapproved of the picnic: she had her work to do, she said, and couldn't take time for such affairs—and besides it seemed too soon after, we were supposed to be in mourning, weren't we? She had spoken as though there were a statute that should govern us all, but her voice had a bitter little note of jealousy in it. "It isn't up to me to tell them what to do." And I said it might be the last time we could ever all be at Bell's Landing. I ought to sell it, oughtn't I? I put the case bluntly. Was there any sound reason why I shouldn't sell it? We were in the bare little sitting room she used at the hospital and she was standing by the table in her posture of foursquare defiance; her face had flushed from the issue of the picnic, and she looked ready to fight. "Yes, certainly I think you should sell it." She almost snapped at me. "What else could you do?" I nodded gloomily. The thing was, I said, you did get so attached to the old place, and there were so many things—like pictures and books, and those boats in the cellar. It seemed to me at first that she was angry, and I paused and braced myself for her words, but there was a long silence and then she wiped her eyes with the same gesture, I suddenly realized, she must have used since she was a little girl, curling her two forefingers round to stem the flow. "I don't know, Will—" She got out a paper handkerchief and mopped herself very quietly. "You can't do what you want to —you've got to make up your mind—there's no sense in just hoping—" When she controlled herself she grew angry again. She *worked*, she said with compressed fury. She worked hard. She had no time to waste on picnics—she didn't think I did either. Here I was starting at Tech—I'd better realize what I was up against. It was foolish and dangerous for me to be dreaming about a gentleman's estate on the North Shore. Didn't I have a career to make? Didn't I have to work, work, work? Family sentiment was all very well if you could afford it—*she* couldn't, certainly; she had learned long ago that there was nothing for her but work, hard work. When I left her, some time later, she sent her love to all, was sorry she couldn't be there, and kissed me with awkward and flushed tenderness.

"The practical ones," Jane Safford was saying to me, "think you should sell at once. The romantic ones think you shouldn't."

"Which are you?"

"Oh, I'm romantic." Her voice as always was perfectly flat. "I think you should hold on. To the last. That's why I got up the picnic—to appeal to everybody's sentiment." She took in

my somewhat satiric grin and calmly nodded. "The lobsters
may make us reckless and romantic enough to save the old
homestead—" We glanced round at the self-contained company. Bolles Sumner, I noticed, was working intently on each
small claw; his round face had a gentle shine of anticipation.
"Of course," she went on, "Walter never gets reckless. He is
much too reliable. He doesn't despise sentiment—he is very
nice about it—but the first consideration is always reliability.
That's what it is to be a business man, and the Redferns have
never been good at business—not for several generations,
anyway. I suppose they were once—that's how families get
started, isn't it?" Her voice was like an unruffled brook, gentle
and somehow transparent. "First the money, wickedly acquired. Then the estates and castles and family pride—still
rather wicked. Then the reliability. Then the civilized virtues
—manners, kindliness, responsibility. Then gentleness and
niceness and the cultivation of the impractical arts."

"And then what?"

"Oh, then—well, it would be easy to say degeneracy, but it
doesn't really happen that way. The family cycle seems to
come to an end, and the gentle ones, the impractical ones, just
sort of melt into the social landscape. I'm sure they do it good
in a missionary way—assuming, that is, that civilization is a
desirable state."

We worked on our lobsters for a minute or two. Then I
asked her if she thought the Redfern cycle had come to its
end.

She glanced round at them, sitting on logs and rocks, balancing plates on knees, gnawing at the primeval food. Gener-
alization, she said, was always easy and always wrong. But
what she had in mind was not just the Redferns, but the whole
Boston family: they had all gone through the cycle together,
like a single dynasty. They had all made money wickedly long

ago, they had built castles and lived in pride, they had acquired manners and wonderful virtue and had cultivated the arts— Here for the first time I felt something vibrant in Jane's voice. "I really think they came to be the most civilized people on earth. Is there anything about your grandfather's life here at Bell's Landing that doesn't have a kind of absolute goodness about it?" She said it with careful precision. "I don't mean it sentimentally—I mean it as literally as possible. There were no vices here, no ugliness really—except for the inevitable Victorian gingerbread: they were kind, modest, unselfish, unbelievably honorable, devoted to the noblest ideals. They rejoiced in the sea and its ways, and the land and the farm; they were social—they had loyal friends everywhere, and they took part in city affairs. They were very good and happy people. If civilization means anything at all it means what happened at Bell's Landing—as well as at a lot of other places round here."

She stared for a moment at her lobster with an almost visible emotion, and then settled back to her normal placidity. After a while she remarked that no specialized civilization can endure, not as long as the world was predominantly barbarian, as it was. "I can't help being romantic about it, though. I hang on to the hope that if we keep the place itself we somehow keep all that it used to be—though I know quite well it doesn't work that way."

When I walked along the shore with Betsy afterward I felt strangely sombre. The day had grown more gray and steel-clear, and seemed oppressive. But Betsy was as bright as ever and said it would be fun to come out for week-ends in October—and even in winter—and she hoped I wouldn't mind if she got a gang together, specially the ones who liked music: it was a fine place for music.

I mumbled something about Mr. Upshaw but she wouldn't

listen: whatever happened, I was not to sell. If I needed money for taxes or anything, she'd ante up herself—she had a fortune of her own, did I know? A trust fund, anyway, with a little income. She spoke lightly, as though nothing was to be argued. The place was to stay in the family.

But I had begun to realize how it would be. It may have been what Jane had said. I stared at the metallic sea with a sort of clairvoyance.

That night the storm began with rain and a southeast wind. By morning it was an easterly gale, and by noon a northeast hurricane whipping the trees and flinging spray against walls and windows. I paced from room to room, watching the white froth and sheets of spindrift above the breakers, hearing the crack of branches over the general roar, feeling the house shrink and vibrate in the gusts. It seemed vast and very lonesome to me. The white oak in front snapped above the base and crashed along the unused drive—the oak my father used to say would make good ship timber, and my first thought was that it should be carefully saved and seasoned. But the house itself stood firmly, and when the wind began to ease off in the afternoon I inspected everything and then took ax and saw and began to cut and clear the fallen trees. The damage had not been great, but I felt subdued and even melancholy as I cleared away the big branches. When Mr. Upshaw drove in about five o'clock to see how things were, the sun was out and the wind was off shore though a range of mountainlike clouds lay in the north.

We settled the deal, at least verbally. I said that Mr. Guptill would handle all the legalities for me. And I'd have to have time to consult the family about the furnishings. Mr. Upshaw said he'd buy whatever we wanted to leave, but he understood all about family possessions. He was a close-mouthed, rather dry man who made quick decisions and prided himself on fair dealing. "It's the best thing about being rich," he said. "You can afford to be fair. You aren't obliged to take advantage." I remember how he looked round the yard and gestured stiffly. "If it was mining property I'd probably have to cheat you. Or try to, anyhow."

And after that, when he had driven away, the solitude of Bell's Landing grew unbearable to me. The sea still rolled in against the west wind and surged up the beach and the roaring sound of it rose and fell like doom. The blue expanse was empty: no boat, no wink of sail anywhere. There must be wrecks, I thought, and a few drowned men. Air was growing cold, and the level sun struck everything with a white glitter. Yellow leaves lay in heaps on the ground—the trees had been blown bare, and the house stood up massively but somehow faded and a little shoddy, like a cardboard castle. I walked into the dusky rooms, upstairs and downstairs. I took a flashlight and descended into the cellar to see if the little white yachts were still sitting in their cradles as they had been for fifteen years. I poked into corners and closets and storerooms as though something I had never seen might be there. I climbed to the top floor and looked through the unused rooms, the locked and secret places Aunt Evelyn had never let us see, full of round-topped trunks, cardboard boxes, discarded chairs—a white baby's chair with a tray—and in the center of all a dressmaker's form like a presiding deity. The evening sun splashed over the piled-up stuff and made bright rectangles on the plaster of the inner walls. On the side of a square box I could see the words "Mama's Spring Hats" and I recognized Aunt Evelyn's vertical hand.

The sunlight faded as I watched. The walls darkened as though an oil lamp had been turned down and then blown out. And almost at once it seemed that the rush and break of the sea grew louder, and I felt the tremor inside me like quicksilver exactly as it had been when I was little and lay listening in the night. There was no one below, no one there at all but me; the house seemed to tremble with silence. I tiptoed into my old room, aware of the squeak of floor boards.

And then I thought I heard a voice calling my name. The word rang clearly in my ear: "Will!" I waited, listening, hearing nothing but the rumble of sea along the beach. I started down stairs, very dark now in the interior of the house. There were steps down there, and a faint voice calling out again. "Will!" I stopped now with the fantastic notion that it must be Sally, that she had come after all through storm and chaos; in a flash I believed in the miracle, accepted it as a special act of fate on my behalf. The time and setting were right. We were there again and alone in the castle, she and I against the world. I called her name: "Sally—is it really you?" I could touch her, sleep with her in the turret chamber protected by moat, portcullis, and drawbridge. The certainty of it rushed upon me—it all happened in one electric shock, and I found myself plunging down the stairs and along the second-floor hall to the top of the wide oaken flight that led to the main hall. But by then I knew it couldn't be so, it wasn't possible— at least it wasn't likely, not really likely . . .

"Will—hello! I've been hunting all round for you." It was Betsy, cool and crisp and self-contained. "Did you think I was somebody else?"

"I didn't know—" the flashlight in my hand was on, I found; I switched it off.

"Wasn't it terrific? I wanted to be here—it must have been wonderful—but I couldn't get here. I tried—no trains. Have you seen the trees down—goodness, it came straight in, didn't it? Is the house all right?"

We stood at the east windows looking out at the luminous water, and then Betsy said she wanted to see things before it was too dark. The boathouse, I told her, was a little crooked, the wooden ways were all gone, but a nice new bed of sand had been dumped on the north end of the beach. We walked about. "I'm sure they didn't have hurricanes in the old days," she said. "It's queer, isn't it?" She kept saying she wished she had been there to see it. "Are you going to sell it, Will? Bell's Landing?"

"Yes," I said.

We were back in the yard, near the kitchen door. I had been trying to tell her—all the time we walked on the rocks and beach I had been saying the words to myself. I think she must have known.

"Is it that you have to have the money?"

I thought a moment. "I don't really belong here," I said.

"Will! Why—" She stopped as though a switch had been turned.

"If I tried to keep it and maintain it—even if I could I'd be—I'd feel like an impostor."

"But you aren't, Will; you couldn't be."

"I would if I stayed here."

"No." She stopped again. "What makes you think so?"

"Well, I've been thinking about it—or trying to—for a month. I suppose it was something Jane said that made me understand—it was about how good they were."

"Don't be absurd, Will."

"Oh, more than good: they lived up to a vision—they literally did. I couldn't—or wouldn't—" I gestured vaguely. "If I ever did have a vision, a good one, it wouldn't be the same at all—it wouldn't belong here. And if I tried to stay I'd do nothing but remember how it used to be. They'd be testing me and I wouldn't measure up. I'd be a faithless caretaker —I mean I'd feel like one all the time."

"But you—you—" Her quick voice darted at it with ex-

asperation. "It's just spooks, Will. You don't have to be an-
cestral and all that. All you have to do is be here. I know it
would take money, but why couldn't you rent it for a while—
I mean, houses are in terrific demand these days—and then in
the long run you'd have it."

"Spooks," I said, nodding. "I guess I'm afraid of them. I
think I'm a little bit haunted already, and it isn't good. All
those old people—it's bad enough being old anyway but when
the only world you believe in is dead and gone you get so you'd
be much better dead yourself. Maybe it doesn't have to be like
that, but it often enough seems to—round here, anyway."

She looked at the ground for a long time, making marks with
her sneakers and smoothing them over again as though she
were intent on a design. "What about going back to Cambridge tonight? Are you going?"

"Why, we'd better, I suppose."

"Will." She still looked down. "What about Sally? What
are you going to do about her?"

She must have heard me call Sally's name, I thought.

"It's all done. Sally's gone away—to Mexico."

"For ever, you mean?"

"Well, it's as good as for ever."

"So, now—" She drew a line in the gravel with her toe and
looked at it carefully; then she brushed it out. "You begin all
over again, huh?"

"I begin, anyway."

"Tell me, Will—am I a spook too?" Then she kicked at the
gravel, lifted her head, and smiled. "I hereby testify that I'm
not a spook, nor do I intend to be until I'm sixty-eight at
least. I am hungry, though—I haven't had a bite: you haven't
either."

"I've still got some eggs," I said.

"No—I have a whim—a whim of iron, as you'll find out

when you get to know me better. I want to go back to the joint we went to the first time—remember? McGinty's Diner. I feel in a commemorative state of mind."

I collected a few things and we closed and locked the doors and walked out to the car.

"I really know," she said. "It's dead—it died with the poor old dears. But I can't help wanting to hold on. I wanted you to hold on. It's foolish of me."

The west was a band of yellow. Stars shone overhead, and a sickle moon hung in the blue-green sky behind a corner of the barn roof. I put an arm round Betsy's shoulders and she brushed her cheeks on my jacket. "It's such a huge house, Will—I'm glad you aren't trying to paint it all. Look at those cornices or whatever you call them. I can't help crying, though. It's a sort of event, isn't it. Farewell to Bell's Landing. *Vale*, as we used to say in Latin class. Good bye to all that."

I leaned down and kissed her. "Betsy—" Her lips and cheeks seemed as cold as snow. I felt her draw away, but I held my arm round her shoulders. "Can you do something for me?"

She relaxed a little warily. "I might, Will." But there was a note of mockery and I looked down to see her smile.

"Well," I said, "I'd like to try to do the best I can do." It was hard to say what I meant and I felt as though I were stumbling. My life was all there in my mind like a vast dumb show, but I couldn't speak.

"You want me to help you do that, Will?"

"Yes—yes, that's exactly it."

"Maybe you won't need help—once you get going."

"Everything up to now—everything I've been doing—is a kind of dream—"

"You mean spooks, Will?"

It wasn't what I meant but there seemed to be no other way of saying it. I thought again. "A pretending, maybe. Or a retreat. Do you see what I'm trying to say, Betsy?"

She looked at the ground. "Do you mean Sally too?"

"Yes, Sally too." My voice shook. "She kept trying to tell me."

You have to subdue yourself for a good end—Betsy herself had used those words, long ago it seemed. I repeated them to her and she stirred under my arm and lifted her head and smiled. "Very good, Will. But you still haven't told me what I can do."

"Just stand by me." I shook her a little. "You know what I mean—don't be perverse about it."

She took my hand and rubbed her cold cheeks with it. "All right, Little Will, I'll try to stand by. Let's get on to McGinty's, shall we?" She gave me a bright smile. "It has to work two ways, you know—I mean the standing by and the doing and the subduing and all." Her voice was buoyant and clear, and she seemed about to say more, but then she turned and got in the car. "Uncle Will, I should have said. Aren't you starved? I am!"

We sat and listened for a few seconds to the low grating sigh of water on the sand shore and the sharper crackle and splash against the rock of the headlands.

Date Due

DEMCO NO. 295

FEB 20 '66				
FEB 25 '17				
AUG 7 '70 CANISIUS				